Between Classes

~Between Classes~

Anne Willingale

Matador
9 Priory Business Park,
Wistow Road, Kibworth Beauchamp,
Leicestershire. LE8 0RX
Tel: 0116 279 2299
Email: books@troubador.co.uk
Web: www.troubador.co.uk/matador
Twitter: @matadorbooks

ISBN 978 1838594 374
British Library Cataloguing in Publication Data.
A catalogue record for this book is available from the British Library.

Printed on FSC accredited paper
Printed and bound in Great Britain by 4edge Limited
Typeset in 11pt Minion Pro by Troubador Publishing Ltd, Leicester, UK

Matador is an imprint of Troubador Publishing Ltd

My thanks go to my dear friend Alan Bricknell who proofread this book for me while he was on holiday, [that's dedication] and my cousin Brian Phillippo, who lives in Australia, and took the time to check the book for its Australian authenticity. [The landscape and journey time through the bush.]

1.

The New World, 1802

The drumming of Black's hooves vibrated through Emma's tense body, blotting out all feeling and thought. Earth spewed out behind them as she rode Black hard. Her tanned legs hung free and bare below her skirt that lay in folds around her thighs as her body stretched forward. Her face, almost touching the animal's neck, was lost in the mane that flew wildly about her head, mixing with her own loose sun-bleached hair. Reaching a wooded area, she encouraged him uphill, passing a group of eucalyptus trees baked dry and bent at strange angles by sun and fire. The dead leaves covering the ground crackled beneath his hooves, causing a dust that released a powerful aroma that she didn't like.

Breaking out of the shade allowed by the trees, they zigzagged carefully through the low brush and scattered boulders spread out before them. On reaching the top of the rise Emma pulled Black to a stop. Exhilarated by the ride she bathed in the smell of her horse and patted his neck to calm him. He whinnied in reply and, dipping his head sharply, almost unseated her.

The stress that had built up within her body during the day had for the moment found its release; she wanted to scream but dared not spook her horse. Tethering him to the branch of a small tree she tied her skirt in a knot and, with slim legs exposed, climbed the red sandstone stack in front of her. There were plenty of handholds and places for her toes to grip where the weather had gouged small pockets into the soft rock. On reaching a ledge where she felt safe to stand she viewed the land below her. From here, the territory stretched for miles in all directions over the never-ending flatness towards the mountains in the west and the distant hills in the east. Within this landscape, she could see nothing to account for her anxiety which had grown within her over the past days until this morning when she could stand the feeling no longer. Now, filled with the exhilaration of the ride, she observed the distant Tate homestead. It was easy to find in the vastness of this land, its location identified by following the river to a wide patch of grey eucalyptus trees in front of which the log cabins sat in blistering silence. Tate Farm's surrounding barns and water towers appeared in miniature from this distance and she could just make out her own cabin on the far side of a space that was Black's paddock. Nothing moved in the heat haze that blanketed the land and choked the day.

Her brother, James Tilby, and stepbrothers, Jack and George Tate, now all in their teens, were on their horses somewhere off towards the hills looking for stray bullocks. Her mother, Martha, and stepfather, Andrew Tate, were also away checking the health of their herd and fourteen goats.

Nona, her sister, now twenty-three and still unmarried, had left hours ago in the cool of early morning with their cart pulled by their brown mare. She was heading for the small township that had started to take shape some six miles upriver. It consisted of a dozen houses, a tavern, a forge and general store from which she would collect their supplies, accompanied as always by her dog, Bart.

Beyond this enclave settlers had been claiming land and putting down roots, as the spread of small shacks attested. Some were badly built, standing on poor soil, and those inhabitants were barely surviving. The evidence of this being in the spread of makeshift wooden crosses in the cemetery.

It had taken Emma's family more than two years to understand the weather patterns in this new land, and they were thankful to John Brisket, their tenant farmer on Andrew's farm back in England, for sending the rent regularly at the end of each year. Without it they could not have managed.

Unlike England, this New World was hot and sometimes arid, and when it rained it rained so hard that the land was unable to absorb the water quickly enough. Deep gullies opened up, filling with water. Rivers appeared where no rivers were before, death traps for animals and humans who could be swept away on a frothing red surge. The steamy silence after a torrential downpour always excited Emma. Cleansed, the land seemed to vibrate with expectation, waiting, hormonal, pregnant with hidden promise. In the following days after the infrequent rain, the land was awash with colour. A rainbow of flowers spread like a soft carpet across the earth and both Martha and Emma gave thanks to the Goddess for this occasional beauty.

Emma's brow furrowed as she looked again east towards the hills and then west, her eyes following the direction that Nona had taken earlier. There was still no movement in the landscape.

She'd taken off without her bonnet, a stupid thing to have done she now realised as the sun bit into her neck and arms. Seeing nothing in the landscape to alarm her she lowered herself carefully down to her horse before easing him back down the slope, guiding his feet where she could see holes in the dry earth. This far out from the homestead her life depended on his fitness. Back on level ground his muscles rippled, he was ready to run and she gave him his head.

On reaching the homestead she returned Black to his paddock; giving him water she rubbed him down. The ride had given her some relief even though it had been a fruitless journey.

Entering her cabin, she felt the coolness of the dark interior sucking the heat from her body and was grateful that just before her marriage two years ago, Andrew and the boys had built it with thick walls to keep the heat of the day at bay.

Emma's husband, Richard, was younger than she, and at first Martha and Andrew had been happy with the match.

The stranger calling himself Richard Ladd had arrived when they needed extra help with branding and harvesting. They knew nothing of him, but he had convinced them that he was a good worker and was not a deportee from Britain; that he was certainly not a criminal and came from a good family – although he didn't say who that family was until the day of their marriage. When Martha and Andrew learnt that he was really a Laddisbrock, gentry from their own village, Haddenford, back in England, they had reservations about the union. But they had agreed on the marriage later, having long since realised how few neighbours they had and there being little possibility of their girls finding a decent law-abiding husband.

At first, Richard was a loving husband and worked well alongside Andrew and the boys, but gradually the call of the township with its bar and gambling room became a bigger object of his desire. Emma believed that she loved Richard, but was becoming tired of placating the family when he wasn't pulling his weight.

Sighing, she washed her hands in a small bowl of water and splashed her face. She was twenty-five, and after twelve years had still not settled in this hot country. She longed for the greenery of England with its cool dark lanes, their banks filled with flowers and herbs. The forests of recognisable oak, chestnut, beech and willow, the snaking silver rivers that ran gurgling gently between fields and under trees. She wanted to see again the gold and bronze of an English autumn; see the beautiful whiteness of a hoarfrost, and feel the coldness of a snow-filled day.

It was during the afternoon that she felt the pang of impending doom return. It rose as a panic in her chest and prickled in her head. She could hardly breathe for the feeling of fear that almost choked her.

The worry of the unknown about to be visited upon her was as real to Emma as the table at which she sat sewing.

Going to the door she once again looked towards the horizon and waited. It was coming, approaching fast and yet she could see nothing. Every muscle in her body was taut, cramped with anxiety. For an hour she stood watching, and then, through the heat haze she saw a shadow, a distorted blue-grey movement that disappeared as quickly as she had seen it. She waited, her mouth dry. It appeared again a little closer, the outline of men on horses. Dust rising from the ground told her they came at speed.

Opening the drawer in the dresser that stood by the door she snatched the pistol that lay covered by a cloth. She had no means of firing it, as ammunition was on Nona's list of things to buy, but the feel of it in her hand gave her courage. This was a lawless land and she was alone.

Running outside she hoped that they were sufficiently far away not to see her. Taking Black from his paddock she led him into the barn and tied him loosely to a post in case she needed to escape quickly.

Standing in the shadow of its large warm interior, Emma observed the fast-moving group. As they came closer she saw another horse bringing up the rear, moving slower, throwing up more dust than the first group and knew it was pulling a cart.

The horses and men thundered into the yard before her cabin, and as the dust settled her heart thumped in her chest as she recognised them. The Logan brothers; what could they want out here on Tate land?

The hat was pushed back from the face of the leader, the eldest of the four brothers, and the look on Neil Logan's scarred face blanched Emma's skin. As he pulled his horse to a stop Neil slid a bullwhip from the back of his saddle. Holding it tightly in his right hand he let the narrow end fall to the ground where it lay curled ready for use.

'Get yourself out here, Tate, and watch your boy die,' he shouted.

Emma couldn't move, couldn't breathe, her mouth was dry. The heat of the day seemed to have swallowed all the oxygen.

The horses in the yard moved restlessly, snorting, ears back, the veins standing proud on their necks, adding to the feeling of danger.

What boy? she thought desperately.

5

She knew who they were; she had seen them in the township, lounging outside Anna's Bar. Notorious criminals, gamblers with several murders attributed to them, but in this lawless land so far from the military, they ruled with impunity.

'Search the place,' Neil Logan directed his brothers as he sat nervously watchful from his saddle.

Emma watched as Morrie dismounted and crept, bent low, towards the cabins, while the youngest boy, the sallow-faced Clem, turned his horse toward the barn.

As Clem rode slowly in the direction of the high wooden building he looked edgy; his hand lay limply on the pistol at his hip.

Hiding her unloaded gun in her skirt pocket Emma stepped from the shadow of the barn and into the sunlight.

Clem pulled his horse up, fixing her with a malignant glare; the atmosphere in the yard was static with danger.

The moment was broken as the cart, driven by Nona, arrived in a cloud of dust. Beside her sat Jed Logan, a cocky fellow who, people said, had been born without the knowledge of fear.

'Get yourself out here!' Clem demanded as he saw Emma. His eyes did not leave Emma's face as the cart moved past him, drawing up outside the cabin. 'Come see what your sister brought you,' he smiled, revealing yellow teeth.

Emma ran forward, fear welling up inside her. Nona and Jed were already moving to the back of the cart where Bart lay across the prone body of Emma's husband. He wasn't moving and blood was staining the boards on which he lay amongst their supplies.

Nona's face appeared grey beneath her tan as she saw Emma approaching.

'They shot him, Em,' was all she could whisper.

'Why?' Emma looked at the handsome face of her young husband, his lips now as pale as his face. 'What happened?'

Nona could not answer, could not look her sister in the eyes; instead she called Bart off the prone body. Obediently the dog jumped down and sat at Nona's feet.

6

'Where's the rest of you?' Neil's voice was threatening, demanding. 'The rest of the Tate clan, where are they?'

'Working,' Emma retorted, with a look in her eyes that portrayed it to be something that these men knew nothing of.

'You got nerve looking at me like that, lady,' Neil sneered. 'But we'll see how stuck up you are after we give you a dose of what your husband gave our sister. But first, we'll show you how we deal with men like him.'

He nodded to his brothers, who leant into the back of the cart, pulling Richard by his boots unceremoniously to the ground. Bart growled. Morrie pulled a knife. 'If he jumps me,' he said to Nona, 'he'll jump on my steel.'

'Bart! Stay,' she demanded. The dog lay down, but his eyes never left the men.

'Take him to the barn.' Neil spat on the ground. 'We'll deal with all of them in there.'

Inside the barn Morrie indicated the girls sit on a bench near a pile of straw, while Jed threw a rope over a roof-beam making a loop in one end. Black snorted nervously.

The full horror of what was happening hit Emma. Leaving the bench, she threw herself on top of her husband. 'No. You can't. It's murder. I won't let you.'

'Make your peace with him, lady.' The scars that were cut deeply in the flesh around Neil's eyes seemed to tighten. 'It's the last day any of us will have to look at his pretty face.'

'What has he done?' she cried, her hands feeling Richard's chest for a sign of life. When a faint beat told her that he was still alive she was even more scared for him.

'You can't kill him without telling me what he has done,' she cried, looking back at Neil.

'Don't tell me you don't know what he's been up to. What wife wouldn't know what her husband was doing in town if he didn't come home nights?'

'He was staying with friends,' she cried in Richard's defence.

'Is that what he told you? Ha! What he was doing, was sleeping with our sister, and now she's pregnant and he's going to pay, and so are you.'

Emma couldn't move; it was a shock to hear it said. Yet she had suspected through his recent coldness that he had found someone else.

Neil bent and whispered in Richard's ear, 'You're going to pay, Mr High and Mighty, and we're going to dance on your grave, after we've tasted your goods, like you took ours. Pull him up, Morrie.'

The noose was deftly placed over Richard's head as Jed and Morrie lifted the limp body with difficulty into a sitting position. Without thought for her own safety Emma threw herself at the men, knocking them all to the floor. Morrie cursed and kicked out at her with his boot. Bart was on the man's leg in a second and Morrie yelled as the dog's teeth sank into his leg.

Jed had fallen with Richard's weight on top of him, but was fighting his way up as Nona hit him across the head with a spade. He fell across Morrie's waist, pinning the man's arms to the floor. Neil pulled his gun and fired at the dog. Bart yelped, but didn't let go of his prey. Morrie screamed, 'Get it off me, Neil.'

But Neil's eyes were looking somewhere else. He was facing the barrel of a gun.

'Put it down, lady, or I'll blow your head off.'

Emma didn't lower her gun as Neil looked towards Nona.

'Call the dog off,' he shouted.

'No!' Nona stood solid, watching her sister.

'Don't shoot it, Neil, you might shoot me,' Morrie screamed again as the dog bit harder, growling and twisting its head.

Neil swore as the dog shook his brother's limb like an empty cloth.

'What does it matter if I shoot you anyway? You'll recover,' he told the terrified man as he took aim. The shot rang out around the barn.

Frightened by the sound, Black reared up, loosening his tether, and in his panic to escape careered into Neil, knocking him to the ground.

As the horse raced from the barn, a man's boot put pressure on Neil's neck and he felt the cold metal of a gun pressing painfully into his temple. Turning his head, Neil came face to face with Andrew Tate.

Andrew's voice was tense. 'Throw your gun and get up.'

The gun landed at Nona's feet. She picked it up and, looking around the barn, asked Emma, 'Where's Clem?'

Emma turned and saw a movement a few feet from Andrew. Clem had his gun pointed at Andrew's back. She watched, frozen in time, as his finger squeezed the trigger. The click, as the hammer came down, cut through their senses like an ice shard. It didn't fire. Clem looked at the gun, a question in his eyes.

The sudden roar of a gun sent that look into a fleeting horror as a bullet thudded into his chest. His body left the ground, landing heavily on the bench where earlier the girls had been sitting. A patch of red spread quickly across the front of his shirt; he didn't move. Nona was holding Neil's smoking gun in her hand; her face was pale.

Andrew's eyes flicked from Nona to Emma, his gun still pointing at Neil.

Running quickly to her sister Emma held her close. 'It's alright, Nona, it's alright.'

Emma's closeness brought Nona out of her daze and, recovering quickly, her eyes searched for Bart.

'Bart!' she called, her voice holding a note of panic.

Morrie was on his feet, his hand on his gun; as it cleared the leather of his holster a flash of black came from nowhere. Bart's teeth bit into Morrie's throat, ripping the flesh. The gun that had been pointed at Andrew and Nona went off, but the bullet slammed harmlessly into the roof as Morrie fell backwards, the dog still at his throat. Nona screamed at the sight of Bart covered in blood. Morrie was dead. A small whimper came from the blood-matted dog that lay beside him.

As Nona held Bart's body in her arms, his tongue lolled from the side of his mouth, his eyes glazed and he lay still.

'What the hell, happened here?' Andrew Tate looked from one to the other.

Nona couldn't speak.

'Can we look at Richard?' Emma was quickly on her knees beside Richard's prone body and, loosening the noose, she slipped it over his head.

'Richard!' she called to him, her voice full of anxiety. He didn't respond but was still alive.

Andrew took Neil and Jed to the storeroom and tied them tightly by their hands and feet. Jed had a split in his scalp that bled profusely, covering his face and filling his eye sockets. Andrew left the bodies of Clem and Morrie where they lay.

'Let's get Richard into the house.' Andrew took charge, as he always did. 'We'll lay him on the table and have a look at him.'

Emma's heart was racing as she looked towards Nona who was still kneeling, head bent, with Bart draped limply across her lap. She obeyed Andrew, quickly lifting Richard's feet as Andrew hefted him under the arms.

Inside the cabin, the stillness made the situation seem all the more unreal as they laid Richard on the table. 'Get his clothes off, Emma,' Andrew instructed, 'we have to see the damage.'

Richard's neck was red where the noose had tightened during his fall with the weight of the men on top of him. When he was undressed they could see that he had been shot in the stomach. His trousers were soaked with blood, but the wound was already drying around the edges. They rolled him onto his side to find the angle at which the bullet had left his body, but could find no outlet.

'The bullet's still in there,' Andrew said, 'but I don't know if we should try to get it out.'

'Can a man live with a bullet in him?' Emma asked, looking at Andrew.

'Maybe.' He frowned.

'Maybe! Don't you know?' Emma's voice rose in panic.

'I'm not a doctor, Emma.' His voice was more anxious than she had ever heard it.

'It can't be much different from working on an animal, Andrew, surely.'

'Of course it's different, Emma.' Anger suffused Andrew's face. 'His muscles, his organs and body fat are different to a cow. If I lose a cow it's money lost but if I lose a man because I don't know what I'm doing it could be murder.'

'How can it be murder if you're trying to save his life? Please, Andrew,' she beseeched in desperation.

At the sound of a wagon pulling up outside Andrew looked towards the door. 'It's your mother. She's been anxious all day and made me come home to see that all was well. I told her to stay at the camp, but she seems now to be here. I have to talk to her. Cover the wound, Emma, I'll be back.'

His feet stomped loudly on the wooden floorboards as he left the cabin and crossed the veranda.

Emma stood beside the table and in the silence studied Richard's face. He was handsome, even when unconscious. As the shock of all that had just happened rose to the surface, tears flowed over her cheeks. 'If only you had been different, Richard,' she whispered. 'Why did you marry me?'

In England, she mused, she wouldn't even have considered marrying him, nor would he have considered her.

Then, suddenly making up her mind, she ladled water from a churn into a pan, before placing the pan over the fire to heat the water. Taking a long sharp knife from the drawer, she pushed the blade carefully into the hottest part of the fire.

The door opened and her mother hurried into the room followed by Andrew. With her came the cool smell of herbs; Martha was still beautiful, her long hair still black.

Going straight to the table she placed her hand on Richard's head, then lightly onto his chest, feeling the temperature of his skin. 'He's clammy,' she said, looking at Emma.

'He's lost a lot of blood, Mother.'

Martha nodded. 'His body is in shock. I'm not sure if he'll survive us cutting into him, Emma,' she said quietly, looking at her daughter with sad eyes.

'But we have to try something!' Emma knew without doubt that she desperately wanted Richard to live.

Martha looked from Emma to Andrew. 'He has a good chance of dying either way, Andrew. Can you do it?' Her voice was soft.

'I don't know,' he replied, looking at Richard's young body.

In the coolness of the cabin Andrew's tanned face had taken on a grey sheen and while the women waited for his decision a heavy silence fell between them.

'If he was one of your boys, Andrew, would you do it then?' Emma asked.

'I might have a look. See if I can find the bullet, but it's risky.'

'If the risk is the same either way, then we should try. Don't you think, Andrew?'

Martha laid her hand softly on his arm and looked into his face.

He nodded agreement.

Emma pulled the knife from the fire and brought him hot water to wash his hands.

As Andrew stripped to the waist Martha forced a leather strap into Richard's mouth to stop him biting his tongue if he came to. Seating herself at the top of the table she held Richard's head between her hands, closed her eyes and prayed to the Goddess to give Richard the strength to survive.

Positioning herself at the foot of the table, Emma held Richard's legs as Andrew cut into the bullet hole to make it larger.

A groan emanated from the patient and his eyelids fluttered. Andrew put pressure on the wound as the blood began to flow freely.

'I can't see anything, there's too much blood.' He spoke to himself. Then, taking a deep breath, he pushed his finger into the bloody hole, feeling for the bullet.

Richard screamed and brought his legs up, pulling Emma forward, almost onto the table, as blood spilled onto the floor.

'Hold his legs!' Andrew shouted as his finger probed the path of the bullet. The pain became too much for Richard and he fell into unconsciousness.

In the following silence they all visibly relaxed. Andrew pushed his finger deeper into the soft tissue for what seemed like an age to Emma. At last he said, 'It's in too deep, I can't feel it.' Richard's blood could be heard running onto the floor. 'I have to stop.' Andrew was sweating. 'I'm sorry. I can't reach the bullet. If he loses any more blood he will die anyway.'

He looked first at Martha and then Emma; they nodded agreement, both also being alarmed by the amount of blood on the floor. Andrew removed his finger and put pressure on the wound.

'Get your sewing box, Emma, and I'll sew him up.' His voice was tense. 'God, I hope we've done the right thing. If he dies…'

'If he dies, Andrew, at least we tried to save him. We cannot reproach ourselves for that,' Martha said quietly while soaking a cloth in the now warm water and gently wiping Richard's face and damping his lips.

After the wound had been stitched Richard was tightly bandaged with a torn sheet and put into the bed, where he lay pale and silent.

After washing in the yard, Andrew entered the kitchen, pulling his shirt on over his head. 'Now, will someone tell me what happened?'

Martha and Emma had been scrubbing the floor and the table when he returned. Standing, feet apart, he looked from one to the other. It was Emma who took a chair by the fireplace and indicated her parents to sit down. Only Martha sat, as Emma's hands fluttered like leaves in her lap and she tried to find her voice. She was, after all, trying to work it all out herself and was still in shock. When she did speak, she hardly recognised her own voice.

'Richard got one of the Logan girls pregnant, Andrew. He was in town when her brothers shot him and came here to take their revenge.' Emma felt nothing as she spoke into the silence; it was as though she were repeating someone else's story.

'They brought him back?' Andrew's voice, almost a whisper, seemed to match her own.

'Yes, in our cart.' Her voice trailed off for a moment. 'Nona drove with Jed's gun in her side.'

Andrew was silent a moment before saying, 'So what happened in the barn?'

'They were going to hang Richard and then give us a taste of what Richard had given their sister.'

For a moment Andrew's face was blank before realisation dawned. 'Where's Nona?' His voice was strained.

Both women looked at each other, suddenly alarmed; they hadn't thought about Nona since bringing Richard into the cabin.

Andrew turned on his heel and ran out into the yard followed by Emma and Martha.

The storeroom was now unlocked, the door ajar. Andrew's heart was in his mouth as he pulled the door open and saw Nona sitting calmly on a sack of flour. His gaze turned slowly from her to where he'd left the men. Jed was dead, his lips blue. Neil had now been shot between the legs; he was still alive, but his life was ebbing away as Nona looked on.

'Nona?' Andrew stepped slowly into the storeroom, watching her face carefully. She looked up, but showed no recognition. 'Nona,' Andrew spoke softly, 'give me the gun. It's all over.' The blankness he saw in her eyes frightened him. 'Come,' he said gently, and warily stepped towards her. 'Let's get you to your mother.'

She allowed him to help her to her feet and take the gun, and without looking in the direction of the men she walked with Andrew to the door, where Martha held her gently, leaving Emma to do what she could for Neil Logan in his last minutes on earth.

~

Darkness was pulling in as the cart with its gruesome cargo pulled up outside the Logan cabin situated in an area of uncultivated land a mile outside of the township. A washing line, strung between the trees, held faded clothes. Rubbish and broken tools littered the ground around the cabin. The area had a feeling of neglect and Andrew's heart was heavy.

The door opened immediately the cart came to a stop and several women spilled out led by Rilla Logan, the men's mother.

'I'm sorry, Rilla,' Andrew said, from his seat. But the women weren't listening. They were running to the back of the cart, where they cried in horror at seeing all four of their men laid out.

'You killed them,' Rilla Logan wailed accusingly.

'It was self-defence, Rilla. They came to kill my family.'

'No, Tate. If I know anything about my boys they were going to get revenge, not kill anyone.'

'And we were supposed to let them hang Richard and rape our women? Is that what you're saying, Rilla?'

But she wasn't listening.

Jack, James and George, who had accompanied Andrew, dismounted from their horses and pulled the dead men from the cart. With the help of the women they carried the bodies into the ramshackle darkness of the Logan cabin. The women, who ranged from twelve years to twenty, were the men's sisters. They were rough women, well built with muscular arms, their faces already hardened by the harsh weather and the will to survive.

As Andrew and the boys went to leave, a pretty girl in a faded pink dress ran out and held the side of the cart. Andrew pulled the horse to a stop.

'I'm Lizzie, Mr Tate. How is Richard?'

Andrew looked kindly on the girl who was probably the one carrying Richard's child. 'We can't reach the bullet, he still has it in him.' Andrew was blunt. 'He may not live.'

Lizzie nodded and, biting her lip, let go of the side of the cart and turned away. Andrew flicked the reins. With a toss of its head the horse moved forward into the night and Andrew was glad to get away from the heartbreak and squalor, glad that he had his sons and stepson with him.

2.

It was a month before Richard was strong enough to sit in a chair for any length of time. 'How are you this morning, Richard?' Emma asked as she handed him his clothes. She had nursed him, hardly leaving his side, yet as the weeks passed she felt confused about their marriage. Would he leave her when he was well and where did that leave her?

Each day she stared out from the cabin door through the heat, across the vast stillness of the land and felt the stirring of an emotion deep down in her soul. It was something that she had not given herself permission to give in to. But now, knowing she was married to a man she could not trust, she acknowledged that she felt restless and could see no role for herself here anymore. The heat stifled her and she longed even more now for the coolness of England.

'Will you sit out on the porch for a while before it gets too hot?' she asked Richard.

'Yes, I'll sit outside.' His voice was flat, petulant. 'I hate this place. I want to get out of here.' He didn't look at her as he moved with the stiffness of an old man pulling at the bed covers.

Every day she tried to hide how his attitude, his anger, hurt her, and when she spoke it was quietly so as not to make matters worse.

'When you're well enough, Richard,' she said, 'you can go where you like, but for now you don't have the energy.'

Helping him from the bed she let him lean on her until he could stand up almost straight. It was always an effort for him first thing in the morning when his wound was tight.

He walked slowly, holding his stomach. Helping him out of the door she lowered him into a chair on the veranda where he could see the distant blue mountains. As she turned back into the cabin she noticed her mother skirting Black's paddock.

'Good morning, Richard,' Martha called. He didn't answer; the effort of walking had robbed him of speech and his face was pale.

'It's good to see Richard up and about,' Martha said cheerfully as she entered Emma's cabin.

'He manages a couple of hours a day now in the chair, Mother. I don't know if he will ever be strong enough for manual work.'

As she spoke, Emma felt a twinge of the old embarrassment. She was still making excuses for Richard's lack of ability to do his share of the farm work. Except that now it was true; he was no longer the vital young man he'd been before he was shot.

Martha was aware of her daughter's feelings, not that Emma had said anything to her, but she felt it.

'I have a confession to make to you, Emma.'

'A confession, Mother?' Emma looked up sharply, her hands covered in flour ready to spread on the table before kneading her dough.

Martha looked uncomfortable. 'Without saying anything to you, and probably I should have, I wrote to Richard's parents and told them that their son had been shot and that he was very weak. I also told them of his marriage.'

'I see.' Emma looked at her hands and kneaded the dough with more vigour.

'You see what?' Martha asked.

'I don't think that was something that Richard wanted, Mother.'

'They had to know, Emma. They had a right to know that their son had taken a wife.'

'We both know why he didn't tell them, Mother. He is the son of gentry and I the daughter of a carpenter and a mother who's a farm worker.'

18

Martha flinched. 'We own two farms, Emma. Andrew may not be your father but he is a landowner.'

'You know what I mean, Mother. Andrew wasn't born into gentry any more than I was born into it. Here in Australia it doesn't matter, we're all equal, but back there I wouldn't be accepted into Richard's world.'

'Even so, I believe that you should both go back to England. Let Richard see a doctor. Give him a chance to get his health back. Then you can return if you feel you want to.'

Emma threw the dough into a greased bowl and covered it with a cloth. 'Our marriage won't last five minutes back in England, Mother,' she said over her shoulder as she placed the bowl on a small table near the door for the warmth.

'But you want to go back, don't you?'

'Yes, I do. I'm sorry, Mother, I long for the greenery of home.'

'Then you shall go. Andrew and I have saved enough money; you will have it for your passage.'

Emma felt a weight lift from her shoulders. She was going back to England; the only worry was that she would have to live with her in-laws and that put fear into her heart.

'I'm worried about Nona,' Martha continued. 'She hasn't recovered. She's taken to her room and doesn't leave it, not even for food. I try to tempt her out to help with the chores, but she's unresponsive.'

'None of us have spoken about it, Mother, but Nona killed Neil Logan in cold blood. He was tied up. He couldn't get away. I know she loved Bart, but to shoot a man...'

A flash of anger crossed Martha's face. Her features set like a mask as she looked directly into her daughter's eyes. When she spoke, Emma knew her mother was trying to keep control of her feelings, something that she had not witnessed before.

Martha's voice was clipped with anger when she spoke. 'Have you such a short memory, Emma? Did what happened to your sister in England mean so little to you?'

19

Emma had forgotten. After all, she wasn't living at home then but was in the service of the Brack family. Now she felt ashamed.

'I'm sorry, Mother, I had forgotten. I thought that this was about Bart.'

'Well, now you know. She loved her dog, but this goes much deeper.'

'She still killed Neil Logan in cold blood, Mother.'

'Did she, Emma? Was it Neil Logan that she killed, or someone else?'

'It was Neil Logan. You know it was, Mother.'

Emma was confused; she had never had to stand up to her mother before. Martha was being irrational. She'd seen the body. She knew who he was.

Martha raised an eyebrow, staring at Emma before she silently turned away and walked out of the door into the heat of the yard, leaving Emma perplexed.

~

Later in the day Emma walked slowly to her mother's cabin. It still felt like home as she entered, with all the familiar smells invading her senses. Knocking on Nona's bedroom door she asked, 'Can I come in?' She was careful to use a gentle tone of voice. When there was no reply she knocked again. Not waiting for Nona to respond she opened the door slowly. The room was dark, the shutters closed, and Emma felt like an intruder. Nona was sitting on the edge of her bed in the cool gloom.

'Are you alright?' Emma whispered.

Her sister didn't answer; she didn't even acknowledge that Emma had entered her room. Emma moved quickly to her side. The young woman was still in her night smock, a shawl wrapped around her shoulders, her hair untidy in its night plait, which hung down her back.

'Do you need to talk, Nona?'

Taking her sister's brown work-worn hand in her own, Emma held it quietly and waited. When there was no response she tried another tack.

'Nona, who did you shoot?' she whispered.

Nona flinched. 'Do you know who you shot?' Emma persisted. 'Tell me who you shot, Nona.'

Her younger sister raised her head; an angry fire burnt deep in her eyes. 'You know who I shot, Em, and I would do it again and again.' Her voice held such venom that Emma was shocked. 'I *want* to kill him.' Nona choked with emotion.

Emma held her sister's body tightly and could feel the shaking of pent-up rage. Moments later Nona stood suddenly and so violently that Emma was thrown to the floor.

'I want to do it again,' she cried. 'When I find him I will kill him again.'

Nona's bare feet slapped on the wooden floor as she ran wildly about the room. 'Where's the gun?' she shouted, looking deranged, her eyes wild. 'Get me the gun.'

As she screamed her demands she pulled the drawers from a cabinet that stood near the door. As the contents fell to the floor she dropped to her knees, rummaging amongst the spilled items. Her fingers were like claws and her eyes glowed with the light of insanity as she glared around the room as though she might see the gun. Throwing the closet door open she pulled at her clothes. When she couldn't find the gun, she swept her mirror and hairpins from her dressing table in anger before Emma could reach her. Her voice rose louder. 'I want to kill him. *Get me the gun*. I want to *kill* him.' Tears ran relentlessly over Nona's face and dripped onto her night smock.

The door burst open and Martha ran into the room; grabbing her daughter she held her in her arms and in that moment Nona's manic fury seemed to dissolve.

'Mother, Mother,' Nona cried into Martha's hair, her body jerking with each sob.

'It's alright, Nona, it's finished.' She stroked Nona's back. 'It's finished, little one.'

Leading her back to the bed, Martha sat holding her daughter in her arms reassuring her, just as she had all those years ago when she had discovered the bruises on Nona's tiny thighs.

~

Emma was sitting in her mother's kitchen when Martha entered and joined her at the table.

'I'm sorry, Mother, I shouldn't have asked her who she thought she'd shot. I've just made it worse.'

'No, Emma, you did the right thing. It was what was needed. I guessed that it was Beemer she was shooting in her own mind. She was just a child when she was raped and has buried that trauma all these years. Let's hope that now she can live a life of happiness.'

In the silence that followed, Martha looked at her hands and arms, brown and hardened by working on the land. 'Emma,' she continued, 'I want Nona to return to England with you and Richard. This is no place for her. It's too rough.'

'I will be glad to have her join us, Mother.' Emma felt relieved. 'It will be good to have a supporter when I meet Richard's parents.'

'That is settled then. We will do our best to get some clothes together for you. You cannot run around as you do here. You will have the grey costume and green jacket that I wore to Beemer's trial in London, and we will put together something for Nona. You will both have to buy another outfit when you get there.'

The following weeks were spent sewing and altering the best of their clothes. The time passed quickly, too quickly for Emma, who felt certain that she would not fit into the society in which Richard's family were born.

3.

They had started out around midnight, which gave them some hours of cool relief at the start of their journey to the coast. Five hours later, while the sun was still hidden behind the distant mountains, they stopped to rest the horse and eat the food that Martha had packed for them.

The air was already warm as the dark blue mantel of darkness receded before the rising sun that bathed the land in shades of apricot. By midday the heat was relentless, stiflingly hot beneath the canvas that Andrew had rigged up for their shelter in the back of the wagon. Their journey through the bush to the port was slow. The Tate homestead was many miles from Port Jackson and the tree- and shrub-covered rocky land that they had to pass through made travelling difficult. Andrew did his best to drive the cart smoothly, but Richard was in a great deal of pain by late afternoon when they camped under trees near a spring. After eating they retired early, sleeping together in the cart across its boards. Starting again around midnight they reached their bustling destination mid-morning.

The area that they viewed from the wagon had changed in the years since the family had arrived as free colonists. Emma remembered how, twelve years before, the convicts, some in chains, were moving large rocks and cutting back dense forest. Gangs of men were digging out tree stumps and clearing the ground. Emma and Nona had watched a group of women prisoners grinding clay and mixing it with water to make bricks. There were prisoners sitting on the beach in the hot sun; their pale flesh, unused to the heat, glistened red and sore. Some had covered themselves in wet mud as a protection which dried and cracked within the hour. Housing had already been built for the military officers by the time the Tate family had arrived, although the houses were little more than shacks.

The family had watched as women prisoners swam in the rough sea, diving again and again to gather oyster shells for burning and crushing into powder to make lime. And beyond the beach, more women and children were hoeing and digging the cleared ground for growing food.

At that time the convicts had been living in a guarded compound of makeshift huts and cooked on open fires. They were dirty, wearing torn clothes, and some were almost naked. An atmosphere of depression and violence seemed to enfold the area and Emma had been afraid of the prisoners, even the women.

As their wagon now approached the port she and Nona saw that some of the buildings were now built like grand English houses and had spread far beyond the area that they remembered. They noted a large building as they passed, standing alone in a vast open space which, they agreed, must be a prison, as soldiers walked the walls, guns leaning on their shoulders.

Emma could see children running around in the streets that had sprung up, and it was obvious to her that the convicts who had worked out their sentences were setting up home. Most, she knew, would never see the land of their birth again and were trying to start another life as best they could here.

Andrew and Nona walked to the dock to arrange the passage home, while Emma stayed with Richard in the wagon.

Situated to one side of the dock, the Custom House, unlike the buildings around it, had two floors. The lower part of the building was built of brick and the upper floor, which was no more than wooden boards nailed together, was reached by an outside staircase and had a thatched roof to keep the sun off.

As Andrew and Nona entered on the ground floor, the clerk, a man in his thirties, looked up from his desk, quill in hand.

'May I help you?' he asked, screwing up his face as the stark light from the doorway cut through the cool darkness of the interior.

'I wish to purchase three tickets to England on the next ship going home,' Andrew announced calmly.

The clerk blinked at Andrew as though trying to get him into focus. 'Long hours looking at figures,' he said apologetically, 'have made it difficult for me to see, sir. Please tell me who will be going aboard. I have to keep tally of everyone who sails.'

'I would like to purchase passage for Mr Richard Laddisbrock and...'

'Age... if you please, sir?' the clerk interrupted him apologetically.

'Um, twenty years.' Andrew looked at Nona for confirmation, but she wasn't sure and shrugged her shoulders.

'Occupation?' The clerk didn't look up from his work.

Andrew thought for a moment, before saying strongly, 'Farm worker,' then thought that perhaps he should have said gentleman. The dilemma was, did he say what Richard once was, or what he was now? He watched as the man dipped the quill into the ink and wrote the figure 20 into a column next to another in which he had written Richard's name and then wrote farm worker in the following column.

'His wife, Emma Laddisbrock, aged twenty-five years, and...' The man wrote slowly and deliberately, placing Emma's name in the column below Richard's and the word 'wife' under occupation. When the clerk paused Andrew continued, 'And, Mistress Nona Tilby, sister-in-law to Mr Laddisbrock, aged twenty-three years.'

The clerk wrote steadily, his quill scratching loudly on the parchment in the silence of the dimly lit room. His nose almost touched the page as he methodically wrote the information into his book.

'Can you tell me when the next sailing will be?' Andrew asked as the man finished by sprinkling sand onto the ink-wet page from a small box on the desk.

'You are indeed lucky, sir. Another day and you would have missed the ship and there would not have been another for at least four months, maybe longer.'

Andrew looked at Nona with relief. Richard could not have made the journey back to the farm without risk.

'One of the passengers travelling is unwell,' Andrew said. 'Is it possible at this late stage to purchase a cabin?'

'I'm sorry, sir. The ship's full. There is only room on the deck for late passengers.'

'But my son-in-law is very ill. He may not survive the journey exposed to the elements on deck for many weeks.'

'We take so few passengers to England, sir, mostly soldiers returning after a two- or three-year duty. The ship carries prisoners here and cargo back, and unfortunately,' he squinted at Andrew, 'this time there are other passengers, wives and children of soldiers.'

Andrew's jaw clenched and Nona noticed a twitch in his facial muscles; she could see that he was not going to let the matter rest. Before he could speak she stepped forward and looked straight into the watery eyes of the clerk and smiled gently. The man's face flushed and he seemed uncomfortable.

'Sir,' she said, 'I can see that you are a man of great importance to the shipping company, and that it takes a great deal of knowledge and competence to do this job. I can also see that you are a man with a big heart, who would not see my sister and myself travelling on the deck of the ship. Please. Would you look again, just out of kindness, to see if you could find us a place below the deck?'

The man cleared his throat and, blushing, pulled another book from a shelf at his side and opened it at the last entry page. Running a finger up and down the columns, his eyes squinted at the copperplate writing before he said, 'I believe, mistress, that if you arrive on board early, then there will be a small cabin for your use on the lower deck. It will not be pleasant, as it is above the hold in which the animals are held. I will speak to the Captain and arrange it.' His voice had a break in it when he spoke. 'I don't get many young women in here and you remind me of my sister back home, she would be about your age now.' He nodded his head as though agreeing with himself, and his weak grey eyes glazed in remembrance of family life so far away.

'Thank you,' Nona said quietly, pulling him back from his daze.

Coughing to cover his embarrassment he blushed again.

'Get there early or someone else will have it,' he warned, pushing his quill once more into the inkpot.

'Do you know of anyone who could put my family up for the night?' Andrew asked, having calmed himself.

The clerk wrote on a piece of paper and handed it to Andrew. 'Take this to the address written there.' He jabbed at the paper with an inky finger. 'The wife of Captain Fry will likely give you lodging and if not, she will know of someone that will.'

After taking Nona back to the wagon, Andrew walked the streets that bore names from England such as Norfolk Street, York Street and London Road. The home of Captain Fry and his wife, Diane, was of brick and wood, in a style that could have been seen in any English village back home. The front garden was neatly kept, with flowers growing at the front door. As he stood on the step Andrew could have imagined that he were back in England, if it were not so very hot.

A maid showed him into a low-ceilinged room that was wonderfully cool. When Mrs Fry entered the room Andrew could see straight away that she was a genteel woman. Her personality was warm as she greeted him.

At his request of rooms for one night she smiled serenely. 'I shall enjoy the company of your family, Mr Tate,' she said smiling assurance. 'I shall look forward to looking after them even though for only one night.'

An hour later Emma and Nona were sad to see Andrew leave and hugged him as he wished them all farewell before he headed back to the homestead and Martha.

The Frys had five children, all girls, who were introduced as Molly, Amy, Beatrice, Dorcus Mary and Hephzibah, the youngest, who was four years old. After a convivial meal when both families exchanged information about their lives over dinner, Richard, who had become pale with pain, went to bed.

Emma and Nona sat on soft chairs listening to the children reading and were overjoyed to be cradled in a family atmosphere after the hard journey.

'You have made a comfortable home here, Mrs Fry,' Nona said, as she turned the page of a book for Hephzibah.

'Thank you, Mistress Tilby. Although, it takes a great deal of patience to await things that I need brought by ship from home.' Going to a drawer she took out a letter. 'I wonder if...' she held the letter out to Emma, '... if you would take my letter to London and give it to a messenger, Mrs Laddisbrock. It is addressed to my parents.'

'I would be very pleased to hand it to a messenger for you, Mrs Fry,' Emma said, putting it into her purse.

'Thank you.'

For a moment Diane Fry looked sad and Emma realised that moving to Australia with a military husband, leaving her family behind, was in itself a prison sentence. She changed the subject.

'The port has changed a great deal in twelve years, Mrs Fry.'

'It has indeed, Mrs Laddisbrock. The prisoners were soon put to work in 1788, cutting back the thick forest and building houses with the materials to hand. It was good for the convicts to have something to do; it focused their minds from other distractions.' She blushed and, taking a deep breath, continued, 'It made it easier for the officers to manage them. They discovered amongst them carpenters, masons, a blacksmith, fishermen and farmers. Harnessing their knowledge has saved us, for we were at one time in danger of starving to death, when our expected supply ship did not arrive.'

'When my family arrived here,' Emma said, 'the convicts had started to build brick houses in the style of home and they looked strange in the unfamiliar landscape. Now twelve years on the area has become a large village.'

Diane Fry smiled gently. 'It makes it easier for officers' wives, who join their husbands, to settle here. Captain Fry and I will, I think, only be here another year. I worry about my parents who are ageing, and I do miss my siblings who have married and had children that I have not yet seen, nor they mine.'

It suddenly brought home to Emma that she and Nona may never see their family again, and the emotion of that thought caught in her throat and brought tears to the rim of her eyes. She looked down quickly. Diane Fry said nothing, although Emma knew that she must have seen. Were not all the women here feeling the same loss, a feeling that bonded them together?

The evening was spent in the comfort of female company, and they were sorry to leave Mrs Fry and her children behind when, next day at an early hour, they boarded their ship and were shown to their cabin.

It was narrow, with two berths, one above the other against one wall, and beneath the bottom berth, a cupboard that held a sack of straw to be used as a third mattress. There was, Emma noticed with relief, enough space in the cupboard for their essential clothes, as there was nowhere to hang or place anything.

A chair stood against the back wall and above it a shelf to be used for writing. On the wall opposite the bunks was a short corner shelf on which stood a jug and bowl and beneath that a small cupboard holding a bucket and a cloth. It was sparse, but private.

The ship was soon crowded with people, their footsteps loud upon the wooden deck above. All was busy as the crew hurried about their duties, getting the ship ready to sail. On board, the military that were returning home were finding their allotted accommodation or places on the deck. The hold below was stacked with cargo and provisions for the long journey, including barrels of drinking water and live animals.

Only one day out at sea and Richard became sea sick and unable to face food. At first Emma and Nona felt confined in the narrow wooden cabin allotted them, with its bunked berths and one chair. However, they soon realised that they were lucky to have a small private place to share. Most of the military returning home were single men who lay in hammocks hung at night in the passageways beside their meagre belongings, or slept on deck.

Below them in the hold live animals complained with a cacophony of noise – cows for milk, hogs for meat and chickens for eggs. Most, if not all, would be slaughtered on the journey home to feed the crew and passengers. The stench of the animals rose up through the deck boards adding to Richard's sickness and bad mood.

Emma and Nona had, after twelve weeks, settled into a routine, walking the upper deck daily for exercise and to leave Richard in peace. After the freedom of the Tate homestead they were stifled by the bad air below deck where passengers and crew slept, cooked and ate shoulder to shoulder in a stench far worse than any farmyard.

'I'm getting tired of this endless view, Em,' Nona complained as she shielded her eyes against the sun that shone relentlessly on the water. The sparkling stars that glittered off the waves bit painfully into her eyeballs. 'There has been nothing to see but water for months.'

'We must find a way to endure this torment, I agree.' Emma's voice was quiet.

Nona had a serious look on her face as she studied her sister. 'You don't want to go to England, do you, Em?'

'Oh I'm sorry, Nona, yes, yes I do, more than anything in the world. It's just that I am nervous about meeting Richard's parents.'

'What are they like?'

'I don't know. When we lived in Haddenford I saw them the few times that I had to go to church on Mother's behalf, but they didn't speak to anyone lower than themselves. I'm not sure anyone we knew would have known them.'

'I saw them once when they attended a fair held in the church grounds,' Nona offered. 'You remember when that awful Mrs Fearling abused Mother?'

'I don't remember that,' Emma said, 'I must have been in service by then.'

'The Laddisbrocks, Emma, are far above ordinary people, they have servants.'

Emma sighed; looking at the sea she thought about the life they'd had before the death of their father. A happy family life without cares, without struggle.

She took a deep breath and exhaled loudly, before saying, 'I know that Father was employed by them until his death. But they didn't help Mother in any way when she was widowed. We were lucky that Father had decided not to live on the estate, but rented the cottage near the village, or we might have lost our home sooner.'

'Do you really think so, Em?'

Emma shrugged. 'I don't know. I wish that I knew more about them.'

'Why don't you ask Richard?' Nona squinted into the sun, her hand shielding her eyes against the painful glare.

'Richard doesn't like talking about his parents. He believes that he was a disappointment to his father. That's why he ran away to somewhere where he could be free to do what he wanted.'

'And what was that?'

'I think he was too young to know, after all he's only around twenty now.'

'If he ran away from home, do you think that they will welcome him back?'

Emma pulled a face and with raised eyebrows said, 'I wish I knew. I'm not looking forward to arriving at the Laddisbrock estate. I'm so glad that you are with us, Nona.' Emma placed her hand on her sister's. 'I may need a friend and who better than you.'

They walked the deck arm in arm, nodding to the people that they had come to know. A small girl ran towards them, blonde hair bouncing. 'Hello, Lilly,' Emma said. 'How are you?'

'About the same as yesterday, thank you,' she said with a smile. 'Mistress Tilby, will you play catch with me? My father has made a ball out of cloth and I need someone to throw it to me.'

'I would like to play with you, Lilly, but where is your mother?'

'Mother and Father are below, they want some peace. They made me come up here to play.'

'Then I will be very happy to throw the ball for you, Miss Lilly, but we must be careful that it doesn't fall into the water.'

With her hair bouncing about her shoulders Lilly skipped across the deck to a wide area and Nona followed, leaving Emma to her thoughts.

After another turn around as much of the deck as could be manoeuvred, Emma stood by the rail and looked at the endless sea. She sighed deeply; she missed the family but more than anyone she missed Martha. The growing expanse of sea that lay between her and her mother weighed heavily upon her heart with every nautical mile. The pain of missing her family, she was discovering, was just as bad as the longing that she'd had for England. *Am I to be doomed with these feelings of melancholy wherever I am?* she asked herself as her thoughts deepened her loneliness, as though admitting it made it so. She might have cried in that moment had she not become aware of a shadow that suddenly covered the rail to her right. Turning her head, she was surprised to see a young man in thickly woven, home-spun clothes, the sort that farm labourers had worn when she was growing up. He didn't speak and, like her, stared at the endless sea in silence. Emma had noticed him before, loitering about the deck; he wasn't military and seemed to be travelling alone. Could he be a prisoner returning home? She had heard that one or two did, although the majority could not afford the passage after serving their sentence. She viewed him critically from the corner of her eye, noticing his weather-worn face, his skin pulled tight across his high cheekbones; his hair, uncovered, was a thick blond mop that fell across one eye, and his slightly darker beard hid his age from her. She was intrigued, yet did not have the courage to start up a conversation; he could, after all be a thief or worse.

Later in the afternoon Nona looked at the horizon and commented, 'It looks different today, don't you think, Em?'

Emma followed her sister's gaze and saw a shadow darkening the line of the horizon. A strange stillness had settled over the ship; the general noise that they had become used to had died. No flapping of sails, no slapping of ropes and rigging. 'I don't think we're moving, Emma, we seem to have stopped. How can that be?'

Emma looked up towards the sails that hung deflated and silent. 'There's no wind to fill the sails, that's why we seem to have stopped.'

The air had become heavy, sultry, and she shivered in the ominous stillness. Even the gulls that had followed the ship in recent days, filling the air with their awful shrieking and constant quarrelling, had faded away.

'Shall we take a seat on this box and watch the sky for a bit?' Emma indicated the box, trying to sound relaxed.

As they watched, the distant black line grew in height, until the sky seemed cut in half; above them blue sky and in the distance, roiling purple clouds approached at an alarming speed. They sat together in silence, fascinated by the lights that flashed within the turmoil of storm clouds rushing towards the ship. As a deep rumble reached their ears they felt the sudden power of the wind that preceded the storm. The waves grew ever larger until the colour of the sea mimicked the blackness of the sky. Salt tingled on their lips as the ship suddenly rose and then dipped in response.

'Perhaps we should go below.' Emma raised her voice above the wind as sailors hurried about the deck, taking down the sails and lashing down anything that would move.

'What is going to happen to the people travelling on the deck?' Emma shouted above the wind to an old sailor who was strapping a water barrel to the mast.

'As many as possible should get below or take shelter where...' His last words, caught by the wind, went unheard as a huge wave broke across the deck, washing it in a sweeping movement, like a monster hunting its prey.

Emma grasped Nona's hand, but before they could move, rain struck them with a stinging force that whipped across the deck, forcing them to stagger towards the hatch and the safety of cover. As the wind pulled at their clothes and took away their breath, they moved slowly, hanging onto anything solid so as to keep their balance, and with fear in their hearts they made it to the safety of the hatch, helped by a sailor.

Below deck they found the gangways crowded with soldiers, women and children. The first of the storm's large waves hit the ship with a bang that made many shout out in fear. The ship shuddered, tipping downwards. Those that lost their footing fell upon a pitching floor, laughing hysterically or screaming in terror as they slid one way and then the other in a heap of arms and legs. The ship rose to the top of each large wave only to drop suddenly to the depths beneath a wall of black water that followed them down, crashing onto the deck. After the initial screaming, a silence of fear held them in its grip; pale-faced and wide-eyed they held each other close, ready to endure whatever was to come.

In their cabin, Emma tied Richard into his bunk to stop him falling out. His groans, as the ship plunged and rolled, went unheard above the noise of the howling wind and crashing of waves. Many prayed. Emma, although feeling powerless on water, also prayed to the Goddess for deliverance and wondered if she would ever again see a tree or feel a summer breeze. Her heart was pounding as she thought how deep the water might be below the ship. Nona, who lay with Emma on the top bunk, dug her nails into her sister's arm as the ship was tossed in a cauldron of angry water.

In the gangways people scrambled to tie down anything that moved as suicidal lamps swung from the low wooden ceilings, swiping at the heads of any who didn't duck. On deck, some possessions were lost as huge waves of water swept thunderously across the deck, tearing even heavy items from their tethers. The storm raged for nine hours before calm returned to the ocean and the sails could again be raised.

Many of the animals in the hold were dead or injured and the sailors, their bodies shining with sweat, dragged the corpses to the edge of the ship and threw them over the side, as nothing could be kept in the sweltering heat.

In the days to come passengers and crew fished from the side of the ship. Emma and Nona tried without success to catch something on the fishing line given to them by the crew. The journey, from this day, seemed endless.

The Captain rationed the drinking water for the passengers, and the crew were on half measures of rum. Emma shared her water with Richard who seemed permanently hot or sick in the cabin below, where she worried that the bullet might be travelling to his brain or his heart.

The crew spent the next few days repairing the damage done by the storm and Emma was surprised to see the mystery man naked to his waist, hanging with a sailor over the side of the ship, hammering at the wood. He was slim and his torso, she noted, was solid and darkly tanned – an indication that he had been doing manual work. She stood for a moment fascinated, as his blond hair flipped about his face in the breeze. Her eyes were exploring and appreciating his body when suddenly he turned his head and looked straight at her. Embarrassed, she turned quickly away and went below to see Richard. He had been up on deck a few times since they set out, but the effort of getting up and down the steep wooden ladder exhausted him.

She was, therefore, glad as she entered their cabin to see that he was out of bed and sitting on the chair reading by the light of a lamp.

35

'It's good to see you up, Richard.' She smiled, for it was a relief that he was at last moving about on his own.

He gave her a cursory glance before saying, 'You look pink.'

'It's the air on deck, it brings a bloom to the face. Would you like to come up and look at the sea?'

'No!' His tone was peevish. 'Why would I want to look at endless water?' He turned the page of his book sharply.

Ignoring his ill-tempered behaviour, she smiled, saying, 'The breeze on deck would do you good, Richard. You have become pallid shut away down here, it's so airless.'

Snapping the book shut he stared at her in silence, his mouth set in a hard line, one eyebrow slightly raised. A warning. She turned away and he reopened his book.

~

The morning was bright on the day that England appeared to rise from the sea, a speck on the horizon. The cry of 'land ahoy' brought everyone onto the deck, eagerly looking for the shadow that appeared and disappeared in the swell.

After their months at sea, passengers and crew alike were relieved to eventually see the cliffs of England slowly appearing. Some of the women passengers cried with relief at the sight, falling onto their knees; some hugged their children and gave thanks to the Almighty for their deliverance, although they were not yet safe, as England was known for its treacherous rocky coastline.

Standing on the deck with Nona, Emma was overwhelmed as she looked at the land which she had thought never to see again and which she had craved for so long.

Watching a flock of gulls wheeling over the sea and around the cliffs, her heart soared with them and yet, were their shrill cries a welcome or a warning? Feeling a sudden coldness creep over her skin, she shivered and pulled her shawl tighter.

As the ship followed the coastline, a westerly caught the sails, the rigging slapped loudly on wood and the ship increased its speed. With nothing else to do, Emma watched in silence as the waves crashed upon the rocky shoreline, leaving a white spume in the air and foam at the water's edge. A feeling of dread was already creeping into her heart as she took Nona's hand and squeezed it. In response, Nona slipped her arm around her sister's small waist and Emma felt the comfort of belonging.

'Let us wash and help Richard to get ready,' Emma tried to sound cheerful, 'even though we may not dock until the morrow.'

They docked next day during the early afternoon in Portsmouth with all the usual quayside pandemonium playing out below. Emma and Nona looked over the side of the ship, watching the sailors run up and down the gangplank carrying empty water barrels which were quickly piled up on the side of the dock along with the passengers' larger pieces of luggage.

The first passengers to disembark disappeared into the waiting crowd that surged forward at seeing them; shouting greetings they hugged and kissed before walking away arm in arm, children carried shoulder high.

Traders mixed with the crowd, trying to sell their wares, their shouts adding to the general noise, and over the top of all the quayside mayhem, a church bell peeled relentlessly.

After the relative silence of the outback and the long voyage, the hubbub that rose from the dockside was overwhelming, and it was with some trepidation that Emma and Nona eventually left the ship with Richard.

Stepping onto the quay they found themselves engulfed in the stifling bedlam, their movement impeded by the sheer number of animated people.

Emma felt lost within the crowd, like a stranger in a foreign land, a land where she no longer understood the rules. When she looked at Nona, she witnessed her own feeling of panic reflected in her sister's face.

The two women had carried their own valises off the ship and had paid a sailor to carry their trunk. The man also helped Richard down the gangplank, as he was frail after the long journey, having only left their cabin for short exercise when he felt strong enough. As the months had passed, his leg muscles, Emma noticed, had softened until he had little strength left in them.

A smartly dressed mature man in brown livery, sitting high on the seat of a carriage at the back of the crowd, saw them and waved his hat in the air.

'Sir, Mr Laddisbrock sir,' he called, before disappearing from view. Moments later, accompanied by a small pale-faced boy, he arrived at their side.

'It's good to see you, sir, let me take your valise.' Taking Richard's bag from the sailor the man shouted an order to the boy. 'Jacob, help the ladies with their bags.'

'Yes, sir, Mr Larch.' The boy almost jumped to attention.

Dressed in cream trousers and a brown jacket like that of Larch, Jacob quickly grasped the handles of Nona and Emma's bags.

'Let me help you,' Emma said, holding tightly to her valise.

'No!' Jacob replied sharply, glancing quickly at the retreating Larch, a look of horror on his face. Noticing the relief on the boy's face when he saw that Larch had his back to them, Emma realised that she had made her first mistake and, of course, he was a servant, not a child being asked to carry something far too heavy for his small frame.

Meanwhile, Larch pushed a pathway through the crowd as another man, dressed similarly, held the door of the carriage for them as they approached. When Richard was seated inside, a blanket was placed over his knees.

Emma gave Mrs Fry's letter to Jacob, with instructions that it be given to a messenger. As he ran off on his errand Emma and Nona took their seat opposite Richard. Blankets were also placed over their knees, for although it was April the air felt cold.

When the boy returned, the coach set off, rolling raggedly over the uneven cobbles until it cleared the dockside.

Emma felt suddenly weak with the realisation that she

was sitting in a high-class carriage with a husband who she suspected did not love her, heading for a family who she also believed would never accept her. *How did I come to this?* she asked herself and her fingers searched for the comfort of her sister's hand on the seat.

Through the carriage window the streets passed quickly, clothed in grey and tightly packed with houses. As Portsmouth was quickly left behind, Emma feverishly drank in the sight of the green countryside that she had so craved in the red dust of the outback. With the energy of all this greenery to support her, she thought, how could she not endure her in-laws, if endure she must?

Richard looked pale, and Emma had to admit that he was not repairing as quickly as they had all hoped and the long uncomfortable journey had taken its toll. At least now, she thought to herself, he would receive medical attention.

'Would you like the carriage to stop for a while, Richard?' she asked as she noticed him wince when the coach lurched over a bump in the road.

He opened his eyes briefly. 'No!' he replied sharply and closed his eyes again.

Embarrassed and hurt at being dismissed so brusquely, she turned her head to the window to hide the flush of her cheeks and saw nothing of the passing scenery as she struggled with her emotions. She was even more convinced now that life with the Laddisbrocks was going to be difficult. Without the support of her husband how was she going to manage?

4.

Haddenford hadn't changed at all. It was just as she remembered it: thatched cottages with gardens growing a confusion of vegetables and flowers; the village green dominated by the church on one side and the hardware store, blacksmith and cottages on the other three. They swept quickly past the blacksmith's and Mr Rudd's hardware store where, as a child, after the death of her father, Emma had exchanged the church 'widows and orphans' docket for food.

The carriage dragged on uphill, passing fields and orchards. Everything looked so small and green. Suddenly, an overpowering and desperate urge to get out and walk amongst it all rushed over her. To see butterflies, to hear the birds, to smell the grass. But not yet, she must wait and she could hardly contain the feeling rising within her.

'We're nearly there, Richard,' she said instead.

He didn't open his eyes, but acknowledged that he had heard with a slight nod.

The coach turned onto the Laddisbrock estate and travelled quickly along the well-tended drive edged with mature trees. Beyond that she could see what appeared to be a large green park, dotted with oak, walnut and horse chestnut trees. Both Nona and Emma were wide-eyed at such tended greenery.

The carriage slowed, coming to a stop before a magnificent red-brick building with stone pillars at the front door. Steps led down to the gravel driveway and already standing on them were several servants. A welcoming committee.

The carriage door was opened by the man who had held it at the dockside. Richard was helped down and then Emma followed by Nona.

The party walked slowly together up the steps, with Richard leaning heavily on Larch as servants hurriedly removed their bags from the carriage.

Two women servants, dressed alike in long-sleeved black dresses with high necks, watched the men impassively. The eldest woman, her grey hair tucked under a white bonnet, bobbed as Richard passed.

'Good to see you back, Master Richard.' Her voice was thin with age. The second woman kept her eyes to the ground, acknowledging them only with a small bob.

A tall male servant standing stiffly to attention beside the women, and also dressed in a black jacket, now stepped forward at their approach.

'Thank you, Larch.' His voice held authority. 'Please take Master Richard to his room, I will be along shortly.'

Turning to the two women waiting on the steps he frowned, unsure, before appearing to make up his mind and stepped forward smartly.

'I am Patrick, Master Laddisbrock's man.' He bowed as Emma and Nona moved forward. 'This is Mrs Jenk, the housekeeper.' He indicated the older woman with a sweep of his arm, but didn't look at her. 'This is Martin.' He indicated the younger woman. 'She will be of assistance to you and will show you to your rooms. Dinner is at four o'clock. Martin will show you to the dining room at five minutes to the hour.'

Emma's stomach tightened before the sternness and assured manner of this man and, swallowing her fear, she held her head high. 'Thank you, Patrick.' She spoke in a strong voice that surprised even her.

As a look of satisfaction crossed Patrick's face, Emma realised that until that moment he had not known which woman Richard Laddisbrock had married.

Entering the house, Emma and Nona followed Martin up a steep flight of stairs which ascended to a dark landing above the main hall. The walls, Emma noted on her way up the stairs, were festooned with the portraits of dour-faced people. A large wooden clock standing on the landing ticked and clunked in the otherwise silence. Small, elegant tables stood at measured distances along the landing at the top of the stairs, on which ornaments or vases had been placed, and it was obvious to them both that this house was richly furnished.

Nona was shown into a room and Emma into the room next door which was heavily furnished with large furniture stained black. The dark brown curtains hanging at the window made the whole place seem utterly dispiriting.

Two male servants placed her trunk on a low table at the bottom of the double bed as Martin opened the door of a heavily carved closet and started to hang Emma's clothes on the posts within.

'I can do that, Martin,' Emma said, feeling embarrassed about the condition of her clothes.

'I'm sorry, madam, but it's my job to help you. Hot water has been placed in your dressing room, if you would like to freshen yourself after your journey.'

Emma gave in gracefully and was happy to shut herself in the dressing room and wash the dust from her face and hands. Sinking onto a chair that stood next to the washstand she covered her face with the soft towel left on the side. She sat for what she feared was a long time with her face covered in the comfort of the material. And when at last she went back into her room Martin had dealt with her few clothes and set out her hair dressings.

'You will dress for dinner, madam.'

It was a statement. Perhaps the young woman realised she needed guidance. 'I have put out the best of what you have.'

Emma was now aware of the tone in Martin's voice. The maid had seen that Emma did not have anything that would come up to the standard of the Laddisbrocks. Why should she have? She'd had no use for such frivolities in the outback. There, she had worn hard-wearing material, most of which was faded by the sun.

Martin had laid Martha's grey skirt and a white top on the bed, and Emma noticed that her little black boots had been polished.

'Thank you, Martin.'

'I will dress your hair, madam, and then I will help Miss Tilby to select something suitable.'

'Thank you, Martin,' Emma said again and wondered if she would ever say anything else to the young woman.

Martin dressed Emma's hair in a fashionable collection of curls, pulled high behind her head, adding combs that Emma had not seen before.

When the maid left, Emma sat in a comfortable chair beside a large window overlooking the grounds and wondered where Richard was. A thought occurred to her and, standing, she went to the closet to find what she was beginning to suspect. His clothes were not there. Where was he, and was she to sleep alone? What if he needed something in the night and she didn't know where he was? Worry creased her face as she closed the closet doors.

A light knock came at the door and Nona entered in her best maroon dress; her hair, beautifully dressed in long blonde curls, hung behind her head almost touching the nape of her neck.

'What do we do now, Emma?' Nona asked, looking uncomfortable.

'I don't know!' She shrugged her shoulders. 'Wait, I suppose, until we are summoned to dinner.'

'I don't like this very much, Emma, I feel lost. I don't know what we are supposed to do.'

'Nor I.' Emma found it hard to keep the desperation out of her voice. 'We will both have to learn as we go along.'

'They will know as soon as they see us that we are not of their class.'

'I know, and as soon as that hurdle is crossed the better. We cannot pretend to be something that we are not and I fear that this may be just as hard for Richard.'

~

Martin arrived at five minutes to the hour of four o'clock. 'Please follow me, madam,' she addressed Emma.

They followed the maid along the silent corridor towards a door with a long table placed beside it. Memories of carrying food and laying the dishes on such a table leapt into Emma's mind. Having been a servant, she was transported back to that position. Nerves now fluttered in her stomach. What was she doing, being shown into the dining room as though she were one of the privileged? She hoped desperately that Richard was on the other side of the door.

Martin knocked, then opened the door, slowly announcing, 'Mrs Richard Laddisbrock and Mistress Tilby, madam.'

A woman in a dark blue dress was sitting elegantly on a leather-bound chair beside a writing desk as they entered. She wore a grey wig with long curls and her makeup was so pale that Emma was reminded of a street player.

As they entered, Charlotte Laddisbrock looked up, folded the paper on which she had been writing and stared with a sharp eye at the two women standing before her.

They bobbed, ducking their heads in respect.

Charlotte's tone was blunt as she addressed them. 'Which of you married my son?'

The question was direct and Emma wasn't ready for the hostile tone of it.

'I am Richard's wife, madam,' Emma said confidently, and was surprised at the clarity and strength in her own voice as she returned the direct stare.

The woman nodded sagely. Her demeanour, as Emma expected of someone of her class, was haughty as she looked unfavourably on the two women standing before her.

'Richard will not be joining us for dinner,' Charlotte stated, 'the journey has tired him.'

She spoke, Emma realised, with an air of possession, and panic began to rise in her throat, yet she managed to keep her tone even as she replied, 'Will I be able to see Richard after dinner, madam?'

'I think it unwise,' his mother said carefully. 'He is not a well man.'

'Richard is my husband, madam, and I have nursed him since the day he was shot. I am aware of the state of his health.'

'Then you will know that what he needs is rest.' Her tone left no doubt that she knew best and that the matter was closed.

The two women glared at each other across the room until the uncomfortable silence was broken when a door on an inner wall opened and a male servant, no older than their brother James, stood in the doorway looking nervous.

'Dinner is served, madam.'

Charlotte nodded and rose from her seat. Without any indication that they should follow her, she left them and entered the adjoining room.

It was the servant who extended his arm towards the door and Emma and Nona, moving after her, were shown to their seats at a large polished table.

The three women sat in silence, their hands gently folded on their laps. The table, Emma noticed, was laid with good china and silver. In the centre was a large bowl of roses, picked in the garden she supposed. The walls, papered in a dull cream with repeated patterns of embossed flowers, were covered in portraits and pictures of landscapes. Nona, she knew, was squirming with embarrassment in the silence, as was she.

'We will be ready to eat, Gant, as soon as the master arrives.' Charlotte addressed the servant who stood beside the door, looking straight ahead into space, seeing nothing.

'Yes, madam. Thank you, madam.'

Gant left the room, moving out backwards. Emma almost smiled. She knew how a delay annoyed the servants in the kitchen. She could imagine what they were saying, the kerfuffle this caused below stairs. The three women continued to sit in silence.

Eventually the door opened and Richard's father entered slowly. He was not as tall as his son and rather portly. The skin on his round face was a ruddy pink, his nose wide and pitted below his wig of short grey curls. His eyes, although grey like Richard's, were smaller and hooded with folds of puffy skin that hung beneath them, giving him an air of tiredness. In that moment Emma realised that Richard did not take his looks from his father and was glad.

As George Laddisbrock's eyes swept the table he merely grunted at seeing the visitors. As he seated himself heavily in a chair held by Gant, he said, 'So which one of you married my son?'

'I am Mrs Richard Laddisbrock, sir,' Emma spoke up.

He said no more, acknowledging her with a nod as three servants entered and began serving the meal. Four meats – venison, lamb, pressed ox tongue in aspic and a goose – were served to them with a mixture of sauces, followed by a watery soup. The Laddisbrocks drank large quantities of wine during the meal which was followed by a serving of egg and rose-water pudding with strawberries, all eaten in an uncomfortable silence.

The servants moved like shadows around the room in which nothing was heard but the movement of cutlery and the sound of eating.

After the meal, George Laddisbrock left the table without comment, and Emma and Nona followed their hostess into a pleasant sitting room that overlooked the parkland.

As they took their seats Charlotte looked straight at Emma, asking, 'Why did you marry my son?'

Once again Emma was unsettled by the directness of her mother-in-law and decided to be as direct back. 'I loved him, madam.'

46

'How interesting that you use the past tense,' Charlotte replied sharply.

Emma realised her mistake and also that here indeed was a clever woman.

'And why was my son shot?' She spoke with such a matter-of-fact air, that it sounded as though she was scarcely interested and only a little intrigued.

'He had gone to the outpost, madam, a small hamlet, and was shot by a man called Neil Logan, a criminal. A murderer.'

'And why did this man shoot my son?' There was no facial expression for Emma to read, as only the mouth moved in the heavily painted face below the grey curls.

Emma had hoped not to be asked such a question and had not in her dreams thought that it might be Richard's mother who would ask it. She didn't answer at once and was struggling to think how to phrase her answer. She had the feeling that whatever she said would make her look bad in the eyes of his mother.

'You will not shock me, my dear. I can tell that you are struggling with the information.'

Emma studied the face of Richard's mother for the first time and was surprised that she was not as old as at first thought. There appeared a softness in her eyes as she waited for the answer, but still Emma was unsure of how much she should relay, though the softness in the eyes of a mother who needed to know what had happened to her son almost made Emma tell the truth.

'The Logans were a bad bunch,' she started. 'They were always looking for trouble. I wasn't there. I don't know why they got into a fight with Richard.'

'And were these men dealt with?'

'Yes, I believe that they were.' Emma continued to be cagey, not wanting to implicate Nona.

'I see.'

Emma wondered what she saw. Was it that Emma was trying to protect her from knowing the truth about her son, or that she had not been told everything?

'I am sure that we will learn more about it as the days pass.' The softness in her eyes had been withdrawn. 'Tell me about your past, I should like to know who it is that my son took it into his head to marry.'

Emma's heart pumped in her chest; she should enlighten Charlotte of what it was like to live in Australia, the hardship.

'The New World is not at all like England...' she started.

'Does that have some bearing on your marriage?' Charlotte interrupted.

Emma bit her lip; to answer was difficult. Why was she not telling his mother what she wanted to know? She was not fooling her for one minute. The woman knew that Emma was not one of them and then she realised that what her mother-in-law wanted to know was how big a mistake her son had made.

With no clear idea of what she was going to say Emma began again to try and help Charlotte understand why they had married. 'In that country, madam, everyone is equal.' But even that was wrong, she knew it as soon as she had opened her mouth. Of course, she and her family were better than the criminals that had been transported there. She continued, 'My family and I lived for some years in this village, until, after the death of my father, my mother married the landowner Andrew Tate.'

Emma noticed one eyebrow twitch slightly, but otherwise the woman sat impassively. 'My parents decided to start a new life in Australia. We went as free colonists and were given a hundred acres of land. We have lived there for more than twelve years. We now farm cereal, beef and goats.'

'And why did you marry my son?' The question was again direct as though she had dismissed everything Emma had just said.

'Richard came to our farm looking for work. Mr Tate took him on.'

The eyebrow rose again, and Emma suspected that this was a revelation to Richard's mother and now she knew why. 'He worked very well alongside Mr Tate and my brothers; he was an asset to the farm,' Emma emphasised. 'When Richard asked me to marry him I agreed. It wasn't until the day we married that I knew his surname; until that moment he had called himself Richard Ladd. I know that if we had been in England that we would not have married. We would not even have met, but in Australia things are different. It is a vast land and a hard life where the people become equal in their efforts to survive. I am truly sorry if our return may have embarrassed you but Richard needed medical attention.'

'May... have... embarrassed me?' Her voice rose to a shriek. 'He was to be engaged to Sylvia Brancumbe, Lord Brancumbe's daughter. It wasn't something that he wanted, but he had a duty to this estate. After my son's disappearance we discovered that he had paid his passage to the New World but, until we received your mother's letter telling us the name of the ship you were on, returning to England, we did not know if we still had a son.'

'I'm sorry.' Emma didn't know what else to say; she had not known why Richard had run away from home other than he was a disappointment to his father.

The woman stiffened. 'Rooms have been made available to you and Miss Tilby on the other side of the house. Whether my son wants to continue with this charade of a marriage will be up to him. I should like to see proof of the marriage, after all it took place in a barbaric country.'

'The service, madam,' Emma justified, 'was conducted by a priest of the Crown.' She would like to have said church, but as it was conducted in her cabin, she left it at that. 'Your son and I are married, I can assure you.'

'How long have you been married? Three years, is it not? And you have no children, why is that?' There was a hint of mischief behind the eyes of the woman who sat opposite Emma.

'I don't know why I haven't conceived, madam, but I do want children.'

'I need a grandson.' Her words bit deeply into Emma's heart. 'A grandson, who will have breeding and connections, do I make myself clear?'

'No, madam. Not entirely.'

'I want this farce of a marriage dissolved. Until then, you and your sister will have food brought up to your rooms. You will not be treated as family nor even guests in this house.'

'And Richard?' Emma's courage had left her.

'Richard will do as he pleases, as he has always done.'

'Richard may not want our marriage dissolved, madam.' Emma could feel herself shaking with emotion and knew that she was not sure of Richard at all. Not sure what he wanted or if he would stand up to his mother.

'Oh, he will want it dissolved. I can assure you of that, madam. Now, if you will excuse me.'

Emma and Nona were dismissed with the turning away of Charlotte's head toward the window.

Martin stood in the hall. Emma was in no doubt that she had heard the conversation and would report back to the staff below stairs.

'If you would follow me, ma'am.' Martin turned along the passage in a different direction. 'Your things have already been moved to your new rooms.'

Emma said nothing, she wasn't going to say, 'Thank you, Martin,' again. She wanted to see Richard and she would see him, even if it meant entering every room in the house until she found him.

Martin stopped before a large door and opened it for them to enter. 'You have four rooms, ma'am: two bedrooms, a sitting room and a room in which to prepare for the day.'

Emma nodded, giving the rooms a cursory glance before she said, 'I want to see my husband, Martin. You will take me to him immediately.'

Emma's voice carried authority, just like that of Miss Brack, her old employer, and she was pleased that she copied the tone so well that Martin flinched. The maid looked indecisive.

'Are you going to disobey me, Martin?'

'No, ma'am,' she replied quickly.

Nona's face was a picture of amazement and as Martin turned away, the girls grinned at each other.

'Do you want me to come with you?' Nona asked.

'No. I will tell you about it when I get back,' Emma whispered.

Martin hurried across the landing and to the end of a passage on the other side of the house. The maid then turned right without hesitating into a short passage with a door at the end, which she opened. Behind the door a staircase led upward and Emma followed Martin up the wooden stairs that had no covering other than being stained brown. At the top were three large rooms off a small landing. One door lay open, revealing a comfortable room complete with fireplace and soft furnishings. Emma was shown into the spacious room opposite. At its centre a four-poster bed with thick cream drapes, hung with gold tassels, dominated the space. A large window looked out over the park and a cheerful fire burned in the grate.

Richard was sitting in a large armchair reading a book. When he looked up it was Martin he saw first and Emma noticed a fleeting curious look in his eye that changed as Martin announced Emma's arrival. 'Your wife… sir.'

He nodded acknowledgement and placed his book on a small table beside his chair.

'Don't wait for me, Martin.' Emma looked hard at the maid who still stood in the doorway. 'I'll find my own way back.'

As Martin made her way down the stairs Emma listened until she heard the door shut before she said anything.

'How are you, Richard?'

'Tired, as you can see.' His face was pale, his skin drawn tight around his cheekbones and there was no lustre in his hair, no sparkle in his eyes. He looked ill and much older.

'Why are you up here, Richard, and not with me?' She looked about the room that, apart from its four-poster bed, might have belonged to a servant.

He blanched. 'I thought it would complicate things.'

'What things, Richard? I don't understand what is happening.'

'Do you think that I wanted to come back here, Emma?' he responded. 'I'm trapped and will never get away again. Those damn Logans,' he growled.

'Do you not take any responsibility for what happened to you, Richard?'

'No! They put me in this position, them and your damn mother.'

'My mother?' Her voice rose in surprise. 'You blame everyone but yourself. You are a weak man, Richard Laddisbrock. You have no backbone.'

'Then divorce me, Emma, I won't contest it.' She was startled to hear it from his own lips.

'Oh, and how am I going to do that?' she replied, tears in her eyes.

'My parents will pay.' He sighed and looked into the fire that crackled cheerfully.

'And what grounds do we have for divorce, Richard? I have been a good wife to you.' Her mouth was dry; she could hardly believe that they were having this conversation.

'We can divorce on the grounds of unfaithfulness.'

'You would admit that?' She was shocked. 'I have just shielded your mother from that truth.'

'Good,' he said, looking relieved. 'For me to have the marriage my parents would want, a society marriage that will bring money to our family, you will have to say that you have been unfaithful.'

Emma's eyes and mouth widened in disbelief. Her legs almost let her down and she reached for the chair to support herself as his unexpected words hit her like a physical blow.

'I will do no such thing. How dare you ask me to say that, when there is no truth in it.'

'You don't have to say anything, Emma, because I am going to tell my parents and the solicitor.'

As anger rose within her she balled her fists until her nails dug into her flesh; she wanted to hit him.

But the conversation had left him weak and he started to cough. Holding his stomach, he groaned. There was a jug of wine resting on the table beside him and she poured some of the liquid into a cup, handing it to him when the spasm had passed. He drank the wine slowly and she noted that his skin was clammy as he sank exhausted into the chair.

When he spoke, his voice had no energy in it. 'As you can see, Emma, I am still not well enough to do battle with you, or my parents. Please do not come here again.'

Her voice was bitter as it escaped through clenched teeth. 'You are in no position to ask me anything, Richard. You are my husband and I am worried about you. We once loved each other. How can you forget that so easily?'

'Did I love you? I don't know what love is, Emma. I don't understand the need for one human to possess another. Having to give up my freedom, being told what to do, when to work and where I can go. Is that what love is, Emma?'

She was shocked once again by the depth of anger in his outburst, yet knew that this was his truth. He was not a man that could settle down to what he saw as a mundane life with one woman. Or perhaps he just had not yet experienced love and couldn't differentiate between it and lust.

Standing up for herself, she said, 'I will not say that I have been unfaithful to you, Richard, for that is not the truth.'

His eyes flashed with anger. 'And who do you think will listen to you, Emma, a trumped-up servant?'

Her hand connected with his face so hard that his head rocked on his neck. A red mark was already blooming on his skin as she left. The stairs and landing were a blur as she ran back to her rooms.

Nona jumped in fright as the door burst open and Emma sank to her knees just inside the door, crying.

Running to her, Nona held her sister in her arms for some time before helping her to a chair. When the sobs had subsided, Nona's voice trembled as she asked, 'What happened, Em?'

Pulling on an inner strength deep in her core, she told Nona what had happened between them. That she was to say that she had been unfaithful.

Nona stared at her, unable to comprehend that Richard could be so cruel.

'This is wicked beyond belief, Emma. After the way that you fought to save his life, surely there is nothing they can do about your marriage?'

Emma sighed. 'How could I live in the face of such a lie, Nona? We are already treated as less than servants here.' She wiped the tears from her face with the flat of her hand as she spoke.

'What will you do?' Nona's voice was bleak.

'I don't know. I need time to think.'

'How much time do we have?'

'I don't know that either, but I am sure that my mother-in-law will soon enlighten me.'

5.

Mary Martin opened the door of the terraced cottage behind the church on her day off and called, 'Cooee'. Hearing a little giggle, she played along with the game. 'Now where can that boy be?' she said, looking behind a painting on the wall. 'No, he isn't there.' She moved to a little cupboard in which her mother kept her china. Pulling the doors open she looked inside. 'No,' she said, 'he isn't in here.'

'I'm not here,' a little voice called.

She went to a high-backed chair and looked over the top. 'Boo,' she said.

A brown-eyed child, curled cross-legged on the floor, laughed up at her. He threw up his arms and she pulled him from behind the chair, holding him close. She kissed his face and stroked his hair, loving the smell of her child. 'Mother's home, Thomas, do you love me?' she said quietly into his ear.

'Yes,' he squealed, wriggling to get down. 'Gwanny, Gwanny, Mother's home.' He was three years old and still mastering speech.

A woman in her late fifties, plump and silver-haired, entered the room. 'How's he been, Ma?' Mary looked at her son.

'Oh, just the same, full of interest, he runs me ragged. I'm getting too old for this game, Mary. The sooner you find a husband the better.'

'Oh, Mother, don't start that again. Who is going to take on a woman with a child, a child out of wedlock?'

Celia Martin changed the subject; she'd had her dig at her daughter. 'So, what's going on up at the Castle?'

55

Mary laughed. Her mother always called the Manor House 'the Castle'. She had no time for the Laddisbrocks, the biggest employer in the county, who would set people off at the drop of a hat with no care for their support when times were hard.

'Richard Laddisbrock is back. He turned up a couple of days ago. He is not a well man.'

'No, really!' Celia looked interested. 'I think they thought they would never see him again. There was talk in the village that he was dead, eaten by bears.'

Mary ignored her mother's thoughts on the subject; she hated village gossips.

'And, he came back with a wife,' Mary continued.

'No, really!' Celia's face looked eager for more.

'If you keep saying that, Mother, I won't tell you anything else.'

'You don't appreciate how boring my life is, young woman, with only a three-year-old for company.' Her mother pouted like a young maid taken to task.

'I know, Mother. But without my job we would all starve.'

'True,' Celia was quick to concede.

'So, what is she like, this wife of Master Richard?'

'Do you remember Emma Tilby, Mother?' She used to live in the village about thirteen years ago.

'Yes, sweet girl. A bit weird like her mother, I always thought. We never saw Martha Tilby in church, you know. The widow Fearling put it about that the woman was a witch.'

'No, really!' Mary's eyes were wide now, searching her mother's face for proof.

'Martha Tilby went to work on the Tate farm after the death of her husband.' Celia continued, 'There was something funny going on there.'

'No, really!' Mary was now looking interested.

Celia gave her daughter a look and continued, 'Andrew Tate's wife had died. He took Martha Tilby in to look after his children. For some reason the village rent collector, Barney

Beemer, took against Andrew Tate and burned his winter barn down, almost putting the poor man out of business. It would have been bad for the village, Tate was a good employer. He cared about his workers. If I remember right, he sold some of his fields bordering the Laddisbrock estate and with the money he went to London to find Beemer with the intent of bringing him to justice. He and the vicar went to Beemer's trial. I think Beemer was hanged in London. Although some say he got off. Anyway, I heard that Andrew Tate married Martha Tilby and they went to Australia, free colonists, to start a new life, leaving John Brisket running Tate Farm as their tenant.'

'So, Emma Laddisbrock is well known in the village and for all the wrong reasons.'

'I wouldn't say she was well known. She went into service at the age of twelve and wasn't seen again.'

'So, Mother, she is only a servant?' Mary's nose turned up and her face became serious.

'Yes, I guess she was.' Celia nodded.

'Well, trumped-up little madam, the way she spoke to me. I'm not having it.'

Celia's eyes narrowed. 'However she spoke to you, Mary, you will have it, or lose your job and then where will we be?'

But Mary's jaw had a set of determination about it. Celia had seen that look before and only trouble would come out of it. She was sure of that.

6.

Emma and Nona had stayed in their rooms for two weeks, walking the floors and looking out of the windows. Emma had been staring across the park when she suddenly turned to Nona who was sitting in a chair looking equally bored. 'I can't do this anymore, Nona. I have to get out. Come for a walk with me.'

'Do you mind if I don't, Emma? Perhaps tomorrow.'

'Don't you need air? We could just walk here on the estate.' She had a sudden thought. 'Nona, let us cut across the fields and visit Tate Farm. I have a letter for Dolly from Mother, and it would be good to see Dolly and Alice again. Then you could write to Mother and Andrew and tell them all about it. Please.'

'Alright. As long as we can cut across the fields. I feel so conspicuous in these faded clothes.'

'It's not like you to care, Nona.'

'I didn't even think of it in Australia. I mean, who was going to care what we wore? I was a child when we left here and now I want to be dressed properly as a woman.'

'Yes of course you do, Nona. I'm sorry. We just didn't give enough thought to our clothes. We had been away so long.'

Donning their cloaks, they set off across the park, walking under the ancient oaks and horse chestnuts. Emma looked up into the branches of the trees and breathed in the energy and fresh air. 'Oh, Nona, isn't this all the medicine that anyone needs to stay well?'

'It is good to be back and out of the hot sun, but I'm cold.' Nona pulled her cloak tighter around her slim body. 'I haven't been able to get warm since we came back.'

'We'll get used to the English weather again soon, Nona.' Looking over her shoulder Emma grinned. 'We're out of sight of the house, let's run.'

The soft green grass seemed to fly beneath their shoes as they ran downhill before pushing through a small gate on the edge of the park where they entered a wild meadow.

Emma stretched out her arms and ran in circles, breathing in the air. Kicking off her boots she lifted her skirt and felt the luxury of the grass beneath her feet and its soft sweeping fingers on her shins. She was ecstatic. Nona laughed at the sight as she followed sedately at a short distance. Since being back in England the old aches and pains in her joints had returned. Emma dropped to the ground and lay on her back with her eyes shut. Nona joined her, and together they lay hidden in the meadow grass listening to the buzz of insects and smelling the familiar fragrances of their childhood.

'Isn't this wonderful, Nona?'

'I believe, Emma, that your mother-in-law would not approve of your lying in the grass with your skirt around your knees,' Nona giggled.

'I don't imagine that she has ever touched the grass, Nona. And her life is the poorer for it. I could lie here forever, I'm so happy.'

Nona's stomach grumbled. 'If we stay here forever we will surely starve to death.'

'Come on then.' Getting up Emma dragged Nona to her feet. 'Let us visit the farm, where hopefully we will be given normal food.'

They entered Tate Farm from the back, behind the winter barn. The last time Nona had seen this building it was blackened by fire, but there was no evidence of it now.

They walked unchallenged into the farmyard and stood in front of the brick-built house with its sullen empty windows that still stared mournfully at the stables and barns opposite. 'It's strange,' Emma said, 'not to be attacked by the geese.'

Nona smiled. 'They were tyrants. Better than a dog for letting us know someone was at the door.'

Emma stepped forward and knocked.

Moments later, the door was opened by a small dark-haired boy with a dirty face. 'What do you want?' he asked, pulling himself up to look bigger than he was.

'Is anyone at home?' Emma asked.

'Yes,' he said, continuing to stand in the doorway.

'Who is it, William?' a voice they recognised called from within.

'It's Emma and Nona, Dolly. Can we come in?'

A small woman with red hair pulled the door back sharply away from the boy, exclaiming, 'My God! I can't believe it. You're on the other side of the world.' And coming out into the yard she felt their arms. 'You are here. I'm not dreaming.' She stood back and viewed them. 'My, how you've changed. You're all grown up. Come in, come in, there's so much I want to ask you.'

Emma and Nona embraced Dolly Mott, almost crying at the warm welcome.

'William,' Dolly spoke to the boy, 'go and get the milk jug and get the box with the cake from the cupboard.'

The boy ran off to do as he was bid. 'My grandson,' Dolly said proudly. 'He's three years old and as sharp as a knife.'

'Can I have some, Granny?' William asked, kneeling down to open the door to the cupboard.

'Course you can, my darling. He's such a good boy. He works hard too, don't you, little man?' she said, watching him.

'Yes, Granny.'

'What do you do, William?' Emma asked.

'I collect eggs and run errands for Granny,' he said, pulling a box onto the floor.

Emma smiled and nodded. 'He must be the son of Alice and John.'

'Yes, the others are at school.'

'How many do they have?' Nona asked.

'William is the youngest for the present. They have four others. Now, I want to know what life is like in the New World. Although I get a letter every year from Martha, it's not the same as getting it from the horse's mouth.'

'That reminds me, Dolly, I have a letter for you from Mother.' Taking it from her pocket Emma laid it on the table.

'I'll read it later,' Dolly said, pushing it to the side. 'There's so much that I want to know, and now I can ask you and have a proper conversation and not have to wait nearly a year for the answer to a question that by then I can't remember asking.'

Emma laughed. 'Where shall I start? Unlike here, Dolly, it's very hot and when it rains we get too much at one time. Andrew has fixed up water towers to save some of it for our use. Work on the land is hard, but James, Jack and George have settled very well to the work. They are on horseback most of the time, riding for hours managing the stock. I believe that they will make good farmers themselves one day.'

'And Martha?'

'Oh, she and Andrew work well together. It's a harsh country for a woman, but Martha loves Andrew and as long as he is there, so will she be.'

Dolly seemed suddenly to remember her manners. 'I must give you something to eat as well as cake.' She looked apologetic.

'We would love something to eat, thank you, Dolly,' Nona said, before Emma could.

As Dolly gathered together plates and cups, she took a quick look at her letter. Putting it down on the table she looked up at Emma. 'I see from the letter that you married Richard Laddisbrock. I guess that you are staying at the Manor House then!'

'Yes.' Emma felt uncomfortable, not wanting to tell Dolly of her troubles.

'I can't compete with the food you get there,' Dolly said, looking worried.

'We will be very grateful for that,' Nona said without hesitation as Emma laughed and Dolly looked confused. 'The fare is much too...' Nona searched for a word.

'Much, too... much?' Emma helped out.

'Yes, exactly, there's enough at each sitting to feed a poor family for several days.'

Pushing her letter into her pocket, Dolly laid the table with bread, cheese and cold pheasant.

William, unable to reach the top of the table, gave Dolly the cake box.

'Thank you, young man,' she said, taking the box that was almost too large for his small hands to hold.

The afternoon passed quickly as they answered all of Dolly's questions and caught up with the village news. Most of the children they'd grown up with were married, had left the area or were dead. And Emma tried to remember everything that Dolly said, so that she could write to Martha.

'Now, how are you getting on with your mother-in-law?' The question was quite sudden and Emma was not prepared.

'I... oh, um...' She frowned.

'I'm sorry, Emma, I shouldn't have asked.'

Emma sighed. 'It won't be a secret for very long, Dolly, that she doesn't see me as a daughter-in-law. She would have preferred Richard to marry into money and their own class.'

'Well of course she would, but he couldn't have a better wife than you, Emma.'

Emma felt a pang of pain but said nothing as Dolly continued, 'It must also be very hard for you, landing in that society. You must feel like a duck with no water to paddle in.'

'It is hard, Dolly, not being one of them and I will never be one of them, you can't jump class and be accepted.'

'Well, I wish you luck, Emma. You know you can come here any time you need a change of scenery. Your mother's letter states that your husband isn't well.'

'Yes. That's why we've returned to England, the climate here is better for his recovery.'

'Is it consumption?'

'No, nothing like that. He became unwell and wasn't getting better. Too much heat perhaps.'

Nona gave Emma a strange look and Emma could see that Dolly knew she hadn't got the whole story, but she could wait, it would all come out in time.

The door opened suddenly and a young man with hooded eyes gave a flicker of surprise as he saw the visitors. Dan, Dolly's son, nodded at them as he sat heavily on the chair by the door, removing his boots. He said nothing.

'Do you recognise our visitors, Dan? It's Emma and Nona who used to live next door to us before we came here.'

'Yep.' He didn't take his eyes off his boots.

Dolly looked exasperated. 'Come to the table and eat with us, Dan.'

'I'll have mine in the other room.'

And without looking at the people around the table he took a slice of bread and some meat from the plates and left the kitchen.

An uncomfortable silence was left in his wake; Emma and Nona looked at Dolly questioningly.

'I'm sorry,' she said. 'He's a man of few words. Keeps himself to himself, but works hard.'

'Does he have a girl?'

'No, Emma, I've suggested one or two. But he's not interested, so he says.'

After they had eaten and heard all about the work being done on Tate Farm, Emma looked at Nona who'd hardly said a word all afternoon. She looked tired and Emma decided that she had probably had enough of visiting.

'I'm sorry but we have to go now, Dolly.' Emma stood up, smoothing her skirt with her hands.

'Oh!' Dolly looked sad. 'Do you have to go so soon? I was enjoying your visit so much.'

'We have to go back. Can we come again?'

'Of course you can. I'll be very hurt if you don't. And next time you'll see Alice and John.'

'Thank you for everything,' Emma said, wrapping her arms around Dolly.

Dolly raised her eyebrows in surprise. 'I haven't done very much.'

'Yes, you have.' Emma smiled. 'You made us feel welcome.'

After saying goodbye to Dolly they walked back across the meadow and through the park. But their mood had changed. Neither woman felt as elated as they had, and as the house came into view both hid their dark thoughts from the other.

Alone in her bed that night Emma wondered why the joy had gone out of the day. Perhaps it was seeing Dolly and remembering the past. Or Dan, who they'd played with when young and who couldn't now bring himself to look at them. Was it because she, Emma, was living above her station? She sighed; perhaps he'd just grown into an angry man.

That night she tossed and turned in her bed for what seemed like hours, unable to sleep, unable to stop her mind going over the day's events. Eventually she couldn't listen to her active brain a moment longer and, sliding from her tangled bed, wrapped a large shawl around her shoulders, opened her door and stepped out onto the cold landing. It was late. The servants had retired to their beds and in a few hours would be sleepily moving about the house again, preparing for the day. It was this time of complete stillness that Emma loved. Everywhere smelt different, felt different; there was freedom in the darkness. She became a ghost, a secret observer, a non-entity; stretching out her arms she padded slowly along the landing, enjoying being alone, an unobserved escapee. Hearing a sound below, she looked over the banister and observed Martin, in white night attire, stepping stealthily into the hall, drawing her shawl around her body. From the darkness of the landing Emma saw her close a door quietly behind her and tiptoe towards the servants' quarters and back stairs.

Emma stood uncertain, staring after the young woman. Where had she been, creeping around in the night? Frowning at the closed servants' door, Emma moved silently down the stairs and into the hall, finding the door from which Martin had just emerged. Pushing it open she felt cool air coming up a flight of stairs, accompanied by the nutty smell of dampness, and in front of her a flight leading upwards. Stealthily, she climbed the three flights of wooden stairs and on reaching the top was shocked to find herself in the attic where she had last spoken to Richard.

Going to his room she found him in his bed sleeping peacefully. Staring down into his face, she thought that he looked healthier. Gone were the gaunt lines of the sick man she'd brought home to his mother. She looked carefully at his bed; there was no sign that another person had been in it. So, what was Martin doing up here in the middle of the night? Had she come to Richard hoping for sex and found him asleep?

Returning to her own bed, she vowed to watch Martin more closely; she didn't trust her, and she no longer trusted Richard.

In the darkness of her room, Emma lay back on the pillow feeling desolate. As unwanted thoughts tumbled around in her head she heard a soft click and watched with fear in her eyes as the door opened slowly and a figure in white silently crossed the room towards her bed.

'Nona, what's wrong?' Emma raised herself up on one arm.

'Nothing! I couldn't sleep. Can I get in with you?'

Emma pulled back the covers and Nona climbed in, snuggling up. 'You're so warm, Emma.'

'And you are very cold, where have you been?'

'Nowhere! My room is cold. I keep thinking of when I lived on Tate Farm with Mother and Robert and how happy we were growing up there. Seeing Dolly living there now has brought back happy memories and left me feeling sad.'

'I wish that I could have known it, Nona.'

'I also wanted to thank you, Emma, for not telling Mrs Laddisbrock or Dolly what happened in Australia.'

'I don't think Richard will speak of it. I'm sure he won't want his parents to know why he was shot.'

Nona pulled the covers up over her shoulders and wriggled down into the warmth of the bed and sighed. 'Are we going to have to live like this for long? I hate being the hidden relatives, the embarrassment of the Laddisbrock clan.'

'Nona!' Emma was shocked to hear it voiced, although she also knew it to be true.

'I'm sorry, Em, but we have no clothes to be seen out in, and we're asked to stay in these rooms as though we don't exist.'

'I believe that my mother-in-law wishes that we did not exist. This is truly a difficult state of affairs. Somehow all will come right in the end,' Emma whispered.

But as Nona slept, Emma lay on her back unable to sleep. Did Richard really want to end their marriage or was that his mother's plan. But either way, she would not say that the fault was hers. She would not say that she'd had an assignation when she had not.

7.

By the end of May the walls of the house were closing in on Emma as she and Nona sat in their rooms with nothing to do but talk about the past and read. By mid-morning Emma could stand it no longer. 'Nona, I have to get out of here, come with me. I'm going to the stable to find a horse.'

Nona looked at her sister in amazement. 'You can't just take a horse, surely you would have to ask permission.'

'Who of, Nona? Who should I ask?'

Nona looked distressed. 'Emma, don't be reckless, you don't know the nature of the horses here.'

'I know that having nothing to do all day is the worst torture in the world. Come with me, we will explore the house together instead then.'

'I'm sorry, Em, not today. I'll stay here and rest.'

'Are you ill?' Emma was quickly at her sister's side. 'You are a little pale.'

'My bones are sore, that is all. You explore and then tomorrow if I'm feeling more able you can show me what you find.'

'If you're sure, Nona. I don't want to leave you if you're ill.'

'I'm sure.' She touched Emma's arm. 'It's no more than the rickets set off by the cold English weather.'

'I won't be long, I promise. I just have to escape for a little while.'

'I know.'

Emma stood in the corridor, having shut the door behind her, and wondered what to do next. Should she explore inside or outside? It was the bright sunlight shining through a window that decided her. Moving quickly down the stairs she made her way towards the back of the house. There would be a way out at the back, she didn't want to be seen by Martin; she couldn't say why she felt that the servant was watching her, but she did. She knew that it was probably childish but it would give her great joy to avoid the servant and do something that she, knew nothing about.

The house was silent; the only person Emma met as she descended a narrow staircase into a long passage was the boy Jacob.

He gawped at seeing her. 'You lost, missus? You shouldn't be down here.'

'No, Jacob, I'm not lost. I want to get out of the house without anyone seeing me.'

'Well, you better not go that way or Mrs Jenk will see you from the kitchen.'

'Will you help me, Jacob?' she whispered.

'I don't know.' He pulled a face. 'Mr Patrick will flog me if I do something wrong.'

'How can it be wrong, Jacob, when it's Mrs Laddisbrock who asks you?'

The boy frowned, looking uncertain.

'I will say that I was lost while finding my way around the house. I will keep our secret, Jacob.'

His face lit up. 'Secret!' he said. 'Martin has a secret.'

'Does she, Jacob, and what is that?' Emma was alert; she'd somehow known Martin was hiding something.

'I don't know,' he shrugged. 'It's a secret.' He raised his eyebrows, looking at Emma as though she were stupid.

'Of course, you're right, Jacob, how could anyone know, if it's a secret?'

'Mrs Jenk knows,' he offered, wide-eyed.

'Does she?' Emma raised her own eyebrows. 'How interesting.'

'We better go this way,' Jacob said, pushing past Emma to a door beside the stairs. On the other side of the door they went quickly down a short flight of stairs to a passage that led to a small door. As it was opened, Emma recognised the nutty smell on the air and realised that this was the bottom of the stairs she'd seen last night. At the end of a short passage, Jacob opened an outer door and Emma saw a damp, square courtyard about fifteen feet across in either direction and completely walled in by the house. The walls here were covered in vines that snaked up to higher windows. The brickwork and the cobbles were green with slime and there appeared no way out of this damp area.

'This way,' Jacob said, crossing the courtyard and bending below the foliage that grew on the wall opposite; beneath it Emma could see a hidden door.

It opened easily as the boy pushed it. Passing through the door she found herself in a passage similar to the one that the servants were currently using.

'This is the old servants' quarters,' Jacob whispered. 'When they built the other part of the house they left this as it was. We sometimes use these rooms for extra storage. He shivered, Martin says it's haunted.'

'You're very brave to show it to me, Jacob, thank you.'

He brightened up at her thanks and said, 'If you go through the door at the end of the passage, you'll come out in the old stable yard.'

She nodded her thanks and the boy disappeared back the way they had come.

Left alone in the deserted servants' passage, Emma stood in the silence. It was a place that she understood, a place that gave her comfort. The air was cool, but not haunted. Haunted was something she would be aware of. She walked softly down the arched passage, looking into all the rooms. It was easy to identify what had been the larder with its marble shelves and marble-topped bench. And the apple storeroom that still held the faintest aroma of apples. There was the washroom and the small room where the herbs were dried, prepared and hung from the ceiling; the butler's quarters and the cook's parlour with its fireplace and shelves. There were many rooms, mostly empty, leaving no trace of their use.

Putting her head around an open door she was surprised to find an unmade bed, the sheets folded back as though someone had just got up, leaving the bed to air. There was a half-burnt candle in a holder on a table and a large jug and bowl on a marble stand. *Perhaps*, she thought, *the place isn't used just for storage, someone comes here. Perhaps it's Martin; is this where she was coming from in the night and if so why?*

Opening the door at the end of the passage, she viewed her escape route – an abandoned stable yard. Some of the stable doors hung open, and a mounting block green with moss and weeds reassured her that no one came here anymore.

She was about to step into the yard when something stopped her. Retreating back into the shadow of the doorway, she waited. A window above closed loudly, a warning that the area was overlooked. Hardly breathing, she waited. When she decided that she would go, she went boldly, because if she was supposed to be lost then she had nothing to hide.

Hurrying across the yard towards the arched exit, she felt as though every window behind her had a face at it, watching her progress. She didn't look back, and as she passed beyond the arch felt a change in the atmosphere.

Seeing the path to the current stables, she took it. The smell of horses informed her that this was a working stable, not abandoned like the yard she had just left.

Here, the low buildings in front of her were built on two sides of a quadrangle, facing each other, before opening up into a large green paddock at the far end.

A thin young man of about fourteen, who was wielding a laden shovel from the doorway of a stall to a small handcart, stared at her. She smiled, but felt unnerved as he scowled and stared in return. It was then that she noticed that his face was a strange shape, dented in above the left eye; the left side of his face dropped, so that his eyes did not match up and his nose lay flat across his face. Not wanting to appear rude, she nodded to him and walked on, feeling his eyes on her back. To relieve the feeling of being watched, she poked her head around several doors. One, a room with horse bedding, another holding tack. Even the carriages were under cover. Everything was tidy. A horse snorted and a hoof struck wood; Emma smiled, her spirits rising. As the strange boy had departed with his now full handcart, Emma crossed the quadrangle and entered the stable block unobserved. She found three horses stabled and several stalls empty, the doors hanging open. She spoke quietly to each animal, and they responded by hanging their heads over their doors and nuzzling her hand.

A small brown mare was in the last stall watching Emma approach with rolling eyes and ears flat to her head. Opening the door Emma entered and stroked the animal's body. Its muscles twitched at her touch but it stood quietly as she stroked the veined face and scratched behind the soft warm ears. 'You're a beautiful girl,' she whispered.

The mare's ears pricked up as the slow clop of hooves approached from outside. A missing horse was being returned to its stall. Emma, shielded by the frame of the mare, watched as a man led a large white horse through the doorway. She heard him whispering gently to it but couldn't catch his words, as he was at the other end of the building. Then, to her horror she heard a noise closer; he'd thrown the saddle up onto a shelf nearby.

Realising that she had stopped breathing and felt dizzy, Emma leant her head on the mare's belly, letting out a long breath.

Turning, the man came towards the stall, addressing the mare. 'So, madam, you have quieted down.' And then his voice changed. 'Who the...?'

There was no hiding now. Emma stepped out and said, 'I was just admiring the mare,' and grinned cheekily.

The man stared at her from a weather-beaten face, his skin as tanned as she had been herself not so many months ago. For a moment his expression was serious; he frowned and then said cautiously, 'Do I know you?'

Emma was about to say no, but there was something about the voice, and perhaps the eyes. Then it was she who gasped, 'Matt, is it you?'

For a moment he seemed confused as he stared at her. Then recognition swept across his face.

'Emma? It can't be, after all these years.' His eyes sparkled with gladness. 'I always wondered what became of you after the day you set out to find your mother. My mother and I often spoke of you.'

He stepped back and looked at her in more detail. 'You've grown into a fine woman, Emma. But what are you doing here, have you taken a job?'

Sadness flowed over her as the gap between the classes was once again reaching out and smothering her joy. She played for time. 'How is Nell?'

He looked pained as he answered. 'My mother died some time ago.'

'I'm truly sorry to hear that, Matt, what happened?'

'After you left, Mother and I were dismissed and the mistress moved to France. We tried, but we couldn't find work. The mistress wouldn't give us a reference.' His face was suddenly sad. 'Mother was ill. Her chest couldn't take the damp weather sleeping wherever we could. Eventually we went back to Claydon House. Alf was glad of the company and Mother's cooking.' He smiled, remembering. 'Her health improved being back beside her fire. We were lucky to have a roof over our heads, even though we didn't have a wage. She died the following year with a fever and Alf died the year after of old age. The horses had been sold, so there was nothing for me to do. The furniture was left in the house in case Mr Oliver returned, and I stayed on for a few more weeks trying to decide where to go.'

'Did he return?'

'No.'

A familiar feeling of fear crept over Emma as she remembered her cousin Oliver Brack, standing over Polly's shallow grave in the forest clearing, and she shivered.

'Are you alright?' he asked, noticing the movement.

'Yes Matt, just forgotten memories. How long have you worked here?'

'Ten years, about.' He changed the subject. 'But what are you doing here, Emma? You're not dressed like a servant.'

She sighed and bit her lip; her secret, though of course it was no secret, was going to be exposed and it seemed that it was she who was going to be doing the exposing. She played for time.

'Mother married Andrew Tate and we all emigrated with them to Australia. It was a hard life, Matt. If it hadn't been for Mother and Andrew's strength and courage we wouldn't have survived. It's a hot, strange land, Matt, with strange trees and animals that you couldn't imagine. Huge things, a cross between a horse and a rat that hops at speed balancing on a thick tail.'

'Is it dangerous?' He looked shocked.

'I don't know, we keep away from them. Mother shoots over their heads when they get into the area where we grow our food and herbs.'

His face now showed astonishment. 'Your mother shoots?'

'Yes, we all shoot. It's a violent, lawless land, Matt. The military try to keep some order, but they are few in a vast land and are taken up with their duties of looking after the poor wretches that are sent to the penal colony. Some are murderers and many, Andrew believes, innocent souls. They work under the eye of the military, constructing housing, making bricks, growing food. We live some forty miles inland from the colony. Andrew found an area for us to live that had a river and we cleared the land and built cabins of wood.'

He stared at her, saying nothing. She stopped for breath; she wanted him to understand the harshness of the environment that she had come from before she continued. 'We were many times on the brink of starvation.'

Unexpectedly seeing him was exhilarating and her heart fluttered. The handsome boy that she'd loved as a child was still there; now older, he was muscle-toned, weather-beaten and rugged. She wanted to run to him, throw her arms around him, have him hold her close. She wanted to smell the scent of him, and blushed at the thoughts and feelings that were rising in her body. He might be married. *Oh, good Lord*, the thought came to her, *I am married*.

'I have something to tell you, Matt. While I was away I changed my name. I didn't know that I would be returning,' she faltered.

His eyes narrowed; his voice held a note of suspicion when he spoke. 'Are you the new...?' He didn't finish the sentence, he'd seen the answer in her face. His shoulders stiffened, his face froze. 'Why are you here in the stable, madam?'

'Matt, don't be silly, I just want to talk.'

'If you order me to talk to you then I will, madam, but I have to get back to my work.'

He turned away, walking quickly out of the stable block, leaving Emma saddened by his sudden change of attitude. Now a new emotion was rising in her chest. Anger. How dare he just abandon her? He'd been like a brother, she'd looked up to him.

'Wait,' she called sharply, going after him. 'I want to ride, that is why I came here.'

He stopped, flinching as though an arrow had struck him unexpectedly between his shoulders.

He turned slowly. 'Do you have permission to ride one of these valuable horses?'

'No, I don't have permission.' Her eyes flashed as she struggled with the anger that was being prodded by the intensity of his demeaning tone of voice.

'Then I'm sorry, madam, I can't let you ride until I know that you have permission.'

He walked away, disappearing around the edge of the building.

Emma stood in the yard, fuming in her anger, and wondered what to do next. Determination suddenly took hold over sensibility, and with chin jutted forward and teeth clenched she turned abruptly; entering the stable she approached the mare.

'How would you like to run, my beauty?' As she stroked the animal's nose, it nuzzled at her fingers with soft, hairy lips. 'You are a beauty,' Emma whispered as the mare's hot breath caressed her hand.

Standing on a stool, she laid across the mare's back, speaking quietly into her ear. Then, carefully brought one leg across the horse and sat up, holding onto her mane. It felt good to be up high on a horse again, to smell the sharp, sweet smell of horse sweat.

The mare, suddenly backed into the corner of the stall, shook her head violently and kicked out at the wall behind her, before bucking and lowering her head. Emma's arms were unexpectedly wrenched forward. Losing her balance, she slid over the mare's head, landing unceremoniously face down in the filth of the stable floor, her clothes over her head. Mixed in with the mare's snorting, Emma heard a giggle.

Standing up, she brushed herself down. Her clothes were covered in muck but she wasn't hurt, only her pride was hurt.

'You alright, missus?'

Emma saw Jacob's cheeky face peering over the dividing wall.

'Thank you, Jacob, I'm not hurt.' And balling some straw in her hand she tried to wipe the muck from her skirt, bodice and arms.

'You're supposed to put a saddle on the horse, one of those things on the shelf.' He pointed.

'I know what a saddle is, Jacob, thank you.'

He raised his eyebrows. 'She can't be rid.' He flicked his head towards the horse. 'She's a demon, so Ames says.'

'Ames? Oh, you mean Matt. Well, she didn't want to be ridden today.'

'Nor any day, she's going to need some training, Ames says.'

'I'm sure Mr Ames knows best, Jacob, he has been around horses a long time.'

'Do you know him then, missus?'

Emma became wary; this child would tell the staff all that she let slip, she was sure of that. And, sadly, also what he'd just witnessed. 'What are you doing in the stable, Jacob, shouldn't you be in the house?'

'I like horses and would like to train under Ames, but I have to stay in the house. I'm a boot boy and my father, a boot boy before me. I took his job when he died. He wanted to be a footman one day but it never happened. So, I just comes and watches Ames when I can get away. I learn a lot, just watching.'

She changed the subject. 'Who is the tall boy who cleans out the stables?'

'Oh, that's Simeon Larch,' he said, pulling a grotesque face. 'He's dippy.'

'You mustn't say things like that, Jacob, it's cruel. Something must have happened to him.'

'Oh, it did, missus. Larch said that when Simeon was about four years old he was kicked in the head by a horse. They thought he would die, but he didn't.'

'So, he's the son of Larch?'

'Yes, missus, but he's not good for nothing but sweeping.'

~

Returning to her rooms the way she'd come, through the old stables yard, Emma went to her dressing closet and poured cold water from the jug into the bowl. She smelt of horse and wanted to wash it off. Removing her skirt, she poured water over the stains and rubbed.

Hearing a noise in her bedroom she opened the door, but it wasn't Nona as hoped. Martin stood in the room, trying to conceal the smug look on her face.

'I heard that you'd had an accident, madam, and thought that you might need help.'

Emma noticed the twitch of a smile in the corner of the woman's mouth and the glint in her eye. 'Do you find it funny, Martin?'

The woman stiffened. 'No, madam, not at all. I'm glad to see that you're unhurt. Mrs Laddisbrock would like to see you as soon as you're dressed. Leave those clothes with me, madam, I will tend to them.'

As she spoke, Martin was laying out a change of clothes on the bed.

'Do you know what your mistress wants to see me about?'

'No, madam, it's not for me to know the mistress's business.'

Emma flushed; she knew it was a put-down and also that Martin probably did know what her mistress was going to say. In a big house like this the walls had ears and eyes, and those ears and eyes were called servants. She couldn't make out why Martin was so hostile towards her, unless she was in love with Richard. Emma knew that she needed an ally in the house and she could do without another enemy.

8.

Emma swept down the stairs behind Martin who knocked on a large polished door.

'Mrs Richard Laddisbrock, madam,' she announced.

Emma stepped through the doorway, her head held high. She wasn't going to show Richard's mother that she was worried.

Her mother-in-law was sitting on a chair in a room the like of which Emma had never seen before. A carved stone fireplace dominated one wall. The light from two huge windows set each side of it highlighted the stonemason's skill, as the carvings of leaves, fruit and flowers in sharp detail crept up the stone supports. Books, in varying shades of leather, decorated the walls, on shelves of varying height to suit the size of the displayed volumes. It was the only decoration that this room needed.

'Please sit.' The voice was high and haughty.

Emma seated herself in an upholstered chair opposite Richard's mother. The door opened and a maid entered with a tray. 'You'll take tea with me, I hope.'

Emma nodded in agreement, completely disarmed by the woman's friendliness. As the tray was placed on a low table between them and cups set down before each woman, Emma became aware of a prickling in her hair, as though she were being watched. Turning her head, she saw no one else in the room, yet suddenly she was on her guard.

Charlotte Laddisbrock was holding her teacup mid-air as the servant who had poured the tea left the room and closed the door.

'Have you given any more thought to our proposal?' Charlotte asked.

'Proposal?' Emma felt confused; she'd thought the interview was going to be about the stables.

'I haven't, madam,' she said, quickly gathering her thoughts.

Charlotte looked annoyed. 'You must see how unfortunate this marriage is, not only for Richard, but for yourself.'

'Mrs Laddisbrock, your son and I are legally married. I am his wife and as such have been very badly treated since our return to England. At first, I understood that you wanted to have Richard nursed and that he was given rest in his own rooms. I have since seen that his health is much improved and I would resume our relationship as man and wife.'

The hand holding the cup dropped. The cup hit the saucer with a clunk. The older woman's mouth puckered. 'You seem to be under some misapprehension, madam. You see it is also Richard's will that this marriage be dissolved.'

'But he has no grounds for dissolving our marriage.'

The woman opposite was silent, then, staring straight into Emma's eyes, she said, 'What were you doing in the stables?'

Once again Emma was thrown by the sudden twist in the woman's thoughts. 'I wanted to ride. I'm sorry that I didn't ask permission.'

'You crept out of the house like a common thief, madam, and were found by one of the servants with your clothes in disarray, I understand.'

Emma gawped. She could hardly believe what she was hearing. 'I fell from the horse, madam.' She watched as Charlotte raised a questioning eyebrow.

Emma's spirit spiralled downwards. 'You believe that I went to meet someone. How dare you. You know very well that is not true.'

'I know only what I have heard. It is common talk amongst the servants. I think that we have our proof, and our solicitor will be drawing up the papers for submission to the court. I would of course be glad if you would leave as soon as possible.'

'You will turn me out with nothing, with nowhere to go?'

'You had nothing when you met my son.'

'I had a family, madam, land and a home. I left all that behind so that Richard could have the medical attention that he needed here.'

The older woman's rouge-covered cheek twitched. A momentary admittance to Emma's care for her son showed in her eyes, but was gone in an instant.

'We will make a one-off provision for you. Enough money for you to support yourself until you can return home.'

Emma knew that it was no use fighting; they didn't want her and she would never fit in. She didn't even know how to fit into their lives. Her best option now was to bargain for what she could.

'My sister and I need clothes. We came from a very hot country where there was no society and to live here we must have something decent to be seen in.'

Charlotte nodded. 'Yes, I understand. I will see to it that you will have enough money for you both to buy what you need.'

'Thank you. We will also need a horse and carriage.'

Charlotte's voice was crystal sharp. 'Do not try my patience too far, madam.'

Emma continued, 'We will need transport. Can you imagine how it will reflect on this family if Richard's wife is seen walking from the estate with her bags?'

'Do you imagine, madam, that anyone will care when they know why you are no longer Richard's wife?'

'But that is an untruth.' Emma's eyes filled with tears at the injustice being heaped upon her. 'I have done nothing wrong as a wife and you know that.'

'I only know what the servant saw.'

'Servant?' Emma's voice was raised now. 'A boy finds me face down in the straw having fallen from a horse. That is all that happened.'

'No one believes that. Martin found you removing stains from your clothes. You have brought dishonour to yourself and to our family. If, madam, I hear any more of this you will leave with nothing.'

Emma stood so suddenly that the woman sitting opposite flinched, but Emma was already making her way across the room to the door.

Upstairs she entered Nona's room without knocking. The room was empty. Going to her own room she found that also empty. She couldn't think where her sister could be. Turning swiftly, she hurried down the corridor and entered the door leading to Richard's apartment. He was standing in the window dressed ready for the outdoors. Patrick was handing him his hat.

'Emma! What's wrong?' Richard looked concerned. 'I'll call if I need help, Patrick, you can go.'

Patrick bowed, gave Emma a withering look and left the room.

'I have just come from your mother, Richard. She tells me that it is common gossip that I have been with a servant.'

'You were found in a compromising position, Emma.'

'I'd fallen off a horse, Richard, that is all that happened.'

'As you say, Emma.' He raised an eyebrow. 'Can you deny that you didn't already know the man that you met in the stables?'

'I'm not denying it, Richard. I did know Matt Ames at Claydon House. We were both servants of the Brack family.'

'And?'

'And what, Richard? I was a child.'

He looked out of the window into the park. 'You gave us no option, Emma, this marriage has to be dissolved.'

'And if we were still in Australia?'

'I would have left you for Lizzie.' His voice was low, strained.

Hot tears rolled down Emma's face. Now she knew that he didn't love her. 'Did you ever love me, Richard?'

'I thought I did at first.' He sat slowly in the nearest chair. He looked pale. 'I didn't want what came with you. Working on the land isn't what I was groomed for.'

'You would rather have lived in that hovel with the Logans?'

'No! I had no intention of living like a rat in dirt with those women.'

'You would have left Lizzie unsupported with a baby?'

'She'd only just told me when her brothers arrived. I hadn't had time to think that far ahead. But you're right, I wouldn't have stayed around, she had plenty of women to support her.'

Knowing now that there was no longer any reason to be married to Richard her heart was heavy. 'I will go quietly, Richard. I ask you please not to tell this untruth, and to give me enough money to live on until Nona and I can be settled somewhere.'

He nodded agreement, closing his eyes. 'Our solicitor will draw up the papers. I will tell my parents what we have agreed.'

Emma let out a sigh of relief. 'Thank you, Richard.'

Leaving him sitting in the chair she went to look for her sister.

Seeing Martin in the corridor she asked, 'Have you seen Miss Tilby?'

Martin appeared to look down her nose as she spoke. 'She went for a walk, madam.'

Emma felt the strangeness of that statement, as Nona hadn't wanted to go out because of her aching joints. She kept an impassive face as she replied, 'Which direction did my sister take, Martin? I will join her on her walk.'

'I'm sorry, madam, I didn't see which direction Mistress Tilby took.'

Emma's emotions were at boiling point; she was sure that this woman missed nothing and was being difficult on purpose. Staring steadily into Martin's eyes until the servant lowered her impudent gaze, she said, 'Go about your duties, Martin.'

But as the servant moved on along the passage, Emma knew that she was still only just holding authority over her.

With her shawl wrapped tightly around her shoulders, Emma stepped out into the grounds where the air felt good upon her face. Walking out into the parkland, she moved with purpose, all the time looking for her sister.

Stepping through the small gate into the meadow she immediately felt a weight lift from her shoulders and relaxed. The air was sweet here; the grass and colourful meadow flowers swaying in the breeze soothed her. Walking through the long grass towards a huge swathe of red poppies she lay down.

Her heart was pounding; she'd always felt at one with nature when she'd lain on the earth, but not today. Today, her heart was aching, her throat constricted as she stared at the small clouds in the sky above, and soon the tears ran unchecked over her cheeks and into her ears. She sobbed until she could cry no more and then, exhausted, she heard the buzzing of the insects, smelt the sweetness of the flowers and was at last at one with the earth.

Since being back in England, trapped in the confines of the house with no privacy from the servants, she had been denied the expression of her faith. Now she got onto her knees amid the colour, raised her arms to the Goddess and breathed in deeply, feeling the strength and energy of the trees beyond the meadow join with the freedom of the birds. As the peace of the Goddess energy entered her, she prayed.

'Sweet Mother Goddess, your daughter links with you after so long a time. In that time, my being has been in turmoil. I have felt no peace and have been unable to link with you or my ancestors because my mind has been too busy with burdens out of my control. Now I realise that all is as it should be. All is well and for the best. My life will go on and I will not forget you again.'

As she knelt in silence, her eyes shut, feeling the love of the Goddess through all her senses, suddenly, and for no apparent reason, a vision of Claydon House flooded her mind. She frowned, wondering why, and as the vision faded she opened her eyes.

Standing up, the vision was forgotten and her thoughts turned again to her sister. Walking downhill towards Tate Farm, she realised that it was the only place Nona could be.

On this side of the hill the meadow and fields were sheltered from the breeze and the air was deliciously warm. She took a deep breath, breathing in the scenery which she had so long craved and, in that same moment, noticed a movement in the field below her: Nona, walking slowly, her hair removed from its pins hanging wantonly down her back. Her skirt, pulled up and tucked into the waistband in front, exposed her bare legs and feet. Shocked, Emma looked about her quickly to see if anyone other than herself was watching. To her relief she saw no one and, grabbing up her own skirt, ran down the hill toward her sister.

The sudden movement from above stopped Nona in her tracks. 'Emma!' She waved a hand in greeting.

'What are you doing here?' Emma demanded as she got nearer.

Her sister looked shocked. 'Walking!'

'Like that! Undressed?' Emma pointed at Nona's hair as it hung down her back, its length falling over one shoulder.

'I was enjoying the weather, Emma, and my surroundings. Surely that isn't also a crime in this country?'

'Yes, it is. It isn't what young women do in this country. Why did you leave the house, Nona?'

'I was lonely.' She looked at the ground and put her arms behind her back like a naughty child, and in that moment she looked very young.

'I asked you if you wanted to come with me and you said not.' Feeling the frustration of trying to do what was expected from those in the house, it made her sad that she would have to berate her sister over something so natural.

'I know, Emma. I'm sorry, but after you'd gone the silence of the house unsettled me. I hate it here, Emma, there is nothing to do but stitch or read their boring books. I miss being useful.'

'You were wild in Australia, Nona. Women here are expected to act differently and even the poor have to show some dignity.'

'Dignity?' A flash of irritation crossed Nona's face. 'Trussed up like a chicken in these clothes with nothing to do all day. It may suit you, Emma, but it doesn't suit me, I want more.'

Anger suddenly flashed through Emma. 'Do you think that I don't want more, Nona? When we leave here we will need to work. We will have no references. I might, if I say that I am a widow, get a position as a governess. You may, if we say you have come straight from your family, get a position, but I don't know in what capacity, as you are headstrong. Getting work is going to be difficult for us both. Now sit down while I dress your hair, I have something I have to tell you.'

Nona sank sulkily onto the ground, and Emma gathered her hair and twisted it, piling it on top of her sister's head securing it with hairpins.

'Mrs Laddisbrock will have my marriage to Richard dissolved on the grounds of my adultery. She will give me enough money to support us until we get passage home.'

'Oh, Emma, what does she mean, adultery?'

'While I was at the stable I spoke to Matt Ames, someone I used to work with at Claydon House. He and I had sharp words. I was angry because he walked away when he found out who I was and why I was here. I needed to ride and mounted a horse that threw me. One of the servants came across me with my clothes over my head. It is now gossip among the servants that I have been unfaithful. My mother-in-law is happy to have the ammunition she needs to give to a solicitor.'

'But that isn't the truth, Emma.' Nona's face had paled.

'They don't care about truth or what it will do to my reputation and yours. They just want to be rid of me so that Richard can marry into his own class and have a Laddisbrock heir.'

'I'm so sorry, Emma. They don't deserve you. You are much too nice to be associated with them.'

'I went to see Richard. I told him what had happened and he has said that if I go quietly and agree their terms, then he will divorce me without saying that I am an adulteress.'

'I will go and see Richard's mother, Emma, and I will put her straight about her beloved son.' Nona's face was flushed with indignation and Emma was afraid how her sister's anger might show itself.

'It won't make any difference, Nona, men can be unfaithful and society think no less of them. I am learning that that is how life is. We will need more money than enough to support us before we are settled, Nona. I am trying to get more for us.'

Nona looked down at her hands and then straight into Emma's eyes. 'You don't intend for us to go home, do you, Emma?'

'No, we are not going back, dear. With the money I receive we will cope with whatever fortune throws at us here. Come.' She pulled Nona to her feet. 'Now you are respectable we can walk back. We will eat and make plans.'

But in her heart Emma had no idea what those plans might be.

~

As they approached the house a carriage stood at the bottom of the steps. A bay horse between the shafts snorted and shook its head impatiently as they approached.

'The Laddisbrocks have a visitor, Emma, should we go in another way?'

'No! We will enter at the front. We do after all live here, Nona. We're not servants.'

As they entered the hallway they saw Charlotte standing at the top of the stairs with a gentleman. He was just taking his leave and saying, 'I hope that Richard will soon be well enough to attend church.'

Charlotte was no longer listening to him; her face had turned from gentle peace to confusion, as below her the two women entered the hall from outside. The gentleman, dressed all in black, turned his face away from Charlotte to see what had distracted her and for a moment stood with his mouth open in disbelief.

'My Lord, an apparition,' he exclaimed, and striding down the stairs towards Emma and Nona he left Charlotte standing alone. 'I can hardly believe it. I thought never to see you again.'

Emma extended her hand. 'Reverend Draycott, how wonderful to see you and how is your wife?'

The Reverend, now visibly older, his face creased with the passing years, took her hand and bowed. 'My wife is very well, thank you, Emma. Are your mother and Andrew here also?'

'I'm afraid not, sir, there is only my sister and I.'

'I can see that you are come to visit Mrs Laddisbrock, so I will not delay your visit, Emma. Would you both come to church on Sunday if you are in the area and take lunch with us after the service? There is so much I should like to know.' A shadow crossed his face. 'They are both well, your parents, are they?'

'Yes, sir, they are both well. They are in the best of health as are my brothers who are now young men.'

'When I tell my wife she will be delighted. I hope to see you both on Sunday then.' He bowed to them all in turn, donned his hat and hurried out of the door down the steps to his carriage.

Emma looked at Charlotte as Patrick shut the door behind the Reverend Draycott. Charlotte was annoyed, it showed in her eyes, and yet her face broke very slightly into a thin smile as she said, 'Please come to my sitting room, Emma, I have a need to speak with you.'

Emma followed Charlotte into the room on the first floor where last they had taken tea and Charlotte had laid down her demands.

'Please sit.' The voice was again sharp.

'I will stand, thank you, Mother-in-Law.'

She could see that Charlotte was irritated with the use of the title. When she spoke, she issued a terse warning. 'You will not attend lunch with the vicar on Sunday, I forbid it.'

'You forbid it!' Emma was aghast. 'You would stop me going to church?'

'You may by all means go to church on Sunday, but you will not go to lunch with the Draycotts, you will make an excuse.'

'I have been invited to lunch and I will be going to lunch with the Draycotts, madam.'

'If you want to leave this family with your reputation intact and money to survive on, then, madam, you will do as I wish.'

Emma was speechless. Charlotte still had the upper hand. 'You may send a note of apology,' she continued. 'One of the servants will get a boy from the village to deliver it for you.'

Emma had a sinking feeling in her stomach. Did no one know that she was Mrs Richard Laddisbrock? Why had she herself not informed the vicar that she lived here, that she was not visiting? In her heart she knew the answer. Politeness had stopped her interrupting him and now she regretted it. Charlotte was trying to keep the marriage quiet. But servants talk, surely there were whisperings in the village?

Charlotte's voice cut into her thoughts. 'There will be no more discussion. You may go.'

Angry at being dismissed like a servant, Emma stormed along the passages to her rooms and when she entered was glad to see Nona sitting in a chair.

'What did Charlotte want with you?'

'I am not to go to lunch with the Draycotts on Sunday. Charlotte does not want them to know that I am Richard's wife.'

'What will you do?'

'If I go, Nona, she will make sure that I am dishonoured and that we are penniless.'

'Then I will go, Emma, she holds nothing over me. I will let it be known that I have been invited to the Motts' for lunch, but will go instead to the Draycotts.'

'She will find out, Nona. No! I think I will write a second note to Mr Draycott explaining the real reason for my not attending lunch.'

'That you are Mrs Richard Laddisbrock, and that you are a prisoner to your mother-in-law! Do you not think that he will come straight here and approach her on the subject?'

Feeling deflated, Emma sighed. 'You're right. I can't do that either. I will, for now, have to send my apologies and hope that I can speak with him after we leave here and everything is settled.'

9.

Mary Martin was excited as she approached her mother's cottage on her day off. She knew her mother would relish the gossip from the Manor House. Bursting through the door she called, 'You'll never guess what's gone on up at the house, Mother.' But stopped suddenly in the doorway, surprised to find the Reverend Draycott sitting on the sofa with her mother.

'Here is Mary, Reverend, come to visit her old mother on her day off.'

Ernest looked at the young woman who had just entered and didn't miss the light in her eyes fade at sight of his presence.

'Is all well up at the house, Mary?' he enquired, smiling thinly at the young woman who, he knew, did not like or respect him.

'Oh yes, Reverend, all is well, just a little female tittle-tattle, that is all.' She felt her mistake before she had finished the sentence, remembering his sermon several Sundays past on the subject of gossip doing the Devil's work for him. She continued to stand in the doorway feeling uncomfortable.

'Come in, Mary, for goodness' sake, you're making the place look untidy.' Her mother's tone was sharp.

Mary moved into the room and looked about for her son. She looked at her mother with a raised eyebrow.

'Sleeping!' Celia replied to the unspoken question.

An uncomfortable silence filled the room, prompting Ernest to stand up saying, 'I will leave you now, Mrs Martin, I can see that you have things to discuss.'

Looking at Mary, he nodded curtly, then bowed to Celia and was gone, shutting the door behind him.

'What did he want?' Mary's voice held a note of accusation.

'What do you mean, what did *he* want? He's the vicar and a better caring man you'd be hard to find, my girl. He came to see if there was anything that I needed and to ask if Thomas would like to start at the Sunday teaching, after church.'

'And what did you say, Mother? Considering that Thomas is my son.'

'I said that I would speak to you about it and let him know.'

Taking a deep breath Mary tried to contain her anger. She always felt guilty and unclean in the presence of the vicar and she knew why. He wanted to know who the father of Thomas was, and she wasn't going to tell him, nor anyone else. It was strange, but while no one had that knowledge she felt that she could hold her head up.

'Now, what were you going to tell me?' Her mother brought her back from her seething anger. 'Something happen up at the Castle?'

The joy of the gossip had somehow disappeared and Mary was in two minds whether to tell her mother at all.

But Celia was eager for some gossip and, turning to the kitchen, called over her shoulder, 'You can tell me while I make you some lunch.'

Mary sat at the table as the small fire over which her mother cooked glowed warmly. Celia cut into a newly baked loaf with vigour.

'Well, go on, Mary,' she said, placing a slice of bread on a plate.

'It's the new Mrs Laddisbrock. It seems that she knows Matthew Ames and was found by a servant in a stable with her clothes in disarray. Later, I found her in her room trying to remove a stain from her clothes.'

Celia stared at her daughter. 'Do you mean that she was caught…?'

'Yes, Mother.' Mary's eyes sparkled. 'It seems so.'

'My goodness, it just shows, doesn't it, that breeding will out.'

'Sooner she goes, Mother, the better, I say.'

'What was Richard Laddisbrock thinking when he married her?' Celia cut another slice of bread with new vigour.

'His mother isn't pleased,' Mary continued. 'I overheard her telling Miss High and Mighty that she wants her to leave and wants nothing more to do with her. There's talk of divorce.'

'Divorce! Really. Can they do that?'

'Yes, Mother, really. But you mustn't breathe a word outside these walls or I could be in trouble. I don't think that the Laddisbrocks have told anyone about the marriage.'

'Really!' Celia looked incredulous.

'Well, why would they want anyone to know?' Mary continued. 'First, he disappears, and then turns up with an unacceptable wife. His mother still wants him to marry into their own class.'

'Well of course she does. We should all know our place, Mary.'

There was something in the way her mother spoke that made Mary look at her sharply. But before she could ask what she'd meant, her mother was speaking again.

'Now! What am I going to tell the vicar about Thomas going to the Sunday school teaching?'

'I don't want him to go, Mother. He's too young. He can't speak properly yet. Maybe next year.'

Celia was not surprised at her daughter's reaction. Nodding agreement, she pushed a plate of bread and an apple in Mary's direction across the table. 'Here,' she said, 'it's not much but then Thomas and I don't have much to live on.'

'Oh, not that old chestnut again, Mother!' Mary raised her eyes to the ceiling.

Celia slammed her hand on the table, making her daughter jump. 'How dare you speak to me like that, Mary. While you live on good food up at the Castle, Thomas and I have to make do on what we can get.'

'I give you good money, Mother,' Mary retorted loudly.

'Your money only covers the rent, Mary. How am I expected to feed two of us on nothing? I have to rely on my few vegetables, our fruit trees and the generosity of my neighbours.'

'Oh, them. Your neighbours. There's always someone to gossip and stick their nose in where it isn't wanted. And you listen to them, Mother, you take sides against me.'

'Don't you sound so bloody virtuous, my lady, if it wasn't for them, then Thomas might have gone into care a long time ago.'

Mary was shocked. 'I'm sorry, Mother, you didn't tell me you were struggling.'

'Well, I'm telling you now and I want Thomas's father to take some responsibility for his son's upkeep.'

'That isn't going to happen, Mother.' Mary's voice was angry again; she hadn't wanted confrontation on her day off, the only day she got once a month to see her son.

Celia felt the usual frustration due to Mary's stubbornness rising within her. 'If you won't tell him, my girl, then I will. Now who is he?'

The atmosphere in the room was charged. But Mary's jaw had set tight and Celia knew that she wasn't going to find out, not today anyway. She continued to glare at her daughter even so, just to let her know how deep her feelings went on this subject.

Mary knew that her mother was set on finding out who the father of Thomas was and tried to deflect the conversation from going further. 'I will help out more with food, Mother, that's all I can do. Next time I come I will bring meat and whatever else I can. They won't miss it, you wouldn't believe the amount of food they eat.'

'It's a start, Mary, but not enough, the boy's growing fast, he needs clothes and shoes.'

Mary sighed. She knew her mother was right and also that her wage wasn't going to increase. She was as trapped as her mother in this spiral of twilight poverty.

~

Matt had been rubbing liniment into the fetlock of the white horse. It had been lame since May, and Matt was at last satisfied that healing was taking place as the June weather warmed the estate. Walking the horse slowly in a circle around the yard he watched its movements. Each day the massage and a little exercise was doing wonders for the strained leg. As he walked beside the horse he noticed Mary Martin standing in the yard.

'Hello, Matt.'

There was a softness in her voice that he noticed, yet he gave no reaction to it as she undid the top of her dress. 'It's so hot today.' She looked at him from under her lashes. 'Wouldn't you like to take a walk with me? I know it's your day off.'

'I don't take days off.' His tone was sharp as he passed her, trying not to look at the open front of her dress. As he continued to walk the horse around the yard she came up beside him, walking with him shoulder to shoulder.

'You don't have any fun in your life, Matt. What harm could a walk in the woods with me do?'

He tried to ignore her closeness by watching the movement of the horse's leg. He patted the white's shoulder. 'You're doing well, Baron.' The horse responded, turning its head to him, laying its nose momentarily on his chest. 'Good boy,' Matt responded, stroking the side of Baron's huge head, and led the horse back inside the stable block.

When Baron was settled with the boy Simeon rubbing him down, Matt crossed the yard to the tack room, putting the liniment safely back on a high shelf.

He flinched, nearly dropping the bottle as the door shut with a bang leaving him unable to see in the sudden darkness. Moving forward, arms outstretched, he hoped not to trip over anything when he felt the warmth of a body close to his, a hand stretched out in the darkness, touching his chest gently. It moved slowly down towards his belt, towards the top of his trousers.

Instinctively he grabbed the unseen wrist, stopping it going any further. He knew who it was as Mary's face came close to his and her body pushed against him. He heard the quickening of her breath, felt her mouth on his lips. For a moment he was overcome with the desire to have a woman. For a moment, his lips responded to a rush of feeling that swept through his loins, a need that almost overcame him. Letting go of her wrist he pushed his hand inside her dress feeling the firmness of her breast. She groaned as he kissed her harder. His other hand swept into her hair, grasping it tightly. Pulling her head backwards violently he kissed her neck before his mouth moved hungrily down inside the open dress. She groaned again as his lips covered her breasts.

A second later the room was filled with light as the door burst open. Over Mary's shoulder Matt saw Jacob standing in the doorway, his mouth hanging open.

'Go back to the house,' Matt shouted at the boy.

Jacob's face crumpled at Matt's unexpected anger and, turning, he ran from the doorway.

The moment had been broken and Matt seemed suddenly to wake up. He looked at Mary who was hurriedly buttoning her dress, her hair was a mess, her top lip swollen.

His sudden and almost uncontrollable lust had been replaced just as quickly by anger. Why had she offered herself to him? Raised a need in him that he'd worked so hard to deny? He'd wanted to... God, he wanted to, but not with her. He'd had women, but none could compromise his job like this one could.

Leaving her standing in the tack room, he walked quickly across the yard and mounted the stairs to his quarters over the stable block. Slamming the loft door, he locked it. Walking over to his bed, he lowered himself slowly and sat with his head in his hands.

~

In the kitchen, Mrs Jenk looked up as Mary entered, adjusting her hair. 'Where 'ave you bin, me lady?'

'I went to speak to Matt.'

'Matt, is it? Don't you go getting any more ideas about men, Mary Martin, because I won't help you again. Next time, you lose your job, understand?' Banging the rolling pin onto the pastry that she had been rolling out, Mrs Jenk made a long dent in it. Scooping the pastry up again she balled it in her hands and, covering the table in flour, started to roll it out again.

Mary's face was flushed with anger as she retorted, 'Yes, I understand. And don't think that I won't tell the mistress that you helped hide it from her. If I go, you go.'

'Why, you little slut, don't go thinking that you can threaten me.'

The cook waved the rolling pin at Mary who tossed her head, her lips twisted in a mirthless grin.

'You'd best be nice to me, Mrs Jenk, because one day...'

The door opened and Jacob entered, carrying an armful of wood. Seeing Mary his small face paled. Putting the wood in a box by the fire he made a hasty retreat into the servants' passage. Mary went after him and, catching him by the ear, she pulled it up so hard that he wailed, standing on tiptoe. 'What did you see, Jacob? Out in the yard,' she hissed.

'I saw you talking to Ames.' His face was reddening and he tried to hold his ear, but she slapped his hand away.

'Saw me talking to Ames, did you?'

'Yes,' he cried out as she twisted his ear harder and brought her face close to his.

'Anything else?'

'He shouted at me, that's all. Please, let me go, Martin.'

'Do you know why he shouted at you?'

'No, no, let me go.'

'You'd be advised to get on with your work and stop hanging about the stables. It's not a safe place for a boy, especially a boy who don't know his place. Now get about it, or it'll be worse for you.'

Letting his ear go she pushed him up the passage towards the back door.

As she watched him run off she felt worried. The boy was in the way.

Her face was set in a scowl as she made her way to the rooms of the unwanted guests.

10.

In the early hours of the following morning Emma awoke from sleep with a start. A deep fear swept through her in the darkness. The muscles in her stomach were taut and a deep emptiness, like hunger, wormed deep in her solar plexus. Her heart pounded, saliva filled her mouth; something was happening, something bad. Every cell in her body was taut, jangling. She knew this feeling all too well. Her senses alerting her to some emotional trauma or danger about to be visited upon her. Staring into the darkness of the room she whispered, 'What is it?' and wondered if something was happening right now. Or had it already happened? Was she being forewarned that something was going to happen? Emma hated this feeling. Hated not knowing what it meant. What was the good of it, she thought angrily, if she didn't know what it meant?

She tried to go back to sleep but by now her brain was far too active. Perhaps it was her mother. Had something happened to her mother, or brothers? Was that what she was picking up?

The bedroom window was ajar and the partly open curtains revealed the sky, allowing a small amount of light to creep across the sill. It was so early that even the blackbird hadn't started singing.

Thinking that perhaps there had been a noise outside that had woken her, she slipped her feet out of the bed, padded barefoot across the room and looked out of the window into the garden.

The moon-silvered flower beds and lawns were held in silence, a magical essence that she breathed in. The air through the casement felt cold to her, as she wasn't yet used to the temperature of the early-morning English air. Shivering, she crossed the room;

taking up her shawl she opened the door. Stepping onto the silent landing she looked over the banister rail to the hall below. All was quiet in the house. Taking a deep breath, she strained against the pressure of foreboding building within her and tried to make sense of it. Could it be because the solicitor would be coming to go over the divorce papers? She pulled her shawl tighter around her shoulders as the cold penetrated her night shirt. Or could it be because she was afraid of what the future held for her and the uncertainty of her life to come? As she stood in the silence of the landing she thought, *that has to be it, that must be what it is*, and shivering returned to the fading warmth of her bed.

She was woken with a start, from a restless sleep, by the sound of running footsteps and a fist knocking upon a door somewhere in the house. She lay very still, her ears straining to hear. Then, quite suddenly, there came the sound of feet running down the stairs and a door banging. Slipping from her bed Emma went into Nona's room and shook her. 'Nona, wake up, something is happening.'

'What!' Nona's voice was thick with sleep as she struggled to open her eyes.

'I don't know. Get dressed, we have to be ready.' Emma pulled a heavy shawl from the top of a chest and threw it towards her sister.

'Ready?' Nona appeared to be struggling to understand and to open her eyes.

'For goodness' sake, Nona, get dressed. I'm going to see if Richard is alright.'

'Richard?' Nona looked dazed.

But Emma had already left the room, the door closing silently behind her.

Hurrying down the corridor and up the stairs leading to Richard's room she found him in his bed, deathly white, but asleep. Her fingers caressed the exposed arm lying on the cover and she bit her lip, relieved that nothing seemed wrong.

Carefully pulling the cover over Richard's arm to keep him warm she left him to sleep.

Returning to Nona's room she found her sitting up in bed with her eyes closed.

'Is Richard well?' Nona sighed, fighting sleep.

'It isn't Richard.'

The relief in Emma's voice was missed by Nona.

'What isn't Richard?' Her eyes were flickering but not opening.

'Go back to sleep, we'll speak at breakfast,' Emma whispered.

Nona didn't answer, she had already slipped down her pillow and was asleep. Emma closed the door quietly. What had she been thinking, waking Nona? She shouldn't give in to these feelings so easily. Running around flapping like a chicken without any good reason. At least it wasn't Richard.

Returning to her bed she slept another hour. It was Martin who awoke her opening the closet door. 'Martin! What time is it?'

'Late, madam. Something terrible has happened.'

There was a break in the woman's voice and Emma saw that her eyes were red from crying or an illness.

'Are you unwell, Martin?'

'No, madam.' Martin laid Emma's clothes over the chest at the bottom of the bed.

'Then what's wrong?'

'It's the master, madam.'

Emma noticed Martin's mouth tighten and her back stiffen as she spoke.

'Tell me what has happened,' Emma asked quietly, yet she already had a feeling that she knew.

'The master died in the early hours of this morning, madam.'

'My father-in-law is dead?' Somehow the words, now spoken, shocked Emma.

'Yes, madam.' Martin was shaking as she straightened the curtains and tied them back.

Moving from her bed Emma sat heavily in a chair beside the fire and addressed the maid. 'Come back later, will you, Martin.'

She needed to think. What would happen now? Would Richard still want to divorce her? Would her mother-in-law still want her out of the way? Did Charlotte still hold a position of power?

Nona entered in a flurry. 'Oh, Emma, you knew something was wrong, but this! What will happen to us now?' She sat on the crumpled bed and stared at her sister, waiting for an answer.

'I won't know until I have spoken to Richard,' Emma said quietly.

At that same moment the door swung open and, as though he had been summoned, Richard entered the room. Both women stood and greeted him as he made his way to the chair that Emma had just vacated.

'I'm so sorry to hear about your father, Richard,' Emma said, approaching him.

'You cannot be as sorry as I, Emma.' His voice was sharp and held a note of bitterness that Emma had not heard the depth of before.

Nona turned away. 'I will go. I'm sorry for your loss, Richard. I will speak with you later, Emma.' And she left hurriedly.

'What is to happen now, Richard?' Emma asked gently, addressing his unnerving silence.

She wasn't prepared for the look of hate displayed in his eyes as he turned towards her.

'What happens now, Emma, is that I am trapped, forever. Even if my health were to improve, I would not be able to escape my duties to this place. You brought me back here. This is all your fault.'

Although shocked by his assault, she tried to keep her feelings calm. 'Richard, I can help you. We could run the estate together.'

He laughed. A sudden explosion of sound that held no joy.

She was shocked and then hurt, knowing that she could be a support to him. She wasn't without experience. She'd watched her mother over the years supporting Andrew. She knew what was expected of a farmer's wife and was prepared for the involvement. Indeed, needed the involvement.

'Well-bred women in England do not get involved in the day-to-day running of an estate. What do you imagine people would think of that, eh? Well, I can tell you. That the man is weak. Doesn't have control of his wife or his own life, isn't up to the job.' The venom in the last words were spat at her with such force that she stepped away from him.

'Why would they think like that, Richard? Surely working together...'

'Listen to yourself, Emma,' he shouted, 'this isn't the bloody New World. This is the mentality of your class.' His temper exploded, his face showing the first sign of colour in months. 'It isn't how it works here,' he continued, 'but what would you know?' Now his voice held a mixture of contempt and helplessness. 'I want you and your sister to leave. I will give you money; there will be no scandal. I will support you wherever you decide to live until the divorce comes through.'

'You will support me until the divorce comes through?' Her voice was almost a screech. 'I am to be treated like some common mistress? I am your wife, Richard, and whether you and your mother like it or not, I am not moving out of this house until the divorce comes through and you hand me the money that you promised. I will leave here with dignity. Do not look at me as though I am some loathsome creature, Richard, it's unfair. I have loved and cared for you only to find that I am to be put out of this house, replaced by a more suitable wife of means, through no fault of my own. I am to be disposed of, as though our marriage had never existed. And I can tell you now, Richard, that I am not going to leave until the divorce is final.'

He stood, weakly holding onto the back of the chair for support. The confrontation, Emma could see, had robbed him of all the energy he had mustered to come to her room. She could not move to help him. She was too desolate now that her bravery had drained away. Where could she and Nona go at such short notice?

After he had left she paced the floor thinking things through. Later when she went to Nona's room she found her

102

sister standing by the window looking out and Emma felt an unexplained emptiness between them. There was something different about the way Nona stood. A self-assurance that Emma had not noticed before and for the first time in her life she didn't know what to say.

At the sound of the door opening Nona had turned around and Emma saw sadness in her sister's eyes before Nona looked quickly away. When she spoke, her voice was almost a whisper. 'I have something to tell you, Emma, something that you will not like, and really, I have been struggling to tell you for some days. I haven't known where to start. And now, even though this is the best time for me to speak out, it's not the best time to be telling you...'

'Telling me what, Nona?' Emma's heart thudded in her chest. What had her sister done, had she spoken to Charlotte as she had threatened?

'I have been going out a little more than I let you believe. I have been going over to Tate Farm.' She bit her lip and turned to look out of the window; when she looked back Emma noticed a strange light in her eyes and a tear on her cheek. 'I have been going there in the hope of seeing Dan, and we have met once or twice and...'

'Oh my God, Nona, what have you done?'

Her sister's difficult childhood flashed through Emma's mind. How she had been abused at the age of eleven and then, after they had all gone abroad, led a wild life. What did she know of life in England and how it worked? How people thought, or how those people could destroy a woman? Emma's mind was in turmoil. Was this what the premonition had been about, her sister bringing shame on herself, Emma, and the Laddisbrock family? Could things get any worse? Her blood seemed to pound through her veins and into her head, forcing her to wait before she could speak, and when she did, her voice didn't sound like her own.

'Have you brought shame on yourself, Nona, on all of us?'

Nona replied with a firmness that surprised her sister. 'No, Emma. I have not brought shame on myself or on anyone else.

Do you remember that first day that we went to Tate Farm and saw Dolly? When Dan entered the kitchen? He didn't make eye contact. Didn't speak. Do you remember, Emma? I was drawn to him in that moment and he to me. Sometimes, when you were out or lying down, I would walk out in the hope of seeing him. We started to meet late in an evening after you had retired to bed and he had finished in the fields. We did nothing but talk,' she added quickly, seeing the look of horror on Emma's face.

'You met a man alone in a field after dark? Do you have any idea how that looks to the gentry, Nona? Even gentlefolk would be shocked.'

'No, Emma, they would not be shocked,' Nona retorted sharply. 'It's called courtship. Dan has asked me to marry him and in the heat of the moment I said yes. I know it seems quick and I should have asked you first, but you had so much to deal with, with Charlotte and Richard and the threat of divorce. How could I tell you how wonderfully happy I was? I even felt guilty for feeling happy!'

A tear made its way over Nona's cheek and Emma wondered how she had been so caught up in the drama of her own life that she had completely forgotten that her sister was alone in this dark, cold house without comfort in the middle of a tragedy that was not her own.

Emma tried to keep her voice even as she spoke. 'I came to tell you that Richard has asked us to leave the house. He is still going through with the divorce but it will happen quietly and he will give the promised money to me without fuss and without blackening my name.' As she spoke, she was amazed at the steadiness in her voice, the quietness of it, and felt the breach between herself and her sister even more keenly. 'I'll not be leaving just yet, Nona, and am happy for you and Dan, that you will have somewhere to live. I suppose,' she said as an after-thought, 'that his family knows?'

'Yes.' Nona looked guilty. 'And Dolly has written to Mother but of course it will take many months to reach her. Dan and I have been talking about returning to live with Mother and Andrew when we are wed. We don't know yet how we will get the money together for the passage, it might take years.'

Emma could no longer stay angry and felt herself relax. 'I'm sorry, Nona. It was a shock and I'm thinking only of myself and how I will miss you. You can have my cabin as a wedding present. I will not need it and you can have Black, if you would like him.'

With these words spoken aloud, Emma realised, without having thought it through in advance, that she really would never again return to her mother and would never again see her family. A lump was forming in her throat, threatening to choke her as she stepped towards Nona and hugged her. 'I'm so sorry for all of this, Nona.'

Nona squeezed Emma tightly as she spoke. 'Please don't feel sorry, Emma. If I had not come back with you I wouldn't have met Dan again. I will thank you for the rest of my life.'

~

The following day, low cloud swallowed the tops of the trees and the air felt damp with cold. As the day progressed it did not lighten as though it too were in mourning at Nona's imminent departure from the house and Emma's side.

Seeing her sister leave, carrying her bags to the cart that Dan had brought to the rear door, Emma already felt the emptiness caused by the loss of her sister's companionship. She watched from an upstairs window as the cart, carrying her sister to Tate Farm, travelled along the driveway, getting smaller and smaller.

The house seemed to close in as a grey mood crept through her, stealing the energy from every cell in her being. Going to her room she stayed there for the rest of the day, sleeping on and off, unable to face life alone. She no longer knew why she was here, or where her life was going, except that, wherever that was, she would be going alone.

Martin brought food to her about four o'clock and by seven thirty Emma had retired again to her bed. She felt lethargic, lost, and more alone than at any time in her life.

11.

In the following days the house was as silent as a mausoleum. The servants, their feet covered with black cloth, moved about their duties like occasional shadows.

Charlotte, Emma heard from one of the maids, had taken the death of her husband badly and was unwell.

Emma did not attend the funeral. She had not been invited to do so and had no clothes appropriate for the occasion and no money was forthcoming to purchase any. It was while the house was empty, with all the staff attending the funeral, that Emma decided she could not live in this situation any longer and that she would leave immediately. She would travel to Claydon House, which she knew to be some twenty-five miles away. She would stay with her brother, Robert, who lived there alone having inherited it from their cousins, the Bracks. Now that she had a plan she felt better and, taking her valise, packed what little she had into it and pushed her clothes into her trunk.

She waited until those friends of the family who had come back to the house had left before she went to see Charlotte. Knocking on the door she did not wait for permission to enter but walked in. Charlotte stood near the window and immediately Emma could see that all was not well. The woman was holding onto the curtain, her body slowly moving towards the floor. Running to her, Emma held her under her arms, dragging her to a chair. Grasping the bell pull she summoned a maid, who turned deathly white at the sight of her mistress.

'Don't just stand there,' Emma shouted, 'get Mr Laddisbrock and send someone for a doctor.'

Patrick arrived first, followed by Richard.

'How did you find her?' Patrick asked. But before Emma could reply Richard was bending over his mother.

'Mother! What has happened here?' His tone, Emma thought, was accusing and, straight away, for no reason she felt guilty.

Standing back, letting them take over, she said helplessly, 'I came to talk with her and found her hanging onto the curtain for support. She is clearly very ill.'

'We must get her to her bed. Summon Martin while I carry her upstairs.' Patrick picked Charlotte up as though she weighed nothing.

'It was the funeral. It must have been too much for her,' Richard was telling Patrick as they lowered her onto her bed. 'She has been unwell since Father died.'

While they waited for the doctor Richard walked back and forth in front of the fire. Emma sat beside Charlotte and noticed that the woman's skin had a yellow sheen and that her flesh was damp. 'How long has she been like this, Richard?'

'I don't know. The servants have been seeing to her. Martin has been looking after her.'

At that moment the doctor, a tall, pale-faced man, strode into the room and took Charlotte's hand.

'This woman is very sick. If you will excuse me,' he said unpacking his small leather bag, 'I would like to examine my patient in private. Please send a maid up with water.'

Richard and Emma stood on the landing outside the door, while the doctor examined Charlotte and a maid bustled back and forth at his bidding. Patrick had brought a small chair for Richard to sit on, and all that could be heard as they lingered on the landing was the tick of the clock that stood at the top of the stairs.

Eventually the door to the bedroom opened and the doctor stepped out looking grave. 'I believe,' he said, 'that your mother may have eaten something that has not agreed with her. I fear that because of the shock of her husband's death she has been too frail to fight it. I have bled her and she must eat nothing for the next twenty-four hours. She must be encouraged to drink as much as is possible.'

'The staff will see to it, Doctor.' Richard gave his assurance and the doctor left saying, 'Call me if anything changes.'

Returning to her room Emma unpacked her valise; this wasn't the time to be leaving.

Each day Emma sat with Charlotte for a short time in the morning and again in the early evening; each time she tried to encourage her to eat. But Charlotte could keep nothing down, suffering from stomach cramps. Emma could only manage to get her to drink what lay in the cup beside the bed.

One afternoon she noticed that the whites of Charlotte's eyes were becoming a different yellow and the doctor was called again.

'She is being poisoned,' he told Richard. 'I want to know what she is eating and who is administering it to her. I will need to speak to your staff, sir.'

~

Mrs Jenk shook uncontrollably as tears ran down her face. The doctor, standing grey and imposing before her in the sitting room, waited for an answer to his question.

'You must tell me, madam, all that you have given your mistress to eat.'

'I have been making very bland food that comes back to the kitchen almost untouched, sir.' She twisted her hands in her apron as she spoke. 'I wouldn't poison my mistress. I wouldn't know how to.'

'Who has been feeding her?'

'Martin looks after her, sir, also Mrs Laddisbrock.'

Martin was leaving the sitting room after being questioned by the doctor as Emma, who had also been summoned, approached along the landing. There was unbridled hostility in Martin's eyes as she thrust her chin out and walked past Emma towards her mistress's bedchamber.

Shaken by the maid's boldness, Emma stood with her hand on the sitting room doorknob and took a deep breath. She was nervous. She knew that she shouldn't be, that there was no reason to be, but she couldn't stop the fluttering taking place in her stomach.

The doctor, who was sitting at Charlotte's desk, looked up as Emma entered. 'Mrs Laddisbrock, please be seated.'

It felt wrong to Emma that this man should be in her mother-in-law's sitting room offering her a seat.

'You have been sitting with your mother-in-law, I understand.' His voice was quiet and authoritative and Emma suddenly felt that she was on trial.

'Yes, sir.' She spoke quietly.

'I am trying to find out what ails Mrs Laddisbrock. I am sure that you understand my concerns. Can you tell me what she has eaten?'

'She has eaten very little, sir. Mrs Jenk has tried with good food – eggs, broth, bread soaked in milk. But Mrs Laddisbrock refuses to eat, because she cannot keep the food down.'

'And what has she had to drink?'

'I have offered her whatever was beside the bed, sir. I knew that you wanted her to drink.'

'Thank you, madam.' He looked grave. 'I will not detain you further. Something has poisoned her and we must find out what and how.'

He stood up and, gathering papers from the desk where he had been writing, he pushed them into his bag. 'I will return tomorrow and see how the patient is.'

As Emma left the room she wondered what was in the cup beside the bed. What was it that she had given Charlotte to drink? Hurrying to Charlotte's room she found the woman asleep and the cup that was normally beside the bed removed. Hurrying to the kitchen she asked Mrs Jenk about the liquid.

'I think that it was a little wine mixed with fruit juice to fortify her. I told the doctor.'

'Yes, I know, and who makes up the liquid?'

'Sometimes myself and sometimes Martin. Is something wrong?' She looked worried.

Ignoring the question Emma asked, 'Why has the cup been removed from the mistress's bedside table? She has nothing now to drink.'

Mrs Jenk looked towards the scullery door and inclined her head in that direction.

'Martin came back with the empty cup.' She paused. 'It's being washed and will be back with the mistress soon. Is she asking for something to drink?'

'No, she's resting. But we must not leave her without liquid.'

'I'll see to it,' Mrs Jenk said, staring at Emma, an eyebrow raised waiting to see if there were any other instructions. But there was nothing else that Emma could say. A niggle of a thought was worming around in her head. Was there something in the drink and who would gain by hurting Charlotte? The only person who would gain by her death, Emma realised, was herself. Charlotte was the one standing between her and Richard. Without Charlotte, things might be different. Her heart was fluttering as she hurried to her room, shut the door and sat quickly on a chair as her legs gave way.

Although it wasn't she who was poisoning her mother-in-law, she felt guilty, felt as though everyone must be thinking it.

For the next few days Emma mulled it over until, with a decision made, she went to the sitting room where Richard had taken to spending time reading.

He looked up as she entered, as though expecting someone else, and frowned when he saw who it was. Clearing his throat, he looked back at his book and turned a page.

'Richard, your mother has improved a little and I have made a decision. I would like to take some time to visit my brother. While I am there perhaps we can both think about our situation.'

'Our situation, Emma, does not need thinking about.' Richard didn't take his eyes from the page in his book. 'The decision has been made.'

She had difficulty in stopping her emotion welling up into her eyes and there was a catch in her throat as she spoke. 'I will go for a short while, Richard, and ask my brother if I might live with him. I am sure you will allow me that.'

'Take as much time as you need. I will arrange for Ames to take you in the carriage.'

A silence fell upon the room. It had been easy to ask and he had been too ready to agree. There was no regret in his manner, and it was with a sudden clarity that she realised her marriage was over and that she was the last to come to terms with that fact. Leaving the room, she went to pack.

Matt Ames brought the carriage to the front door and Patrick secured her valise at the back. She was shaking as she sat in the open carriage and Patrick shut the door.

'I am afraid, madam,' he said, 'that Larch cannot be spared today.'

She nodded. 'Thank you, Patrick. I understand.'

She didn't look back at the house as they moved away. What would be the point? There would be no one waving goodbye, no one who would miss her. But she was wrong. In two different parts of the house eyes were watching her departure from the shadows with satisfaction. Charlotte and Mary Martin were smiling in triumph as the carriage disappeared up the drive between the trees.

12.

It seemed strange to Emma to be sitting in the carriage looking at Matt's back having once been like brother and sister. They had been through so much working for her cousin, Amelia Brack. They had faced so many horrors at Claydon House that it seemed unreal now that there was an awkward space between them. When they passed slowly through the village, Emma's childhood memories came flooding back. She called to Matt as they passed the church. 'Can you stop, please? I would like to visit my father's grave.'

Matt eased the horse to a stop beside the lychgate and, after tying the horse to the hitching rail, helped Emma down. 'Thank you, Matt, I won't be long.'

'It's Ames, madam.' His back was stiff and his face showed no recognition of her at all. Trying to ignore his dismissal of their past friendship she turned towards the churchyard, a lump in her throat.

Passing beneath the lychgate she walked the gravel path with its graves each side and felt the silence. The trees seemed taller now and the shadows deeper than she remembered, but then she had only been a child when her father had died and had not been here at all when her baby sister Charity was buried. As she passed the front of the church she remembered being told of the day when all the villagers had come here to take part in the village fete and how it was gay with laughter until old Mrs Fearling had verbally attacked her mother for being on holy ground. Emma had not understood at the time. But now, as a grown woman, she did understand the danger that her mother felt, being Pagan.

A coldness closed about Emma's heart. She, like her grandmother, was psychic, and knew that it was a gift that could also be interpreted wrongly. She hurried on around the church to the spot where her father and Charity were buried. There was no headstone, just a large rock that Martha had laid down to mark the spot. The ground, now flat, was grown over and she smiled to find herbs growing in the grass, her mother's doing she was sure. Emma found it hard to recall her father's face as she looked at the ground below which he was buried. She remembered the smell of his pipe smoke and laughter in the house when Charity was born. Then started to remember the struggle of that first winter without him. Without money to buy food or pay the rent. How they had had no help from the Laddisbrock estate on which her father had worked. How they had struggled to keep warm and how she had been sent to work at Claydon House as a maid, not knowing that the mistress there was feared by her servants, or that she was a distant cousin of the mistress and her brother.

Trying to push those thoughts away, she concentrated on remembering the last time she had seen Charity with her little arms and legs waving in the air as she lay on Martha's bed in the smoky little cottage that they called home. Home! Suddenly, the loss of family and home overwhelmed her and she fell to her knees on the grave and sobbed, pushing her hands into the grass as though she could reach her father and her sister, to touch them, to feel their love. But there was nothing. No energy came back to her and she knew that they were gone forever.

Returning to the carriage she ignored Matt, too forlorn in her own grief to acknowledge his coldness. Sitting back in the seat she pulled a blanket around her body for comfort. Closing her eyes, she saw nothing of the passing English scenery that only months ago she had been so desperate to see.

As the carriage slowed, Emma opened her eyes; they were turning into the driveway that she remembered with so much fear. 'Stop, Matt. Stop.'

He pulled the reins, shouting, 'Whoa.' Turning to look at her he saw her fear.

'It's alright, Emma, she's not here,' he said, forgetting himself.

'I know. Will the horse go up the drive?'

She was remembering when she had arrived on this very spot in Mim Buckle's cart as a twelve-year-old and how his horse refused to go up the drive and that Mim wasn't going to make the horse take her any further. She remembered vividly Mim driving away and leaving her standing in the road in front of these gates with the long driveway ahead of her, and that she couldn't see the house.

'If she won't go,' Matt broke through her thoughts, 'then we will know that things haven't improved, won't we?'

Emma's breathing was coming in short bursts as she remembered the hex her cousin had put on the driveway and how she had been caught up in it on her first day when she couldn't find the house. How she had been lost in the forest that grew each side of the driveway and how she had spent the night alone in the wooded darkness crying for her mother. Then, how she had met a man the next morning sitting beside the river, who directed her, and how she had found out much later from her mother that he was her cousin Oliver, possibly murdered in the forest by his sister Amelia. And how Matt Ames, the housekeeper's young son, had found her and taken her to the house smuggled under a filthy horse blanket so that she wouldn't get into trouble with their mistress, Amelia Brack.

As the thoughts tumbled at speed through her head she felt overwhelmed.

He watched her face for confirmation that she was ready. 'Shall we go?'

She nodded assent.

The horse didn't hesitate in trotting up the driveway and soon the house came into view. It looked grey and forlorn. The drive and the space before the front door were green with weeds. And Emma noticed that weeds grew from the windowsills and the roof. That the windows in the west wing were still empty and hollow without glass, or shutters, where the fire had taken the life of Mrs Shillabeer and a baby, and where Emma and Matt had been burnt trying to rescue them.

Emma was silently wondering if anyone was living here at all, when Matt voiced the same thought.

'Are you sure that your brother is here?' He had pulled the horse up in front of the house and was looking back at her questioningly. It seemed that being back here he had forgotten his place.

'I wrote to him,' she said, her eyes scanning a property that looked abandoned.

'Did he reply?'

'No.'

'What do you want to do?'

The unwelcoming front door with its faded wood and tarnished doorknocker worried her. 'Can we go to the servants' entrance? I would be happier going in that way.'

Matt flicked the reins and they were soon in the little quadrangle outside the kitchen door.

Helping her down from the carriage, he followed her to the door with her valise. The door felt familiar to her hand as she pushed it open, revealing the kitchen. Although it didn't have the memorable smells of Nell's cooking, it welcomed her all the same.

There was no one in the kitchen, although a fire was in the grate and a large black kettle straddled the bars at the side. Emma lifted the kettle with a cloth and, feeling that it had water in it, pushed it onto the grid over the heat, adding more wood.

'Well! Someone is living here,' she said in relief. 'Matt, would you go outside and pick me a handful of camomile if it still grows by the gate next to Alf's vegetable patch.'

He went without query and was soon back with a large bunch of the herb in his hand. Its fragrance, a smell of ripe apples, filled the room as Emma tore it up and placed it in a bowl, then sat in the chair by the fire to wait while the water in the kettle got hot.

'I'll go.' Matt turned toward the door.

'No, stay awhile, Matt, and have some camomile tea with me before you go back.'

'It's difficult, Emma.' He looked uncomfortable. 'So many memories. This was my mother's world. She loved this kitchen and we had some good times with Alf, didn't we?'

'Yes, Matt, and it seems strange in here without her. She is in every item in this kitchen, she is even in the walls.'

He looked suddenly at the walls and Emma laughed. 'Not literally, Matt.'

When the water was hot Emma poured it over the herb, releasing the wonderful fragrance of camomile, then covered it with a cloth to allow it to steep.

'When did you last see your brother?' he asked, having taken a seat at the table.

'It was in London, over twelve years ago, just before we boarded the ship for the New World and a new life.'

'Didn't he want to go with you?'

'No, he was just starting out on a new life himself. He wanted to be a priest.'

'A priest? So how did he come to have this house?'

'When Oliver Brack hadn't made an appearance in the given time after he'd vanished, my brother inherited the property, being the next of kin.'

'Next of kin?' Matt's face changed and a glint of anger flashed in his eyes. 'You mean that you were related to the Bracks and you didn't say anything?' His voice had risen and his look, as well as his tone, were accusing.

'I didn't know that I was related to them, Matt. That was one little fact that my mother didn't tell me for some years, probably for my own protection.'

Getting up she poured the light golden tisane into two cups and handed one to Matt.

'I don't know what my mother would have made of that, Emma.'

'No, nor do I. I do miss Nell, Matt. She was a good woman and like a mother to me.'

He nodded his head and she could see that being in this house again was affecting both of them. He put down his cup and stood up.

'I'll leave you now, Emma. I hope all goes well for you here.'

She knew he hadn't finished the sentence – *It's the class where you belong*. They didn't say goodbye. He left, shutting the door behind him leaving Emma alone in the kitchen with her memories, and as she heard the horse's hooves on the flagstones in the yard retreating, she felt lonely and unsettled. What would Robert be like as a man, as a vicar?

13.

Opening the door from the kitchen Emma stepped into the servants' passage and mounted the rickety stairs. At the top she pushed through the baize door and moved into the familiar hallway. It was exactly as she remembered it. The walls lined with wood. The dark shadows. Where was everyone? Were there no servants? The door banged behind her as she stepped away from it and she was surprised as it used to close silently, with a slight swish, so that Amelia wouldn't know that the servants were about the house. Fearful memories were now re-enacting in her mind as she passed by each door. The room in which Oliver Brack's picture hung with the eyes that followed her around the room. Next to that, the library that faced south and where the sun streamed in most of the day, giving a feeling of warmth to a cold house. She went slowly up the staircase to the first floor, expecting at any moment to be challenged. The now dusty grandfather clock still stood solid and dark at the top of the stairs, the slow clunk, clunk of the pendulum another indication that someone was still living here. At the top of the stairs she looked apprehensively to her left, knowing that the stairs to the west wing were in that direction, and was relieved to see that the passage had been boarded up. Now she turned to her right and walked slowly, noticing that the small tables that used to stand beside each door were no longer there. She also noted faded squares on the walls where paintings she used to dust had once hung. The blood was pulsating in her arms and legs; her stomach did a somersault as it always had done when she stood outside Miss Brack's bedroom, for although she now knew the woman was her cousin she still thought of her by her title and always would. The fear, that had never gone away, stopped her entering. She could not bring herself to believe that the woman was not in there, or that somehow, even if she were not there physically, something of her wasn't left behind, waiting. Passing through a second door that led down to the servants' passage she descended the stairs, feeling the coldness of past ghosts touching her back. Arriving back at the kitchen she opened the door and, seeing a figure in black, she almost screamed.

At the sound of the door opening the black figure turned sharply and jumped in alarm.

'Emma, is it you?' Robert came towards her. 'Come in and sit by the fire, you look as though you've seen a ghost. I didn't know that you had arrived. I was at the church. Although I did wonder who had made camomile tea.'

She wanted to run to him. Throw her arms around him, her flesh and blood. But before her stood a man she didn't know. The boy was gone. Here was a man with receding hair and chiselled features, looking much older than his twenty-seven years.

Instead she said, 'Robert, I hope you don't mind. I walked around the house looking for you. Where are the servants?'

'Ah, well, Emma,' he sighed, 'I can't get servants to stay very long. They are uneducated and naïve and think that the house is haunted. I tell them that there is no such thing as a ghost and it is evil to even think that there is, but they still leave.' He raised his hands. 'So I manage alone.' He pushed a log onto the fire. 'I don't have much in the way of food to offer you – ham, eggs and cheese, will that be enough?'

'That is more than enough, Robert. I'm very glad to see you, brother.'

'And I you, sister. You must tell me all about the new Tate farm and how the family are. I cannot deny that I have missed you all, even though the church is my family now.'

'Let me get the meal ready for us, Robert, I would like to have something to do.'

Emma busied herself around the kitchen, and after eating they sat before the fire in the chairs that she had sat in with Nell so long ago.

When on close inspection of him she noticed that his clothes were fraying at the sleeves and that the material was thin she asked, 'How do you manage, Robert?'

In reply, his smile was thin as he nodded. 'I have an annual stipend and I am very vigilant over what I spend. Although, I am sure that my parishioners would not see me starve.'

'Do you not grow vegetables, Robert? When I worked here, Alf grew the most wonderful vegetables and it kept the house supplied for very little money.'

'Alas,' he raised his arms in submission, 'I do not have the time nor an aptitude for it.'

'But you were learning to be a farmer when Mother left you with Mr Tate.'

'Sadly, sister, looking after cows or putting up fences is not the same as growing vegetables. I have not inherited Mother's skill with plants.'

Emma found flour and lard in a cupboard and began to make sad dough for the bread, as there was no yeast. And while she worked, she told Robert about the hundred acres of land that Andrew had been given on the government's free settlers scheme. She told him of the difficulties with the strange seasons, the heat and the struggle to get the farm going in their first few years; about clearing of rocks and trees and finding water and learning how to store it for the hot, dry months. She told him about their brother, James, and their stepbrothers, George and Jack, and how well they had taken to farming in such a harsh environment. 'You would not recognise them, Robert, they are so burnt by the sun. They are all young men now, and Andrew and Mother would not be able to work the land without them.'

'I am glad, sister, that I did not go with you. Although I have missed you all.'

'And we have missed you, Robert. Letters take so long to arrive. We had one several years ago from you dated thirteen months before it arrived with us, and your life would have moved on so much before we received it.'

He pulled a face. 'No, not moved on so very much, Emma. Life in the priesthood moves at a slow and leisurely pace and I am thankful for that.'

When the dough had rested she kneaded it before placing it on a flat paddle and covering it with the cloth.

'It is so good to have you here, Emma. It's like watching Mother cook.'

Looking at him more closely she noticed the dark shadows under his eyes and the thinness of his face and realised that life had been hard for him also. 'When did you finish your training, Robert?'

He thought a moment before saying slowly, 'About five years ago. I wrote to Mother and told her.'

Emma said nothing, just nodded her head. Martha must have forgotten to tell her. Sometimes, although they lived on the same property, things got missed, perhaps because of a bush fire on the edge of the farm or because of a drought or the upheaval in Emma's marriage. Sometimes, of course, letters didn't arrive; not all the ships setting out from England reached their destination, or even reached it with all their cargo.

'Are you happy, Robert, in your work?' The sudden question seemed to startle him but he recovered quickly.

'Yes, I am happy, on the whole. The Lord has been good to me. I am looking after the flock in a fine church.' For a moment he was quiet, looking at her steadily over the top of his steepled hands, his eyebrows puckered into a tight frown. 'Although, I'm not sure that I was ready for the other side of the calling. Dealing with my parishioners' many problems that they believe I should be able to solve.'

Emma said nothing, hoping that he would say more. But he was silent, staring into the fire, and she noticed that he had retreated into his own world.

Taking up the paddle she pushed the dough into the hot bread oven. As she shut the door she remembered all the times that she had seen Nell doing just that with this same paddle and she missed her again. The kitchen was not the same without Nell.

~

That evening, as they ate the fresh bread, ham and cheese in the light of one poor candle, Robert asked her why she had returned to England. It was a question that she knew he would ask and she had been hoping that he would not ask it so soon. Now she had to tell him the truth. But she wasn't finished telling him about their hard life in the hope that eventually he might understand.

'As I said, Robert, we arrived at Botany Bay with our goats, two cows and a bull, bought from the natives on one of the islands that the ship visited before we arrived. We also bought a wagon and two guns off a man on arrival, before our journey took us further into the interior looking for our given land. There is so much space there, Robert, that you could not believe that a country could be so large. We are settled near a place called Parramatta and, as I said, it took years to get the farm going. Mother eventually made friends with some of the native people, and their medicine woman taught her about the herbs of that strange country and how to find food when there appeared to be none. They communicate by sign language and the medicine woman saved our lives. We would have starved without her knowledge of edible roots, fruit and berries.'

'Who is she?' Robert looked dubious.

Emma shrugged. 'I don't know. They seem always to be travelling, walking in single file, burnt black by the sun. They arrived one day, standing under the trees, staring at our property.

Men, women and children,' she blushed, 'all naked. The women carry the babies, the men carry spears.'

Robert looked appalled. 'Naked, Emma? In front of you and Nona?'

'Yes, they came several times over the years. The first time, Mother was looking for herbs that she might recognise when an elderly woman came alone and stood near her. She showed Mother by signing about the vegetation to eat or use as medicine and what not to touch. Mother is learning some of their words and the name of the plants, although they are hard to say.'

'But why did you come home?' he persisted.

The light went from Emma's eyes as she said slowly, 'I was to be married to our farmhand, Richard Ladd. At the wedding ceremony he told us that his real name was Richard Laddisbrock.'

'Laddisbrock? Not the same Laddisbrock from Haddenford? That would be too strange.'

'It was strange, yes, Robert. But it happened and made no difference to me. I loved him and we were never going to return to England. Where we were living, everyone was trying to survive. There was, and still is, no class system.'

'But you are here!'

'Yes.'

Lowering her eyes, she felt her face become hot and took a deep breath before saying, 'Richard got himself shot by some ruffians. There are many good people in the land, people like us who paid their passage, but there are also some who carry on being criminals after they have done their time.' She hoped that Robert would not ask why Richard had been shot and he did seem to accept what she had just said.

'Emma,' he changed the subject suddenly, 'I retire early. You may stay up as long as you like, but if you will excuse me.'

He stood slowly; taking his bible from the table he held it gently in front of him, a pinched smile on his face. 'I rise early for prayers.'

'Oh! Yes, of course, Robert.' She accepted his apology, even though she had at first felt dismissed. 'Where will I be sleeping?'

'I have made a bed for you on the first floor. It's a small room but I think you will be happy in it.'

Emma knew that she would be happy in anything and was relieved that she had not been offered Amelia's room.

~

The following day, while Robert was gone about his parish, Emma took charge of the kitchen and the supplies. Carrying water into the house from the well she started the same cleaning regime as when she was the servant, although on a smaller scale. By the time Robert came home, Emma had walked to the village and bought six laying chickens, and by the time they were delivered she had cleaned out a shed for them to be housed in.

Having bought a square of yeast she had made bread. It was just out of the oven cooling next to a meat pie, on the table, as Robert entered the kitchen. His face lit up, and for a moment she saw the face of the young carefree brother who had existed before their father died.

'I am glad that you have made so much food, Emma, for I have found a gardener to help me with the growing of vegetables.'

'But how will you pay him, Robert?'

'Oh, I'm not going to pay him, Emma. He approached me while I was about the parish. He has been walking for many days, I believe, and is tired. He will grow vegetables for his food and board. Perhaps you would lay the table for three.'

It was but an hour later that a knock came at the kitchen door and Robert called out, 'Come in.'

The man who entered was tall, clean-shaven, his hair tied behind his head hidden beneath a wide-brimmed hat.

'Ah, Jon, welcome. This is my sister, Mrs Laddisbrock.'

Emma stood to welcome him and then hesitated. She had seen those clothes before, or something like them. When he removed his hat and she saw his blond hair fall over one eye she knew, even without the beard, that he was the convict from the ship.

124

He introduced himself as Jon Benson. Emma asked him to sit and then busied herself so as not to have to speak to him. When Robert had said grace, Jon turned to Emma. 'How is your husband, Mrs Laddisbrock?'

Startled at his revealing his knowledge of her she bit her lip in consternation, before answering slowly, 'He is well, thank you, Mr Benson.'

In the silence that followed Robert looked from one to the other, frowning.

'I am surprised to see you here,' Jon continued as they ate, ignoring Robert's look of confusion.

Emma stared at him but said nothing. It was Robert who cleared the air.

'Mrs Laddisbrock is visiting me for a few days. We have not seen each other in nearly thirteen years.'

'Then, sir, if you would show me where I am to sleep, I will let you both speak alone.'

'Please do not retire on our account, Jon.' Robert looked uncomfortable.

'It has been a long day, sir, and I have much to do on the morrow preparing the ground for seed.'

Jon pushed back his chair. 'Thank you for a fine meal, Mrs Laddisbrock.'

Robert also rose from the table. 'Yes, yes, of course. I will show you to your room. I hope that you don't mind being in the roof, a nice little room, Briar Rose.'

It was silly, but Emma wanted to shout, 'No! Not Briar Rose, that was my room.' But she said nothing as she cleared the table.

On his return Robert seemed annoyed. 'Why would you treat my guest so badly, Emma? I could feel the hostility from you and I am sure that Jon felt it also.'

Emma put the clean dishes down on the table with a bang. 'You know nothing about him, Robert, and have invited him to live under your roof. I met him on the ship. He is a criminal, perhaps a murderer.'

Robert's voice was controlled as he spoke, but there was a flash of disgust in his eyes that was not lost on Emma. 'We will ask him in the morning why he was on the ship returning to England. Goodnight, Emma.' And with that he left the room, leaving her alone with her thoughts.

Next day was bright and the grounds looked different draped in sunshine. Having prepared the dough the night before, the bread had been out of the oven for twenty minutes before she left the house, leaving the table laid for the men to break their fast.

Making her way past what would be the vegetable patch she let the chickens out to scratch around. Then followed the path across the old paddock towards the trees, where she entered and stood very still for a moment in the coolness. Walking to a small clearing where the early morning sun streamed down, she closed her eyes and connected with the energy of the Goddess. The freedom of being able to do this small act made the tears tumble over her cheeks. Raising her arms, she welcomed the sun and acknowledged the energy of every living thing. As she stood, arms raised, she let her energy flow into all of the nature around her. She was completely consumed in the peace that flowed through her whole being and, for Emma, time stood still. It was the sweet song of a robin that brought her back to reality. With a sigh she walked on, knowing her way very well amongst the trees, and was soon on the path that meandered beside the river. She had to know if Oliver Brack was still there, waiting.

The deep part of the river with its rocks had not changed apart from being more overgrown. Removing her shoes, she sat with her feet in the water, embracing this private magical place. The river sang softly and the foliage that sometimes touched the water was greener here than anywhere else. Here, birdsong was the music of joy as she watched dragonflies, their colours flashing as they circled and clipped the surface of the water. She had almost lost a sense of time when she heard movement behind her. Looking around sharply and reaching for her shoes she saw Jon Benson come crashing through the undergrowth.

'I'm sorry to disturb you,' he said looking sheepish and hot. 'I lost my way in the trees.'

Emma stood up, her fragile peace shattered. 'No matter, Mr Benson, I was ready to walk back.'

He looked about, getting his bearings. 'Ah, I see a path. I missed that completely. May I walk back with you, Mrs Laddisbrock?'

Straightening up after putting on her shoes, Emma's stomach tightened with annoyance, yet she would not be rude again to this man that her brother had employed, for she knew that Robert needed him.

'Yes of course,' she replied in a level voice.

'Is there something that you would like to ask me?' He looked straight into Emma's face as he spoke.

As she did not answer straight away he answered her silence with, 'You want to know why I was deported on a convict ship?'

Still she said nothing, embarrassed that he had read her so well.

Ignoring her silence, he determined to tell her his story anyway.

'We lived in the poorest part of London, my mother and I. When she died, I was nine years old, left to fend for myself, having no relatives. I was taken in twice by people who used me badly, and one day I was so hungry that I took an apple from beneath a stall. It was on the floor. What I didn't know was that it had fallen out of a sack and the stall owner caught me and gave me up to the justice. Within the hour I was in the court. I didn't get the chance to speak. The room was crowded with people and no one questioned me. I was told that I could hang for my crime, but instead I was put on a convict ship. I was frightened, but at least I was given food, even if I had sometimes to fight for it. Several men died on the journey and we divided their ration between us. Also, being deported was an innocent man, a man of God, the Reverend Harding. He looked after me like a father. It was hard in the colony but together we lived through

127

it. We did our time and more. Seven years.' His voice held regret. 'And at the end of our time there was no way of getting home. Reverend Harding had the idea that we could start a business to earn money for our fare home. We had found a way to save and dry seed to sell to others. We sold to those who also couldn't get home and to soldiers' wives, and new colonists just arriving. But after a few years the Reverend felt the need to travel, to take God to the natives. He was sad when I did not want to join him. I desperately wanted to get back to England. After he left, I lived alone in a small building of wood on the beach from where I watched the ships coming and going every six months or so and I saved my money.'

Once again Jon looked straight into her face speaking slowly. 'I paid my debt, Mrs Laddisbrock, and I paid my passage home. I am not, nor have I ever thought of myself as, a criminal. How can a starving child be a criminal, tell me that?' There was anger in his voice and Emma knew he had every right to be angry and her heart went out to him.

'I'm sorry, Mr Benson.' As she spoke her face was flushed with embarrassment and grief for the young child; and shaking her head at the unjust criminal system that would send a starving child to the gallows for picking up an apple, she said, 'I can no longer think of you as a criminal. I hope that you will see that I was worried for my brother, who is not worldly and is too trusting.'

He nodded in agreement. 'Your brother is a good man and I will look after him. I am, as you can imagine, grateful for a place to stay as I have been wandering ever since leaving the ship.' When she didn't speak he continued with his story, filling the silence that had fallen between them. 'A week before I left for home a soldier came and found me. He had two books with him. One I recognised straight away as the Reverend's bible. The other was a roughly bound leather notebook and inside was a written account of his journey into the interior. His body had been found emaciated and unrecognisable but for his clothes and his books that carried his name. The soldier brought them to me because there was a letter addressed to me inside the bible, asking that if anything happened to him, he would like me to take the books to his wife.

'When your brother found me, I had been walking for many months, working when I could for my keep. The books are all that I have of a wonderful man who became like a father to me and I must still find his wife.'

A huge wave of emotion flooded through Emma, and it was with difficulty that she stopped herself throwing her arms around him for his comfort. Blushing, she looked at the ground in case he saw the feelings that his story had evoked in her.

As they turned to leave the river bank the hairs on the back of Emma's neck stood on end and she thought that she smelt pipe smoke. She turned slowly, expecting to see Oliver, but the river bank was empty.

After supper, when Jon had retired, Emma approached Robert on the subject of Oliver. 'Robert, I believe that cousin Oliver is dead.'

Robert, who was reading a journal, nodded his head in agreement but did not look up.

'Robert,' she continued, trying to keep her voice even, 'will you please listen to me.'

Lowering the paper slowly onto his knees he gave her his full attention.

'Mother thinks that Oliver is dead and that he lies somewhere near the river.'

There was a sudden glint of anger in Robert's eyes, and he spoke slowly and deliberately as he looked at her.

'Mother has never been here, Emma, why would she tell you that?'

'Because she feels it, Robert. When I lived here I saw him twice by the river in the same place.'

'And from that she informs you that he is dead out there near the river?'

'You don't know the whole story, Robert, because you were living with Andrew and then with the Reverend Draycott. But I feel that Mother is right. I think that Oliver is dead, and that he is somewhere near the river and needs to be laid to rest properly.'

'Oh yes, madam,' there was a sarcastic tone in his voice, 'I had forgotten how you and Mother see things that are not there. Things that no one else can see.' His face had paled. 'I had hoped, Emma, that you had changed since becoming a woman, a wife, but I can see that you are just like your mother and I will not have any of this ungodly talk in my house.' His voice had risen with his anger.

Emma raised her voice in defence of Martha and to some extent herself. 'She is your mother also, Robert, it is wrong to speak of her so.'

'I will not listen to any more of this, Emma,' he shouted, standing suddenly and letting the journal fall to the floor. Snatching his bible from the table, he left the kitchen, banging the door behind him.

Emma sat alone by the fire, shocked at her brother's outburst. How could he talk about their mother like that, as though he were ashamed of her? Tears filled her eyes. God had been thrown back at her just like Mrs Fearling had done all those years ago to her mother. Why couldn't they see that God is not a human man but energy, an energy that is in every living thing? That she and her mother only chose to pray in a different way, in the open air, with nature all around them, acknowledging God's energy? Should it matter what they called the energy that they felt?

But she knew that wasn't all of it. It was that she and Martha saw things. They couldn't help it. It was something born in them.

Sighing, Emma banked down the fire and went to bed, but she couldn't sleep. The sight of Oliver, all those years ago by the river, floated in her mind. A spectre that would not step away to allow sleep to reach her.

14.

Awaking late the following morning Emma did not feel refreshed after a night of tossing and turning. But there was determination in her quick movements as she dressed. During the night she had resolved to find Oliver's resting place and would not leave Claydon until she had laid his body and his spirit to rest, whether Robert liked it or not.

There was no one in the kitchen as she made her way without stopping into the quadrangle. Taking a moment to splash her face with water from the bucket at the side of the well, she moved swiftly towards the gate. Jon looked up as she passed the vegetable garden, but she ignored his good morning and, taking a spade from Alf's shed, walked with purposeful steps across the paddock towards the trees.

On reaching the river bank, at the spot where so many years ago she had seen Oliver sitting with his pipe, she stopped, realising her folly. Where was she going to dig? She had thought that she would know exactly where he was buried and now realised that she didn't. Was he beside the log on which he had sat, if so which side of it or even at one end? He might not be there at all but further along the bank. She couldn't dig up the whole area.

A small breeze moved in the tops of the trees and she no longer felt the peace of yesterday. Today, there was an absence of birdsong, the water looked darker and there were no dragonflies dipping. Yesterday's magic had disappeared and it was as though she had just arrived somewhere that she didn't know, and didn't connect with.

Putting the spade down she wandered up and down the river bank studying the ground. She felt nothing, and saw nothing that was out of the ordinary. Wandering slowly away from the river bank she searched amongst the undergrowth below the trees but still found nothing that might look like a shallow grave.

'Excuse me but what are you doing?'

Her heart almost stopped beating at the sound of the voice. She had been so caught up in her search that she hadn't heard Jon arriving.

'I'm... I'm looking for something.'

'Can I help?' He sounded eager.

She felt guilty, caught out and embarrassed. 'No,' she said a mite too quickly and then realised her voice was sharp so followed up quickly with, 'Thank you.' Being followed made her feel uncomfortable. What right had he to follow her?

It was as though he had read her thoughts when he answered, 'I saw you with the spade. I thought that something was wrong.'

'Why would something be wrong?' She glowered at him suspiciously. She didn't know him. Who was he? If she told him the truth would he laugh at her or fling God in her face like her brother had? As he stood silently before her waiting for her to speak she stared back at him, trying to feel in advance how he would react if she told him the truth.

'Emma?' He raised an eyebrow in expectation of a reply.

It was the first time that he had used her name and there was a softness in his voice, an element of concern that touched her.

'It's difficult, Jon, for me to tell you.'

'Yesterday, Emma, I trusted you with my story. Believe me when I say that I can be trusted.'

Tears rose in her eyes; she knew that he believed what he said, but on hearing her story would his belief change into loathing and would he run, leaving her brother without help?

'Come,' he said, 'sit by the river with me on this log and tell me just as much as you want to.'

132

Now that Jon was here she could no longer search for Oliver's grave and so went to sit with him on the log. They sat for a long while in silence until Emma said, 'I came here to work when I was twelve. My father had died and my mother needed one less mouth to feed.' She nodded her head in affirmation as memories of the past crept into her mind. 'On my first day I got lost in the forest trying to find the house.'

Jon didn't interrupt and she was grateful for that. 'I was in the forest alone all night, and next morning I followed the smell of pipe smoke to the river bank, just here. There was a man sitting on this log and he showed me the direction to take.' Emma stopped; she hadn't revealed too much and decided not to tell Jon about the favour Oliver had asked of her that had led later to the deaths of two people, for she could hardly understand that herself, or why Oliver was unable to leave the forest and how marking a window in the house where the baby was hidden could have caused a fire.

'I came here to replace a maid that had gone missing,' she continued, 'or at least, left without notice. At the same time the owner, Oliver Brack, had also disappeared. Although his clothes were still in the house he didn't return.' She shrugged her shoulders. 'It was a mystery. His sister, Amelia, was mistress of Claydon House and I soon learnt that the servants were afraid of her. She had a terrible temper and of course held power over their lives. Nell Ames, the housekeeper, was like a mother to me, and her son Matt would have left but for the sake of his mother. The mistress had made it very clear that if anyone left they would not get a reference. For my thirteenth birthday my mother gave me my grandmother's ring. She had put it in my bag amongst my possessions for me to open on the day of my birth. It was beautiful, but I couldn't wear it.' She couldn't tell Jon the significance of the ring and how it connected her to her ancestors, even though that fact was ringing in her head as she continued, 'A servant can't have anything of value. I hid it by sewing it into the hem of my skirt.

'The mistress had a friend staying with her, a Mrs Shillabeer. They had been at school together. She was staying in the west wing with a baby, although Mrs Ames, the housekeeper, didn't know that there was a baby in the house and didn't believe me when I told her so. There was a fire, and Matt and I tried to save Mrs Shillabeer and the baby but it was too late.'

She stopped for a moment, overwhelmed by the awful sight of Mrs Shillabeer catching fire and she and Matt being driven back by the heat. Taking a deep breath, her voice was low as she said pensively, 'Matt and I were burnt in the fire, almost killed ourselves. And it was Mrs Ames that nursed us back to health.

'When washing my clothes, she found my ring and gave it to the mistress believing that I had stolen it from her. I went to ask for it back but Miss Brack said that the ring was hers and who would believe a servant above its mistress. I was told to leave. I was in a lot of pain from the burns and damage to my back, and Mrs Ames bravely hid me in the servants' quarters and carried on nursing me. Miss Brack went to Kent for the funeral of her friend and the baby stayed a mystery. It was while she was away that I could openly walk in the forest and again saw Oliver, Mr Brack. He didn't speak to me but indicated that I follow him into the forest, which I did.' Here Emma stopped and took a deep breath. Could she go on without revealing herself to Jon? But he didn't interrupt her silence. She wished that he would so that she could change the subject. Her mind was in a whirl. How could she explain what then happened? 'I'm sorry, Jon, I can't go on. It's too terrible for me to relive.'

Looking up from her hands folded in her lap, Emma saw anger in Jon's face and realised what he was thinking. 'It isn't what you think, Jon, Oliver didn't touch me.'

Jon's shoulders relaxed and he nodded affirmation that he accepted what she said, but still he said nothing.

Emma felt agitated; she had never spoken of this to anyone other than her mother. Here was a man who might help her find Oliver, but if he didn't believe what she said next, her relationship with her brother and Jon could end. She would never be allowed to come back to Claydon House and Oliver would be lost to her forever. How could she tell Jon that she followed Oliver to a clearing, where she found him standing across from her holding a baby, its pink arms and legs moving happily, the same baby killed in the fire? How could she explain that she believed the baby was alive as he lowered it into the ground and why she had run screaming to the spot, tearing at the soft earth with her bare fingers to find the baby before it suffocated, and then, the horror that sent her running home in terror?

'Emma?' His voice broke in on her thoughts. 'You're shaking.' He put his arm around her shoulders and she was glad of the warmth. 'You don't have to say any more.'

She struggled with herself; she had been given leave not to go on, and yet, something within her had moved. The relief that might come from having a friend released her tongue. Nodding that she understood she continued quietly, 'When I got to where Oliver had been standing, he had melted away into the trees. I saw disturbed earth and dug into it with my bare fingers and...'

'Take your time,' he said quietly as she trembled.

She took a deep breath. For even now all these years later she felt the fear that had clutched at her, sending her like a mad dog running wildly, howling, through the trees for the safety of home. Her voice was very small when she could bring herself to say, 'I uncovered a large hand.'

'My God!' There was shock in his voice. 'My God, Emma,' he repeated.

She ignored his outburst, for if she hadn't she wouldn't have been able to go on. 'I brought Alf and Nell back to the spot and Alf went and looked. Then he went for the doctor and the Squire who was the local justice.' She took a sharp breath as the tears ran over her face. 'It was our servant, Polly.'

Emotion caught in her throat. 'She had been there all the time and hadn't run away at all.' Now she openly sobbed and Jon held her close.

'Had she been… murdered?' His voice was very soft, close to her ear.

'No, she had died in childbirth and someone had buried her in a shallow grave.'

'But Oliver knew!' Jon said. 'Why didn't he tell someone?'

Emma looked into the eyes of the man that she barely knew and saw the beautiful concern for her exposed there, making it even worse if she lost his goodwill now. How did she think that he would not ask questions? 'I'm sorry, Jon, I'm not sure that I can explain more to you.'

He nodded and changed the subject. 'So, what is it that you are looking for?'

Emma stood up, she couldn't go on. 'Nothing, nothing at all, Jon. I must go back now.' She felt agitated and exposed; she had said too much. Picking up the spade she turned for home.

'A woman doesn't walk into a forest with a spade not looking for anything, Emma,' he called after her. 'You have trusted me so far, please let me help you.'

Turning to look back at him she said through a deep emotion that was about to choke her, 'You don't realise what you're asking, Jon. Now that you are involved it has become more than what I am looking for. It is about your judgement of me.'

He looked confused. 'Why would I stand in judgement of you?'

She turned away. What could she say? She hadn't told the truth, not all of it. She hadn't trusted him and it was more difficult now to explain the reason why. Leaving him standing alone beside the log she walked away.

She didn't see Jon for the rest of the day and in the evening when all three sat to eat there was an atmosphere.

Robert felt it but said nothing. Emma would be gone soon.

15.

Next day Emma worked her frustration out on the house by cleaning it. She had just taken a seat at the table after washing the kitchen flagstones when the door opened unexpectedly and a pretty young woman stepped inside and stopped abruptly, looking confused.

'Can I help you?' Emma asked equally surprised.

The girl's bright blue eyes searched the room. 'I brought a dish for the Reverend.' She held out an earthenware pot covered with a cloth. 'I sometimes bring him a dish on a Saturday.'

Emma could see that the girl was wondering who she was. Smiling to put her at ease she said, 'Please come in. I'm Emma Laddisbrock, Reverend Tilby's sister. Are you one of Robert's parishioners?'

The girl looked relieved and Emma realised that she was more than just a parishioner to Robert. At least in her mind, for Robert had not mentioned the maid.

'Yes,' she blushed, 'my father and I attend the church.' The girl bobbed politely and stepped into the room, placing the cook-pot on the table with dainty work-worn hands that Emma noticed by their dryness and broken nails. She raised an eyebrow, still not knowing who the girl was.

The girl noticed and spoke quickly. 'I'm sorry, madam. I forgot to say who I am, I was so taken aback.' Her face was still pink with embarrassment. 'I didn't know anyone was here. I haven't seen you in church.'

Emma let that go. She had no wish to make excuses for herself and changed the subject with a question. 'You live in the village, mistress?'

'Yes. All my life. I'm Sarah Poleshore, the daughter of Jake Poleshore.'

The name cut through Emma like a knife. She would never forget the name Jake Poleshore, or the fear that had descended on the servants at Claydon House and the residents of the village, after he had been found wandering speechless in the darkness one night, unable to say what horror he had seen in the forest. Jake, usually a lively and well-liked man, had never spoken another word and had never gone poaching again. In fact, had hardly ever left his house and never alone. Emma gathered her senses and smiled thinly at the girl. 'How is your father?'

'Do you know of him?' The girl's voice was incredulous and her face flushed with uncertainty and a tinge of fear.

Wanting to put her at ease Emma tried not to sound condemning and smiled gently as she spoke. 'I worked here when I was a child. I knew your father from the staff.'

Sarah looked down at the floor and when she looked up again her blue eyes held an intensity of defence that shocked Emma. 'I expect you heard that he'd been scared out of his wits while poaching.'

Emma could not answer for it was true, that was what she had heard.

'My father *never* spoke again. Not even to my mother who has now passed away. I long for the father that I had before that night and wish that he could explain what happened in the forest. I was only three years old. I lost my father that night and my mother lost her husband.'

There was a break in the girl's voice and as Emma stood to comfort her, Sarah turned and ran from the kitchen.

Emma stood with her hands on the table, staring at the empty space left by Sarah, astonished that Amelia's wickedness was still being felt even after thirteen years. Until now, she had forgotten about Jake Poleshore and suddenly realised, in the stillness of the empty kitchen, that he might know where Oliver was buried. Taking up her shawl she left the cook-pot on the table and walked towards the village.

The Poleshores' cottage was small, built at one end of a terrace, with a front garden set to vegetables. A thick hedge ran down the side of the property, a barrier between the garden and the fields. Emma noticed cabbages planted along the bottom of the hedge and could see two traps hidden and primed amongst them. How resourceful to plant cabbages where they could be easily accessed by rabbits creeping in from the field and trap one or two of them for the pot.

Emma stooped under the low thatch and, standing under its shade, knocked on the faded door.

When Sarah opened the door, she looked taken aback to find Emma on her step.

Smiling quickly, in the hope of defusing a situation, Emma said, 'I didn't get the chance to thank you for looking after my brother. I'm sorry that we didn't get to speak further.'

Sarah looked uncomfortable and didn't respond.

Ignoring the silence Emma continued, 'I had hoped that we could be friends as I know no one here.'

Sarah hesitated for a moment before stepping back from the door, indicating with her head that Emma should enter.

Inside, the cottage was clean and bright. A cat slumbered on a wide windowsill, basking in a shaft of sunlight, and a bunch of wild flowers had been placed in a handmade vase on a small table. It was homely.

A slim man with receding hair and a pale young face sat on a high-backed settle beside the fire. He didn't look up. Emma had never met Jake Poleshore, only heard about him, and was surprised at how young he was. She had always imagined him to be an old man, but now reviewed her thoughts. If he'd had a three-year-old daughter at that time he might only have been in his early twenties back then. This knowledge made what happened all the more shocking.

Sarah's voice broke into her thoughts, pulling Emma's gaze away from Jake. 'Your brother visits us. He reads the Bible to Father. I don't read, but I listen. Some of it frightens me. The stories about wars and killing your enemies, and at first, I wondered what it had to do with us. But Robert helped me to see that I had to look beyond the happenings, to the way man conducted himself. The stories, he says, should help us to see the right and wrong way to think and act. He says that God is helping Father.' She looked across the room at Jake. 'But I don't see it yet. Robert says that it is all happening inside of him, he's fighting his demons.'

Emma noticed a twitch in Jake's cheek at the word demons, but otherwise he did not move, nor did he acknowledge her being there, though she was sure that he was listening. Sarah was right, her father was not witless, he was afraid, and even after all these years he was still afraid. How could she reach him? How was she going to be able to ask him about Oliver without upsetting him?

'Sarah,' she said quietly, 'I had hoped that you might be able to tell me what happened to your father the night he became sick.' She chose her words carefully. Sarah looked quickly towards her father who stared unmoving into the fire. 'I'm sorry. I don't know.' Biting at her lip she said softly, 'Shall we sit beside the door? It's sad to miss such a lovely day.'

The women sat each side of a small table beside the open door and the fragrance of a rose drifted into the room. Its heady scent might at some other time have given a feeling of peace, but that, Emma did not feel. What she felt was sorrow for someone so young to have been trapped all her life in a house steeped in fear. She could see that her visit had unsettled Sarah and that for the first time she was thinking about what had happened to her father while he was out getting food for them that night.

Sarah looked at Emma with a face as white as chalk. Her voice was but a whisper when she eventually spoke. 'Before this moment, I had accepted Pa's condition. I was so young. Mother never spoke about it. It was the reaction of the people of the village, who shunned us and talked behind their hands, that I noticed as I grew up. I was a lonely child, for no parents allowed their children to play in our garden and I was not invited to play with them. They were afraid of us and the children became afraid of me. I didn't attend school because the children threw stones at me.' At this she lowered her head and held her hands tightly on her lap.

'I'm sorry, Sarah.' Emma felt that she also had to whisper as Jake sat, still unmoving, next to the fire. 'I have a reason to know what happened to your father that night. I can't tell you what that reason is, but if I can find out, it might help him and me.'

'You?' Sarah looked amazed.

'Yes.' Emma nodded an assurance at the young woman. 'As I said, I was working at Claydon House as a servant soon after that night and I think that your father saw something happen in the forest and I need to know what it was.'

As the girl shook her head Emma knew that she would learn no more and decided to leave before it became more difficult. She might have an ally here that she didn't want to lose. 'I will come again, Sarah, and if you need anything please send a messenger and I will come straight away.'

The girl looked puzzled, but inclined her head and nodded an agreement.

Standing to leave, Emma smiled a thin smile at Sarah, frustrated that the secret of Oliver's disappearance was possibly known by only one person and that person would not speak. Or, could not speak.

16.

When Emma had left, Sarah noticed that the visit had affected her father. He now wore the pinched face that told her he was sinking into one of his moods. His body was bent forward as though in agony and tears rolled over his cheeks as he sat in his silence.

Fear gripped at her heart as she also wondered what had happened that night.

~

Emma walked home slowly. Her heart was heavy for all that this innocent family had endured, and she wondered if she would ever find out what had happened to Oliver, and whether it would change anything for the Poleshores, or even perhaps make matters worse.

~

The sky was black with angry clouds massing in the distance. It was going to rain again, Sarah could smell it. Hurrying outside to bring in the washing she also cleared away her father's wood-handled tools from his work bench in the garden, putting them on a shelf under cover of the low thatch at the back door to keep them dry.

Re-entering the cottage, she saw her father still sitting before the fire but now with his elbows on his knees and his head in his hands. Putting down the washing Sarah went to him, rubbing the flat of her hand over his back. 'Pa!' He did not acknowledge her. She bent down in front of him and pulled his hands from his face. 'Pa, I think that you can talk, that there is nothing wrong with you. I can't live any longer in this silence, so I am going up to Claydon House, to the forest, and I am going to walk through the trees and find out what happened to you.'

His hand moved so fast that she hardly saw it before it clamped like a vice of steel around her wrist. She cried out in pain and tried to wriggle free but it held fast. 'Pa, you're hurting me,' she cried out.

Looking up into his face she saw not anger but fear. Sweat stood out on his brow and the look in his eyes was like that of a wild animal caught in a trap. Her heart pounded in her chest and drummed in her ears; never had her father set about her before. Even so, her jaw set in determination. 'I am going, Pa. I have had enough of this. All my life I have been afraid of the forest up there and not known why. Today I'm going to find out. Let go of my arm, Pa.' She tried to pull her wrist out of his large hand, but he held it fast.

She had never before raised her voice to her father and part of her shrank from the expected retribution. Jake stood up suddenly, pulling her up with him. Sarah yelped as he dragged her by her arm to their small storeroom. Pulling the door open he threw her inside with a force that sent her reeling against the shelves. The door slammed shut behind her and she could hear him dragging something across the floor and wedging it against the door.

Sitting almost in darkness on the floor she shook with alarm. Her father had never shown violence before. Banging on the door she shouted, 'Pa, let me out, please let me out.' She pressed her ear to the door and listened. The house was silent, yet she knew that he was there, sitting before the fire.

For an hour she sat thinking and occasionally knocking on the door. It took some time for her to realise that she was not in complete darkness. A little light came from a small window high up on the back wall. Silently, and carefully, she moved items from the shelves until she could use the empty spaces left behind as a ladder. At the top she had little movement as her body was pressed between the top shelf and the ceiling, which was just above the top of the window.

Pulling away the thin sacking that covered the small aperture she breathed in the fresh air. The aperture was small and she wondered if she would be able to wriggle through it. Lying on her stomach she eased herself through, legs first, but when she got to her middle almost screamed in panic as she became stuck... trapped. Gripped by the wooden frame she twisted and turned until her skin burned beneath her clothes and then, breathing in and tightening all her muscles she was through, falling to the ground with a thud that jarred her whole being. Without looking back at the cottage and ignoring the rain, she ran towards the road and the property known as Claydon House.

17.

It had been raining on and off for some hours and in the afternoon a leaden sky still hung low over the house and forest. The air was close, heavy and sullen. A storm was brewing. Beneath her clothes Emma's skin was damp. Opening the top of her dress for some relief she pulled the back of her hand across her brow to remove the sweat that covered her face.

The silence pressed heavily upon her ears as she walked under the trees. The eeriness reminded her of the first time that she had stepped into this forest as a child, and the fear that followed when she couldn't find her way out. Stopping, she pushed a strand of damp hair behind her ear and looked about her. Today she would find out where Oliver was buried. Nothing would deter her this time. If only she knew how he had died then she might know where to look. She only had her mother's belief that the man she'd met in the forest all those years ago was her cousin Oliver's ghost, and yet, deep down she knew that Martha was right and that he was a troubled spirit.

The dark sky had turned the forest into a different, forbidding place. No sunlight peeped through the overhead branches making random puddles of light on the dry leaf floor. No shafts of light broke through the gloom like a magical stairway, and Emma shuddered. There was an expectation in the air that was so real to her that she could almost touch it. Shaking herself out of the spiral of fear that was starting to grip at her heart, she took a deep breath. Today she would concentrate on the forest floor,

145

think of Oliver, and hope that if he was a spirit that he would come to her and show her where he was buried.

After three hours of wandering through the trees she was depleted, she couldn't go on. She had failed, having been so sure that today she would have been able to put his spirit to rest.

The atmosphere under the trees was heavy, draining the last vestiges of energy from her body. Desperate to splash her face with water she made her way in the direction of the river.

After the rain the river was in full torrent and she could hear its roar before she got anywhere near to it. Suddenly, the air was split by another sound, the petrified scream of a woman. Emma stopped dead in her tracks, her heart beating hard in her chest. She could hardly breathe. The vision of Polly's dead and decaying skin covered in earth was, for the moment, all that she could see in her mind and she wanted to run in the other direction, run for home, run for safety as she had done before.

When more screams split the silence of the inner forest, each more terrified than the last, Emma ran towards the river fearing what she would find. As she broke through the trees she was shocked to see Sarah Poleshore on her stomach beside the water.

Running to her, Emma knelt to hold her. At Emma's touch the girl twisted away violently, her face contorted in a mask of horror.

Emma called her name but she seemed not to hear. One of Sarah's arms hung over the bank into the water and Emma saw lunacy in Sarah's eyes as she looked at Emma and then back to the water. Realising that the girl was in danger of being pulled into the river by the rushing water, Emma took hold of Sarah's free arm and pulled it hard, trying to get her fully onto the bank. That is when she saw it. The skull, green with slime, river weed filling the eye sockets and minuscule creatures writhing within, giving the impression that the skull was blinking as it seemingly devoured Sarah's hand caught in its mouth.

Emma almost screamed herself at the sight of Sarah's hand caught beneath the skull's teeth and she pulled back in shock just as Sarah fainted.

Sarah was now a prone dead weight and, taking hold of the girl's ankles, Emma pulled the inert body away from the edge of the river. The skull followed, bouncing onto the bank.

Emma sat on the ground next to Sarah, unable to take her eyes from the hideous sight until Sarah came out of her faint and her eyes went immediately to her hand. Eyes wide with horror she screamed one long continuous scream that cut Emma to her heart, immobilising her.

A man was suddenly beside them and, falling to his knees, spoke earnestly. 'It's alright, hush, girl, hush.' There was a croak in the unused voice as Jake Poleshore pulled his daughter into his chest so that she couldn't see the skull, and raised his eyes to Emma who was still sitting in shock.

Coming out of her own stupor Emma released Sarah's hand that had been trapped by one of her fingers in a jagged crack in the back of the skull.

Jake rocked his daughter in his arms like a baby and Emma saw tears rolling over his cheeks. 'I'm sorry, girl,' he sobbed, 'I'm sorry. None of this was my doing. None of it.'

At that moment a loud clap of thunder rent the air and they all flinched as huge spots of rain quickly turned into a downpour. Emma pushed the skull, that now she could see had no lower jaw, under a bush and all three ran for cover under the trees.

'We must make our way to the house,' Emma shouted over the thunder.

Bursting into the kitchen as thunder reverberated across a leaden sky, all three stood inside the door dripping water onto the flagstones, their clothes and hair sodden with water.

Startled by the sight, Robert rushed to help them. 'Come in. Come to the fire. Jon,' he shouted, 'can you get blankets from the cupboard in the passage.'

Jon left immediately, looking concerned, while Robert pulled chairs up in front of the fire and threw on more logs.

Soon, all three sat by the fire wrapped in blankets, their

outer clothes drying over a rack as Robert poured brandy into cups and handed them to his unexpected guests.

Emma took Sarah to her bedroom and shared Charlotte's underwear with her. Sarah's face was pale as she looked in the mirror and whispered, 'My father spoke.' There was the sound of incredulity in her quiet voice as she looked at Emma. 'I haven't heard his voice since I was three years old and yet, I remembered it. I recognised it.'

Emma put her arms around the girl, who now seemed so frail, and cried into Sarah's hair for the terrible disservice that she now knew her cousin Amelia's wickedness had caused this family.

When they returned to the kitchen Jon served them a bowl of stew and all five sat in silence as they ate.

When the storm had abated Jon looked at Emma with a raised eyebrow but she ignored him, needing to speak to Robert. But how to begin?

'Robert,' she eventually broke the silence addressing her brother in an uncertain voice, 'I think we have found Oliver's body and he will need a proper burial.'

Robert, who had been clearing the table, looked as though he had received a blow to his face. 'How have you found Oliver? What do you mean, you found him?'

But an even greater shock was to come when Jake spoke. 'Thank you for drying our clothes and for the food, but I have to take my daughter home.'

Robert stared at Jake in disbelief, his mouth open. '*You spoke!*'

'Yes, Vicar, I'm sorry.' Jake started to stand, taking Sarah's arm. But she didn't move.

'We can't go, Pa. I want to know what happened all those years ago and I know that Emma wants to know what happened to her cousin.' Her face was white with compassion as she looked at her father. 'If you know, you *must* tell us, we have all lived long enough with this.'

The legs of the chair made a harsh sound on the flagstones as Jake sat down again. He didn't look at the expectant faces but stared for some time at the wood grain on the table top. When he eventually spoke, it was quietly, his voice cracking with emotion. 'I can't, not in front of the vicar.'

'Yes, Pa, especially in front of Robert, who has helped us all this time.'

'He won't understand. None of you will understand.' And he crumpled, holding his head in his hands. 'My wife,' he sobbed, 'I couldn't even talk to my wife. She didn't deserve all those wasted years.' His tears ran uncontrolled over his cheeks and his body shook with his sobs.

Sarah leant her head on her father's shoulder and cried with him. 'We will never be free of this, Pa, until you tell us what happened to you.'

Blinking back the tears and trying to wipe his face with his large hand, Jake looked at Robert and sighed. 'I'm sorry, this is against all that you believe and I think that you will condemn me to hell for what I am going to tell you.'

As Robert looked at Jake his lips tightened; he took in a deep breath before saying, 'It's not my place to condemn anyone to hell, Jake, but to save them from it.'

Anger flushed Jake's face as he spoke through his tears. 'Then you are too late, Vicar, for I have been there for thirteen years.'

Ignoring his angry outburst Robert said, 'Start at the beginning, Jake, and I promise that there will be no condemning this day, nor any other.'

Jake nodded, taking in Robert's words, although he didn't look convinced when he spoke but defeated, resigned to the fact that he would now have to speak his truth.

'I had a wife and child and little money, there being no work for labourers that year.' He swallowed hard, as though using his voice after so long was painful. 'The winter had been hard and I went that evening to the forest here to try and get some meat or fish. I had traps laid and just wanted to check on them. We were

149

hungry. After we'd fed Sarah there was nothing left for us and my wife was expecting again.'

Sarah's eyes opened wide. 'I didn't know that, Pa.'

Nodding, he patted her hand, a look of pain on his face as he continued, 'I heard voices somewhere amongst the trees and crept quietly to see who was in the forest at night. I saw Mistress Brack and another woman in the light of the lamps that they had with them. They were digging a hole on the edge of a clearing. I couldn't think why they were there.' He stopped and looked briefly at Sarah. 'It was a few moments before I saw the body on the ground. They picked it up and placed it into the hole. They were just covering it with soil when Mr Brack arrived, shouting that they had killed her. I knew then that it was a woman they were burying. He threw himself onto the ground and began scraping at the earth. It was then that his sister took the spade from the other woman and hit him over the head with it. He fell forward. There was a terrible silence before the other woman screamed. Mistress Brack slapped her face, telling her to be quiet or it would be the worse for her. The woman stopped, obviously afraid as she apologised profusely and I could hear the fear in her voice. They were discussing what to do with him, when I stepped on a twig and the crack alerted them to my hiding place. I didn't move, but she knew I was there.'

He stopped for a moment and took a breath, looking at Robert, sorrow covering his face before continuing, 'She called out, "I know it is you, Jake Poleshore. Come here." There was something in her voice, a power that could not be denied. I went forward and stood at the edge of the grave and saw in the light of the lamp the blood on the head of her brother. She commanded me to pick him up, and I did. You cannot imagine the wickedness in her face, in those eyes, in the shadow of that lamp and I was afraid of her.

'I carried him to the river and lowered him into the water on her instruction. While they stood back, I wedged him tight between the rocks under the bank where the water was deep, but not in the fast current, so that he wouldn't be washed away. It was all that I could do for him and I shook with fear in case she realised what I had done. When I had finished, she asked what she should do with me, and put the edge of the spade on my chest, pushing at me until I was on the edge of the river bank. I pleaded that she should spare me for I had a pregnant wife and a small child at home. She told me that she knew everything about me, that I stole from her often, and that now she would have her revenge. I pleaded for my life. I told her how hungry we were, that I took so little, only enough for us, I didn't sell any of it. She laughed. A sound so shrill and wicked that the blood froze in my veins and I couldn't move.'

He looked down at the table again. Sorrowful tears flowed freely from his eyes, dripping onto the wood, where he left them. 'She told me that she would make life easier for me, that my wife would lose the child she was carrying. "That will ease things, won't it?" Her laugh was thick with evil and I shook with fear. Then she told me that if I ever used my voice again or told anyone what I had seen, then my wife would die and so would my daughter.'

He was silent for a moment then seemed to gather himself before saying in a quiet voice, 'I was found next morning by Alf Freeman and some villagers who took me home but I couldn't tell them what had happened. My wife had lost our baby in the night. The floor was covered in blood and she was almost dead. I knew why. I never spoke again for fear of losing her and my little girl.' He broke down sobbing. 'My poor wife.'

He turned his head away from Robert and continued to sob silently, only the movement of his shoulders giving him away.

Robert looked grey, and Emma noticed how he held his bible in both hands slightly off the table between himself and Jake. Was he holding it out to Jake, or was it being held as a wall between himself and evil?

The silence in the room became heavy and Emma could wait no longer for Robert to act.

'As you know,' she said, 'I worked here soon after that night and I can tell you that Polly was not murdered, but died in childbirth. I hadn't realised that Oliver must have loved her. All we knew was that she left suddenly and that he mysteriously disappeared, leaving all his clothes behind. And even though the family solicitor visited Amelia, she didn't say that she knew anything about him. I'm so sorry, Mr Poleshore, for all that has happened to your family.'

Robert seemed suddenly to come alive. 'Jake, would you like to come over to the church and we will pray for your lost baby, your wife and for you and Sarah?'

Jake nodded agreement and stood slowly, following Robert from the kitchen, and Sarah went with them, her arm around her father's waist.

Jon, who had listened to everything in silence, stood up and without looking at Emma also left, closing the door quietly behind him.

Sitting in the kitchen alone with only the sound of crackling logs for company, she sighed. After all these years the mystery was at last unravelled. She sighed again, looking around the kitchen that had not changed since she was a child and thought, *If only Nell and Alf were here to know this.*

Feeling restless, she left the house and made her way to the river. The rain had stopped and she couldn't leave Oliver alone any longer. On the way she picked flowers, which calmed her nervous energy. But as she reached the spot where Oliver's skull had lain, she was surprised to see Jon kneeling over some bones. He looked up as she drew near, a pained look on his face.

'I removed what was left of him, stuck in the bank and caught between the rocks,' he said. 'This is all that's left, the rest I think washed away.' He looked down at the small pile of bones saying quite unnecessarily, 'I laid them out.'

Emma stared at Oliver's skull and one or two bones now placed together on the bank. A shoulder blade, an arm, some ribs and a foot – a sad sight.

'It's not right for a man to lie in pieces,' Jon said quietly to himself. 'Not right at all.'

Kneeling next to him, Emma placed her flowers on Oliver's few ribs. 'Like you,' she said sadly, 'I came to bring him peace.'

Jon said nothing as they knelt together, each in their own thoughts, trying in some way to bring dignity to what was left of Oliver.

'I'll cover him with branches,' Jon said after a while, 'and I'll get a sack to move him. There's no need for you to see that. I'll lay what's left of him out properly in the church and go to the village for the authorities.'

On the walk back Emma felt suddenly empty, traumatised at the way that Oliver had been found and yet happy that he would now be laid to rest. Being here after so long had been difficult and emotional. She had also wanted to get to know Robert, as a brother and a man, but on that level she felt that she had failed.

~

The sun shone on the day of the funeral as Oliver was laid to rest in the family tomb. Robert had taken the service and Mr Redfern, the family solicitor, had attended all the way from London. Afterwards, Emma stood by the tomb door in the silence of the graveyard and felt the weight lift from her shoulders. At last it was over. Oliver was settled, and no longer would she expect to see him sitting beside the river with his pipe when she walked there. Other things had also changed, she had to admit to herself. Having laid her cousin to rest, she had now lost her focus. Her brother was perhaps more aloof. Sarah didn't come again with a cook-pot for Robert, and Robert no longer visited the Poleshores, who he believed no longer needed his help. She felt sad about that, as she had been sure that Sarah had been attracted to Robert. Perhaps it was because Sarah now had no excuse to visit, or perhaps the memories of that day in the forest were too difficult for her to overcome.

Emma decided to take matters into her own hands and invited the Poleshores for a meal on Sunday after church.

~

On Sunday, Sarah looked pretty in a fresh cream dress tied with a deep pink ribbon at the waist. And Emma noticed with satisfaction that Sarah blushed at the sight of Robert, who smiled warmly at her and took her hand, leading her to the table to sit next to him. Knowing that her instincts had been correct Emma hoped that Robert would find a reason to see Sarah again.

When, after the meal, the Poleshores had departed, Jon stood beside Emma as she put the plates away. There was a look on his face that she could not fathom. 'Well done, Emma,' he said, not looking at her directly, 'that was a good thing that you did. Some men find it difficult to approach a woman. It isn't something that we are taught, and Robert, I think, does have feelings for Sarah.'

Before she could reply he turned and left the room. When the door closed she felt his loss. His words played round and round in her mind. '*Some men find it difficult to approach a woman, it isn't something we are taught.*' Could he mean that he likes me? she thought. But don't I have enough trouble? Why, she thought sadly, couldn't it have been Jon that came to the door wanting work, instead of Richard, all those years ago?

Over the coming days Emma realised an immense joy working with Jon in an afternoon on the vegetable patch, when she had done her chores. She loved the chickens and rejoiced in the fact that Robert was beginning to take an interest by collecting the eggs each morning after his prayers.

The library at Claydon was full of books, and Emma and Jon read and discussed them in the evenings while Robert was in church. As a companionship formed between them she found herself surreptitiously watching him out of the corner of her eye when he wasn't looking. Just glimpsing him at any time of the day made her smile to herself. Feeling captivated by him, she went out of her way for an excuse to be near him. They talked about the New World and the animals, the people and the politics. For Emma it was balm, for no one had included her before in discussing anything other than farming or work.

As the three of them sat at breakfast one morning, Emma noticed that Jon was very quiet. 'Are you well, Jon?' She felt concern.

'Yes, thank you.' He seemed pensive and didn't look at either of them as he spoke. 'I have been trying to find the words to speak to you both.'

Emma's heart thudded in her chest, wondering what he was about to say.

When he eventually spoke, after taking a deep breath, his words were so unexpected that for a moment she stopped breathing.

'I have to go away.' He looked at Robert, but his eyes flicked just for a second towards Emma. 'When you took me in, Robert, I was struggling to survive. I had no money and was relying on the kindness of strangers to help me on my journey.'

'Journey?'

Robert laid his bible on the table and concentrated on Jon; he hadn't thought to ask Jon about himself or what plans he might have had.

'Yes, Robert. I should have told you that I was on a quest which I must complete. I have to take the Reverend Harding's notebook and bible to his widow. The names of his ancestors are written at the front and I believe it will mean a great deal to her to have it back. I know that while we were incarcerated, he thought of me as his son. I must do this for him.'

There was a great sadness about Jon and it showed in his face as he continued, 'I know that the book should be with his wife. I also believe that he kept the diary so that she may one day know what he experienced, and why he did not return home at the end of his sentence. That he still loved her and spoke of her often. I feel it my duty.'

As his voice trailed away he looked from Robert to Emma and both stared back at him in silence. He knew that they were digesting what he was saying, and continued apologetically, 'There are enough vegetables in the garden to keep you going for several months, Robert, although if this hot weather continues you must water every day.'

Emma's heart was racing in her chest, already feeling his loss. Unable to speak, because her throat had constricted, she stood slowly and left the kitchen. The tears welling up in her eyes were brimming over by the time she reached the library, where she shut the door, needing to be alone. It was a quiet sanctuary, with the sun streaming in through the window warming a section of the floor.

Feeling cold she made her way towards the pool of sunshine and stood in it, soaking up its warmth. Facing the window and the blur of greenery beyond, she saw nothing through her tears that, now she was alone, rolled over her cheeks. 'No!' she cried in her agony and despair. 'No!' And then remembered that she was married and that there was never going to be any future in what she felt for Jon. Secretly, she had been acting like a young girl with a life ahead of her. A girl with ideas of being loved and cherished. Jon's face loomed before her eyes, his soft blond hair, his broad shoulders and his smile. So great was the loss that she now felt, it frightened her. How could she face life alone now that she had experienced real love? Her heart, that had been so free since Jon arrived, now felt as dense as stone.

It was with great sadness that Emma realised she must return to her husband, and she had never felt so alone. Richard didn't want her as a wife and Jon was leaving, perhaps never to return. He had said nothing to her of love and she had kept her feelings to herself whilst secretly enjoying his company in a silly girlish way.

The following day, knowing that her brother would not now starve to death, she knew she had to face her own troubles. It was with a heavy heart that she made plans to return to the Laddisbrock estate and Richard.

'Robert,' she said after breakfast, 'I feel that I must return to my husband. I have perhaps been here a little too long.'

In reply, Robert slowly lowered the letter that he had been reading and stared at her.

'Sister,' he smiled, 'at first, I found it hard to have company, but now, I have to admit that the changes you have brought about here have made my life more enjoyable. When you go,' he looked at her with a fondness in his eyes, 'I will miss you.'

'Thank you, Robert, I too have enjoyed the *latter* part of my visit.' And for the first time since they were children they laughed together. While he appeared to be in good humour she added, 'Please write to Mother, Robert, when you have the time, she truly misses you.'

'I promise,' he said, folding his letter and standing up. As he passed he kissed her on the cheek, taking her completely by surprise.

18.

Several days later Matt arrived in the carriage to collect her. 'No Larch?' she asked.

'No, madam.'

Matt's face was stiff and she could see that he could hardly bring himself to look at her. With a sigh she accepted the gulf between them and stepped into the carriage, realising that nothing had changed. The Laddisbrocks were showing her that she was still not worthy of the service of Larch.

There was little breeze other than the movement of air caused by the carriage, which moved swiftly through the countryside towards the Laddisbrock estate. The nearer they got, the heavier Emma's life laid itself upon her shoulders.

The sky had become grey with scudding clouds, reflecting the beating of her heart and her mood, as the carriage approached the house along the tree-lined driveway. As the house came into view, the windows, it seemed to Emma, were staring with malevolent eyes at her approach. Her mouth became dry and a coldness crept over her skin. A feeling of foreboding crept across her shoulders as though the ghost of an ancestor sat next to her and was letting her know that they were there.

This time, there were no servants to greet her on the steps and she made her own way to her room, knowing that eventually her trunk and valise would arrive.

As she washed her hands in the small bowl there was a timid knock on the door.

'Come in,' she called.

Emma was wiping her hands as a small girl entered and curtsied.

'I'm Rosie Carter, madam, and I will be looking after you as Martin is looking after the mistress, who is unwell.'

Emma was feeling uncharitable towards Charlotte but asked out of politeness, 'Unwell in what way, Rosie?'

Too late, Emma saw Rosie blush and realised that the girl would expect to be addressed as Carter. Passing quickly over her mistake Emma asked, 'Has the doctor seen her, Carter?' Emma hoped so. If Charlotte was ill while she was away, then this time the finger could not be pointed at her.

'I've been told that the doctor has seen her, madam, but I don't know what's wrong, only that it's something that she has had before.'

So, it was happening again. Looking at Carter, Emma changed the subject.

'Would you ask Mrs Jenk to make me something to eat. I will eat here in my room.'

Carter gulped and tears flooded her eyes. 'I'm sorry, madam, but Mrs Jenk is dead.'

'Dead?' Emma looked sharply at the servant. 'When did this take place?'

'Two weeks past, madam. She was found with head injuries on her way to the village.'

Emma could hardly believe it. 'How did it happen?'

'The authorities say that a tree branch may have fallen on her, madam. There was one near the body with blood on it.'

'So, she was on the footpath when she died?'

'No, madam, she was a little way from the footpath.'

Emma wondered why the cook would not be on the path, but did not pursue it as she could see that the girl was upset.

She changed the subject. 'Do we have a cook, Carter?'

'Yes, madam, Mrs Martin.'

'Mrs Martin?'

'She's from the village, madam, Martin's mother.'

Emma felt a tremor of suspicion. 'I will come with you to the kitchen, Carter, and meet Mrs Martin.'

Carter's face drained of colour and her eyes opened wide in shock. 'Oh, please, madam, don't come with me, they will think that I have brought you to the kitchen.'

'They, Carter?'

'The Martins, madam.'

'I see. Then I will give you time to ask cook to get me some food and I will come down later to meet Mrs Martin.'

Carter was now twisting the edges of her apron in her shaking hands. 'Is something else wrong, Carter?'

'They will know that I told you about Mrs Jenk not being here.'

Emma wondered what had gone on in her absence. It seemed that Martin was now ruling the kitchen staff. 'I will make an excuse to visit the kitchen, Carter. I will not mention you,' she assured the trembling maid.

An hour later the heels of Emma's shoes seemed to clunk loudly on the bare wood as she descended the servants' stairs. As she entered the kitchen a small woman sitting at the table, reading, looked up then stood up sharply.

'Where is Mrs Jenk?' Emma asked innocently.

The little woman looked nervous and tried to cover a child's toy lying on the table with a cloth.

'Mrs Jenk had an unfortunate accident, madam. I am Mrs Martin, the new cook.'

'I see. Did Mrs Laddisbrock hire you, Mrs Martin, and have you been in service before?'

Looking uncomfortable, the little woman started to stutter something unintelligible as Mary Martin entered the kitchen.

'Mrs Laddisbrock, do you need something?'

'I wished to speak to Mrs Jenk, but I see we have a new cook, Martin?'

'I'm afraid Mrs Jenk is no longer with us, madam.'

The voice of the servant held no deference, in fact there was an edge of challenge, that for the moment Emma ignored.

'Mrs Martin has stepped in, in the emergency,' Martin continued.

'I hope that you will be happy here, Mrs Martin,' Emma said sweetly, while thinking *I am going to get to the bottom of this.* 'Would you have some bread and cheese brought to my room and perhaps something sweet.'

When later the maid arrived with her food on a tray Emma asked, 'And where is Jacob, Carter? I didn't see him in the house. I hope that he isn't annoying Mr Ames up at the stable.'

Carter shook her head. 'I don't know, madam, he just disappeared.'

'Disappeared!' The word held a significance that Carter would not understand. After what had happened to Polly when she worked at Claydon House, Emma wondered how many servants just disappeared.

'Yes, madam. Martin says that he has run away and that we should forget about him.'

'But he is a small boy. Does he have family living near?'

'No, madam. He has no family. We all searched for him in the house and in the grounds but he couldn't be found.'

'What would have made him run away, Carter, do you know?'

There was something hidden behind the girl's eyes as she shook her head in denial.

Emma was worried, but had to let it go. What could she do?

That night she had little sleep as a storm raged outside. Rain battered the windows and lightning lit the sky with ragged white and blue flashes that flooded her room, followed immediately by the sound of thunder that boomed and rumbled above the roof. It felt like an omen as she stood at her bedroom window watching the garden illuminated by sudden light, before being shuttered into darkness, on and on and on, until she turned away, getting into bed and pulling the covers up over her head.

The following day, the sun was shining as Emma left the house to walk. She had not seen Charlotte or Richard and had not searched them out. Since returning from Robert, she felt even more lost and abandoned.

It was mid-morning and the day was going to be hot. Heat was already radiating from the bricks as she rounded the corner of the house and smelt the honeysuckle that sprawled up the walls, giving off a sweet scent that at any other time would have filled her soul with delight.

Apart from last evening's storm, they seemed to be in the grip of a heatwave. As she walked through the garden, the warm air was filled with the perfume of roses. She stopped to watch a blackbird pulling at a worm in the flower bed, and in the trees along the driveway she could hear the birds singing. A glorious English summer day, and yet for all its beauty and all the yearning she had had for it when living on the other side of the world, she shivered. There was something brewing, she felt it in the pit of her stomach. She hated this side of being psychic. Knowing that something was heading her way but not knowing what it was. She tried to shake it off, walking across the fields towards Tate Farm, she looked forward to seeing Dolly and Nona. At least she would receive a warm welcome there. As she walked she remembered the Mott children, Dolly's eldest, Dan, a little older than Robert, and Alice a little older than Nona. Those days, growing up just outside the village, living in the cottage next door to the Motts, seemed to her now to have been very happy. It was strange, she thought, how she no longer felt a part of anywhere, not part of her husband's family, or her parents' lives in the New World, or even Nona's life now. There was no feeling of belonging anywhere. Why, she wondered, could she not feel that she belonged somewhere? Why could she not feel more than a visitor? She had looked forward to returning to England so much, that it had filled her every waking moment. Yet now, although nature and the climate did not disappoint her, everything had changed, as things always do as the years go by, and she had very stupidly and childishly thought that all would be the same. Of course, rural life had not changed in hundreds of years, and the village and the farms were still the same, moving at a slow pace. It was, she knew, that it was she that had changed. And it rubbed inside her like sand in the shell of a mussel, an irritation that she couldn't shake off, couldn't escape from. And what would she do if Nona and Dan found the money to live on the other side of the world with Martha and Andrew? Robert and she had little in common. Living with him, she realised, was not an option unless she was destitute. Soon, she would be without a home, and although she knew that Dolly would offer shelter for a short time, she was not in charge of Tate Farm and the house was full now that John Brisket had married Alice and they had children.

The farmyard was as dreary as ever. The plain square house, with its soulful windows looking across the yard to the barns, did not feel any more welcoming today.

She'd just lifted her hand to knock on the door when it opened and William's small face stared up at her.

'Hello, William, is Grandma in?'

'Come in, Emma,' Dolly called from inside. 'I saw you from the window but had my hands full.'

Dolly was just tipping two large loaves from the paddle onto a substantial bread board at one end of the table. Her face was flushed from the heat of cooking but her smile was as welcoming as ever. 'It's good to see you, Emma. Have you seen Nona?'

'No, I only arrived back yesterday and had things to sort out up at the house.'

'Well, you must tell me the latest. How did you find your brother? In good health, I hope.'

'Yes, by the time I left he was in good spirits and, I think, falling in love.'

'Is he allowed to fall in love?' Dolly looked surprised.

'Pardon?' Emma felt a little shocked at the immediate reaction to her good news. 'What do you mean, Dolly?'

'Not all vicars are allowed to marry, Emma.'

'I didn't know that, Dolly. But... the Reverend Draycott is married.'

'Oh yes! Ignore me.' She raised her shoulders and continued, 'I don't understand it either, Emma. I don't know why I said it. Look, I've got some cake about to come out of the oven, so why don't you go and see Nona, she's outside somewhere and has something that I think that she would like to tell you on her own.'

Emma's heart sank again. Nona couldn't possibly have managed to get the money together for the trip home already, surely. As she walked across the farmyard and put her head around one of the doors she wondered if Dan had had some savings. When Nona wasn't in the barn she walked out towards the stables and saw there in front of her an amazing sight. Nona, wearing a long cotton coat over her dress, which was tied in a knot at the front to keep it out of the muck, was shovelling steaming manure from the heap onto a low pushcart. Emma stopped in her tracks at the sight. Nona, who hated smells, who cried as a child when asked to do the most menial task, was shovelling something that normally she would hold her nose to walk past.

'Nona!' Emma called.

The girl looked up and, seeing her sister, threw down the fork and ran to her, throwing her arms around Emma who took a step back in shock but could not avoid the hug or the smell.

'Oh, Emma, you're back. I have wonderful news to tell you and I wanted to tell you in person, not send a letter.'

Emma's stomach tightened with a feeling of loss. But her sister looked so happy that she couldn't let her feelings of despair show.

'Dan and I are to be married by the Reverend Draycott and I want you to be my witness, Emma. Please say yes.'

'Of course I will be your witness, Nona, how could I not? I would have been disappointed if you had asked anyone else.' Her mouth was dry as she asked, 'Does this mean that you've found the money for returning to Mother already?'

Nona stood back and smiled into Emma's tense face. 'We are not going home, Emma. Mr Mott, John Brisket and Dan are doing up the foreman's house and when we are married we will be living there. We are staying here to work the farm for Andrew.'

'But, Nona, how can John afford that? The farm has always struggled and John has to make enough to send Andrew some of the profit once a year.'

'As John is Andrew's tenant farmer, I know that he could not pay me any money. But I don't need money. I will be an extra pair of hands that he will not have to pay, and he didn't want to lose Dan. When we are married I will move out of the house and give Alice and John more room.'

Emma stared at her sister's bright face and wondered why she was thinking of Andrew's profit at all. Nona was staying, and it was the best news that she had had in a long while. 'I am so happy for you both. I really am, you can't imagine how wonderful this news is to me, Nona.' Now she hugged Nona, kissing her muddy face.

'Come on, girls,' Dolly called from the doorway. 'The cake is cut and getting dry.'

With her arm around Nona's waist they hurried together towards the house, where Nona removed the coat, washed her hands in a bucket of cold water and kicked off her boots.

As they sat at the table eating the cake, Emma told them about her stay with Robert, leaving out the information about her feelings for Jon or the finding of Oliver's body.

Looking at Nona across the table Emma saw for the first time how healthy she looked. The weak girl with rickets had been surpassed by a glowing young woman.

'You heard about Mrs Jenk, Emma?' Dolly said in expectation. 'Poor woman, just walking to the village to post a letter, to be struck down like that.' Her voice trailed off and she frowned, shaking her head. 'Strange,' she added.

'Strange, how?' Emma felt a chill on her back.

'We all walk that path. None of the trees as far as I noticed were rotten. We must all be thankful that none of us had a branch fall on our heads.'

'Who found her, Dolly?'

'The young boot boy, Jacob, from up at the house.'

'Jacob!' Emma hadn't heard that.

'Yes, the poor little soul, he went running into the village and told Mr Rudd. A party of men went out and found her. Carried her down to the doctor. There wasn't anything to be done, she was already dead.'

'Was it Jacob who moved her from the path?'

Dolly frowned. 'Moved her from the path?'

'Yes, I heard from one of the maids that she was not on the path when found.'

'Perhaps she crawled away trying to get up,' Dolly mused thoughtfully.

'Yes, perhaps she didn't die straight away,' Nona added.

Emma frowned. 'I wonder what happened to her letter.'

'I don't know, Emma, no one has mentioned a letter,' Dolly said. 'Perhaps someone found it and posted it. You will have to ask Jacob.'

'I'm afraid that Jacob has run away. Everyone searched for him, but he hasn't been found.'

'We will keep watch for him,' Nona said, 'just in case he comes this way or hides in one of the barns.'

'Thank you, Nona. I'm afraid that all is not well up at the Manor. There's a new cook and an atmosphere that I intend to get to the bottom of.'

~

On the walk back to the house Emma thought over the situation and realised that she had not questioned for one moment that Charlotte had not hired Mrs Martin. That was definitely not like her at all. Now she hurried, almost running; she had to see her mother-in-law. Something was most definitely wrong. On entering the house, she took the stairs two at a time in an unladylike manner. Hurrying along the landing she arrived at

Charlotte's bedroom door just as Martin came out of the room. The servant stopped, took in a breath seeing Emma bearing down on her and blocked the door, her hand on the door jamb.

'The mistress can't see you. She is sleeping… madam.'

'Out of my way, Martin, I intend to see my mother-in-law.'

'I told you, madam, that she is sleeping.' There was a determination in the maid's voice that defied Emma to disobey.

'How dare you speak back to me, Martin. If you wish to stay employed here you will move out of the way this instant.'

The look on Martin's face was derisive. 'You are not in charge here, madam, and never were. Only you believe that you could be the lady of this house. You will never produce an heir and that is what they want, an heir.'

'Move away from the door or I will make you move.' Emma knew that she was yelling but was determined that she would not be told what to do by this maid.

For a moment Martin looked unsure, but as she moved away from the door there was a look of triumph in her eyes that puzzled Emma.

The room, when Emma entered, was dark. Walking to the drapes she pulled those nearest to the bed open so that she could look at Charlotte. The woman's face was grey. Not a good sign. Beside the bed Emma noticed that an empty cup had been left, but there was no sign of a vessel holding water for Charlotte to have a drink. In the silence of the room Emma felt unsure what to do. She touched Charlotte's arm, but when she didn't wake she shook her a little until she moaned.

'Charlotte, it's Emma come to look in on you, as I am back from my visit to my brother.'

There was no response apart from the flicker of an eyelid. Emma went to the dressing room and came back with a cloth soaked in cold water and gently wiped Charlotte's face. A long sigh left her lips and the smell upon the breath was so unpleasant that Emma stood back and almost retched. Then she noticed the bottle of laudanum and a spoon. The spoon was sticky, indicating that the dose, whatever that was, had been administered in the last hour. Knowing enough about the mixture, an alcoholic solution containing morphine prepared from the opium plant, Emma knew that Charlotte would not be waking any time soon. Why was she being given laudanum, what was wrong with her?

On leaving the room Emma left the drapes open in the hope that Charlotte might wake sooner with the light, and made her mind up to return in an hour and look at her.

~

Marching along the corridor and ascending the stairs to her husband's rooms Emma was startled to find them empty. The bed had been stripped and all sign of occupation gone. Now that she came to think about it she hadn't seen him or Patrick since her return, not that she had sought him out. Back on the landing she saw Carter with her arms full of linen.

'Carter, can you put that down and come to my chamber, I need to speak to you.'

The girl looked worried and, laying the linen upon the nearest table, followed Emma to her room.

'Shut the door, Carter.'

The girl did as she was asked and, looking even more worried, fiddled with her apron.

Emma noticed, but ignored the girl's nervous habit and asked directly, 'Do you happen to know where my husband is now lodging in this house, Carter?'

'He isn't in the house, madam.' Red spots of embarrassment appeared on the maid's cheeks as Emma frowned at her.

'Not in the house? So where might I find him?'

'He is gone, madam, with Patrick and some of the servants to Freelanders Farm.'

'What is he doing there?' Emma knew the farmhouse and it was not large. Also, that Davy Creel, the Laddisbrocks' estate manager who farmed Freelanders, had six children. There would not be room for Richard and his servants as well as the family.

'Mr Creel died, madam, it was his heart, and his wife and children have left.'

'Left!'

'Well yes, madam, Mrs Creel couldn't run the farm and look after her children, and the tenancy, I heard, was in her husband's name only.'

'Do you know where the Creels now live, Carter?'

'I believe, madam, that they have moved in with her sister but not for long, madam, as her cottage is very small.'

'Thank you, Carter, that will be all.' Looking relieved the girl left quickly.

When she had gone Emma went over all that she had heard. It brought back memories of when her father, who had worked for the Laddisbrocks, had died and there had been no help forthcoming from his employer. Martha had been left with five children and no income. The Laddisbrocks had not even given her mother meat or bread to help her. It was as though Father had not existed. She could be wrong, but if she were not, then she would be angry and would find a way to help Mrs Creel. As her emotions calmed, she began to think. *Perhaps I should look to my own life, for I may be in the same position as Mrs Creel soon, homeless and living unsatisfactorily with a relative.*

19.

The stable smelt sweetly of horses. A smell that Emma had always enjoyed and for a moment reminded her of Black, her own horse. How she wished at this moment that he was here.

The door to the tack room was open and she found Matt cleaning some leather. He looked up as her shadow fell across the doorway, then stood sharply with a nod of deference. It made her sad, pulled at her heartstrings; they had grown up together for a few years while they were in service, they had been through so much, both burnt in the fire and yet, it was as though they were strangers with no history. She would, then, treat him as he now expected to be treated, and she was sad for it.

'Have you seen Jacob, Ames?'

'No, madam, he's been missing for some time.'

'So I understand. I ask only because he thought a lot of you and was hanging around the stable whenever he had a moment. I know that he also loved the horses.'

Matt nodded, but did not reply.

'I need a horse, Ames, please saddle something for me.'

A look of surprise crossed his face. 'A horse, madam? Do you ride?'

Emma raised her head and looked at him down her nose. After all, isn't that what he expected from her? 'I do ride, Ames, and would like you to hurry.'

He did not reply but pushed past her, crossing the yard to the stable block. It was not long before he was leading a horse into the yard and helping her up into the saddle.

'You had better tell me where you're going in case I have to send out a search party, madam.'

'There will be no need, Ames. I am quite capable of finding my way. Thank you.'

And with that she turned the horse's head, setting the heels of her boots sharply to its flanks, and rode out of the yard at speed. She was just sorry that she couldn't see his face as she rode away with such confidence.

It was exhilarating to feel the rush of air once more on her face. To see the ground below her speeding past and feeling a horse respond to her touch. When the ground became more uneven she slowed, not wanting to injure the animal. To be riding through green lanes, the birds singing to her from the hedgerow, was so beautiful that she wanted to cry. The land was green and Emma could smell fragrances that she had almost forgotten. The nutty smell of decomposing leaves, the smell of earth and the glorious fragrance of herbs. She gloried in the sight of the purple blossom of the foxglove standing tall here and there among other plants, and of the gentle toadflax. She was intoxicated by the fragrance of the ancient three-cornered leek as it was disturbed by the horse. And felt the joy of seeing once again clumps of green hairy nettles, a nursery for the chrysalis that would fill the air as a butterfly or moth. She and the horse moved slowly when the lane turned into some trees and rode for a distance through a forest of oak, ash, beech and rowan that felt so familiar. The joy in her heart that had waited so long for this nourishment was almost overwhelming.

As the horse jogged once again along the lanes, pheasants, colourful long-tailed game birds, scattered before her, and a quail with little brain seemed bent on outrunning her horse until it eventually ran beneath a hedge. There were no green lanes back home and this is what she had missed, was what her soul needed. A fox loped out of a field and stopped in the middle of the path to look at her, and then, without hurrying, disappeared through a hedge into another field. She smiled and wondered how her horse would have reacted if it had been a kangaroo.

Exhilarated by the ride Emma reined her horse in as she reached the top of a rise. Below her she could see the fields of Freelanders Farm laid out before her as a tapestry, divided by hedges of bramble, hawthorn, blackthorn and thickets of spindle.

Unlike the Tate farmhouse, which was confined within a square of barns, the Freelanders farmhouse looked out across fields, its thatched barns and stabling standing at a distance behind the main house.

The house, a low-roofed building, its upper windows hiding coyly in the heavy thatch that had seen better days, felt inhospitable to her.

Emma rode bravely up to the front door and was tying her horse to the hitching rail when a young man ran up and asked if she would like it stabled. She replied that she would not, as she didn't know how long she would be staying, and walked to the front door. She didn't knock but pushed the heavy door open.

The kitchen into which she walked was large. Two women who were scrubbing the floor and the work surfaces were taken by surprise. They stopped work immediately, and for a moment seemed not to know what to do. As the taller of the two women stood up she looked at the shorter well-built woman beside her, as though waiting for her to speak, and when she did not, the taller woman asked, 'How can we help you, Mrs Laddisbrock?'

Emma felt shocked that these women knew her and acknowledged who she was. She hid her shock and asked, 'Is Mr Laddisbrock at home?'

It was the taller woman who answered again. 'No, madam, the master is out looking over the land with Patrick.'

The confrontation that Emma had geared herself up for was not to be had and she suddenly felt weak. 'Would you mind if I sat at your table?'

Both women were suddenly galvanised into movement, the shorter of the two pulling out a chair and the taller going to a barrel and drawing off some beer. 'Drink this, madam,' she said, handing the cup to Emma, 'you are as white as a new lamb.'

Emma took it gratefully, drinking from it slowly. Carter had told her that Richard had taken some of the staff with him, but she was surprised that she did not recognise these two women and yet they knew her. 'What are your names?' Emma asked as she placed the cup onto the table.

It was the tallest who once again spoke first. 'I'm West, madam.'

Emma looked at the other woman who was forced then to speak. 'Newman, madam.' She looked down at her feet as she spoke, causing Emma to frown.

'How long have you both worked for the Laddisbrocks?'

West answered quickly. 'Five years, madam.'

'About three years, madam,' Newman answered as Emma stared at her in expectation of a reply.

The prospect of speaking to Richard in front of the servants did not appeal to Emma so she asked how large the house was.

'There is a large living room at the back, madam, that the master likes to use, and he and Patrick eat their meals there.'

Emma nodded; at least she could have some privacy when she asked Richard why he had moved out, and if he knew that his mother was ill. But then quite suddenly she had a dreadful feeling and asked, 'By which means is Mr Laddisbrock looking over the farm?'

The two women looked confused. Emma tried again, a sinking feeling in her stomach. 'Have the master and Patrick gone by coach?'

'No, madam,' West answered, 'they travel in the usual way, by horse.'

A wave of fear swept over Emma and for a moment she could hardly breathe as her head spun and her heartbeat increased in her chest. Feeling dizzy, she put her hand to her forehead and leant forward, trying to get the feeling under control. It was a momentary affliction, but the servants had seen it and rushed to her side. West poured more beer into Emma's cup at which she only sipped before standing. 'Would you tell my husband that I have returned from my visit to my brother and that his mother is ill.'

Emma rode back slowly. Her thoughts were in turmoil; she almost cried at Richard's stupidity. A man with a bullet roaming around his body should not be riding a horse. He knew that.

~

Back at the Manor House, Emma looked in on Charlotte. She was still asleep, even though several hours had passed. Emma could see that she had had no more medicine, as the spoon was in the same place. Shaking Charlotte by the arm she still got little response. The question was, had the doctor prescribed the medication?

Pulling her shawl around her shoulders Emma walked to the village. The doctor's house was in the heart of the community, just off the village green and opposite the church. It was grander than its neighbours and had a small garden to the front. Emma walked through the gate and straight into the house, as the door was open.

The wide entrance hall was neatly kept as would be expected of the house of the doctor. A plainly dressed women of around forty years met Emma in the hallway enquiring, 'May I help you?' Her tone was abrupt and Emma did not like her manner.

'I would like to speak to the doctor, if he is in, madam.'

Emma put full emphasis on the title madam, and saw the woman flinch, confused about Emma's status.

'May I ask what it is about?' The woman's chin rose haughtily as she viewed Emma through squinted eyes without compassion, assessing her.

Emma felt irritated; she didn't know the woman. She could be a servant, or the doctor's wife, but was she also a gossip?

'No, you may not know what it is about. I will speak with the doctor,' Emma repeated, staring into the woman's eyes until she looked away. Nodding, the woman left Emma standing in the hall.

It was only a few minutes before the doctor stepped from one of the rooms off the hallway, looking serious. But when he saw who it was his expression turned to concern. 'Mrs Laddisbrock, my wife tells me that you wish to see me. How can I help you?'

His wife, now standing behind him, bobbed respectfully to Emma as he continued. 'I'm sorry,' he apologised, 'my wife didn't know you. You came on foot...' He didn't finish and Emma realised that of course her mother-in-law would never have arrived on foot.

Emma nodded to the woman as she followed the doctor into a dark but pleasant room filled with books. A large desk at its centre dominated the room and Emma was invited to sit in a chair conveniently placed in front of it. When she was seated, he sat opposite her. 'How can I help you, Mrs Laddisbrock?'

'I came to ask you, sir, when you last visited my mother-in-law.'

'I last visited after the death of her husband, madam. If you remember there was some suspicion that she had eaten something that she should not have, and it had disagreed with her. Is Mrs Laddisbrock ill?'

'I don't know, sir. I have only just returned from a visit with my brother and have found Mrs Laddisbrock under sedation, administered by one of the servants, but I do not know why.'

'And you asked the servant?'

'Yes, and I was told that you had been called and that you had advised keeping my mother-in-law sedated with laudanum. But the servant would not tell me why.'

He raised his eyebrows and looked concerned. 'That Mrs Laddisbrock needs attending to. A servant that does not answer to its master is a dangerous servant to have in one's household. I did prescribe laudanum when last I was called, and can only think that the servant is using that same medication because you were not there.'

'You cannot then tell me what now ails my mother-in-law?'

'I am sorry that I cannot.' He seemed pompous and tight-lipped as he asked, 'Have you asked your husband, madam?'

Emma felt her hackles rising, but replied sweetly with a tight smile, 'I have left a message for my husband, sir. He is called away on the business of one of the farms.'

He nodded, taking in the information. 'Do you wish me to visit Mrs Laddisbrock?'

Emma thought about it and decided not, as Charlotte seemed to be sleeping peacefully. The question that had not been answered was why.

'Thank you, sir, if I need to I will send a servant.'

Emma walked back through the lanes, deliberately walking past the cottage in which she had been brought up next door to the Motts' identical cottage. It all seemed so small now as she passed by. Until her father had died, she remembered it as a happy home, before her mother sent her away to work at Claydon House. She sighed, walking on with mixed feelings. It was there that she had last seen her baby sister Charity, who at the time, she remembered, had been teething. As a tear floated in her eye, Emma realised that sometimes looking up old memories was not wise, and she wished that she could have been a comfort to her mother when the baby died.

~

Charlotte still slept as Emma crept into the bedchamber. Her sleep now seemed more natural as Emma looked down on the woman who did not like her, and who she did not like. And she could only wonder why Martin had lied about calling the doctor. One thing that Emma did feel was that it would be best not to let Martin know that she had spoken to him. The less Martin knew, the more power Emma had. Now knowing that Charlotte was not ill, or at least not ill enough for the doctor to have been called, Emma took the laudanum and poured most of it out of the window before refilling the container to the same level with water from the jug in the dressing room. Placing it back in its position on the table beside the bed, Emma returned to her own room. She needed to talk to Charlotte and hoped that Martin wouldn't notice, when next she administered the dose, that the mixture was different.

~

Emma was in the library reading when Richard arrived, bursting in through the library door and standing looking at her as though she were the Devil.

'So, madam, you are back and already causing trouble.'

The door opening so forcibly had destroyed the quietness of the library and made Emma jump. But on seeing Richard, she lowered her book and replied coolly, 'Good evening, Richard.'

Walking into the room he stood before her, frowning angrily. 'I have looked at my mother and there seems nothing wrong with her. Martin tells me that she is still upset at the death of her husband, nothing more.'

'If I have worried you for no reason, Richard, then I'm sorry. Martin told me that the doctor had been called and when I saw the doctor he said that he had not been to see your mother. I just wanted to find out what ailed her and if you knew.'

'I am too busy, Emma, to be called here every time that my mother has one of her turns. You should let Martin deal with it.'

'Oh, and is Martin qualified in your eyes to deal with so much, Richard?'

His face flushed as his eyebrows knitted together in another frown. 'What do you mean, Emma?'

'Did you know that Mrs Jenk was found dead? And that Martin, a mere servant, arranged her replacement, without interview by your mother or even Patrick, who is a senior servant in this house?'

'Patrick was with me dealing with the problems of a farm and if Martin found a woman to step in, then that is good. Mother will interview her when she is well enough, and I don't think that any of this was cause enough to send for me.'

They glared at each other in the silence that fell upon the room until Emma said quietly, 'Your father, Richard, managed the farms from this house. Why have you moved into the Freelanders farmhouse?'

He spoke equally quietly in reply but there was an edge to his voice. 'I do not have to justify myself to you, madam.'

'But I am your wife, Richard.' Emma felt the hurt and was sure that he saw it in her eyes.

'Wife, Emma!' His voice rose. 'You are not my wife. Not here in this house or ever. Our marriage was a mistake and you know it as well as I.'

He sat heavily into a leather-bound chair opposite her. 'If I were not at this time so busy, I would have sent for my solicitor and the divorce would be underway. I have proof that I have *not* slept with you while you have been in this house and, with no children, I can say that I have never slept with you, that I realised my mistake as soon as the marriage ceremony ended. It could be annulled, Emma. It would be less messy and quicker.'

She fought against the tears that would ruin her fake composure but could not speak because her throat was constricted with emotion. She could only hide her distress by looking down at her hands. Why was she so unwanted even by her husband?

An uncomfortable silence cloaked the room and Emma felt herself receding into a quiet, unresponsive place. It was Richard that spoke first. 'I'm sorry, Emma.'

At hearing the regret in his voice, she lifted her head and looked at him. He looked tired and spoke slowly, as though all the world were upon his shoulders.

'You knew that I didn't want to return here. That I ran away to be free from all of this. With the death of my father, I have no option but to take on the duties of the Manor, looking after the house, the servants, the farms. I'm not a man with that sort of expertise, Emma. I hate it and I'm sinking.'

'You had to come home, Richard.' In her heart she knew the struggle that he was having; that he hadn't wanted to come back. 'The bullet,' she continued, 'is still in your body, you needed to see someone, a surgeon.'

'Oh yes, Emma! I was forced to travel for months on a ship that in itself could have killed me. And after all that, the doctor I saw in London could do nothing for me, but cut off my arms or legs looking for it. And now I am here, the last place in the world that I want to be, with all the responsibilities that I did not want.'

'I'm sorry, Richard. I'm doing my best also. I am not enjoying being here any more than you. I'm also out of my depth in this situation. Could we not help each other, Richard?'

'No!' He stood abruptly, his face set in an unreadable mask. 'It's too late for that.'

Striding across the room without another word, he left. Moments later she heard horses racing down the driveway towards the road and as the sound disappeared into the distance she broke down and cried.

20.

Celia Martin sat in the large kitchen and did not feel at ease. She had often wondered about the place that her daughter worked, but she could never have imagined its vastness, compared to her own three-roomed cottage. The whole move had been a disappointment to her. She had lost her rented cottage when taking this job, and her independence, little though that had been. Here, she was cut off from her neighbours and her friends who had been such a large part of her life after the death of her husband. She and Giles had, until his death, never had a day apart. They had grown up together, their parents being neighbours, and as expected by everyone had married. Their first and only child, Mary, had been a joy to them and maybe she had been spoilt, as every other pregnancy was lost. They had hoped that one day Mary would marry well and were excited for her when she got a job at the Manor House with the Laddisbrocks. That, in the mind of Giles and herself, was an opportunity that Mary would not otherwise have had to better herself, living as they were in the village, where there was little work but in the fields, on low wages, for the men.

Celia was a widow by the time she noticed that her daughter was putting on weight. But she put this down to the good food that Mary was eating, until she arrived home one night in pain. By morning Celia had a grandson and her daughter, against advice, had returned to work, leaving the child with its grandmother. Mary would not disclose the father's name and Celia knew it must be one of the servants. The girl had brought with her some old sheets and an antique feeding bottle to help with the birth, nothing else. It was a strain looking after a baby at Celia's age, but her neighbours had helped. A woman in the village who had, that same week, lost her three-month-old daughter still had milk. Celia remembered vividly how she'd had to find the courage to knock on the woman's door, her grandson in her arms, so soon after the woman's loss to ask for help with the feeding. She expected to be turned away and to be burying her daughter's baby herself. Amazingly the woman asked her in and fed Thomas. She told Celia that she was happy to help, as her breasts were painful with milk. The room in which they sat was not large and there were many children. A two-year-old climbing onto its mother's knee took the other breast from the bodice and suckled along with Thomas. The woman, who had had a child each year, told Celia that the doctor had told her she would have no more.

There was little money coming from Mary and nothing from the father, and Celia had struggled for money and food. Now, she observed the male servants, looking for a trace of similarity to Thomas, but so far no one looked anything like her grandson. But worse than that, Celia had witnessed her daughter bullying some of the servants. Knowing who Celia was, the servants avoided her. She felt lonely and, worse still, so was Thomas. He had no one to play with and got himself into trouble being inquisitive about everything that surrounded him in the kitchen. It had also been made clear to her, behind Mary's back, by a servant known as West, that a child should not have been brought into the house. That the incapacitated mistress of the house would not have given her the job, nor agreed to a child being below stairs. Celia had said nothing to Mary, having seen how she had attacked Jacob, slapping him about the head and yelling at him for something she believed that he had done.

That same night, Celia had heard him crying and had determined to mother him next day whether her Mary liked it or not. But by morning Jacob had disappeared. 'Run away,' Mary had said without any sense of regret that Celia could see. The servants had searched for him, but he had not been found and the bad feeling against the Martins increased.

When the master, who Celia had only seen from a distance, went to live temporarily at one of the farms, taking some of the servants with him, Celia was glad. The staff hadn't even tried to get to know her. She had never in her whole life been unkind to a soul, and here she was shunned, and why? Because of the daughter that she had loved more than life itself.

Celia knew nothing of the upper classes, but like everyone else in the village had thought that the younger Mrs Laddisbrock should have known better than to try to be a part of them. But she had to admit that when the young woman had come to the kitchen she had seemed pleasant, approachable. Celia had in the last few days realised something else that she had not thought of before. And that was, that although living here was better for Thomas, who had good food and saw more of his mother, if she, Celia, lost this job, if the older Mrs Laddisbrock didn't like her, then she had no home to return to. It would be the workhouse for her and Thomas. As a servant, Mary could not work here or anywhere with a child.

21.

It was the day of Nona and Dan's wedding and on Tate Farm the excitement could almost be tasted as Alice and John tried to get everyone ready for the ceremony. Their eldest girl, Lilly, was a quiet child but her sibling by one year, Elsbeth, was demanding and loud. Below her in age was Michael, a robust child who at nine was able to do a full day's work in the fields during summer with his father and Dan. The next youngest was Albert, a thin, pale boy of seven, and then Molly, a bossy five-year-old with red hair, who always knew better than everyone else. She and Elsbeth quarrelled endlessly at full pitch over the smallest of things. The only child that Emma knew was William. He, amid all the chaos, was helping Dolly by putting together bunches of wild flowers, to make posies for his sisters to carry. He sat at the table with Dolly, tying the flower stems together with ribbon, his tongue poking out of his mouth in concentration.

Most of the table was taken up with cooked food and it was obvious to Emma that Dolly, Nona and Alice had worked very hard to get enough food together for them to eat as a celebration on their return from the church. The centrepiece was a goose, golden and plump. There were two chickens, two large loaves of bread, butter from the dairy, apples from the orchard, a large lamb pie, spicy bread pudding and a barrel of cider from last year's pressing.

Nona stepped into the kitchen, smiling at everyone, and Emma's heart almost stopped with the pride that she felt. Here was the girl, sickly as a child, now a grown woman, glowing with the excitement of her wedding day, dressed in a cream top with four tight pleats at the front and a matching skirt with one large pleat forming a panel at the front as wide as the four pleats above. She did a small twirl before the gathered family. Around her waist she wore a wide green ribbon tied at the back in a bow. And Emma wished with all her heart that their mother could have been here to see it.

'Nona, you're beautiful, that dress is so lovely. I have never seen anything like it.'

Nona's face glowed. 'Dolly made it, isn't it wonderful? The wide pleat,' she smoothed it with her hand, 'is so that when I am with child I can still wear the dress to church.' And with that she did another elegant and slow twirl.

'I will try and draw a picture of it and send it to Mother with a letter telling her about the day,' Emma said. 'I know that she craves news of us.'

An hour later the wedding party left the house dressed in their Sunday best; the girls, wearing flowers in their hair, held the posies.

It was an excited and loud wedding party that walked through the lanes to the village. Dolly held her husband Tom's arm and looked younger than usual as she smiled and laughed with the children who surrounded Alice and John like a flock of chicks.

Emma noticed Tom glance at his wife, and witnessed him smiling proudly, their love for each other after all these years wonderful to behold; it was what every woman dreamed of, a life with a good and loving man.

Dolly, Emma knew, was aware of what had happened to Nona when she was eleven at the hands of the rent collector, and the trauma that the family lived through after that. But Emma had not told Dolly how the experience still affected Nona, and she wondered if she should have told Dolly about the death of the Logans, especially Neil Logan, by Nona's gun. If Dolly knew that, would she be so happy that her son Dan was marrying Nona?

Would the wedding be going ahead? She had turned it over and over in her mind. But Nona was happy and the joining of two people in love, in their bed, with Nona's consent and willingness, would, Emma hoped, be different for her. Would heal her.

At the church they were met by the Reverend Draycott, who welcomed each by name as they walked through the door. And it was obvious to Emma that Nona, as part of her new family, was now attending church regularly with them, and that she had in a short time found a place in the community. Something that Emma and her mother had not been able to do.

The Reverend Draycott greeted Emma, who had hung back and was last to step through the doorway. As he took her hand he spoke kindly and with a sense of quiet urgency that unnerved her. 'Please come and see me, Mrs Laddisbrock, when you can.'

And there it was. Out in the open. It was like a blow to her stomach as Emma realised that she had been fooling no one but herself by staying out of sight on Charlotte's orders, believing that no one would know her secret. She felt dazed as she followed the Reverend through the church and took her place amongst the wedding party.

The wedding service was, it felt to Emma, endless. She was not at home in the church and felt hemmed in by the congregation who had turned out in force to see the young people married. As the Reverend Draycott droned on, Emma found herself thinking about her own wedding to Richard. Their joining had happened because a wandering priest had turned up at the homestead and Martha had invited him to stay overnight and to eat with them. A day later, she and Richard were married in Emma's cabin surrounded by Emma's family. They had exchanged their vows, but the long ceremony of today, being so much more involved, left Emma wondering if she was indeed married to Richard.

After Nona and Dan's ceremony it seemed to Emma that the whole village was following them cheerfully back to the farm. A line of bobbing heads and chattering people walked through the lanes to partake of the celebration, dancing and food.

There was much laughter as the bride and groom were toasted during the warmth of the afternoon. Tom Mott welcomed Nona into his family and joked that it was he who should be celebrating, as he had not so much gained a daughter but a cheap and worthy farmhand, as well as more space in the house. As the guests laughed, the fiddlers started up with a happy tune and the dancing and eating commenced in earnest.

Emma stood quietly on the fringe of the merriment and felt the pangs of loss. The loss of her sister, the loss of her husband and of the way of life that she had had here with her family, now so far away.

22.

It was late afternoon by the time Emma arrived back at the Manor House. As she walked up the steps and through the front door an agitated Carter met her. It was obvious that she had been pacing the hallway, and looked relieved when she saw Emma.

'Madam, Mrs Laddisbrock is in need of help, please come quickly.'

'Where is Martin?' Emma's first thought was that Martin should be looking after Charlotte.

'The mistress will have nothing to do with Martin and is calling for you, madam.'

Emma followed the maid up the stairs at speed and took a deep breath at the door of Charlotte's bedchamber before opening it.

What she saw frightened her. Someone had smashed every pot, every mirror in the room. The bedding had been stripped from the bed and torn into shreds, the curtains pulled to the floor, and amidst it all a silent and bloody Charlotte sat on the floor, her hair and clothes dishevelled.

At the sight, Emma was aware of Carter taking a step backwards away from the door.

With her heart beating hard in her chest Emma stepped into the room and closed the door on the maid.

'What has happened here? Who did this?' She was aware that her voice trembled with the shock of what she was seeing, and to steady it took a deep breath.

Charlotte laughed hysterically and pulled at her hair. Her hands, Emma saw, were covered in blood.

Not knowing what Charlotte's reaction would be towards her, Emma moved forward slowly.

'You wanted to see me, madam. I am here.'

Charlotte turned her head and looked with wild eyes at Emma, laughing manically. Then, trying to stand, she toppled over onto her face. That is when Emma saw the extent of the cuts and blood on Charlotte's feet. She must have walked bare foot on the broken glass. Opening the door sharply Emma instructed Carter to send for the doctor, *immediately*.

With the side of her boot, Emma pushed some of the larger pieces of glass and shards of porcelain to the side of the room so that she could walk safely, then tried to help Charlotte to her feet.

The woman leant heavily upon her and they both staggered towards a chair. When she was sitting, Emma took up some of the shredded bedding and wrapped it around Charlotte's feet.

Hearing hooves on the drive Emma was relieved to see from the window Gant riding for the doctor.

'What has happened, madam?' She kept her voice gentle, not wanting to antagonise the woman further.

Charlotte's body seemed to have shrunk since Emma last saw her and now she sat shaking her head in a despair that Emma didn't understand.

'Has Richard been to see you?' Emma asked, wondering if they had fallen out.

Her mother-in-law looked at her with disdain. 'My son? The owner of this estate?' She laughed manically again and tears rolled over her sunken cheeks.

'Something has happened, madam. Tell me what it is. I can't help you if I don't know what is wrong.'

The woman became suddenly serious. '*You* cannot help *me*. *You* have no breeding and clean my room like a servant. One amongst many who would better themselves at the feet of my son.'

There was no ignoring the bitterness in her voice and Emma was at a loss. With Charlotte in this mood she was not going to find out what had been the cause of this disturbing behaviour.

Opening the door, Emma was pleased to see Carter still standing on the landing.

'I thought that I would wait and see if you needed anything, madam,' she said. 'Someone has gone for the doctor.' She looked pale, near to tears, her limbs shaking.

'Yes, thank you, Carter. I want to put Mrs Laddisbrock in her husband's bedchamber for now, until we can repair this room. Would you get a couple of the maids to help you prepare it for her?'

'Yes, madam, right away.'

'Oh, and tell Mrs Martin that I will be eating in the dining room from now on.'

Charlotte was sitting where she had been left, in the chair with her feet bound, but was now rocking back and forth, her arms wrapped around her middle, moaning.

Emma was at a loss. What could she do to help the woman? It was clear she would not be able to walk without a great deal of pain.

She was about to ask again what had caused so much distress when the doctor entered the room without knocking. For a moment he stood stock still, looking around at the devastation, before stepping over it to get to Charlotte saying, 'Help me get her onto the bed, Mrs Laddisbrock.'

He bent towards Charlotte, not bothering to straighten her clothes, and taking a leg and an arm each they lifted and manhandled Charlotte to her bed, where the doctor was better able to remove the glass from her feet and bathe and dress them.

'I don't know the cause of this, sir,' Emma said quietly to the doctor as she pulled a cover up over Charlotte who now lay back with her eyes shut, exhausted. 'I have been trying to ask her, but she doesn't make any sense.'

'I am going to give her some laudanum, but the dose must be kept small, just enough to help her sleep and only for a few days.'

He pulled a small bottle from his leather valise. 'She is having a typical reaction, a side effect of having had too much laudanum and then having it suddenly withdrawn.'

Emma felt the guilt, but said nothing. From now on she would give Charlotte the medicine herself, and would keep the bottle in her own pocket where no one would have access to it.

'I am having her moved to another room, sir. Should I wait until she is settled there before giving her the medicine?'

'Yes, that would be preferable, then she may sleep. People who have had too much of the drug may suffer loss of appetite. But if you could get her to eat something so that she is not absorbing it on an empty stomach, that would help a great deal.'

'I will try, Doctor.' Emma smiled ruefully, knowing that to get Charlotte to do anything that she did not want to do would be a futile struggle.

That evening Emma ate in the dining room alone. The silence cloaked her ears and she did not enjoy the experience. The servant, who would normally have stood at one end of the room waiting for her to finish each course, had been told to stand outside the door and that she would summon him with the small bell that was on the table. That at least gave her some relief from the eyes that constantly watched her. It had to be done. She was taking charge and the servants needed to know that.

The food was not good. The lamb broth was tasteless and greasy. The chicken was dry and the potatoes burnt. She sighed; she would have to speak to Mrs Martin. To have to eat food like this was unacceptable. Leaving the dining room after the meal she made her way below stairs.

Mrs Martin was clearing the surfaces and her daughter was sitting at the table watching her mother work as Emma entered the kitchen. The overall sound in this basement room was of the scullery maids scrubbing at the burnt pans.

'I am glad that you are also here, Martin.' Emma spoke immediately she entered the kitchen, taking the women by surprise. 'I need to talk to you about your employment here, Martin.'

Mary Martin stood up, frowning at Emma. 'And you are going to speak to me, about my work here, in front of everyone?' Martin replied, recovering from the shock quickly.

Emma nodded agreement. 'As you have made it clear to me, Martin, that I am not of the upper class, why should I know any different?'

The sound of scrubbing in the scullery had stopped and Emma knew that the maids were listening intently.

'It seems, Martin, that Mrs Laddisbrock no longer wants you as her maid and there is no other work here for you, unless you agree to help your mother in the kitchen. I give you until the morning to think that over, Martin.'

Without waiting for a reply Emma turned to Celia. 'Mrs Martin, I am sorry, but the food this evening was not edible. Do you have an explanation?'

Celia's hands were shaking as she turned to look first at Mary and then at Emma.

'I'm sorry, madam. I have only ever cooked for three people and in the last few years only two and I have rarely had meat to cook.'

Emma felt sorry for the small woman who was visibly shaken.

'I understand the difficulty in cooking for a large household, Mrs Martin, and I would not have employed you, because it would have been obvious to me that you would not manage. And, I believe that Mrs Laddisbrock would have felt the same. As you know, my mother-in-law is unwell and I need good food coming out of this kitchen. I will give you one more day with the help of your daughter, who knows the type of food that is expected upstairs. And if you fail, I am afraid that I will have to let you both go.'

Both women stood with the same expression of disbelief on their faces.

'I will see you in the reception room in the morning, Mrs Martin, and we will go through the menu for the day together.'

In the stunned silence that followed Emma turned and left the two shocked women standing open-mouthed, staring at an empty doorway.

Smiling as she walked up the back stairs Emma felt that at last she had taken charge. That, she knew, would probably change when Charlotte was better, and/or when Richard returned and their marriage was annulled. But until then she would run the household and she would do it well and take no nonsense.

~

Celia Martin sat down heavily on a chair at the table. All colour had drained from her face as she spoke to her daughter.

'You realise, Mary, that if I lose this job, Thomas and I will have nowhere to live.'

'He will live with me, Mother, don't fret about that.'

Her words were sharply delivered and cut Celia to the bone. In response she shook her head and looked squarely at her daughter.

'No, Mary! Thomas will never live with you. I saw the way that you treated Jacob and he was a good boy.'

'He was not a good boy, Mother. Always sticking his nose in where it wasn't wanted. I couldn't move but he was there.'

'And it would be no different for Thomas. No, I will not let you take him.'

'So, what, Mother? You will take him with you to the workhouse? Will you not be separated then? How is that going to be better for him?'

Mary turned and strode into the scullery. The maids did not hear her coming, and Celia heard her daughter shouting at the two maids and heard her slap them before Mary again came into the kitchen, her face red with anger.

'This, Mother,' she shouted, 'is all your fault. At your age you should know how to cook.' And with that she left the room, leaving everyone stunned.

Celia held back the tears and for the first time approached the scullery maids, and seeing the raised hand marks on their flushed faces she apologised for the daughter she no longer knew.

23.

If Charlotte wanted the medication then she had to eat. If she did not eat, then the food and the laudanum were removed for one hour before being brought back. Soon, she was taking a little beef broth, which had improved in flavour. The food was not as it had been before when Mrs Jenk was in charge, but was no longer greasy or dry.

Emma did not want to start again with another unknown cook and had no idea about interviewing. Charlotte was still without a maid to help her dress and do her hair, and that had to be addressed quickly. With her views on hierarchy and staff positions she would not let Emma help her. There was nothing for it but that Carter was volunteered as Charlotte's new maid.

The girl was terrified of Charlotte and Emma, knowing that this position would also not last very long, sighed.

~

Emma awoke slowly; although she had slept the night through she still felt tired when Carter arrived with her water, placing it in the dressing room. Returning to draw back Emma's bed covers she exclaimed in alarm, 'Oh, madam, where did you get that bruise on your arm?'

Emma looked at the place where Carter stared and saw on the inside of her upper arm a massive bruise. 'I don't know, Carter, I don't remember knocking it, unless it was when I was lifting Mrs Laddisbrock. She was a dead weight. I don't know how anyone so small can be so heavy.'

When dressed, Emma went to visit Charlotte and was surprised to find Richard standing in the room. The pair had been deep in conversation, which stopped as she entered.

In a moment of fear and surprise Emma stepped into the room, slowly turning and closing the door behind her.

'Good morning, Richard,' she said, trying to sound light and friendly. 'It's very good to see you, your mother is now a lot stronger.'

Charlotte reacted angrily. 'Don't talk in front of me as though I am not here, madam.'

Emma ignored the outburst, having become used to them, and turned to Richard.

'Is all well now on Freelanders Farm, Richard?'

'No, Emma, it has become obvious to me that I need someone to live in and run the farm, a new tenant who knows what he is doing.'

'I wonder if you would consider my sister and her new husband, Daniel Mott. They have both been involved in farming since an early age. They are, at the moment, living and working on the Tate Farm, but I am sure, like all young couples, they would be glad to have a tenancy of their own.'

'Your sister!' He twisted his mouth and frowned. Something that Emma recognised he did when seriously considering something.

'You know her, Richard,' Emma prompted, 'and how capable she is.' She wanted to add, 'and she risked her life to save yours, Richard,' but instead said, 'Would you not think about speaking to them both, see what they are capable of together?'

'I will think about it. Thank you, madam.'

Emma stared at him in disbelief. Now she was reduced to madam by her husband?

Unable to stay any longer in the same room with them she turned to leave without another word, but did not miss in Charlotte's raised eyebrows what Emma recognised as triumph.

~

During the afternoon Emma decided to take a walk, needing to shake off the hostile atmosphere of the house. She didn't want to race through the lanes on a horse or get someone to drive her in a carriage as her status would normally require. She wanted to walk. To be in touch with the nature of her country. Only now that she was back did she realise the pain that she had endured being removed from it. She was very aware that she was acting like a servant, or peasant, but that is what she was and that is what she understood. She knew now, that there would never be any reconciliation between herself and her mother-in-law, or her husband, and her coming to terms with that fact was giving Emma some peace. She was who she was, and she could not and did not know how to change.

The day seemed joyful as long-tailed tits made their way down the hedgerow twittering excitedly in a large group. When a robin sang with a loud voice on a branch above her head, she stopped to look up at it. He looked back at her, his head on one side, his perfectly round black eye watching her quizzically. She smiled, staring back, her own head on one side. As he lost interest and started his song again she walked on. At the side of the path she saw meadowsweet and yellow flag standing amongst the hedgerow and a secret crab apple pushing through the unkempt hawthorn hedge.

At the end of the lane she entered a meadow that quietly slumbered on the south side of the village. Walking slowly through the long grass as it dragged at her skirt, she heard the buzz of insects and smelt the fragrance of sweet cicely and Alexanders as they mingled amongst the cow parsley. She'd had no other intention but to walk and get away from the house when she had started out, but now seeing the church steeple in the distance towering over the cottages that made up the village, she decided that she would do as he had asked and call on the Reverend Draycott.

Climbing over a stile, she stepped down onto the road that led into the village. The road into this compact civilisation was narrow and as she got nearer the smell of wood smoke filled the air. This was a smell that Emma never tired of – it, as much as the natural beauty of England, reminded her that she was home.

As she increased her pace she became aware of heads turning, the villagers staring after her. She didn't know them and wasn't sure if they remembered her, or perhaps they thought her to be a stranger in the village. After so many years, why would they remember her?

Passing the lychgate at the entrance to the churchyard, she continued until she came to the largest house within the village. The vicar's house stood back off the road hidden behind a hedge; built of dark red brick with vaulted windows to match the church, it seemed austere in appearance. The winding gravel path to the front door was planted each side with large shrubs and mature trees, and behind them an apple orchard. The overgrown foliage should have given the feeling of shelter and protection but Emma began to feel trapped, nervous and unsure about how much of her story to tell, or even if she should tell the vicar anything. Perhaps what worried her the most was that she didn't know what he would ask her.

Rapping hard on the door with her knuckles she stood back. Pulling her shawl up around her shoulders she chewed nervously at the inside of her mouth as she waited. Feeling relieved when no one opened the door immediately she turned away just before she heard footsteps on the gravel path. Walking towards her, Emily Draycott was smiling at the sight of Emma.

'Mrs Laddisbrock, how wonderful to see you. Ernest will be very happy that you have called. Come inside and I will have some biscuits brought to us and some tea. And no, we have not suddenly become rich enough to buy it, it was a present from Ernest's uncle. I am getting used to the taste. Ernest doesn't like it but you and I will enjoy it with some of Mrs Pendell's biscuits. Being cooked yesterday they are now nice and crisp.'

Emily left no time for Emma to answer as she guided her through the hallway and into the large front room where the smell of soot emanating from the cold fireplace vied with the sweeter fragrance of freshly cut logs stacked in the alcove and candle wax. The room, although large with a high ceiling, was dark with solid furniture; there were two comfortable chairs, one each side of the fireplace, each with its own small table, and another with heavily carved legs stood in the window piled high with papers. Emma was directed to one of the comfortable chairs while Emily went to organise the tea.

As she waited for Emily to reappear, Emma looked around her. Two of the walls she noticed, now that she was seated, were shelved and lined with books. Several of those books she noted were bibles and wondered why the vicar would need more than one. As she sat alone with the silent peace of the room settling about her head and shoulders, she might once have relaxed, but instead was unsettled. Wondering if she had time to walk out and run away before Emily returned, she flexed her muscles to stand just as the door opened. It was Ernest that entered and behind him came Mrs Pendell with a tray.

Ernest took the seat opposite Emma as Mrs Pendell poured the tea, which, she announced, had been steeped for the right amount of time. Emma nodded as though she recognised what the elderly woman was trying to impart.

The plate of biscuits was taken from the tray and placed in the middle of the table. 'This,' the woman told Emma proudly, 'was my mother's recipe.'

Emma nodded her thanks and, smiling up into the wrinkled face, wondered if Charlotte would allow a servant to speak out like that. It was quite confusing.

Noticing Emma's look, Ernest said when the woman had gone, 'Mrs Pendell has been here a long time. Longer than Emily and I. She was with the last vicar who I believe was himself rather outspoken.' The smile he gave Emma was more like a grimace as he continued, 'She follows suit, but is a good soul, even with a mind of her own.'

His smile did not light his face and Emma was reminded of what the doctor had said to her about the danger of servants that couldn't be controlled. Ernest poured himself some red wine from a carafe while Emma sipped the strong tea. The brown liquid brought back the memory of the tea that she and Nell had enjoyed at Claydon House, it being steeped again from the mistress's used tea leaves. Except that this tea was dark and coated her teeth, making her tongue dry. Taking a biscuit offered by Ernest, she found it laced with strong aniseed and, leaving most of it on the plate, sat back in the chair waiting.

Ernest took another mouthful of his wine before placing the goblet slowly on the table, looking at her with concern written upon his face.

'How are your stepfather and mother, Mrs Laddisbrock?'

'They were well when I left them, sir, and of course they send their regards to you and your wife.' She waited; this wasn't why he had invited her to drop in when passing.

'And your brothers?'

'Yes, sir, equally well when I left.' She waited.

'It was your sister that told me of your difficulties.' He frowned. 'May I call you Emma again, Mrs Laddisbrock?'

Emma was glad of it for she would not much longer hold that title. 'Yes, sir, if that is what you would like.'

He looked thoughtful and she could see that he was picking his words carefully.

'When you boarded that ship, Emma, you were a young girl, but you have returned a woman.' Frowning he suddenly changed tack saying, 'Emily and I would like to be your friend and invite you to use our given names, in private.'

Emma nodded, somewhat surprised. Would he feel the same when she was no longer gentry? Was he that shallow?

As he filled his goblet again she thought, *He wouldn't dare call Charlotte by her given name and she's gentry, but he would call a villager Benjamin or Mary.* Confused, she felt her spirits declining. In the silence that followed she took another sip of tea and wished that she hadn't as her mouth became dry again.

'I am glad that your family are well, Emma, but I wonder why you, your sister and your husband have returned.'

'Is it that unusual for people to return home, Ernest?' she replied quickly.

'I believe that the journey is fraught with danger and not something that some would do twice without good reason.'

He didn't look her in the face and she didn't know how much he knew or needed to know, or what Charlotte may have told him.

'What did my mother-in-law tell you, sir?' she countered. She could feel deception, and purposely used the address 'sir' to let him know it.

Ignoring the slight, he said, 'Mrs Laddisbrock did not tell me that you were married to her son.' Now, he looked directly into Emma's face. 'She let me believe that you were merely visiting. Of course, I did think that strange as she did not know you before you travelled and, you are not...'

'Of her class?' Emma finished for him, eyebrows raised.

'Yes. Exactly.' He did not look away.

'In the New World, Ernest,' Emma began, still feeling slighted even though she knew it to be the truth, 'there is no class system. It is a struggle just to survive and everyone pulls together to stay alive. When I married Richard I didn't know who he was. He lied about his name, calling himself Richard Ladd. I just loved him.' She closed her eyes, remembering the first time that she had seen the new farmhand and how good looking she thought he was. 'At first,' she continued, 'he worked well with Andrew and the boys, until he discovered a small township growing up some miles away where he began to spend more time than working.'

Ernest raised an eyebrow, but said nothing, leaving Emma wondering whether she should tell him the truth, but said instead, 'My husband got himself into some trouble and was shot by some ruffians. Andrew and Martha tried, but couldn't remove the bullet. It was decided that Richard should come home and get the medical help that he needed, but the doctors here can't find the bullet as it's moving around his body.'

'I understand,' Ernest said simply, nodding his head sagely. But Emma knew that he could not possibly understand and felt anger rising in her chest. She hated insincerity.

'You have returned,' he continued, unaware of her feelings, 'and found yourself in a class that does not accept you.'

'Yes,' she sighed, 'and they are making it very difficult for me. I may as well tell you, Ernest, as you will soon know. Mrs Laddisbrock wants Richard to divorce me.'

'Divorce!' Ernest retaliated quickly. 'Can they afford that, Emma?'

'I don't know.' She shook her head and tried to deny the tears that were welling up in her eyes. 'It isn't something that I have ever heard of. I worry what will happen to me, for I have no money and no other home here. Sometimes, they say they will give me money and other times not.'

She might have expected him to show some feeling for her situation but all he said was, 'What sort of church did you marry in, Emma?'

'There was no church!' She looked bravely into his face, wondering what he was thinking, and continued, 'A travelling clergyman married us in my cabin. All my family were witness,' she added quickly, knowing that a witness was important.

'So, the reason that you are to be divorced is that the Laddisbrocks find your previous station embarrassing?'

'My mother-in-law wishes Richard to marry into his own class. She needs a grandchild to carry on their line, and a dowry.'

He nodded, seeming to understand her position. 'It is a difficult situation for you, Emma. If this happens, what will you do?'

At this Emma shook her head. 'I really don't know, if I am without money. They have indicated that this may happen unless

I go quietly, and what they mean is if I don't agree to the divorce. Perhaps I will go to Robert and live with him. I could help him with his parish work.'

Ernest raised an eyebrow, a look of surprise on his face.

Knowing why Ernest reacted in this way, she thought that she would put him straight and did it forcefully.

'Just because I do not go to church, sir, does not mean that I do not believe in a God, or that helping others with a kind heart is beyond me.' She delivered this statement with eyes flashing and face reddening, and when she saw that he looked shocked at her outburst, she wasn't sorry.

He apologised quickly. 'I'm sorry, Emma. I didn't mean to upset you. I am just trying to understand what is going on in the household.'

'And of what interest is it to you, sir?' Her anger had not receded with his apology.

Ernest quickly changed the subject. 'I understand that while you were away Mrs Laddisbrock became ill and that Mrs Jenk was found dead in the lane and that a new cook has been employed.'

Of course, Emma realised that he knew everything that happened in the village. He and the doctor were informed or involved in every illness or death, but she still felt anger and it was in her voice as she addressed him. 'You are very well-informed, sir.'

There was no longer any friendliness in her voice as she looked at the man who held such sway in the village and yet was the only one who she could say, other than Dolly, could be called a friend.

'Please, Emma, call me Ernest. I am trying to help you, but I need to know what is happening.'

'I really cannot see, Ernest, how you can help me. I am doing my best to manage in very difficult circumstances. I am given no respect from either my husband or the staff and I have decided now to take charge, whether they like it or not, until Charlotte is back to health and then…' She couldn't finish, there was nothing to finish. It was always going to finish badly for her.

'What is happening with the servants?' he asked.

She blew out a long breath. 'I don't know. It's an unhappy house. I can't say too much as I am trying to find out what is wrong myself. I think that one servant is at the root of the unhappiness but that cannot be proved and I cannot diminish the staff further. Also, it isn't for me to dismiss servants that Mrs Laddisbrock employed. I feel that I cannot do it without her permission and my husband has made it clear that this one servant in particular, that I do not trust, should not be dismissed. Also…' she now unloaded all her fears, 'I don't know what is wrong with Charlotte, why she was given laudanum by a servant who lied that the doctor had seen her. And I am worried about the whereabouts of Jacob, our boot boy, who has no family and is missing. The servants tell me that they searched for him in the house and in the grounds but that he couldn't be found.'

She was aware that she was beginning to sound hysterical but she couldn't stop, this being her first time to tell anyone about the life that she had been enduring. She needed to tell someone that she was out of her depth and worried about the boy.

Nodding his head, Ernest stood and went to the door. 'Excuse me, Emma. I will be back, please don't leave. Will you give me your promise?'

She agreed, shaking with emotion and too wrung out to leave. She wasn't sure that she'd done the right thing in telling him so much; if what she had told Ernest got back to her husband, she would be in trouble and probably destitute.

She was not prepared for what happened next. Emily stepped into the room and, holding back a little, but clearly seen, was Jacob.

Emma stood immediately. 'Jacob!' She held her arms out to him and he ran to her.

'That is what I wanted to see,' Ernest said as he followed Emily into the room. 'You see, Jacob has been here for three days. We found him hiding in the back of the church. He was dirty, hungry and cold. He will not or cannot tell us what has happened to him. He becomes distressed when we suggest taking him back to the Laddisbrocks'. And so, I had to question you, Emma, I am sorry. I don't know who or what is the reason for his running away.'

Emma bent to the boy now standing with his head lowered, staring at his shoes. 'Jacob, can you tell me why you ran away?' Emma asked gently.

He fidgeted as though he had a stone in his shoe but said nothing. 'Will you come back with me?' she asked.

He shook his head violently and when she tipped his face up to look at him his skin was as white as milk, his eyes full of fear, and his breathing had become fast and shallow.

Emily rushed for a small bowl sitting on the bookshelf and held it in front of him just as he retched into it. She looked up at Emma and shook her head. 'Something has really frightened him, Emma.'

'It's alright, Jacob,' Emma said, rubbing his back. 'I won't make you go back but can you tell me what happened to you?'

At that he retched again, and Emily knelt and cuddled him saying, 'Don't worry, Jacob, you can stay here with us.' She looked at Emma, who nodded in agreement. How could anyone force him when he was so frightened?

It was a different Emma that walked back the way she had come. This Emma saw nothing of the beauty of the countryside, so caught up was she with what had happened and with thinking about what she should do about it.

By the time she had reached her room she had decided to keep the fact that Jacob was safe to herself. She wanted to know what had happened to him, but that would have to come in its own time.

24.

A week passed in which Emma suffered stomach pain and several severe nosebleeds, and her tiredness continued. The walk that she had taken so happily on that first day to the vicarage was now beyond her strength. On the following occasions that she had gone to see Jacob she had ridden a horse that Matt had made available for her use. Although Jacob had looked happy to see her, he had not spoken about why he had run away. He seemed at home with the Draycotts and Emma had seen Emily working in the garden with Jacob at her side carrying her basket. And it was obvious to Emma that Emily looked very happy with Jacob in tow and seemed to enjoy his company.

'I hope that you don't mind, Emma,' Emily's sweet voice scattered her thoughts as she approached the pair in the garden, 'but I have been teaching Jacob his letters. It is for something to do more than anything else. For he is lost without a job.'

'I'm glad of it, Emily,' Emma returned, 'for when he is a grown man it will be very useful for him to be able to read.'

'I hoped that you would not be angry.' She smiled in relief.

'I am very rarely angry, Emily.' Emma smiled back. 'Did you know that he loves horses and, if missing, can nearly always be found in the stables yard?'

Emily giggled. 'I think that is one thing that we have already discovered. He spends a lot of time in our stable with Handsome, our grey. And do you know, the horse seems to wait for him in the morning to come and give him his breakfast.'

'Has he spoken yet of why he ran away?' Emma asked quietly. As nothing had been said to her she didn't know if the Draycotts were trying to find out.

'Ernest spoke with him and told him that he could come and speak to us any time he felt that he needed to talk.' She frowned as though wondering whether to say more.

Emma noticed. 'What is it, Emily, do you know something?'

Emily sighed and looked worried. 'I have to trust you, Emma, it was something that we noticed the day we took him in, but, not knowing who to trust we didn't say anything. But now I want to tell you before Jacob speaks to you. So that you are prepared.'

Feeling shocked, Emma wondered what they had known and not told her.

'As Ernest told you, we found him in the church. He was hungry and dirty. We fed him and Mrs Pendell was instructed to wash him. That is when she called us. He had marks on his neck, ankles and wrists. Deep red welts, as though someone had tied him to something. And he'd been whipped by the look of the lines on the top of his legs and across his back. It looks as though he was detained against his will somewhere.'

Emma could hardly believe what she was hearing. 'You think that someone snatched him and kept him against his will?'

Emily raised her shoulders, an indication that she didn't know.

'This is dreadful,' Emma continued, 'there are so many children around the village and on the farms. Are they in danger?'

They stared at each other, neither knowing what to say, before Emma realised what had just been said, an indication of why she hadn't been told.

'Surely, Emily, you didn't think that I would beat a servant like that?' She felt hot with indignation; she had never treated anyone badly. 'You did, didn't you!' She raised her voice accusingly.

Emily looked embarrassed. 'We didn't know what to think, Emma. Perhaps Mrs Laddisbrock, who has been sick, got one of the servants to do it. We just don't know, as Jacob won't tell us anything. Oh, Emma,' she cried suddenly, 'you have a nosebleed. Put your head back while I call Mrs Pendell.'

~

Emma returned home. They were no nearer the truth and nothing was getting sorted out. Her other concern was for Charlotte, who was acting very strangely. Since being on the lower dose of laudanum she was mostly quiet but became stressed at the smallest opportunity. Carter did her best but the girl was constantly being scolded – told that she had brought the wrong dress, or pulled Charlotte's hair when brushing it, or tied her undergarments too loosely or tightly; the washing water was too hot or too cold – and Carter was seen with tears in her eyes more than once. Emma knew that the girl could not take much more, in fact she had lasted longer than Emma thought that she would.

~

It was mid-morning when the library door opened and Nona stood in the doorway.

'I hope you don't mind, Emma, I let myself in.'

'Nona!' Emma put her book to the side and almost before Nona was completely in the room Emma was hugging her. 'It's so good to see you, Nona, come in. You cannot imagine how much I need to talk to you in private.'

She indicated a soft chair on the other side of the fireplace and Nona, with a face flushed from her walk, took it gladly.

'So much has happened and I don't want to talk in front of Dolly when I visit the farm,' Emma said. 'It's difficult to get any privacy there.'

'I know, Emma, but I'm getting used to it and glad that I can talk to Dan in our own home now without someone listening. But I have to tell you, Emma, that we were summoned to Freelanders Farm by Richard. He sent Patrick with a message. We were worried and not sure what he wanted with us. In the end John came with us. But we needn't have worried that we had done something wrong, quite the contrary, he offered us the farm tenancy. We had a look around at the acreage and talked to him about the terms of running it for him and in the end, we decided that we would take it.' Her eyes were sparkling as she continued, 'The papers have been drawn up and Dan has signed them. We move in next week and hope that you will be our first visitor, Emma, if Dolly doesn't beat you to it,' she laughed.

Emma clapped her hand to her mouth; she could hardly believe that Richard had listened to her and given them an interview. 'That is so wonderful, Nona. I know that you can do it, you and Dan are hard workers.'

'It might be that come harvest we will need more help, but John has offered to support us when his harvest is home and of course we will hire workers from the village. When they are finished at Tate they will move on to us. I think that it will work very well.'

When she stopped telling Emma of their plans she asked, 'Now, what do you want to tell me, Emma?'

'I just need someone to talk to, Nona, you know what it's like here with Charlotte.'

Nona nodded; she did indeed know what it was like living with Charlotte. 'I'm sorry, Emma, I haven't asked how you found our brother. Is he well?'

'Yes, he is very well, but I need to talk about another matter.' Emma felt sorry that she had cut Nona off; of course she wanted to know about their brother but that would have to wait. She needed to clear her mind by talking out all that she knew and did not know about the goings-on at the house in her absence.

'Oh!' Nona said, feeling truncated, but could see that something important was in her sister's mind and decided to wait until later to find out about Robert. 'What is it, Emma? You look very serious.'

'While I was away things happened. Charlotte became ill, Richard moved out to Freelanders, Mrs Jenk who seemed so fit died, and Jacob vanished. In that void, Martin took charge, bringing her mother into the house to cover the work of Mrs Jenk without Charlotte's permission. I believe that Martin is a bully and that the other servants don't like her and do her bidding only because they are afraid of her.'

'Can you dismiss her, Emma?'

'No! I suggested it to Richard but he has told me, quite unceremoniously, that I have no rights, that it's not my place to hire or fire servants and that very soon I would have no place to live either.'

'But he allows a servant to hire another servant, Emma, is that not strange?'

'He believes that Charlotte will soon recover and take over again and he is right, that there was no one to cook and that Charlotte and the servants had to be fed. The trouble is that Mrs Martin cannot cook for a large number of people and is out of her depth. I feel sorry for her. She seems genuine and truthful and is as shocked as I at the behaviour of her daughter.'

'You will just have to wait for Charlotte to recover, Emma. How is she?'

'Not at all well. She is even more manic than she ever was. At least then she knew that she was being nasty, it was done on purpose or with a purpose, but now, it is as though she doesn't know what she is doing, she just keeps lashing out, driven by something that is affecting her.'

'Do you think that it's the laudanum?' Nona looked serious, having heard when she lived in London with Martha how that particular medicine could ruin lives and become addictive.

'The doctor said as much, and that, I fear, is my fault. I don't think that Martin knew I was returning and I took her by surprise as she was coming out of Charlotte's room. She blocked me, telling me not to enter. I told her to move and she stared insolently into my eyes. I did enter the room and found Charlotte in such a deep sleep that I couldn't wake her. She was hot and yet her skin was cold and wet, her lips grey. I left her for most of the day and yet could still not wake her. But what I had noticed was a bottle of laudanum and a spoon on the table beside the bed. What I did next was what has caused Charlotte so much pain. I emptied most of the contents out of the window and filled it back to the level with water. When I asked Martin what was wrong with her mistress she told me that she did not know, that the doctor had been called. I walked to the village and asked the doctor about it and he told me that he had not been called to Charlotte since the time after her husband's death when he had left the laudanum. I decided not to let Martin know that I had gleaned this knowledge.'

'Oh, Emma! Are you thinking that the maid is poisoning Charlotte? Why would she do that?' Nona looked troubled; she hadn't liked the maid any more than Emma had.

'I don't know.' Emma spoke quietly. 'Unless it is because Charlotte treats her badly.'

'I don't think that would be enough to risk being found out and hung for the murder of her mistress, do you, Emma?'

Standing, Nona walked to the window and looked out at the grounds. 'If this is what is happening, Emma, then she is a dangerous servant to have in the house.'

'That is what the doctor said. Not for the same reason, only because Martin seems to be challenging the authority of her employer and is insolent.'

'He doesn't know what you suspect?'

'No, I haven't told anyone. How can I, when the doctor says that the maid must have meant that she was giving her mistress the medicine kept from his last visit, to calm her, and other than getting the dose wrong, Charlotte was sleeping as was intended? But it was more than sleep, Nona. I am sure that each time she woke up Martin gave her more laudanum.'

'But you cannot prove it.'

'No.' Emma shook her head and felt at a loss. 'I am so worried for Charlotte, that I have given her Carter as a maid and put Martin in the kitchen to help her mother who cannot cook. I am also eating in the dining room to show my authority, such as it is, as the servants have no leader now that Mrs Jenk is dead and Patrick is with Richard at Freelanders.'

'When we move into Freelanders on Monday, Richard will be coming back home with Patrick. You will be relieved that there is some authority below stairs again.'

'You're right. I wonder if I should tell Patrick of my fears, Nona. I need an ally in the house.'

Nona looked uncertain. 'What if he doesn't believe you? Won't that make matters worse? And, he can turn the servants against you.'

Emma let out a long sigh. 'It seems that I am still on my own in this.'

'Until you can prove anything, Emma, it seems that you are on your own.'

~

Nona had been gone some time and Emma was again reading her book when the door burst open after only a cursory knock and Carter flew into the room in an agitated state. 'The mistress.' She could hardly speak and her hands were covered in blood.

Horrified, Emma stood up, immediately afraid of what she was going to hear. 'It's the mistress, madam, her nose is bleeding and I can't stop it. I have tried everything.'

Emma ran to Charlotte's room with Carter and found Charlotte sitting in her chair, her head laid back, holding a blood-soaked cloth to her face.

'What could have caused this bleed, Carter?' Emma asked, removing the bloody cloth from Charlotte's face and seeing for herself that the nose was still running with blood.

'I don't know, madam, she says that she didn't fall or knock herself, so I don't know.'

Emma held Charlotte's nose tightly between her finger and thumb after they had tipped the chair back by putting books under the front legs. It took an hour, but the bleeding stopped. When her face had been washed and her clothes changed, Emma went to speak to Charlotte who was now sitting, pale and listless, in her bed. It was then that she noticed the bruise on the top of her arm and her swollen ring finger now turning black.

'What is the cause of this?' She pointed to the finger and wanted to call her Charlotte, but had not been given leave to do so and she didn't want to say mother-in-law, as that would make her angry.

Charlotte looked up at Emma, her mouth pulled into a thin line as she spoke. 'What is wrong here, mistress, *is* that you are doing your best to kill me.' She spoke with such venom that Emma was shocked, but before she could answer, Charlotte continued in a voice loud enough for Carter, who was tidying a table near the window, to hear. 'But you will not succeed in taking my place. I am stronger than you know.' And with that she sank back onto her pillow, closing her eyes, having used all her energy in this last piece of nastiness.

Emma felt Carter become very still, then, aware of Emma's eyes upon her, the maid busied herself reorganising the items on the dressing table.

25.

It was a moonless night as a shadow moved slowly and soundlessly along the dark landing.

Charlotte was deep in a drugged sleep and was not aware of the spare pillow being removed from the chair, or of it approaching her face. She went quietly and without a struggle.

Next morning it was Rosie Carter who opened the curtains, allowing the sunshine into the bedchamber. As a shaft of light streamed across the room, alighting on the bed, it highlighted the vivid colours in the silk weave of the top cover. Rosie wondered for a moment why the pillow was on the floor next to the bed and not on the chair, before she saw Charlotte's eyes staring at her out of a waxy face.

Her screams, and her hammering on Emma's door, brought the sleepy and shocked household to the landing.

When the doctor arrived, he asked about the bruise on Charlotte's arm, and although no one had seen her fall, she was having falls and the bruise was put down to that.

'Mrs Laddisbrock has been suffering with her health for some time and was prone to falling,' he said almost to himself as his pen hovered over the death certificate before he signed it. Handing it to Richard he said soberly, 'I am sorry, sir, for the loss of your mother. I am sure that she will be greatly missed.'

Richard hung his head as he took the paper, and Emma saw that he looked pale. He seemed to have aged these last few months, and it was all that she could do to stop herself from putting her arms about him to give him comfort. But that show of affection she knew was the last thing that he would want, and she could not bear the thought of his physical rejection of her in front of the doctor and the servants.

~

Richard was now resident in his father's rooms. He was still making himself busy about the land so that he had no time to speak with Emma. She had no idea if he had been visiting his mother while she was ill, but hoped that he had, for the pain of losing her own mother was unthinkable to her.

The funeral was going to be very different to that of Emma's father, even though it was held in the same church.

Her thoughts moved to Richard and his loss as the day of the funeral arrived with a pale blue sky in which small pink clouds dissolved slowly. He was now alone in the world without guidance and she feared his reaction towards her.

Later that day as the sun rose above the trees that surrounded the churchyard, touching the grass and headstones with a gentle warmth, Charlotte's body was transported from the house in a glass carriage pulled by two sleek black horses wearing black and gold plumes.

As the carriage passed through the village the residents lined the street and waited outside the church. In respect, the men had removed their caps and all stood with bowed heads as the cortege passed. The invited mourners attending arrived in carriages large and small, and these now waited with grooms and fidgeting horses around the village green.

The church was packed with people dressed in muted shades of colour, although none were weeping. It seemed to Emma that Charlotte had a lot of acquaintances, although she had not seen any of them at the house.

The servants gathered in their usual places at the back of the church and in the gallery, their number being swelled by tradesmen who had served the family.

The service that Ernest delivered was fitting for a woman of Charlotte's class and for Emma it was yet again eternally long.

Afterwards, outside in the sunshine, the villagers and mourners dispersed, and the bearers, carrying the casket high on their shoulders, walked slowly along the well-maintained churchyard path with the fragrance of cut grass in their nostrils. Insects buzzed and birds sang high in the surrounding trees, proclaiming the continuation of life.

Emma was told to wait in the coach during the internment where only Richard, the family solicitor, the vicar and doctor witnessed the body being placed into the family vault where Charlotte joined her husband in icy silence, for which, Emma thought, he must be very grateful.

The servants, apart from Larch, who had stayed with the carriage, had returned to the house on foot to prepare for the wake. Emma had arranged for Dolly and Alice to help in the kitchen preparing the food, for which she knew Mrs Martin was relieved.

Emma did not join them for the wake but watched from the landing as Richard, looking serious, made a point of speaking to all the mourners standing in their family groups, talking quietly. With sad faces they paid their respects to Richard. Emma could not help noticing how many had arrived with marriageable daughters in tow who looked coyly at Richard from behind lace veils or fans.

The conversations and lunch went on for two hours before the guests' carriages were brought to the front of the house and they departed with their kind words and their unmarried daughters.

As the servants busied themselves clearing the tables, Richard and three sombre gentlemen dressed entirely in black retired to the library. Until now Emma had not seen the family solicitors and was shocked at how young one of them was. Not that she had ever seen a solicitor before; it was more that she thought a man who learnt the law, which took a long while to do, should be very old, having had many years to learn his craft.

The library door closed, shutting her out. It left Emma feeling distracted and worthless. She knew that Richard would be talking about her and she couldn't help pondering what lies he was telling to give himself a good case for her removal.

26.

The inglenook hearth in the library was filled with flowers instead of the usual log fire, as the day was warm and the room lit by sunshine streaming in through the two huge windows.

Richard sat with his accountant, James Houden, and his solicitor, Marcus Goutch, at a highly polished table.

Moving slowly, Patrick poured an expensive port from a crystal carafe into matching crystal glasses before placing the carafe in the centre of the table so that the men could help themselves. At a nod from Richard, he left, quietly closing the door securely behind him.

Mr Goutch nodded in appreciation as he removed the glass of port from his lips, took another sip and placed it on the table between himself and Richard. His young clerk, Master Molding, sat at a table in the window with his notebook and quill which he dipped into a bottle of ink that he had brought with him. Its silver lid, now unscrewed, lay on the table glinting in the sunlight.

The London solicitors Goutch and Manning had been with Richard's family for years and he knew that their services would not come cheaply. He also knew that he could not put the matter of his marriage off any longer. He had to know the law and where he stood. Although at this moment he had to admit to feeling confused as to why he wanted to continue with divorce now that his mother was dead.

Mr Goutch moved a wad of papers that had been placed before him by Master Molding, who waited patiently in his chair by the window for the meeting to start.

'I understand, sir, from a letter I received from your mother,' Goutch said, looking at Richard, 'that you wish to understand the law on divorce.'

Richard nodded. 'Yes, that is correct, sir.'

'Divorce is unusual, sir, and costly, if it is possible at all. May I ask what your reasons are?'

Richard wanted to say, 'My wife did not suit my mother,' but with her death, that now seemed overly petty. He had thought all night about saying that Emma had been unfaithful with a servant and that he had a witness, but the boot boy was now missing, so he couldn't use that. He played for time by sipping his port while the two men waited in the heavy silence.

'Perhaps I could have my marriage annulled, sir, through non-consummation,' he said eventually.

'You have not slept with your wife since your marriage? How long have you been married, sir?' Goutch raised an eyebrow and looked doubtful.

'About four years, sir.'

Goutch shook his head slowly. 'I advise you, sir, that the law adopts the view that marriage is indissoluble and a lifelong union. Divorce!' He scratched his chin. 'The ecclesiastical courts could grant a divorce *a mensa et thoro*. This is more like a judicial separation than a divorce: the parties are free to live apart but cannot remarry. To obtain a *divorce*, we would have to apply for a private Act of Parliament and this, sir, will be lengthy and expensive. If you wish to take this path, I will find you a lawyer to whom you may speak and instruct, if this is your will.'

Richard shook his head; he could not afford the time or the money. Divorce was then out of the question and so was the judicial separation. He realised now, that his mother had been right. He should have married someone with money, someone of his own class. He needed an heir.

Mr Goutch interrupted Richard's thoughts. 'Can you tell me, sir, about your marriage ceremony? I believe you were married in the New World.'

Richard nodded. He had picked his glass of port up, but now put it down again as he replied, 'I had been on the Tate homestead about six months. I had run away from home to avoid having the responsibility of this place. I knew that I didn't want to follow in my father's footsteps. I didn't want my father's bad humour when I did nothing right or misunderstood what he was telling me. I felt at home working on someone else's land, perhaps because it wasn't my father's and I had no pressure.

'I was attracted to Emma and she to me. A priest, who had served his time as a convict, was passing by and asked for food and rest. It seems he was going to bring Christianity to the new country. I got carried away with the idea of being permanently part of the Tate family and caught up in the excitement. It was he who conducted the ceremony. I had not told Emma who I was, or that we came from the same village. This was a shock to her and her family.' Richard winced and released a sigh. 'I was lulled into a false sense of security, gentlemen. I was still young, only just twenty, and it all seemed like an adventure. I realised as soon as the ceremony was over that it was a mistake, and I moved in with her brothers and did not move into Emma's cabin.'

At this lie he felt his face flush and hoped that they would think it was because he was embarrassed to have to speak of such things.

'I see.' Goutch looked thoughtful. 'And the Tate family will vouch that this is the truth?'

'How can they, sir? They are nine months' journey from here in good weather.'

Goutch nodded. 'That is true, sir, but I must have witness to this fact.'

'And,' Richard carried on, 'another eight or nine months for a letter to return.'

'That also is true, sir. As I said, this will all take time and will be extremely costly. When we have their letter of agreement to the facts that you have told me, the lawyer will proceed with the divorce proceedings governed by the ecclesiastical court and

Canon Law as set out by the Church of England. I must also warn you, sir, that any proposed divorce is also subject to scrutiny by both the House of Commons and the House of Lords where intimate details of your private life will be debated in public. Or, we could go for *a vinculo matrimonii*. Divorce from the chain or bond of matrimony, which declares invalid the marriage itself and thus allows either party to remarry. It could be granted if the marriage were not consummated as you say, or for impotence, frigidity or lunacy, or if the marriage could be shown to be incestuous or bigamous, or carried out by force, or in error.'

'It was most definitely in error, sir. I was too young to know my mind, and did not sleep with my wife as our having no children must prove and I have not slept with my wife here as the servants will support, sir.'

'May I interrupt you at this point, sirs?' James Houden's face was deadly serious as he looked from Richard to the solicitor. 'I feel, sir,' he said, looking directly at Richard, 'that as we have not this day had the time to speak, that I must speak now, before I let you commit to something that you may regret.'

Richard frowned. 'Regret, sir, what should I regret?'

'I have to inform you, sir, that since you took over the estate from your father, that the estate has been losing money. It seems that it can no longer support itself.'

'How is it losing money, sir?' Richard felt his energy draining away; money was something he had never had to deal with.

Houden threw his hands up and, shaking his head, looked incredulously at Richard. 'Sir, I cannot tell you where you are losing money or why, it is for you to find that out and to show me what is happening. I can tell you, sir, that unless you sell this property, and possibly the farms, that you will not have enough money to pay for a divorce.'

Richard was stunned. He hadn't known that the estate was in such poor shape. He poured a glass of port and drank it straight down. Both men seemed to understand as he refilled his glass and then theirs. 'I didn't know,' he said, looking at his glass. 'I didn't know, and I don't know why it is so. I don't understand finance, that is why I didn't want this job. I didn't want to come home.'

His shoulders drooped and the life seemed to ebb from him on the sigh that left his mouth.

In the silence that filled the room all the men drank their port and seemed to be thinking. It was the solicitor that spoke first.

'Mr Laddisbrock, might I suggest that you take some time to think about what you will do now that you have all the information.'

'Yes, thank you, sir.' Richard's voice had no life in it. He felt trapped, just as he always knew that he would, given the unwanted responsibility of running the estate.

The gentlemen took to their carriages soon after, and Richard shut himself away in his rooms. It had been a distressing day and now he would obliterate it with a carafe of dark rum and be damned.

Later that evening Patrick, finding Richard slumped in his chair in front of the fire, put him to bed.

~

Emma felt uneasy. She would dearly like to know what had been said, what arrangements, if any, had been made. But she would have to wait until Richard deemed to tell her.

Sleep seemed beyond her. Her brain was too active for sleep, going over all that had happened since she came to this unwelcoming house. Strangely, she felt sorry for Charlotte, and wondered what sort of upbringing she'd had. What love she had received as a child, for she showed none of it as an adult. Was she the product of her upbringing as Emma was of hers? In that, Emma was glad that she had had the freedom to run about the countryside with her siblings. That she had received the wisdom and love of her mother and grandmother.

Unready for sleep she moved to her desk, intending to write to Robert and her mother, but in the end did neither, as her brain would not let her form coherent sentences. Like a grasshopper, her mind jumped from one happening to another without structure. She sighed, and walked the floor, a great unease falling about her shoulders. As time moved into the early hours she still had not attempted to lie in her bed. Something was coming, she knew it. How she hated these feelings of approaching doom. Suddenly she grabbed the chair beside the dressing table and carried it to the bedroom door, wedging it under the doorknob. A doorknob she realised was not like a handle and would still turn with no restriction. Pulling the chair away she pushed the chest of drawers in front of the door; she knew that this would hold the door back from opening and if the furniture was pushed out of the way she would hear it. She then leant a chair backwards on two legs so that it leant against the dressing room door. If that door were opened it would fall, waking her.

The clock on the landing struck twice and now she felt tired. Pulling back the covers she climbed into bed and lay acknowledging the sensation of fear running through her body. Unable to deny sleep any longer her eyes closed slowly and she drifted into an uneasy slumber.

It was the sound of a floorboard creaking that brought her eyes suddenly open. She lay listening. Had she imagined a noise? Realising that she had stopped breathing she took a deep breath. The room was in total darkness as she slipped from the bed and tiptoed towards the chest of drawers where she stood watching the door. The silence of the night sat heavily upon her ears as she listened to her heart pumping. Gradually all warmth left her body and she shivered. Pulling on her shawl she moved to the bed where she sat, still listening, her mouth dry.

It was the sound of knocking on the door that brought her out of her sleep with a start.

'Madam, are you alright? I can't open the door.' The knocking came again more urgently. 'Madam!'

Pulling herself from the bed Emma went to the door and pulled the heavy chest of drawers away just enough to let Carter in. She felt like a small child caught in the act of doing something that she shouldn't.

Carter looked at the chest and then at Emma with an enquiring look that faded quickly as she asked, 'What would you like for your breakfast, madam?' as though the chest being in front of the door was the most normal thing in the world.

Unable to explain to anyone else the feeling of fear and approaching doom that she felt, Emma also ignored the furniture.

27.

Below stairs Patrick could not deny the atmosphere that hung like a mantel of ice and saw it reflected in the faces of the staff. What used to be a busy working kitchen, with Mrs Jenk giving instructions, was now a silent and sullen place. It was obvious to him that Mrs Martin was out of her depth, not only with cooking but with managing the staff. He had also seen Thomas in the kitchen, which was not the place for an inquisitive child, and had asked the Martins to make arrangements for him in the village. But this morning he had seen that the boy was still there, sitting on the flagstones in the corner, playing with some jelly moulds.

Patrick opened the door to the room off the passage opposite the kitchen. The room, which had been for Mrs Jenk's use, doubled up as her quarters and office. The room was tidy and clean and for Patrick full of memories. He had on many occasions sat with Mrs Jenk in this room of an evening with a glass of port or a cup of chocolate discussing household matters. He stood for a moment with his hand on the back of one of the comfortable armchairs placed each side of the fireplace and sighed. He hated change and the room now seemed so empty. Unconsciously he straightened the knitted blanket draped over one chair arm and noticed that the cushion in her chair still held an indentation made by her body. Unhooking the keys from her chatelaine he opened her desk. In the drawer he found an old work staff roster dated the week that she had died, but what he couldn't find were any up-to-date staff rosters that would have helped him. Finding her accounts book in the drawer he saw that she had been diligent in her bookkeeping but that nothing had been entered since her death. The question was, who had been ordering the provisions and who had been paying the bills? He closed the book and looked around the room. Try as he might he could not find where any bills may have been placed for later entry. It was clear to him that they needed a qualified cook-come-housekeeper, but also needed to keep Mrs Martin until they had secured the service of someone else. Until then he had to rethink the below-stairs staff. In his mind he saw each category of staff and thought about how he could make what they had work better for them. Taking staff to Freelanders Farm he realised had been useful. He would not otherwise have known the capabilities of West and Newman. He made a note to interview the two young women who worked in the laundry. He had found them hard working and able to cook for at least four people, and they could possibly help Mrs Martin until he found someone else. Work in the kitchen was full time; they would not also be able to do the household laundry. He wondered if he could put the scullery maids, Palmer and Ike, in the laundry room for most of the day and back in the scullery after meals.

Then there was the question of Mary Martin. Now that Mrs Laddisbrock was no longer here Martin had no place to fill. She would have to go, along with her mother, unless she agreed to work in the scullery. These were just ideas. But first, he decided he would try to find out what was wrong. Why the girls who had worked in the kitchen with Mrs Jenk had left, and why the boot boy Jacob had run away.

He stared out of the window. To his left he looked at the arched entrance to the stable yard set in a high wall; it was wide enough to let the coaches through, and behind the wall he knew were a line of stables and coach houses. Larch ran a tight ship. There was never a grievance or any bother with the lads, everything neat and tidy. He sighed, thinking that men were so much easier to deal with than women.

Looking to his right, at the other end of the house he could just see the old part of the house reflecting the style of the new stable block, with a matching archway that led into a now derelict yard. The bricks of that wall were greying with age, and he could see that the roof of the unused building behind was now a garden for moss and weeds. He sighed again, shaking his head. Where was all this going to end? Things were not right and he had tried to ignore it. But with Creel, the estate manager, and both Mr and Mrs Laddisbrock now dead and Master Richard out of his depth not understanding the business, he felt that his own life was set like a horseless carriage running downhill towards disaster.

~

Lunch for the staff was just finished when Patrick asked West to accompany him to the office. She followed him, looking worried.

As they left the kitchen and crossed the passage to the room opposite, both were aware of the eyes that followed them.

'What do you think that's about?' Ike asked, addressing no one in particular.

Newman looked concerned and, frowning, left the kitchen quickly, going to the wash house to take the linen from the boiler and push it into the cold water sink where she pummelled the material with vigour to remove the soap and dirt. She found, lifting it from the sink to squeeze the water out, that it was too heavy for her on her own and so she attempted the smaller items first. This was too big a job for one person and she hoped that West would soon be back, and also wondered what West had done to attract the attention of Patrick.

In the office Patrick was looking at a nervous West as he asked her to close the door and take a seat in the hard chair he had placed in front of the desk.

Now West was really worried. She had never been asked to sit before. Mrs Jenk expected them to stand. Not that they were ever in here long, only long enough to pick up their wage in its little brown envelope and sign for it.

Patrick sat opposite her and, putting his arms on the desk, stared at the willowy girl of indefinable age sitting before him. His thoughts were whirling around in his head as he tried to decide which subject to broach first.

His staring unnerved West, who was convinced now that she had done something wrong. Her lip started to quiver and she blurted out, 'I'm sorry, Mr Patrick sir, I didn't mean to do it.'

Patrick was taken aback. 'What didn't you mean to do, West?'

'I don't know, sir, but I must have done something wrong. I didn't know it was wrong else I wouldn't have done it.'

Patrick shook his head and sighed. 'You haven't done anything wrong as far as I know, West, so please let me think.'

He decided to start with why the kitchen staff had left. 'West,' he said slowly, 'do you know why the staff that worked under Mrs Jenk walked out the day after she died without telling anyone and without references?'

West's face took on the look of a trapped animal as she sat before him. Her mouth was open in shock and her eyes staring. Biting her lip, she looked behind her at the door as though she were going to bolt. When she looked back at Patrick she was shaking.

'I'm sorry, sir,' she said in a voice so low he almost didn't hear her reply, 'I can't say why another leaves a job.'

Patrick realised that he needed to put her at ease and smiled. 'Of course, you can't, West, so tell me what it was like working under Mrs Jenk.'

The girl before him relaxed. 'Oh, sir, it was so sad. She was like a mother to us. If we had any worries we could always go to her. If we were ill she looked after us as good as, and in some cases better than, a mother. We were all so sad at what happened.'

As tears floated in the rim of her eyes she wiped them away with a toil-worn hand.

'Yes,' Patrick agreed, 'we were all truly sorry at her loss.' Now feeling that he had broken the ice and that she was more pliable he asked, 'Now tell me what it has been like in the kitchen since we lost Mrs Jenk.'

'Oh, sir, it has been truly terrible, we don't get our orders anymore and we have been trying to keep the routine going, but when the mistress died, and with me and Newman being away for a time, we have come back to mayhem, sir.'

He nodded. 'And how have you found working under Mrs Martin?'

'She don't give the orders, sir, it's her daughter who is running the kitchen.'

'I see.' He nodded sagely. 'And how do you get on with Mary Martin? Would you be able to work under her as the cook/housekeeper?'

The speed at which West stood up, pushing her chair back, took Patrick by surprise. The girl was as white as a sheet and yet a flush of pink was now appearing on her cheeks.

'If you employ Martin, sir, to give us orders, then I will leave right now, knowing that by walking out I will also forfeit my reference, for I will no longer take her slapping and punching me whenever she feels like it.'

Patrick was now the one with his mouth open and in shock. He'd been brought up in a family of boys and was not used to managing the emotions of women. Trying to bring some order to the moment he said, 'Please, West, sit down, I have no intention of employing Mary Martin as cook.'

West sat slowly back onto the chair and looked embarrassed. 'I'm sorry, sir. Martin is always hitting one or other of us, it seems to give her pleasure. Mrs Jenk handled her carefully, but I think Martin also had something on her, sir, some secret they seemed to share. Something that allowed Martin to get her own way a great deal.'

'Do you know what it was?' He was hopeful.

'No, sir, and I don't want to know, I value my life more than that.'

Patrick let that outburst go and asked, 'What of Jacob? Do you know what happened to the boy?'

'No, sir. I joined everyone else searching for the poor little thing.'

'Do you know why he might have run away, if that is what he did?'

'Martin was always hurting him. If I was Jacob I would have run away before she killed me, like she threatened.'

'She threatened the boy?'

'Yes, sir. Sometimes Newman and I let him sleep in with us as he was scared to be on his own sleeping in the boot room.'

'Thank you, West. I have something else to ask you. I am going to advertise Mrs Jenk's position later today and I want to ask you if you would work in the kitchen under the next cook.'

'You mean leave my post as laundry maid, sir?'

'Yes, West. And I am going to ask Newman to work with you. I will give you until tomorrow to let me know and to talk to Newman. Now I want you to go back to your work and ask Newman to come in and see me. But I don't want you to talk to anyone about this on your way through the kitchen, nor to Newman, just ask her to come to the office, please.'

Celia Martin and Mary had been watching the office door with interest, wondering what was going on. When West came out and, head down, walked quickly through the kitchen without stopping, Mary called, 'What's going on, West?'

The question went unanswered.

They were just getting the flour out of the pantry when Newman hurried through the kitchen and into the passage. She knocked on the door and entered slowly, looking upset as she shut the door behind her.

'What is going on?' Mary spoke to no one in particular. 'Well, there's just one way to find out,' she mumbled and, walking across the passage, put her ear to the door. All she could hear were muffled voices, so pressed her ear harder to the wood.

229

'Did West tell you what this is about, Newman?' Patrick asked the pale girl who stood in front of him.

'No, sir,' Newman answered as she too sat tentatively on the edge of the chair before the desk.

'I want to ask you, Newman, as I have West, would you consider working in the kitchen?'

He watched the grey eyes of the small maid open wide in shock.

'Oh no, sir. Please don't make me work in the kitchen.' And she started to wring her hands as though they were cold.

Patrick, now more enlightened asked, 'And why would you not like to work in the kitchen, Newman?'

The maid looked behind her at the door and then back at Patrick, the colour having drained from her face.

Nodding, Patrick stood slowly and walked quietly to the door, opening it suddenly. Martin fell into the room looking shocked.

'Do you want something, Martin?' he asked fiercely.

Gaining her balance Martin looked suitably embarrassed and straightened up, saying, 'No, sir.'

'Then get back to your work and I will interview you later.' He shut the door hard, leaving her standing in the passage.

'Interviews,' she said to her mother, 'I am to have an interview. I expect they will be offering me another position now that the mistress is no longer with us. I will be glad to get out of this kitchen.'

Mary watched as Palmer and Ike entered the office together looking nervous. Why, she wondered, were the scullery maids being interviewed? Something huge must be afoot and it was driving her mad not knowing. She was determined to get it out of the two maids on their return, even if she had to beat them black and blue. She waited, and was confused when, instead of returning to their duties in the scullery, they made their way out of the house towards the laundry room.

When after a few minutes the office door opened sharply, Mary put down the rolling pin, wiped her hands on her apron and untied it. But Patrick ignored her and walked upstairs.

'What the hell is going on?' she said out loud.

Thinking that her daughter was speaking to her, Celia said, 'I have no idea.'

Mary gave her mother a look of pure dislike and ignored her.

28.

Emma was sitting at the desk in her room writing a letter to her mother. As she bent over the paper she noticed a large blue bruise that had appeared on the back of her hand and tried to remember when she had knocked herself. Then, ignoring it, she started to write. She had already written and sent a letter to Martha telling her about the wedding and about Nona's dress. She had also added a drawing of it that had not done it justice. She also wrote about Dolly and the children, knowing that Martha was always desperate for news of friends. Then she started out on the pages about Robert, telling how she had found him looking rather thin, and then about Sarah and Jake Poleshore. It took her a long time to think about how to tell her mother about the happenings involved in the finding of Oliver's body.

You were right, Mother, she wrote.
Oliver was not only buried near the river as you imagined, but was in it, and it was poor Sarah who found him quite by mistake. The miracle, Mother, is that Jake, hearing Sarah screaming, came to her rescue and spoke for the very first time. We were all amazed. And we later learnt from him about the demise of his poor family, and that it was all down to the wickedness of our cousin Amelia. Jake had seen Amelia kill Oliver while she and her friend were burying Polly and had threatened Jake with the death of his family. I am heartsore at the terrible things that she did to that poor

232

innocent family, Mother. But there may be good news. Robert had been visiting the Poleshores and he and Sarah, I think, are attracted to each other. I believe that she would make a very good vicar's wife and her father could live on the estate and help Robert a great deal. I fear that Robert has been too long without a family.

I send an assurance, Mother, that Nona and Dan are very happy and will soon have a home of their own, having been offered the tenancy of one of Richard's farms.

My love to you, Mother, and to Andrew and the boys. I hope that all is well with you.

Your loving daughter Emma.

She was just folding it when a knock came at the door. 'Come in,' she called, and was surprised to see Patrick enter and close the door behind him.

Emma's heart jumped into her throat. 'Is it Richard, Patrick?' She stood quickly in a panic. 'What has happened?'

'Master Richard is safe and well, ma'am, but I need your help. May I talk with you?'

'Yes, of course, Patrick,' she said sitting back at her desk relieved. 'How can I help?'

It took him some time to tell her about the fear that the staff seemed to have of Martin and of his ideas for shaking up the staff and advertising as far afield as London for a new cook/housekeeper.

Emma listened to his ideas, wondering why he was including her when she was so little thought of and may not be here herself much longer. As she listened she realised that her dislike of Martin had not been misplaced after all. She also felt guilty when he spoke passionately about the missing boot boy and his fears for Jacob's safety after all that he had learnt about Martin. But she held her peace for now, wondering why he was telling her so much.

'I know, ma'am,' he said, his usual impassive face beginning to frown, 'that I am in charge of the staff below stairs, but I am not used to dealing with the women. Mrs Jenk did that, then reported to me. If it was something that we could not deal with, then I would take the matter to Mr Laddisbrock or the mistress, but now...' he hesitated, not saying, 'now that they are dead,' but, 'I have no one else to turn to. Would you, ma'am, be in the room while I interview Martin and her mother?'

'Yes, of course, Patrick, when do you want to carry out the interview?'

'I think, ma'am, that now would be a good time if it is no bother to yourself. Only, Martin is already interested in what I have been saying to the maids and I am afraid that if I do not do it today she will beat it out of them and they will leave.'

'Beat it out of them, Patrick?' Emma was shocked.

'Oh yes, ma'am, I believe that there has been a lot of bullying going on below stairs.'

'Then we will interview them together, Patrick. Let us do it in the library, that way we will be away from all the staff.'

He looked so grateful that Emma almost cried for him, such a large, strong, sensible man, unable to cope with the emotions of women.

'I will go to the library straight away, Patrick, while you bring them upstairs.'

~

Mary could not settle to any work and had combed her hair and removed her apron twice. She had thought hard about what job was vacant and she could only think that it must be either that of Mrs Jenk, or that Mrs Laddisbrock was not happy with that silly little girl Rosie Carter. What was she anyway, but a jumped-up laundry maid who knew nothing about being a lady's maid?

Celia had been continuing with the pastry that Mary had abandoned in her state of agitation. She said nothing to her daughter, who was pacing the kitchen, having learnt quickly that silence and keeping any questions to herself were her best option. She lined the tins with the pastry and stirred the beef sitting in its gravy, having been removed from the heat. It was now cooling in its huge pot on the end of the table and she was about to ladle it into each lined tin when Patrick appeared in the doorway.

'You can finish that later, cook. I will see you both in the library in three minutes.'

'You're going to interview us together?' Mary questioned, looking annoyed.

Patrick ignored her, saying sharply, 'Three minutes,' and, looking stern, made his way back upstairs.

In the library Emma sat behind the large polished table, having removed the newspapers to a sideboard. Patrick was standing behind her as the two women entered.

Martin was irked at the sight of Emma. But then, she thought to herself, if she was to be Emma Laddisbrock's maid, then of course she would be at this interview, but why were they interviewing her mother?

Celia Martin was trembling, having never stood before anyone in authority before.

Patrick looked kindly at her as he spoke. 'Mrs Martin, you have stepped into the shoes of Mrs Jenk and we are grateful that your efforts have kept the household fed. But, I think that you will agree that this is not a situation that you are happy in.'

Tongue-tied, Celia could only nod in agreement.

'I have today placed an advertisement in a London newspaper for a replacement cook/housekeeper. I have to ask you, madam, did any of the tradesmen give you their bill when you took in the orders?'

Celia looked confused and looked at Mary, who ignored her. 'I'm sorry, sir, I don't know?' She sounded worried.

Patrick tried again. 'Let us say that when the butcher's boy brought the meat, there would have been a sheet of paper with that order. What did you do with the paper?'

'I threw it on the fire, sir, I didn't know what it was,' she qualified.

'You didn't read it?'

Celia looked at her feet and shook her head.

An uncomfortable silence followed, with Patrick scowling at the small woman standing in front of him.

'Can you read, Mrs Martin?' Emma asked kindly.

Celia did not look up as she shook her head, conveying that she could not read.

'Did you show the bills, papers, to anyone else who could have helped you, Mrs Martin?' Emma asked.

Celia's eyes flicked towards her daughter, who said nothing to help her mother. But it was obvious to Emma and to Patrick that she had asked Martin.

'Thank you, Mrs Martin,' Patrick said kindly. There was a pause before he said, 'I find that since the deaths of Mr and Mrs Laddisbrock, that I need to reorganise the staff. And it gives me no pleasure at all, madam, to have to inform you that when I have employed a new cook there will not be a place here for you.'

Celia nodded. She had already worked that out for herself but had hoped that they could offer something. 'Sir,' she spoke, looking straight at Patrick, 'if I am sent from here, I will have no home to go to and I have a grandson.'

'I'm sorry, Mrs Martin, but I cannot help you.' His eyes flashed in Mary's direction, just for a second, but it was enough to convey to both the Martins who he held responsible. 'The scullery maids,' he continued, 'have spoken kindly of you, madam, and I am inclined to keep you on until we find a replacement. Both West and Newman will be taking over your duties and you will assist them until the new cook arrives.'

Celia looked relieved and tears rose into her eyes, but she kept control.

Now Patrick turned to Mary who he noted looked expectant and boldly at him. 'As for you, Martin, I have learnt a great deal about you in this last day. You, I am informed, are a bully and

236

get your way by hitting the staff, who I am sad to discover are afraid of you.'

The expectancy on Martin's face slipped away, replaced by disbelief and then anger.

'I am afraid,' he continued, keeping his eyes level upon her, 'that I cannot have a bully in this household and I give you one hour to gather your belongings and leave. You will see me in my office and I will give you your wage and a reference that will enlighten any new employer of your nature.'

Martin had her mouth open in disbelief, a brief expression, before the look on her face became more calculating and she smiled.

'Oh, I don't think so.' She spoke with confidence. 'No, I will not be leaving and nor will my son, and I would advise you, sir, to hold a civil tongue when you speak to me.'

Emma, Patrick and Celia Martin were for a moment stunned at her reply, and in that silence, Martin continued with a smile on her lips and satisfaction in her eyes. 'You see, my son is the heir to this estate. Yes,' she said, looking directly at Emma, 'I have carried an heir that you have not. My son is the brother of your husband.'

'This is preposterous,' Patrick shouted, making everyone in the room jump. 'Do your lies hold no bounds, mistress?'

'You can shout at me all you like, sir,' she sneered, 'but it is true.'

'No, Mary!' Celia looked on the edge of collapse. 'All these years that you wouldn't say who the father was and now I see why.'

'Yes, Mother. He promised that Thomas would be recognised as next in line after Richard.'

'How dare you use the master's given name!' Patrick shouted again, glaring at her. But this time Martin did not shrink or jump; she felt that she had the power and was glad that they all now knew who her son was.

'Who else knows of this?' Patrick asked.

'I told Mrs Laddisbrock, sir, but she would have none of it so I had to quieten her until I was ready. Unfortunately, or perhaps fortunately, she died.'

Emma now found her voice. 'So that is why you were giving her large doses laudanum.'

'Yes, you cannot know how aggressive she was. I had no choice but to keep her sedated until I could speak to the master. But he moved out before I could speak to him, and you,' she looked distastefully at Emma, 'moved unexpectedly back in.'

The woman's attitude and actions were becoming clear to Emma now. She could see the struggle that Martin must have had, believing that her son was heir to the estate and that she, a mere maid, would be sent away with nothing if the news came out at the wrong time. In fact, many maids who succumbed to the sexual wishes of their masters were repulsed when pregnancy was discovered. And many died of starvation, or, with no husband, had to take to prostitution to stay out of the workhouse. They were often not supported by their master and were looked down upon by both their families and society.

Emma looked puzzled. 'How did you keep your pregnancy a secret from the staff, Martin?'

Martin's face flushed and she looked uncomfortable as she said, 'Mrs Jenk covered for me. I wore a larger uniform. The staff thought I was putting on weight, and that only.'

'So how did you have the baby without anyone knowing?' Emma asked.

Martin seemed to take time to answer that question.

It was Celia that broke the silence. 'She came to me late one evening and had Thomas at home. She was very near to delivery. Afterwards, she left in the morning early, returning to work. She left me to look after my grandson, only hours old and without any help.'

'Without help?' Emma questioned.

'Yes, madam. I had nothing for him, no milk, no clothes. She just left and expected that I would manage.'

'That is enough.' Patrick held his hands up. 'I can hear no more. I will have to speak to Mr Laddisbrock before we go any further. But I think I know what the outcome will be. Thank you,' he said sharply to the two women. 'You can return to your duties.'

When they had gone Patrick looked shaken. 'Do you believe anything Martin said, ma'am? For if you do, then she may have killed the mistress.'

Emma weighed that up in her mind, but as far as she knew there was no proof of it. 'But,' she said to Patrick, 'it does explain her attitude. Her thinking that she has the right to be acknowledged as the mother to the heir, and it enlightens us as to why she has been throwing her weight around.'

'I find it hard to believe that Mrs Jenk went along with this and didn't dismiss her straight away.'

'Perhaps she also had reason to be afraid of Martin.'

'In my mind Martin can't stay,' Patrick said. 'She is too dangerous to keep and the staff don't like her. I want harmony below stairs.'

'I agree, Patrick, but what about Mrs Martin? She will be homeless.'

'There is nothing that can be done about that. I have been kind in keeping her to help West and Newman until she can find a place.'

'Yes, Patrick, you have.' Emma had to agree but looked troubled. 'Will you speak to my husband, Patrick, or is it my place to do so?'

'I will speak to him, ma'am. It is my place to employ and dismiss in the stead of Mrs Jenk, but in this case, I feel that he should be told about his father and the boy.'

Emma nodded agreement and it was with a troubled mind that she watched Patrick leave the room to find his master.

~

Richard, who had been pouring over the accounts, was in bad humour when the knock came upon the door. 'Go away, Patrick,' he shouted, recognising the knock.

'I'm sorry, sir, but this cannot wait.' The voice was muffled through the door.

Sighing, Richard bade him enter and was disturbed by the look on the man's face.

'What has happened now, Patrick? Is it not something that you can manage without disturbing me?'

'No, sir, this is far too serious for me to deal with.'

Richard took time to look properly at his manservant and was disturbed to see the worry lines on the usually impassive face.

'What is it? Speak up.' Pushing the papers away he now gave Patrick his full attention.

On his journey to Richard's rooms Patrick had been trying to work out how to tell his master about Martin, his father and the boy. Where should he start, how should he tell it?

Patrick stood almost to attention before Richard and slowly started. 'Sir, I am sorry to inform you that during the rearrangement of the staff I have discovered from her own mouth that the maid Martin is claiming that she has a son who is heir to this estate. A child that is your brother, sir.' He qualified his statement as Richard looked blankly at him.

'My brother, Patrick?'

'Yes, sir.'

'Do you believe her, Patrick? She is saying that she and my father...'

'I don't know the truth of it, sir,' he said quickly, 'I can only say that it was found out because she was being dismissed for bullying the servants, who are afraid of her. At that point, sir, she told myself and Mrs Laddisbrock that her son was heir to the estate and, in that, she could not be dismissed.'

'Huh, we will see about that, Patrick. What proof does she have?'

'I don't know that she has any proof, sir. But I can tell you that she told us that she had spoken to your mother, sir, and then had to keep her quiet with laudanum because she became hysterical.'

'When was this, Patrick?'

'It was when we were away looking at the tenant farms, sir.'

'Yes, I remember it was my wife who came to tell me that my mother was unwell.'

'Yes, sir, but Mrs Laddisbrock didn't know why your mother was suddenly taken into such delirium. And she did try to help her, but of course she didn't know what Martin was up to.'

'And what was she up to, Patrick?'

'She was keeping your mother on high doses of laudanum, sir, so that your mother could not speak to you.'

Richard was quiet for a moment while he thought. Then, turning back to his paperwork he said dismissively, 'Get rid of her, Patrick.'

'I gave her until this afternoon to get her things together, sir, but she laughed and refuses to go. She says that her son is the heir to this estate, after yourself, and that he will be recognised.'

'Oh, will he? Send her to me, Patrick, I would hear this for myself and have Gant, Larch and Ames ready in the hall to help you with her ejection from this house, and the boy.'

'Yes, sir.'

Out on the landing Patrick felt shaken by what was happening. In all the years he had worked for the Laddisbrocks there had never been anything like this. He knew it went on in other houses; maids were now and again dismissed or left with no references. He could not believe that it had happened here and that he had not known. If indeed it did happen. He could only think that it was after he had put his master, the older Mr Laddisbrock, to his bed and when the staff had retired for the night.

While Patrick had gone to summon Martin, Richard thought about it. Was that why his parents had taken separate rooms? Did his father often have his way with the maids? Did his mother know? He decided not. She would have dismissed Martin straight away. Surely the maid was just trying to save her job, but then he thought, *No, she wants to rule this house. Was it she who made my mother ill?*

He was still debating when Patrick ushered the maid into the room.

For a moment Richard ignored the woman who stood boldly before him, but spoke to Patrick. 'Is all arranged?'

'Yes, sir, in the hall.'

'Thank you, Patrick. You will stay here by the door.'

'Yes, sir.'

Martin frowned at being kept waiting. Being kept standing. Surely she should be asked to be seated as his brother's mother.

Richard got up and stood only inches from her. Being much taller he looked down on her, wanting her to feel threatened, a mere servant taking on her master.

'So, mistress, it comes to my attention that you say that you had a liaison with my father.'

'Yes, sir.' She felt weak inside but turned her face up to his, not wanting him to see that she was intimidated. 'Mr Laddisbrock,' she continued, 'is the father of my son.' She took a step back from him to give her more space to look at him.

'I do not believe you,' Richard said, with eyes that held danger, 'and I give you one minute to show me the proof.'

'I cannot show you proof, sir,' she frowned, 'but the master is my son's father. He promised that if I said nothing, then he would eventually tell his wife and write my son into his will.'

'I can assure you, mistress,' Richard could not hold back his anger, 'that this was not written into my father's will as you may have realised after his death, as nothing was said to you.'

'I believe, sir, that he died before he could write it.'

Richard nodded, a small smile touching his lips. 'I give you immediate notice, Martin. You will not have time to gather your possessions and can send for them later. There will be no reference and you will take your son with you.'

'I will *not* be dismissed.' Her voice rose in heated passion. 'My son is the *heir* to this property!'

Now Richard shouted louder than Martin, leaning close to her face. 'I will hear no more of your lies, mistress, you will leave immediately. Patrick, open the door.'

He was red in the face with anger as Patrick opened the door and Martin made no attempt to move.

She shook her head. 'No,' she said, 'I am not moving.'

'Gentlemen,' Richard nodded to the men who, now on the landing, were exposed, 'remove this woman from the house immediately.'

The men entered the room and seemed to hesitate. 'Do it,' Richard demanded.

Martin lost her composure at the sight of the men and took a step away from them. They moved forward under Richard's gaze and tried to lift her under the arms. She beat at them with her fists and kicked out with her legs as they carried her shouting down the stairs to the front door and deposited her none too gently on the top step where her son was already waiting with his grandmother. They closed the door behind her with a bang of finality.

The men stood in the hall looking uncomfortable, not knowing what they should do next, until Patrick came down the stairs, saying to them, 'You did well, men. I want you to keep a watch and make sure that she does not re-enter the house or stables. If you see her you must come and tell me.'

'Yes, sir,' they spoke together and made their way down the servants' stairs and out into the yard.

'What was that about?' they asked each other as they went back to work. One amongst them kept quiet and was glad that he had not got involved with Martin. She was sheer poison and he had always known it.

~

Mary looked furious as she straightened her skirt and looked at her mother, who stood at the bottom of the steps holding Thomas by the hand.

'This is all your fault, Mother. Now I am homeless with a child and with no money and no reference, how can I survive?'

'I will not be blamed for your misdemeanours, Mary.' Celia tried to keep her voice level but that wasn't what she was feeling as she bent to the child saying, 'You have to go with your mother, Thomas, but I will be along to see you very soon.'

Holding onto Celia's skirt he started to cry. 'I want to stay with you, Granny.' Celia stroked his blond head and made soothing noises. 'It will be alright, little one, you must go with your mother.'

Mary pulled her son roughly away, saying, 'Come with me, Thomas, and stop that snivelling or I will give you something to snivel about. You're a big boy now and Granny doesn't want you anymore.'

And with that she walked away at speed, pulling the crying child with her along the drive, shouting at him each time he stumbled.

Celia could only stand and watch them go, her heart filled with dread as she watched the child that she had grown to love try unsuccessfully to keep up with his mother.

~

At four o'clock Emma sat alone in the dining room and looked at the food placed in front of her. It was probably beef, she surmised, that sat in the gravy below the pastry crust, but she could already see that the meat was dry and overcooked. The servant she had come to know as Gant had brought it to the table and departed to the other side of the door where he would wait to hear the bell ring when she was finished.

The room was quiet. The Laddisbrocks of the past, who watched from their picture frames, seemed to be either scowling at her or looking over her head into the distance as though she did not exist. As she took up the fork that lay on the table beside her plate, the hair on Emma's head moved as though someone were touching it. She looked around. There was no one there, but a feeling of unease was upon her, tightening the skin on the back of her neck and on her shoulders. Something was wrong. Her ancestors were drawing near but, as always, she didn't know why. She thought for a long time about all that had happened since her return, before pushing her fork into the food and placing a piece of the beef in her mouth. She was right, the beef was dry and the sauce had a taste that she didn't much like; there was a sharpness to it. A taste that was like a smell. She chewed several pieces without enthusiasm and tried to think where she had smelt something like this taste before. Swallowing, she held the next piece of beef on the fork in front of her nose and sniffed it before putting it in her mouth.

Her face changed as realisation dawned and she knew suddenly where she had smelt it before. It was not something that Martha would have used, it was something others in the community bought. Rat poison. She had smelt it in Mr Rudd's shop. She dropped her fork and spat the meat from her mouth. Standing, she pushed the chair back. She was shaking as she pushed her fingers down her throat. Pushing hard on the back of her tongue she heaved. Her body convulsed, her eyes watered and she vomited, bringing some of her dinner back. Feeling dizzy, she pushed her fingers down her throat again, and retched twice. Darkness was already taking over her senses. As she fell she grabbed the bell and heard it clink as it toppled with her to the floor. Liquid, warm with a metallic taste, leaked from her mouth and stained the wooden floor beneath her face as she lay unmoving beside the table.

29.

Emma realised that she was in trouble, that she was more than ill, but had no energy to fight the terrible pain in her stomach, her back, her legs. There was no strength in her body as she gave herself up to the pain and then the blessed darkness that swept over her. At some point she opened her eyes and realised that she was lying on a bed, staring at a ceiling, but before she could get her bearings she drifted away.

There were times that she was aware that someone was trying to help her. There were distant voices, one angry, but mostly whispered that she couldn't recognise. Strong hands turned her body from one side to the other. Hands that pushed rolled-up material between her legs against which she grumbled but was helpless. Strong arms that held her on the commode. Hands that wiped her. There were times when she was aware of her clothes being lifted and her body washed. The air cold on her wet skin bringing her partly conscious, making her shiver. And when she was clean, covered up and warm again, she drifted away into darkness. Most awful of all was waking to feel cloth placed under her chin and ruffled up under her ears before hard cold porcelain was pushed into her mouth, bruising her lips, forcing her to drink a foul noxious liquid that leaked out over her cheeks and into her ears before being dabbed away when her throat refused to swallow. She was drowning in a thick mass that filled her mouth and coated her teeth, choking her.

In a dream, she was in her grandmother's house and Selina was telling her that she must drink. Emma took the cup offered

246

in the dream but was distressed to find that it held the same foul liquid. Selina's kind eyes encouraged her to drink and Emma could not disobey her grandmother who knew so much about preserving life.

Sometimes Nona's face drifted before her and sometimes Emily's, and Emma tried to think why Emily would be in her bedroom.

One morning Emma awoke to the sound of rain on the window and a blackbird singing. For a while she listened to the joyful sounds and when she looked around her saw that she was in her own room. The drapes around the bed were pulled, and the room, in half-light, seemed so peaceful and quiet that Emma lay relaxed, absorbing that peace. Gradually, she remembered that she had been poisoned and the full horror of that showed in her eyes. Lifting her arms from the covers she noted how thin they were, like bone covered in a layer of yellow, wrinkled skin. They looked nothing like her arms. She called out for Carter, but when the door opened the woman who entered was not known to her.

'Ah, at last you are awake.' The woman smiled. 'Can I get you a drink, madam?'

Emma didn't want to be difficult but could only say, 'Who are you?'

'Mrs Jeffries, madam. I have been employed by your husband as cook, but because we are understaffed,' her voice dropped, 'because of what has gone on, I pop up now and then to see if you are awake since you have been looking like you might live,' she added with a genuine smile.

'Might live?' Emma copied.

'Oh, I'm sorry. I always say too much. Let me just say that we are relieved that you are much better.'

'Thank you, Mrs Jeffries. Can you send Carter to me, I would like to sit up.'

The plump matron made a clicking noise and screwed up her face as she handed Emma a glass of water. 'That won't be possible, madam. But I can wake your sister. She hasn't left your side and she will be glad to see you awake and talking.'

As the woman bustled out of the door Emma wondered if Carter had left, or perhaps she had been given another job in the house by Patrick.

It was only moments before the door burst open and Nona, in her night attire, her hair dishevelled around her shoulders, burst into the room and ran to the bed.

'Oh, my goodness, Em, we thought that we had lost you. It was Mother who saved you, amazingly.'

'Is Mother here?'

'No, no, Mother is not here but she sent a letter, Emma, that arrived the day you ate the poison telling me what to do to save you.'

Emma stared at Nona, trying to take in what she had said. 'A letter posted nine months ago arrived the day I was poisoned?'

'Yes, and it gave me a recipe to save you.'

'What was it?'

'Blood, Emma, blood.'

'That was the awful taste! You were feeding me blood!' Emma's voice rose in shock.

'It saved your life and I am grateful for it. And so should you be. But I can't be cross. I am so thankful to be talking to you, Emma. I didn't think that we would ever talk again, you were so ill.'

'Can you help me get up, Nona, I would like to sit in the chair, and could you pull the drapes open at the window?'

'Well, it isn't the best of days, Em, it's raining.'

'Can you also open the window, Nona, I would like to smell the rain.'

'I don't know if that's a good idea, Em,' Nona frowned as she pulled the drapes back, revealing the trees in the grounds, 'you might get cold.'

'Then give me a blanket off the bed and tell me how long I have been ill.'

Having got Emma settled in an armchair, Nona was tucking the blanket in around her knees as the door opened and Mrs Jeffries waddled in, carrying a tray.

'I've brought you a coddled egg, madam. You need food inside you, you're as thin as a stick and you must be hungry. My old mum used to say you won't start getting better until you eat something.'

She smiled kindly as she placed the tray on Emma's lap and, turning away, said, 'I don't want to see any of it left, mind, when I come back for the dish, and there is hot buttered milk in the glass. We have to build you up.' And with that she left the room.

Emma was bemused by her. 'How long have we had Mrs Jeffries?'

Nona smiled. 'She has been here three weeks, Emma, and has made such a difference.'

'So, Mrs Martin has gone. Did she go to the workhouse? I hope not, I wanted to help her find a place.'

A look of pain crossed Nona's face, but all she said was, 'Let us talk about what has happened here after you have eaten something, you can't let the egg get cold.'

Emma struggled to eat the egg. It was good, cooked well, but her stomach became full very quickly. After eating she felt quite exhausted as Nona took the tray away and put it on a table.

'You're looking tired, dear, would you like to sleep?' Nona looked worried.

'The food has made me surprisingly tired, but I need to know what has happened to me, Nona. Please start at the beginning. I remember realising that the food had been poisoned and recognised the smell of rat poison. Someone tried to kill me, Nona. Why?'

'Are you sure that you wouldn't like to sleep first, Em? You do look dreadfully drained of colour.'

'No, Nona, I must know and you will tell me right now and from the beginning.'

As she spoke, she pulled the blanket up to her chest. She was getting cold. The pitter-patter of rain falling outside in the grounds continued and she could smell the wonderful fragrance of wet earth and wet brickwork. 'Nona!' Emma looked expectant.

Her sister sighed. 'I'm not sure if you are well enough yet to hear about the events of three weeks ago. It seems so long past now, Emma.'

'Not to me. To me it is like yesterday. I remember people lifting me, turning me in my bed. Start at the beginning with what you know and then I will sleep.'

With resignation in her voice Nona started. 'The food that you ate that day was poisoned. When you didn't ring the bell, Gant, in some trepidation, he said, opened the door to see if you were ready for your plate to be removed and found you on the floor, blood flowing from your nose and your mouth. At first everyone thought that you had hit your head on the table as you fell, but when you could not be roused the doctor was called. Gant and Patrick had carried you to your bed and Gant went for the doctor. This saved his life.'

'Saved *his* life?' Emma interrupted.

Nona looked pained. 'Please, Emma, don't interrupt, it's hard enough trying to remember all that has happened.'

'Sorry.' She let her head fall onto the padded chair-back and tried to relax, but had a terrible feeling of foreboding.

'When the doctor arrived,' Nona continued, 'he examined you and found that you had not knocked your head and that the blood you were losing was the wrong colour. You were losing your lifeblood through your nose and the bleeding was also coming from your gums. On further examination he found bruises on your legs and arms that you had not mentioned to anyone. Richard asked Gant to find me, as the doctor didn't think that you would see the end of the day.

'This is where it gets very strange, Emma. I had had a letter from Mother delivered that morning. In it, she said that if anyone were poisoned, I was to feed them ground oats soaked in blood. I put the letter in my pocket and went to see Dolly, as there was a message in it for her also. When I got to Tate Farm, John was about to cull an old bull that could no longer perform, and he asked me and Dolly to help him. Just as John was about to kill the bull, and Dolly and I were stroking its head and talking quietly to it, Gant arrived with the news. On hearing it and remembering the letter, I asked John to save the bull's blood in a bucket and hurried here.' Nona put her hands over her face. 'Oh, Emma, it was truly awful. I don't know how any of us will be able to live with it.'

Emma turned her face to her sister, thinking she was worried about her. 'I'm alright now, Nona.'

The young woman lowered her hands and, with a thin smile that did not part her lips, nodded and carried on with the story of events.

'By the time I arrived to see you, Richard and Patrick were here sitting with you and you were covered in leeches. The doctor had been called to the kitchen where someone else was ill.' Again, she stopped. Then stood up and, going to the window, closed it. When she turned around, Emma could see that she was very pale and her face troubled. 'I am not sure that you are well enough to know any more, Emma.'

'I am stronger than you think, Nona. I have to know all that has happened. Please do not try to protect me from something that I have to know.'

Nona sat again in the chair next to Emma and with a resigned look on her face continued, 'It had been many hours since the staff had eaten the pies that were cooked that day, and while the doctor was still here Mrs Martin collapsed and later died. She had been poisoned. We know that now, because the staff ate the same food as you.'

'Mrs Martin! Oh no, Nona, that is very sad for poor little Thomas.'

Nona ignored her sister and continued, 'Before several days had passed many of the servants had died in agony – the two scullery maids and Carter. I'm sorry, Em, the doctor tried to save them but it was too late. West and Newman have been very ill, and the doctor thinks that because they were older and strong women they survived, but they are still ill. They all had internal bleeding as did you, but we are hoping that they will make a full recovery.'

'What about Matt, did he eat any of the pie?'

'No, the men who work in the stable see to their own food, as their day can be erratic. This saved them.'

'And Richard, what about Richard?'

'He and Patrick are well. Helping with you they missed their meal. They had intended to eat the pie cold later but luckily the doctor realised where the poison had been placed, but sadly not in time to save Mrs Martin or the three young maids.'

'How did the poison get into the pies without anyone noticing?'

'If you remember, Emma, it was the day that Mary Martin was dismissed. We have found out that she had been poisoning you a little, every day, since your return from Robert. We know that now by the bruises on your arms and legs and that they were the same as Charlotte's, who she was also slowly poisoning.'

Emma's eyes widened in shock. 'We thought that was caused by her falls.'

'Yes. That also fooled the doctor when signing the death certificate, as he thought the laudanum was making her fall and bruise herself. An easy mistake that he now regrets.'

Emma was silent for a moment, thinking. 'If Martin had been dismissed how did she poison the pies and without anyone seeing her?'

'When she was out of sight of the house she placed her son in the bushes and returned to the kitchen. Mrs Martin was upstairs packing the belongings of Mary and Thomas into a parcel, and West and Newman were showing the scullery maids their new duties in the laundry room. Finding the kitchen empty, Martin took the poison from her hiding place and laced the meat that was still sitting in the pot cooling before it went into the pastry cases. She stirred it in and left. Not knowing this, Mrs Martin cooked the pies, and the staff, knowing that she was not the best of cooks, ate it anyway, even if they thought that it smelt or tasted strange.'

'Where is Martin now?'

'She's in prison awaiting trial for murder and attempted murder.'

'How did they find her so quickly, Nona?'

'She hadn't gone very far on foot. Perhaps she thought everyone would die and she could get a long way away. She left Thomas on the village green crying for his granny and then seemed to disappear.

'Richard had raised the hue and cry with the Squire and his deputies and they quickly found her making her way towards the road to London. She denies it all of course.'

'But to kill her mother, that sweet woman.' Emma was aghast. 'How can a child do that to a parent?'

'Sadly, that is not the only murder that has come to light at her hands.'

'There's more?' Emma shook her head in disbelief.

'It was Ernest Draycott who found the child and took him home to Emily. He had recognised Thomas, as he used to visit Mrs Martin where he helped out when he could with food and clothes. Thomas was crying for his granny, and it was Jacob who played with him and distracted him while Ernest came here to find out what had happened, why Thomas was left alone in the village. That is when Ernest walked in on the terrible scenes here. Returning home, as he could not help in any way, he was telling Emily that they should for now keep Thomas and look after him until the authorities decided what to do with him. He was telling her all that he had learnt about what Martin had possibly done, having forgotten about Jacob who spoke up, "She killed Mrs Jenk with a lump of wood."

'So that is why Jacob was so frightened of her!' It was all clear to Emma now.

'Yes, as it was he who had found the body in the woods and raised the alarm. Martin took him from his bed and hid him in an old part of this house. She tied him to a bed there and beat him, trying to get him to talk. When he was missed by the staff it was easy for her to say that she had searched that part of the old building and found nothing. She kept him without food or water, abandoned him, just walked away and left him to die. He told the Squire, once he knew that they had her behind bars, that on that day he had followed Martin, who he saw was following Mrs Jenk on the path through the forest. He saw Martin catch her up and speak to her. They seemed to argue. He saw Martin hit Mrs Jenk on the head with a lump of wood and when she was on the ground saw Martin search the cook's pockets. He saw Martin take her letter and then pull her off the path. He hid until Martin had gone. Then when he thought it was safe went to Mrs Jenk who he said was looking at him, but didn't see him. He ran to the village as fast as his little legs would take him and told Mr Rudd, who was in his shop, but he didn't mention Martin, only that Mrs Jenk couldn't speak or stand up.'

'So, five people have died.'

'Well, six, if the jury decide that Charlotte's death was because of the poisoning. Martin will hang. Although I think hanging is too good for her, Emma.'

'If only we had known what she was capable of we could have been rid of her sooner.' Emma's voice was full of regret.

'No, Emma.' Nona shook her head. 'How could you have known that your father-in-law was the father of Martin's child, and that she wanted this estate for her son, and that it meant more to her than the lives of others?'

'I'm not sure whether she was thinking of Thomas or herself, Nona. She didn't treat the boy well, didn't seem to love him. Was he just a means to an end?'

'Well, unless we go up to London to the trial we will never know.'

'I won't be going, Nona. I have problems of my own. Richard made it clear to me that he wants me to leave.'

Nona felt the anger rising in her chest. 'You will never be homeless, Emma. You will come and live with Dan and me at Freelanders. You will always have a home with us, you know that, don't you?'

'Yes, thank you, Nona.' A wan smile that barely touched her pale lips showed that she was grateful and, pushing the blanket aside, Emma started to stand up. 'I think I do need to sleep now,' she said, as she put her hand out for assistance to rise.

Helping her to the bed, Nona was aware of how thin her sister had become and how frail. Tucking her in and kissing her forehead she left her to sleep.

30.

Ten days passed in which Emily had visited twice and given Emma updates on Jacob and Thomas. Nona had gone home to her husband and Richard had not visited, something that Emma found deeply hurtful. In her poor mood she wondered if Richard wished that she had died; it would, she thought, have solved his problem.

The morning air was cold; a blanket of grey cloud hung depressingly low over the gardens. As Emma looked from one of the windows, a movement on the drive brought her aimless gazing at the vegetation to sudden attention. A black coach was making its way along the drive and the fact that it was pulled by four horses told her that it had come a long way.

Being unable to see the front door from her window she went to stand on the landing, looking down into the hall to see who it was that was calling.

Gant opened the door to two gentlemen in black, professional gentlemen, who she recognised from the funeral, although she had not been introduced to them.

They were shown into the library and she heard Richard's voice greet them before the door was shut.

Returning to her room Emma needed to be dressed and soon realised that she didn't have a maid, or if she did, she didn't know who she was. She paced the floor for several minutes before stopping dead and throwing her hands in the air. What was she doing? Before coming here, she had not had a maid and had been very capable of dressing herself, and doing her own hair.

With that in mind she opened the closet door, only to find that her one decent dress was not there. Opening the lid of her trunk she found only her travelling clothes and boots. She had nothing else, as Richard had not kept his promise and bought her new clothes to wear in public. For a moment she felt weak and sat on the bed holding her head. Headaches seemed to arrive when she was stressed and right now she felt like a prisoner.

Walking slowly along the landing to Charlotte's room she opened the door and walked in. It felt strangely empty without Charlotte. It had been tidied and there was no sign of the past drama that had taken place.

Going to the closet she found all Charlotte's clothes still hanging there and chose a day dress that was not too old-fashioned. Slipping it on, she soon realised that she could not fasten it behind her, so pinned it at the nape of her neck, and wrapped a shawl around her shoulders to hide the open back. Moving to the mirror to do her hair she was shocked at the sight of the thin figure staring back. Her eyes, she saw, were sunken into shadowed sockets and the facial skin was pulled tight over her cheekbones; her face seemed wasted, giving a sharpness to her chin. Hardly recognising the woman sitting reflected before her Emma's eyes filled with tears. Gently brushing her hair, she did her best to pin it up with arms that ached at the effort.

Leaving the room, she had meant to go to the library and confront Richard, but felt too weak and dizzy. Instead, she descended the servants' stairs to the kitchen where she found Mrs Jeffries happily mixing something in a bowl and the sound of singing coming from the scullery. The woman looked up as Emma entered. Shock shadowed across her face as she exclaimed, 'My goodness, madam, what are you doing all the way down here, and on your own? Come take a chair and sit at the table.'

The woman was quickly at Emma's side, pulling out a chair and helping her to sit. 'I have to say, madam, that you do not look well.'

Emma was touched by the woman's care and wished that she had been here when she had first arrived, and fleetingly thought that Mrs Jeffries would not have put up with Martin.

Now the homely woman stood before her with a look of expectation on her face. And Emma realised that she had come here just because she needed company, but in her position needed more than that for a reason to be sitting in the kitchen.

'As you know, Mrs Jeffries,' she started, 'I have not been well for some time and in that time much has changed that I don't know about. Could you tell me what staff we still need to employ?'

Mrs Jeffries shook her head in understanding. 'If you are well enough, madam, we can talk about it. But please, I have made cinnamon biscuits and I think that you should have some with hot milk before we talk.'

Emma was grateful, and hungry. Feeling the care that her own mother would have shown her, she almost broke down and cried.

The housekeeper busied herself around the kitchen while Emma ate and drank, before she also seated herself at the table.

'Now, madam, if you really feel that you are well enough?'

'Yes, really I am ready. Thank you, Mrs Jeffries.'

'Then, madam, I need two more scullery maids and another to help in the kitchen. Someone older with a little understanding of food would be helpful, or who at least could read and follow a recipe. West and Newman are back to work, they help me in the morning and do the laundry in the afternoon, but honestly, madam, it is too much for them, they are still weak, and they need two girls to take over from them if not three. The master has employed a new boot boy as the last is not coming back.'

'Oh!' Emma was surprised. 'I thought that Jacob might return now that...' She couldn't finish the sentence.

'I understand, madam, that the Draycotts would keep him to help in their stable, as that is what the boy wants to do, and came to see the master in the hope that Jacob could be released.'

'Oh!' was all that Emma could say again.

'His replacement has been here two days, madam, and is learning from Gant what is expected of him.'

'I see.' Emma nodded. Of course, they had to start hiring staff, even though she had not been able to be a part of it. 'Have we advertised for the new staff, Mrs Jeffries?' Emma asked, feeling rather left out and needing to feel a part of it again.

'Yes, madam. We have had several replies, which I have already gone through and written back. I am sorry, I didn't know that you were well enough to be consulted.'

'I would like to be at the interviews, Mrs Jeffries, especially for the hiring of my own maid.'

The homely woman looked uncomfortable, but only for a moment before she said, 'As you know, madam, I take my orders from the master through Patrick, and there has been no mention of a maid for yourself. Perhaps that will come later after the below-stairs staff have been found.' Her face was kind as she spoke and Emma wondered how much she knew of her situation with Richard.

Standing slowly Emma thanked the woman for the biscuits and milk before she made her way on painfully weak legs up the stairs.

In her room, she lay down on the bed, surprised at how much energy that little excursion had taken from her.

It was a quiet knocking on the door that later woke her. 'Come in,' she called in a voice husky with tiredness.

Emily put her head around the door. 'I'm sorry, Emma, did I wake you?'

'No, I'm just resting. Come in, Emily, it's good to see you.'

'I have been to see Richard about Jacob and thought that you would like to know what has been arranged.'

Emma slid from the bed and sat in the armchair. Emily sat opposite, declining the offer of tea.

'Is Jacob returning, Emily?'

'At this time, he does not want to return but I have agreed with Richard that I keep Jacob until he is twelve. He will have bed and board and will help my stable hand who will teach him all that he needs to know, until at twelve he will return here and work under Larch and Ames and will then receive a wage. I am happy with that and I think that Jacob will be too.'

Emma had to agree that it couldn't be better; his heart was in working with horses.

Emily looked sharply at Emma, a sad look on her face. 'I think that we are friends enough, Emma, for me to ask what you are wearing. It hangs on you and makes you look like an old lady.'

Slightly put out by Emily's directness, but knowing it to be true, Emma could only tell the truth. 'I have nothing to wear, Emily. My husband has not bought me the clothes promised. I have taken this from Charlotte's cupboard, it was the best I could find.'

'Then we will go through Charlotte's things together,' Emily said kindly, 'and choose the best material for daywear. We will alter it to fit you and in today's style. Come, let's go to her room and have a look.'

They chose a dress which had a jacket that hardly needed altering.

'From this, Emma,' Emily said, 'we can make you a decent outfit. Come to the house with me now and help me sew. We will sit before the fire and talk and design them. It will be fun.'

Not wanting to be seen out in the awful dress that she was wearing, Emma reluctantly declined.

Guessing the problem, Emily was quick to reassure her. 'No one will see you, as I have the carriage outside.'

Taking the dress back to the vicarage a difficulty soon became clear. A delicate matter. The dress laced up at the back because affluent people had maids. How would Emma dress herself if secured at the back? And if they changed the style to fasten at the front, it would put Emma immediately in a lower class. Emily looked perplexed.

'I am not of Charlotte's class, Emily,' Emma stressed. 'My clothes always did up at the front. I don't know what the future holds for me. We should put the fastenings at the front. I would be more comfortable.'

'If you are sure, Emma, then that is what we will do.'

Mrs Pendell, who had been looking at the clothes with interest, spoke almost to herself. 'Why not change it to do up at the side?'

'Mrs Pendell,' Emily almost shouted with excitement, 'that is a wonderful idea. What do you think, Emma?'

'I think, Mrs Pendell, that you are wasted as a housekeeper,' she laughed and saw the woman's dour face break into a confusion of pride and pleasure.

As they worked, Emma couldn't remember one day since being back in England that she had felt so happily engaged and a part of something.

~

Emma hadn't experienced cold November winds in thirteen years and back at the house had to raid Charlotte's shelves again for warm undergarments, of which there were many. She packed them into her trunk, knowing that she would have a need of them soon.

Her existence here was nearly at an end, she could feel it. She would have gone sooner if she'd had somewhere to go and hadn't been ill. But even as she thought it, she knew it wasn't true. She needed an income and that was what she was holding out for.

The first snow had fallen during the night and Emma, now sleeping with the drapes open, was woken early by the light and the quietness. Pushing her arms under the covers for warmth she lay, still afraid of the sense of anxiety that crept into her soul each day. If it were the herald of change, then it would be a relief, but she knew from experience that even at its lowest ebb, life could get worse.

She was sitting up in bed when the door opened suddenly and a young maid entered, holding a large bucket. She bobbed. 'Good morning, madam,' she murmured, before going to the fireplace and placing the bucket on the hearth where she knelt to salvage the fire.

'Good morning,' Emma returned, not having the will to learn the girl's name.

'Mrs Jeffries said to build it good and hot today. It's cold enough to freeze the nose off an 'orse.' She spoke head down over her task, letting the shovel scrape loudly as it moved under the ash.

Emma pulled the bed covers up over her head and closed her eyes to shut out not only the maid but the world.

She must have slept, for when she awoke the maid had gone and the fire was settled and hot. Her clothes were warming on the guard before the fire and the maid had placed a jug of water before the fire to keep warm. Washing and dressing for the day, Emma left her room, wondering what to do to keep herself amused, when she saw Ernest below in the hall, being shown into the library.

She had just decided to take a walk when a new maid hurried up the stairs with a message from Richard asking her to join him in the library.

Entering as she did now unannounced, she felt a flutter of apprehension as two serious faces turned towards her.

'Ah, Emma, please take a seat.' As Richard spoke he had a strange look on his face, one that she couldn't read. Ernest, she noted, was pale; a look of pain crossed his face as he acknowledged her with a slight nod.

'Is something wrong, Richard? Have you heard from my mother?'

'No, I have not heard from your mother, but I do have some news that will affect you.'

She took a seat and waited for him to begin.

Richard turned to Ernest and, nodding, he gave permission for him to speak.

Emma looked from one to the other and noted how nervous Ernest appeared. She smiled to encourage him, although her heart was pounding.

His voice held such sadness that panic rose in her throat and, feeling dizzy, she realised that she had stopped breathing. He was saying, 'Believe me when I say that I am truly sorry, Emma.'

Sorry for what? shot through her mind. And he had never called her by her given name other than when they were at his home or alone.

'I have just informed Richard,' he continued, 'that I have been in touch with the Church about your divorce as he asked of me, and it is with regret that I have to inform you...' he stopped, closed his eyes, just for a second before he sighed and carried on as though having taken strength from some invisible force, '... that you are not married and never were married in the eyes of the Church.'

In the silence that followed no one moved, no one said anything. Only the sound of the fire crackling filled the room that could otherwise have been empty. Emma felt the room swim around her as the enormity of that statement hit her. They had never been married! She had been living, not only out of her class, but out of wedlock, passing herself off as Richard's wife. How would she ever be able to face the world? Society would have no mercy on such a woman as she.

'Emma! Drink this.' Richard was holding a small amount of brandy in a glass before her face. She took it but could not raise it to her lips. There was no energy in her arm, so she held it between her hands in her lap, feeling abandoned.

'I'm sorry,' Ernest was saying, 'I had to tell you in person.'

'Yes, of course, Ernest, thank you for coming.'

Her voice seemed far away, floating somewhere in front of her, and the men standing before her seemed blurred. They were talking, yet her ears seemed to have shut out the sound; she watched their lips moving, but heard nothing.

Ernest took his leave, full of apologies to which Emma could only nod.

When they were alone Richard said, 'I have to speak with you on a more urgent matter, Emma.'

Dully, she wondered what could be even more urgent than the devastating news that she had just received.

Richard paced the room. 'I have been in touch with my accountant and we are deeply in debt. It is as I thought. I am inept in business and have been advised to employ someone to help me. It means, Emma, that although I need the income from the farms, I cannot keep all three and might even lose the house. I have decided to sell back to John Brisket the fields that my father bought from Andrew Tate and to sell at least one if not two of my three farms to allow money for wages.'

It all seemed to be going over her head until he mentioned selling a farm.

'I hope, Richard, that you will not sell Freelanders. Nona and Dan are making a real difference there.'

'Yes, Emma, and that is why someone would see it as a great prospect.'

'Have you no heart, Richard?' She raised her voice. 'That girl could have died saving your life and this is how you repay her. I see very clearly now that I married a coward. You have proved to be the worst kind of husband, a weakling, afraid of his mother and afraid of hard work. You have kept me hanging on all these months with promises that you never intended to keep. What am I to do now, Richard?'

In reply he shook his head and she saw that he looked sorry. 'I have no money to give you, Emma. I am afraid that you must do as you wish.'

'Then I will leave as soon as I can.' She spoke bravely, although her eyes flooded with tears and her heart pounded in her chest.

With that she stood unsteadily and he rushed to get the door for her. Without a second glance at the man who had never been her husband she stoically walked up the stairs with a straight back, her head held high. In her room she broke down and sobbed at the horror that had befallen her. She had brazenly lived in public with a man to whom she was not married. Now she knew that she was tainted. No man would want her for a wife. Robert would probably not want her under his roof. She was an embarrassment. In these circumstances she could not stay in the area living with Nona or with Dolly. She had no money to travel and would have to walk, taking only what she could carry.

31.

An ice-laden wind howled below a leaden sky as Emma left the Manor House, in which she had never been happy and in which she could have died. In one way it was a relief to be leaving, walking away, yet she now felt more isolated and lost than ever. Dan had been to collect her trunk and would deliver it to her when she had a place to stay.

All that she now owned was on her back. She wore two sets of Charlotte's winter underwear beneath her day dress and her travelling coat on top. The new going-out dress and jacket had gone with Dan in her small trunk.

As Mrs Jeffries gave her a hat to keep her hair dry and a thick shawl to go around her shoulders, Emma was sorry that she wouldn't get to know her better. She had made such a difference. The staff smiled and laughter was often heard coming from the kitchen. The food was good and Mrs Jeffries was a good manager. Richard did not come to say goodbye and had given her no money for a carriage.

She had barely walked eight miles when darkness fell quickly upon the deep lane in which she walked beneath skeletal trees, already fallen into their winter slumber.

Sitting on a milestone to rest she knew that she was in trouble. A woman alone on a dark lane with no destination on a winter's night would be in danger. She wanted to cry, but instead pulled the shawl tighter around her shoulders and thought about looking for a piece of dry ground on which to lie down and see out the night.

Her hands were frozen with cold as she pulled herself up the high bank at the side of the lane by the tree roots that stuck out like handles, and used them also as footholds. By the time she reached the top of the bank she was hot with the effort and muddy, but safer than if she had stayed in the lane. Dropping down the other side she found herself in a wood and walked with difficulty in the darkness between the trees, her hand outstretched to feel for obstacles, and still she stumbled over ground roots, falling several times.

The fierce wind that had been stripping the leaves from the trees all day seemed to hold no sway in the depth of the wood. Shielded amongst the trees the leaves here lay deep and unmoving upon the ground. She had just chosen a tree under which to lie down when a sharp bang split the silence, making her jump. Standing still, her hand against the tree, she steadied herself, unsure of the direction of the sound or what it was. When it came again she recognised it immediately and moved towards it; perhaps help was nearby.

The sound of a door banging in the wind came again, leading Emma not to a house as she had hoped but to a dilapidated shack, a storehouse, hidden in a small clearing. There was just enough light as she approached to see that the walls were rough-hewn planks that did not meet and that the roof had been turfed to make it watertight.

The wind was taking the door and blowing it against the wooden wall as she approached. Looking inside she could see sawn logs stacked floor to ceiling and there was just enough room for her to wedge her body inside. Taking two small logs she put one behind the door and one in front to stop it banging, then sat in the small space against the plank wall, hoping that the log pile wouldn't move and kill her.

She sat for a long time listening to the silence of the wood, too frightened to feel hunger, and was soon in a restless sleep.

It was the grating sound of the door being pulled back sharply that woke her. Through bleary eyes she faced an elderly man holding a whip in one hand. He was staring down at her, his face contorted with anger.

'Git up, thief,' he shouted, flicking the whip at her to emphasise his meaning.

Her limbs were stiff with the cold as Emma stood with difficulty in the small space. 'I'm not a thief,' she retorted, 'I was sheltering, that is all.'

'I knows you be stealing me wood and now I have you caught hot-handed. Git out. I'm taking you to the magistrate.'

'But I haven't stolen your wood.' She felt afraid. Why would the magistrate believe her? 'I don't have a home to burn it in and I didn't even burn some to keep warm last night.' Her voice begged for understanding.

'You knozs you're only allowed to glean the forest floor, yet you steals me livelihood. Git outside where I can see you better.'

As she stepped outside she caught a better glimpse of the whip. The handle was of plaited leather; she had seen one like it before. Looking closer at the angry man she noticed his thick neck and strong arms and thought that she recognised him.

'It is Mr Buckle, isn't it? Mim Buckle?' she said, as she moved through the door into the icy morning air.

He frowned. 'Many people would know me but that don't mean that they wouldn't take anything they could without paying.' His old eyes searched her face for some recognition.

'I'm Emma...' She was going to say Laddisbrock but of course she wasn't and it felt strangely alien to her to say Emma Tilby after so long, but she did.

'Emma Tilby!' he said, not looking convinced. 'I 'eard you went to Australia. Tuther side of the world. How could you get back from there?'

'It's a long way, sir. It took nine months to travel home.'

'If that be the case, what you doing in me wood store?'

'I'm travelling, sir, but it got dark before I could reach where I was going.'

Mim looked suspicious. 'Women don't travel alone. No woman should be alone outside at night, especially in this cold. Why didn't you leave yoursel' more time?'

'It was further than I thought. But I'm glad that it was you that found me.' She smiled at him, for it was the truth.

Ignoring her smile, he said suspiciously, 'And you're not taking me wood?' He looked for a bag.

'No, sir! I can assure you that I have no luggage. I am wearing all the clothes that I possess. Please search me if you don't believe me.' She held her arms open ready to be searched.

At that his face flushed red and he declined, turning away. 'I won't detain you further, Mistress Tilby. You be on your way.'

'How is Lady?' Emma asked, remembering his long-suffering horse. Mim and Lady were famous.

He looked sad, stuck out his bottom lip and made a clicking sound with his cheeks. 'She died. Old age. She was a good 'orse.'

'I'm sorry.' Emma didn't know what else to say, she just kept making the situation worse.

'I got another 'orse now. Me daughter named her Prickle, cos that's 'er nature. She's a good strong 'orse but tetchy, specially first thing in the morning when I needs 'er to get going for a long journey. Good luck with your travelling,' he said, moving off towards where Emma could now see his cart and a large black horse, a white blaze between its eyes.

As Mim approached her, Prickle shook her head and stepped back away from him snorting. 'Don't be so daft, you stupid 'orse.' He caught the reins and pulled the animal forward. It shook its head violently, stretching Mim's arm high above his head. He spoke quietly to the animal, stroking her nose, and eventually she came, slowly, but there was, Emma thought, a manic look in her eye.

'I wonder, Mr Buckle, if you could take me some of the way.'

'Some of the way to where?' He frowned. 'I don't give lifts for free.'

Emma knew that she looked crestfallen and that he saw it. 'I don't have any money.' She raised her shoulders at the inevitability of her situation. 'But I could help you load your cart,' she said with sudden inspiration.

His eyebrows knitted together in a frown that completely changed his face into something she had seen on a church wall, a gargoyle, and a snort issued from his nose. She was about to admit she shouldn't have asked when he said, 'I will give you a lift to the next town and no further.'

32.

Emma looked around her in amazement, seeing Horsham for the first time. She wasn't really sure what a town would look like, but knew that it would be a whole lot bigger than Haddenford. The streets, as Mim entered the town, were busy with every type of conveyance imaginable. In the square a stagecoach was pulled up outside an inn where people were alighting. Another group of people in travelling attire were waiting to board, surrounded by their bags and trunks that lay in the road. There were two drivers in black livery and a boy helping with the unloading and loading. The horses, being removed from the shafts, were being taken to the stable behind the inn.

They walked slowly, almost regally, and it seemed to Emma that the stagecoach looked sad and abandoned without the horses.

The town's buildings, she noticed as they carried on down the wide main street, were mostly two-storey and made of brick with wooden-faced upper floors. She wondered vaguely how anyone kept warm behind wooden boards. They were unlike the buildings in Haddenford that were mostly thatched and one-storey with thick wattle and daub walls which kept out the cold and the heat.

The street was busy and noisy with people walking and riding in carriages. The noise, she thought, was almost as bad as she had endured in London the short time that she was there with her mother thirteen years ago.

They passed shops with living accommodation above unlike that of Mr Rudd's general store in Haddenford, where he and his family lived in one room at the back of his shop. Emma craned her neck to see what the shops were selling, but the windows were so small and dark below her that in the end she had to be content with reading the shop signs below which men, women and children walked in great numbers.

It seemed from the signs that many items for sale were being made and sold on the premises. She saw, as they passed, a furniture and tall clock case maker. A master clock mender, a coach builder, a draper's shop and a butcher's that had a slaughterhouse at the back. Further down the street, set back, a smithy with horses waiting patiently and a group of men talking in a group. She didn't get to see much more as Mim pushed Prickle on through the mayhem, and just after they left the square with its market stalls, Mim turned the horse and cart towards a scruffy-looking tavern. As they approached she tried to read the sign that hung from an iron bar above the entrance, but the picture and words painted on it were peeling and unreadable. Compared to the inn, in the marketplace, this building looked desolate.

Mim manoeuvred them skilfully through a narrow gap, and the sound of Prickle's hooves clipping the cobbles was heightened by the tall walls on each side. Having left the busy street behind, peace descended upon their ears and anxiety now pulled at Emma's stomach, knowing that this was the end of her journey.

They broke out from the passage into the tavern's yard at the back where a stable block stood on one side and on another a row of barrels were stacked three high against a wall. At the end of the stable block, in front of a tiny wooden closet with a broken door, a small two-wheeled pushcart was tipped on end, its long handles in the air.

'This is as far as I take you,' Mim said as Emma was looking around, and getting down from the cart he started to unhitch Prickle.

Emma descended slowly from the high seat and stood, feeling lost and vulnerable, wondering what she should do next.

The stable block housed three horses whose heads hung over their stalls watching the newcomers with interest.

Mim, having released Prickle, walked her across the yard to the water trough that stood solid and grey beside a rough door. Leaving the horse to drink, he patted her neck and returned to the cart for a sack of feed, which he then hung on a hook set in the wall a small distance from the trough.

Looking around the yard Emma noted that the air smelt strongly of horse, beer and urine, and that the straw and manure that littered the cobbles hadn't been swept. The wall nearest the back entrance to the tavern had a wide patch of yellow upon it that had crystallised. There were runs of yellow and a pool of it on the ground. It stank of human urine, which was not as pleasant as horse. This, she guessed, was where the men relieved themselves of the ale they'd drunk inside the tavern.

The building was wide, with a small mullioned window on the ground floor overlooking the yard. Above that, a line of six windows on the first floor lay in the shadow of the roof, where plants grew unattended between the wooden roof tiles. A small window in the roof, its glass broken and cobwebbed, contributed to the overall look of neglect and desolation.

Her anxiety grew as she turned to face the man who had saved her from the vagrancies of walking the roads and lanes alone.

'Thank you, Mr Buckle,' Emma said quietly as he returned to the cart to unload it. Now she was here she was unsure where to go so asked, 'Could you tell me where I might find work? Perhaps recommend somewhere.'

His brow knitted in a frown as he weighed her up with serious eyes, shrugged his shoulders and looked at a loss. 'What can you do?' He sounded uncertain.

She thought about it. What could she do in a town? In the end she said pathetically, 'Clean.'

He shook his head and sighed. 'Try in there, in the Standard.' He nodded towards the rough back door to the tavern. 'Beth might need someone. No one stays long and my God it needs a clean.'

As Mim unloaded the logs from the cart Emma entered the door beside the stinking yellow patch on the wall. Inside, a narrow passage was lined with more barrels, and in the semi-darkness she knocked into one with her knee and yelped. A door opened at the far end of the passage and a maid's head poked out.

'What you doing in the passage? You thieving?'

'No!' Emma retorted, struggling to speak as she rubbed the pain from her knee. 'I'm looking for work.'

'Well you won't find it in there.' The head withdrew from the gap, leaving enough light for Emma to find her way to the end unscathed.

Walking through the half-open door she stepped into a large flag-stoned kitchen unlike anything that she had seen before. Two walls were lined with shelves on which sat dusty bottles, flagons and stacks of bowls, plates and drinking pots, lamps and candles. A shovel leant against a barrel without a lid, in which Emma thought there was flour, and noted the mouse or rat droppings on the floor around the bottom of the barrel. There were four other barrels stacked one upon another beside a door that was hung with a hessian curtain.

A small table stood in one corner and a long table filled the middle of the room. Upon this lay half-gutted and quartered bloody animal carcasses crawling with flies. Sawdust, turning red, soaked up the blood that pooled on the floor beneath the table. Pans bubbled noisily and steam rose towards the high beamed ceiling. The heat from the huge fire, before which a carcass turned on a spit, filled the room. For a moment, Emma thought the warmth wonderful as she stood just inside the door. But the cold of the outside had hardly left her body when the smell and heat in the kitchen began to claw at her throat.

The young maid that had spoken to her in the passage stood before three cook-pots, stirring one with a large wooden paddle. Not as tall as Emma, she seemed frail. Skin and bone.

As the maid turned to look at her, Emma noticed that her skin was grey with dirt and her hair lank with grease. The bottom of her grey skirt was stained brown, which Emma thought must be blood and dirt soaked up from the floor.

Smiling at the girl Emma hoped for friendship. But without a word the girl turned back to her task.

'Who should I see about work?' Emma asked above the noise of the boiling pots and the sound of loud voices coming from the other side of the curtain.

The maid gave a sharp nod towards the next room from where the voices rose.

Walking across the kitchen and pulling the curtain back, Emma stepped into a crowded room and found herself standing behind a long narrow table where she was assaulted by a hubbub of men's voices. Conversations were loud, mixed with shouts for more beer, the clanking of pots and the sound of a piercing laugh as the landlady served her clients.

A man sitting at a small table nearby noticed Emma and raised an eyebrow. Licking his lips, he shouted to no one in particular, 'Well, men, things are looking up,' and continued to leer at her over his pot of ale.

A cloud of smoke suddenly billowed out from the fire in the inglenook further up the room; mixing with the smoke from the men's pipes it caused a deeper haze that hid the size of the room from her. People sitting at tables or standing in conversation became distant shadowy outlines to Emma. The overriding smell of smoke, beer and male sweat caught in her throat and made her cough.

The landlady, a large woman, tall with muscular arms, was handing two pots of ale across the table from one of three barrels on the wall behind her when she turned and, seeing Emma, looked surprised.

'You want something?' Her voice had a deep gravelly richness caused by years of smoke inhalation. Emma noticed that her bodice was cut very low at the front and that her huge breasts had a need to escape the confines of the dirty material that encased them as they heaved in the face of the drinkers.

Faced with such a woman Emma felt out of her depth and embarrassed. 'I'm looking for work,' is all she could shout above the noise.

Beth Standard, a woman with greying hair, stared hard at the young woman who had just appeared from her kitchen. Wiping her hands on the hessian apron tied around her waist, Beth frowned, considering Emma. 'What can you do?'

'I can do anything that you ask.' Emma tried to look eager.

A man near enough to overhear whooped with mock joy. 'Come 'ere,' he laughed, 'I can give you summat to do.'

'Shut up, Skilly,' Beth sneered as she walked past him looking Emma up and down. 'I'm usually a good judge of people, mistress, but not with you.' She frowned. 'I don't ask questions, but you don't look strong enough to work for me.'

'You won't know if you don't let me try.' Emma was quick to respond out of desperation.

Beth screwed up her face; wrinkling her wide nose she weighed Emma up. She mistrusted a woman who arrived in clothes of quality, covered in mud, as though she'd been sleeping in the open. Observing in that short moment that Emma had the face and body of someone who knew hunger or sickness, Beth wondered if she was going to bring trouble to their door.

'Are you sick?' Her words were delivered sharply. 'I don't want no sickness here.'

'I'm not sick, mistress.'

'Are you running from the law?' The landlady scowled. 'I don't want no law breakers working for me.'

Emma was shocked at her directness. 'No, mistress, just fallen on hard times.'

Beth stared straight into Emma's eyes, looking for the lie, but didn't find it. 'I'll take you on and see how you do. You can sleep in the kitchen, all the rooms are taken.'

The men were banging their pots on the table and Beth shouted to someone called Bishop to come and serve. She held Emma's gaze for a long moment before saying, 'How do you want to be paid, money or food?'

Emma thought for only a moment and although she was hungry decided on money. With money she could buy food and get a lift to somewhere else if life didn't work out here.

'Money,' she said strongly.

'As you said money I will give you a try.'

Beth moved through the curtain and into the kitchen with Emma following. Reaching up she took a bowl from a shelf. 'I'll give you a small bowl of food to stop you eating my profit. If you had said food, I would have turned you away.'

Emma looked askance. 'Why?'

'Why!' Beth shook the bowl at Emma. 'Is because as soon as you'd eaten you would've left. I've seen it before.' She sounded resigned. 'The starving will do anything to get food. Sit there in the corner out of the way and eat this.' She handed Emma the bowl filled with boiled mutton.

'Joan!'

Beth turned away to speak to the maid.

Emma ate with such speed that she almost forgot to breathe and became dizzy.

After Beth had gone back to the bar, Joan took the empty bowl from Emma's hands.

'You got to set to and work now. And you better take them fancy clothes off.'

Emma removed her travelling clothes, leaving them in a pile in the corner of the kitchen on the dirty stone floor. There was nowhere else to put them.

Joan gave her a filthy hessian apron and a large knife, telling her to get chopping the carcasses on the table.

The work was difficult for Emma, the bones resistant to her feeble hacking with the knife, and she was soon exhausted, covered in blood and almost in tears. 'Here.' Joan elbowed her out of the way, taking the knife from her. 'We can't wait all day for you.' She spoke sharply. 'You stir the pot and fill three bowls and take them through to the bar. And don't dally with the men or Bishop will clip your ear.'

'Bishop?' Emma queried as she took a bowl to the boiling pan.

'The landlord. He'll likely take to you and give me a rest. Mind,' she snorted, 'you look too good for the likes of 'im.'

Beth's loud voice came from the bar. 'Joan, where a them bowls?'

'You better hurry,' Joan said with a smirk. 'It won't please them if they have to come looking for them bowls.'

Taking two filled bowls Emma hurried through the curtain and into the thick fug of the bar. Beth took the two bowls and Emma hurried back to the kitchen for the third.

The day progressed so quickly that Emma had not realised night had arrived. She had poured beer, stirred the pans, cut bread and ripped meat from the bones of the carcasses ready for the pot. By midnight she was exhausted and sore where men had pinched her backside, hips and arms. Eventually, the last of the customers had gone, the travellers were to their beds and the doors had been locked. Joan had been instructed to collect the 'all-sorts', the dregs from the pots left on the tables, and she was tipping those leftovers into a small barrel; the contents, Emma was told, would be for sale at a cheaper price tomorrow.

Beth and Bishop Standard were sitting in the silence of the bar before the fire, with a pot each, talking. Bishop was not an attractive man, rotund like his wife and squat with a bloated face. His small eyes were almost hidden by large dough-round cheeks, below which a large mouth turned down in constant disapproval. His short muscular arms Emma had seen were useful for lifting barrels and rowdy customers, and she'd taken an instant dislike to him.

It was late, and Emma had done her best to sweep the stickiness from the bar floor with water and a broom as instructed by Beth. After covering the floor with a fresh coating of sawdust she emptied the spittoons and washed them in the dirty floor water, before throwing the contents out into the dark yard. Turning the bucket upside down she left it by the door before returning to the kitchen to see where she would sleep.

Joan indicated the corner where Emma had left her travelling coat and where a thin blanket had been left on top. Picking it up, Emma looked at Joan with a question on her face. 'Is there nothing to lie on, Joan?'

The maid shrugged her shoulders. 'You could pull the bench over.'

Emma looked at the filthy bench with its layer of encrusted blood sitting beneath the table and decided that the floor in the corner was probably cleaner, and she was too tired and sore to drag a long heavy bench across the flagstones.

Having removed her dress, she laid the blanket on the floor and lay down in her shift. The floor felt hard beneath her back. Pulling her coat up over her aching body she slept instantly.

Dreaming that she and Richard were back on the homestead in her cabin, she dreamt that he was climbing into their bed. It was late; he was whispering lustful thoughts into her hair. She woke with a start as something touched her ankle. The solid body of a man on his knees was leaning over her. Bringing her free arm up fast, her fist connected with his nose and she screamed as loud as she could. He cursed and held his face. Bringing her legs up, she planted her feet in his chest and pushed hard. The man fell heavily to the floor cursing. He was trying to get to his feet using the table to pull himself up when a lamp swung into the room and Beth shouted, 'What the hell is going on down here?' Then seeing her husband leaning on the table said, 'What are you doing, Bishop?'

'I'm sorry, my love,' he croaked, 'I bumped into the table in the dark.'

'Well I'd appreciate it if you wouldn't wake me with that screaming once I'm asleep. I work hard, Bishop, and I don't like being disturbed.'

'I know, my love. I'm sorry. I just couldn't see.'

'Well maybe if you drank less of the profits,' she retorted, 'you would be able to see better. Now get to your bed before I make you scream again.'

'Yes, my love,' he whined like a miscreant child who'd been caught being naughty.

Emma watched from the floor as he shambled slowly in the poor light across the room towards Beth's lamp. The door at the bottom of the stairs shut behind them. Their footsteps clumped loudly on the wooden stairs as they ascended to their room. The floorboards overhead creaked, marking their passage across the floor above, before a door closed with a bang and silence fell upon the tavern. Mercifully the kitchen was left in the peaceful glow of the dying fire.

Next morning, Joan shook Emma awake at four thirty, just as Bishop was bringing in a sheep carcass which he laid on the long table. He looked in her direction and scowled, his red nose standing out between his puffy cheeks. Getting up quickly, Emma pulled her dress over her head and asked Joan where she might relieve herself. She was directed to the closet with the broken door in the yard. It stank and buzzed with flies but she had to use it.

Back in the kitchen she and Joan worked together to get the bread and meat ready for the travellers' breakfast. The preparation of food went on all day and Emma's hair was now as greasy and lank as Joan's as the day passed quickly, in a spin of preparation and delivery of food to the bar.

The winter nights pulled in early and the doors were never shut before midnight. Emma felt exhausted. She and Joan ate late, sitting together at the small table on which the bread was kneaded.

'How long have you worked here, Joan?' Emma asked, curious about the girl.

Joan raised her shoulders. 'Don't know.'

'Why don't you know, Joan?'

The girl shrugged her shoulders again but didn't stop eating. 'You'd better eat,' she observed. 'You won't get no more.' And she continued to concentrate on her bowl, her dirty hands and arms working quickly to get the food to her mouth.

Emma followed suit. When they had finished she asked Joan where she could wash.

The girl looked at Emma, eyes wide with curiosity. 'Why would you want to wash?'

'I need to wash, Joan. I feel dirty from the meat, the smoke, the food that we just ate.'

'If they,' Joan nodded towards the bar, 'find you washing in their time, you'll be out of here with no money. And anyway,' she frowned, 'it's a strange thing to do. I hear it can kill you stone dead.'

'But at day's end, Joan, surely I can rest and not be on their time.'

The girl laughed. 'If they employ you, every hour is their time. Even when you sleep it's because they let you.'

Emma started to worry. When it was time for her to leave, would she get her money? But right now, she had nowhere else to go.

At the end of each day Emma was so tired that it was harder for her to wake in the morning. Joan had to rouse her twice before she could stand up and put her dress on. The work was constant and she didn't know how much longer she would be able to continue, and had come to admire Joan who just kept going.

On Saturday evening the men were asked to urinate into a bucket in the yard until it was full. After Bishop tipped some of it out onto the cobbles Joan carried it in, her back bent, to the fire in the kitchen where it stayed heating and steaming all evening giving off noxious fumes.

After midnight when the doors were locked Beth instructed Emma to take a hard brush and scrub the sticky bar floor with the hot liquid in the bucket. A great protest born of revulsion swelled into revolt and Emma told Beth that she didn't want to do it.

Beth's thin smile did not reach her eyes as she calmly said, 'If you want your coins, mistress, you will scrub that floor with your own blood if I tell you to.'

Not wanting to lose the money that she had already worked for, Emma hefted the bucket away from the fire. Joan had already swept the sawdust out into the yard, leaving the stone floor of the bar exposed.

Kneeling with the scrubbing brush, Emma hesitated, not wanting to put her hands into the dark yellow liquid.

Still scowling at her whenever his wife wasn't looking, Bishop shouted at her from his position in front of the fire, 'Get on with it or you'll feel my boot.'

Emma sunk her hands into the warm liquid and with tears in her eyes started scrubbing. The smell made her nose run, and soon her dress and knees were soaked where she knelt. When finished, she threw the contents of the bucket into the yard, rinsed it and left it upside down beside the door. Her wet dress clung to her legs and she needed to wash, hardly able to bear the smell of herself.

In the bar Joan was distributing clean sawdust to the floor while Bishop and Beth sat by the fire with their night-time nip of brandy.

While no one was watching, Emma went to the yard and broke the ice in the horse trough to wash her hands and face. It was a quick affair that froze her face and fingers, and although it woke her brain, it did little to move the greasy dirt that was now ingrained in her skin.

It was five in the morning and still dark as Beth unbolted the front door, letting in the cold morning air. The first travellers would be arriving before seven and they would want to be fed. Emma knew that this would be the only time that she would have to talk to Beth about her wage.

As Beth moved sluggishly across the room between the tables, Emma approached her with a small glass of brandy. She had learnt that you could not speak to Beth before she had had her liquid breakfast. Taking it and downing it in one gulp, she looked at Emma with a raised and questioning eyebrow.

Emma was almost unnerved; if Beth wanted she could sack her on the spot and send her away with nothing. But she came straight out with it. 'Could I have the money that I have earned, Beth?'

'You thinking of leaving us, mistress?' The woman's bleary eyes had narrowed.

'I don't know. Maybe not today, but I will soon have need of the money to continue my journey.'

'But not today?'

'No.'

'Then you don't need the money.'

'I do want the money. I want to have what I have earned so that when I'm ready I can buy a coach ticket.'

Beth stared at her for what seemed a long time in silence but Emma stood unmoving; she would not back down.

Beth sniffed. 'See me at the end of the day. I will have you work for me at least for today.'

Pushing past Emma, she shouted over her shoulder, 'Don't just stand there, madam, you're on my time, get the fire lit.'

Emma smiled as she cleared the grate of ash and rebuilt the fire. The travellers would want to warm themselves before catching the coach, and if they were warm they would buy food before their journey. This is where Beth and Bishop made most of their money.

Although tired, Emma started the day with hope in her heart and worked harder than she had any other day. Her employment had lasted for three long weeks in which she had not been out in the air, had eaten very little and always in a rush. And, through sleeping on a stone floor without a proper bed or covers, she felt old, crippled, every muscle in her body ached and she could hardly stand upright anymore without pain in her back. If she didn't leave soon she would die before she could.

That evening, when the doors were locked, Beth gave her a small bag containing the coins that she had earned.

And next morning Emma walked towards the office of the coach company in Market Street to buy a ticket that would take her as far as a town near Robert. Although, what his reaction would be to her dirty appearance or the story that she would in all honesty have to tell him, she could not imagine.

Aware of her dirty appearance as she walked along the unfamiliar street she kept her head down. As she came to the corner of Market Street she almost bumped into a man who apologised and stepped back to allow her to pass.

'Mrs Laddisbrock, is it you?' The voice sounded unsure.

In response to the question Emma looked up and was horrified to see Jon's face staring back at her. Although he wore a hat, his blond hair still fell over one eye. His clothes, she noticed briefly, were now of good quality, making her even more ashamed of her own appearance.

'No, sir,' she replied quickly, 'I'm afraid you have the wrong person.'

Walking hurriedly on, she weaved between people and market stalls until she felt that she was hidden from him. A heaviness had fallen upon her. Never, in all her romantic thoughts, would she have believed that she would want to turn away from Jon. What terrible quirk of fate had brought them to the same town when she had fallen so far from the grace of decent society? A woman who had lived openly and unmarried with a man. A woman who had let all and sundry think that she was married. And now, although she was not ashamed that she was working, after all this was her true class, she was ashamed that she was so changed and so dirty on both fronts.

~

Jon stared after the woman he had just spoken to and felt confused. Perhaps it wasn't Emma. The woman was grey with dirt, her clothes stained and creased as though she had slept in them, and there was an unholy smell about her. But as he walked on he couldn't get her out of his mind. The voice was the same. She was thin and dirty, and the hair that hung below the hat was thick with grease, but there was something about her that reminded him of Emma. Perhaps, he thought, he had been thinking of her for so long that he was now going mad.

~

Emma bought the cheapest ticket, to sit out on top of the coach as she knew that she smelt of fat, smoke and urine and could not bear the thought of people inside the coach turning their heads away or complaining to the driver. At the booking desk the clerk had stared at her for longer than was necessary and she wondered if he thought that she had stolen the money.

With her ticket for the afternoon coach in her pocket and a little money left for food, she ate some cooked pork and bread from a market stall and asked the stallholder if there was a stream in Horsham. The woman nodded. 'River's that way. Walk down the Causeway to the church.' She pointed briefly before turning to another customer.

Emma followed the woman's direction away from the market and entered a wide road lined with beautiful houses. She walked quickly not wanting even a servant to see or smell her. At the lower end of the road, on her left, a huge house with a massive garden stood behind a high wall and on the other side of the road small cottages slept before the magnificent church that blocked the end of the road. Emma could see that to get to the river she would have to walk through the graveyard.

Pulling her coat tighter around her frame she enjoyed her anonymity and the silence as she made her way along the path and around the church to the river flowing at the back. After what she had been through at the tavern, she felt a tremendous feeling of freedom as she walked in the silence and came to the water. But the edge of the bank was a tangle of impenetrable frosted plants making the water difficult to reach.

Walking on a short distance she found a spot where the bank had eroded enough for her to stand on a small shingle beach. Bending to the cold water she gave thanks to the Goddess and washed her face and hands vigorously. The water was so cold that her hands soon became red and her fingers ached. Seeing her reflection in the water she was appalled at her appearance and realised that there wouldn't be any use her washing the dirt from her clothes, as she would then have to wear them wet and would freeze to death. Also, that the cold water would not remove the grease from her hair.

Standing up, she twisted her hair into one long tight mass behind her head. Then, pushing the end into the start of the twist at her scalp, she pulled it through, twisting it into a bun. Hoping that it would hold she replaced the hat and returned slowly to the market from where the coach would leave at half past noon.

As she hurried she mused ironically, If Charlotte could see the state of her clothes now, she would believe that her assessment of me was right. I'm nothing but a filthy homeless servant. Lower than the servants in her home. I'm where she always thought that I belonged.

~

When he had arrived in Horsham, Jon had taken a room in a lodging house near the church of St Mary. He had previously found the small hamlet where the Reverend Harding had lived with his wife and preached, but she was not there. He found the latest incumbent, a grossly overweight man, unhelpful, pretending that he didn't know the woman or where she had gone. It was a chance meeting with a child who told him that she had gone to Horsham to live in her parents' cottage. Jon set off again and would not settle until he had found the widow and given her her husband's bible and notebook. As he had walked the lanes towards Horsham he had hoped that he would find her still alive.

What he eventually found was a frail woman, who had suffered during the long absence of her husband and his unforgiving congregation who had turned their back on her. And Jon quickly realised that she was bitter and unforgiving of her husband.

She had read the notebook and given it back to him, not wanting it, but had kept the family bible. Out of respect for the Reverend, Jon had stayed to help her with her vegetable patch and done small jobs around the cottage that had been neglected because of her frailty. They had, in the end, enjoyed a sort of relationship akin to aunt and nephew. But she had not allowed Jon to speak of her husband, a man that she felt had let her down, betrayed her and left her destitute. It made Jon sad, as he had had such high regard for the man that had protected him from the abusive violence of some of the prisoners in the penal colony.

He was then shocked when one morning the doctor had knocked on his door to tell him that Mrs Harding had died in her sleep during the night. It was, for Jon, a sad day when he attended her funeral, a poor affair with only himself, the vicar and her doctor in attendance.

With the object of his need to stay in Horsham removed, Jon took time to think about whether he should stay here or move on. He had decided that as he had no roots it mattered not where he lived. His one sadness was that he had met and fallen in love with Emma Laddisbrock and that she was married. That fact, he had the proof of in the notebook, and he decided in his moments of despair that his life had started as a sad life and would probably end as an even sadder life. That was, until a letter arrived from Mrs Harding's solicitor asking Jon to come to his office where he was told that Mrs Harding had no living relatives and that she had made her will, fifteen days before her death, leaving everything to Jon. Her money, although small, was more than he currently had. And then he realised that if he sold her cottage and contents the sale would make him a rich man. After paying her outstanding bills, he bought clothes, as he had only what he stood up in. Beyond that, he could not imagine any sort of life for himself and had wandered the streets for exercise and air while he thought about what to do next.

~

Emma arrived back in time to board the coach but not mix with the other travellers. She had expected to see them boarding, but instead they were standing in the street, and the coach, which she had been told would be on time, had not arrived.

Staying on the edge of the crowd she listened to their mumblings of dissatisfaction. It was an hour before a horse, ridden hard, arrived and the rider in the livery of the coach company went inside the inn, followed by the loud questioning of the travellers who were by now irate and asking for compensation. Moments later, the booking clerk faced the crowd with the information that the coach had broken a wheel and until another could be taken to it they would not be travelling until late afternoon.

Emma was in a quandary. She had nowhere to go and did not want to join the other passengers inside, even though they were to be given lunch as compensation. Knowing that they would be warming themselves by the fire, she felt wretched, cold and smelly with nowhere to wait.

The bells of a church rang out across the roof tops and Emma's spirits rose. She would ask the vicar's wife for charity in the form of warm water to wash. She knew that in the same circumstance Robert would not turn a traveller away.

Following the sound of the bells she found the church with ease. The minister's house was pointed out to her by an elderly man, and moments later she was knocking on the door of a large brick building. The door was opened by a male servant who told her that she could not enter and take her clothes off as the current incumbent was not married, and he shut the door on her. Deflated and cold she stood on the step, staring at the door. Disappointed that no charity would be shown her she walked slowly back down the path.

Seeing a small cottage with a well-tended and welcoming garden next door she felt the psychic energy rise within her, directing her to call there. She hoped that the woman who lived in this cottage would take pity on her and give her a little warm water.

Walking up the short path she knocked lightly on the door. It had started to snow and she shivered. When no one answered she was about to turn away when the door opened slowly and she could hardly believe her eyes as Jon stood in the doorway.

It was obvious to him now, because of the recognition on her face, that this was Emma, and he almost cried, looking at the state that she was in.

'Emma!' is all he could say.

'Oh.' She felt confused, she wanted to run, but it was too late. 'Could you let me have a little warm water, Jon... to wash,' she added, feeling embarrassed at having to ask such a thing of a man.

'Come in before you freeze to death, Emma.'

He opened the door wider, revealing the sitting room and its fire.

'Sit by the fire while I heat some water,' he said, hardly able to take his eyes from her or able to believe that she was here in his home and beside his fire.

'Thank you, Jon. I'm sorry that I smell so.' Tears filled her eyes. Of all the people that she would not want to see her like this, it was Jon.

He brought her a bowl of warm water and left her to wash. She started with her hair before her body, all the time watching the door and listening in case he returned.

Later as she sat by the fire, her hair drying, Jon came in with a tray of meat and bread.

'I thought that you might be hungry.'

'Oh, Jon.' She almost burst into tears. 'I'm very hungry, thank you.'

Looking around her for the first time she wondered whose cottage she was in, and would the mistress be annoyed that he had entertained a woman alone. And worse still, was he now married?

'Jon,' she said pushing the plate away when she had finished eating, 'I must go before I get you into trouble. I feel so much better now that I am clean.'

'Please don't go yet, Emma, there is so much to talk about.' The thought of her leaving again so soon filled his heart with dread. 'Where were you going?' he asked quickly.

'I, I thought that I would visit my brother. I was going to ask if I could live with him.'

There was silence between them as Jon took in what had been said. 'You are leaving your husband? Or has he died?'

'I'm sorry, Jon. I can't talk now, it's all so raw.' She was holding back the tears. 'I need time.'

'Time for what, Emma?'

'Time to think. Time to come to terms with all that has happened.'

He touched her shoulder and looked into her eyes. 'Emma, we are friends, more than friends in my heart. But you are married, I know that. Please, tell me what has happened so that I can help you.'

The warmth of his hand penetrated her clothes, her skin, her bones and a sudden, deep sigh caught in her throat as the words tumbled out.

'What has happened, Jon, is unthinkable. I'm not who you thought, nor who I thought I was. I am tainted, Jon. I have a reputation now of indecency that will follow me for the rest of my life. No man would ever want to have me as his wife.'

'Emma!' He was stunned at her outburst. 'Tell me what has happened for I cannot believe that you were knowingly any of those things.'

'It's true, Jon.' She hung her head. 'None of it was of my doing. Yet it happened and I am ruined.'

'I cannot believe that, Emma.' Holding both her hands he shook them as his words were delivered with passion. 'I cannot believe that.'

If she had not been so forlorn she would have been angry that he was dismissing what she had said, but instead the tears flowed and he sat beside her, his arm around her shoulders until she stopped crying.

'I must go, Jon. I have my ticket.' She held it out.

'This ticket, Emma, is for a seat on top of the coach. You will freeze to death in this cold and it's snowing hard now. You must stay here with me and I will look after you until you decide what to do tomorrow.'

She pushed him away. 'You would make me again what I have been accused of?'

'I don't understand,' he said, looking startled.

'You are offering me a place to stay all night without another woman in the house. Don't you see what people will think, Jon?'

Picking up her travelling coat that had been sponged and lay drying at the edge of the fire she started to put it on.

He stood up; worry carried in his voice as he asked, 'Where are you going?'

'To the inn and the coach. I have to get away from everything. Leave me be, Jon,' she shouted at him as he stepped towards her. 'No one can help me the damage is done.' And with that she threw open the door, rushing out bare-headed into the storm.

Reaching the inn, she stood uncertainly in the snow before the door. The coach was not there and she didn't have the confidence to enter and ask of its whereabouts, so stood beneath the large arch through which the horses were taken to the stable at the back and sometimes the coach, if it stayed overnight.

She stood back in the shadows as the snow drove in hard beneath the arch, covering the cobbles at the entrance. She could see the lights and the warmth within shining through the mullioned windows and realised that she could not stand here all night and prayed that the coach would soon arrive.

She was banging her arms with her hands and stamping her feet when the door opened and the landlord came out.

'Can you tell me, sir, have I missed the delayed coach?' she asked quickly.

'No,' he said shaking his head, 'because it isn't coming today. When they took the wheel to mend it they discovered that the axel was also broken. They brought the passengers in and everyone is waiting until the morrow. Try again at midday. Though,' he said poking his head outside the shadow of the arch, 'if this weather gets worse it won't run the morrow either.'

He was about to leave her when a voice in the darkness asked, 'Would you have a room for the mistress, sir?'

The man looked past Emma and saw Jon. 'I would normally, sir, but all the delayed travellers have taken the rooms. There's another inn at the other end of the town, the Standard, they might have a room.' He left, walking quickly towards the stables.

'I don't have any money for a room, Jon. And why did you follow me?'

'Do you really have to ask that question, Emma? I am the only friend that you have in this town. Do you think that I would let you stand in the cold all night alone? I will walk you to the Standard and get you a room there.'

'No, Jon. I can't go to the Standard, they were unkind to me. I can't face them.'

'Then you have no alternative, Emma, than to stay here in the cold all night without the promise of the coach leaving on the morrow and with the possibility that you will not be able to catch it then, having died of the cold. Or you could come back to my cottage and stay warm by the fire all night if you wish, or take the bed... alone, Emma.'

The snow was now several inches thick on the ground and didn't look as though it was going to stop falling.

'Your cottage, Jon?'

'Yes, Emma. And I am not married and I have no disapproving servants. The property was left to me.' He shivered. 'Come back with me, Emma, we can talk through this and I will tell you my story and you can tell me yours. We will sit up all night in the chairs by the fire. Please.' He held out his hand.

Emma took it and was grateful for his companionship. He wrapped a blanket that he had brought with him around her shoulders, and together they hurried, heads bent against the snow, back to the warmth of Jon's cottage.

As they sat beside the fire he told her of his travels and of finding Mrs Harding and of her attitude towards her dead husband and Jon's sadness because of it. But feeling that he had a duty to the small woman and the Reverend Harding's memory, he had stayed on and would have done so indefinitely had she lived.

Emma listened, getting the measure of the decent man before her. And over a mug of warmed rum laced with cinnamon she started her tale. She left nothing out and in doing so saw for the first time from this distance that none of it was her fault. She saw also that nothing could be changed. As she spoke, she came to terms with the situation and told Jon that she was unsure if her brother would let her stay once he knew.

'Emma,' Jon took her hands in his, 'I have loved you since that time I stood beside you on the ship. I didn't know you were married and when I did, I felt the greatest loss that I have ever known. When I arrived at your brother's house, I was surprised to see you there and found it hard to hide my joy at being able to get to know you and live alongside you for a short time. Those days tending the vegetable garden together and reading books in the evening were the happiest in my life. And it tore me in two to have to continue on my journey searching for the Reverend Harding's widow and leaving you behind. I had to go.

I knew that you would have to leave Robert eventually and go back to your husband. I stayed with him longer than I should have. I was a coward,' he smiled into her eyes, 'unable to watch you go because I love you, Emma. It matters not to me what others may think. They are in another part of the country. I can hardly believe that you are free, that you are not married, and I'm overjoyed that one day you might agree to marry me.'

His eyes were so full of love that Emma's own eyes filled with tears. 'You would marry me, Jon? After all that I have told you?'

'I would marry you tomorrow and bring you here to my cottage as my wife. I know that we would be happy, for haven't we already lived under the same roof together and known each other as friends and got on well?'

Looking deeply into his eyes Emma saw the honesty that he had shown at her brother's house. He had not changed and she could no longer hide the love that she held for him. A love that had grown at Claydon House, where she realised that love had been a stranger to her before.

Looking at him now, with the snow on the window masking the outside world and the firelight dancing on his face, she said quietly, 'If you were to ask me, Jon, I would say yes.'

Pulling her up out of the chair he took her in his arms and kissed her with soft, gentle lips.

There was a break in his voice as he asked, 'Will you marry me, Emma Tilby?'

'Yes, Jon, I will,' she replied quietly.

Bibliography

[1] *A Voyage to Terra Australis* by Matthew Flinders

He wrote: 'If I had permitted myself any innovation upon the original term, [name] it would have been to convert it into Australia; as being more agreeable to the ear, and as an assimilation to the names of the other great portions of the earth.'

Flinders' chart accompanying the book was entitled 'General Chart of Terra Australis or Australia'. However, Flinders' patron, Sir Joseph Banks, preferred 'Terra Australis'. In 1817, Governor Macquarie of New South Wales received a copy of Flinders' book, and started to use 'Australia' in his official correspondence. Later, explorer Phillip Parker King also used 'Australia' on his maps of the northern and western coasts, and by the end of the 1820s 'Australia' was commonly used as the continent's name.

For this book set in 1803, I have used Australia for easy reading a little sooner than it might have been officially used.

[2] Divorce

Before 1858, divorce was rare. In 1670, Parliament passed an Act allowing John Manners, Lord Roos, to divorce his wife, Lady Anne Pierrepont. This created a precedent for parliamentary divorces on the grounds of the wife's adultery, according to the **National Archives**.

This was the start of modern 'divorce', says Professor Rebecca Probert of the University of Warwick School of Law.

It also set the precedent for more than 300 cases between the late 17th and mid-19th centuries – each required an Act of Parliament. It was only in 1858 that divorce could be carried out via legal process. Even then, divorce was too expensive for most people, and there was the added challenge for wives of proving 'aggravated' adultery – that their husbands had been guilty of cruelty, desertion, bigamy, incest, sodomy or bestiality.

[3] Obtaining a divorce

Before the mid-19th century the only way of obtaining a full divorce, which allowed remarriage, was by a Private Act of Parliament. Between 1700 and 1857 there were 314 such Acts, most of them initiated by husbands.

[4] Divorce granted by Parliament only

Divorce was granted by Parliament only for adultery. Wives could only initiate a divorce Bill if the adultery was compounded by life-threatening cruelty. Because of the high costs, only the wealthy could afford this method of ending a marriage.

[5] Special court set up

A movement for reform of divorce law emerged during the early years of Queen Victoria's reign. In 1853, a Royal Commission recommended the transferral of divorce proceedings from Parliament to a special court.

[6] Matrimonial Causes Act 1857

These proposals were carried out in the Matrimonial Causes Act of 1857, but the grounds for divorce remained substantially the same. Adultery remained the sole ground for divorce, although wives could now allege cruelty and desertion, in addition to the husband's adultery, in order to obtain a divorce.

ABOUT THE AUTHOR

Anne Willingale was born in London, where she lived for twenty-eight years, before moving with her family to East Anglia. Her first book, The Key to the Street, was based on the history of how London dealt with the plague and indulges her love of both London and Cambridgeshire. Her second novel Revenge, also draws on finely researched social history set in London and a fictional village called Haddenford. Anne is a member of the Society of Authors and now lives in Devon where she enjoys both the sea and the wildness of the moors.